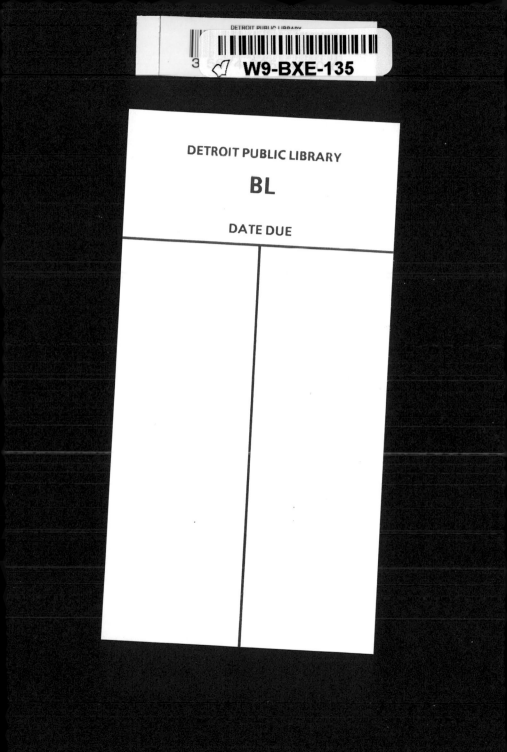

Simon and

Schuster

■　■　■　■　■

New York

London

Toronto

Sydney

Tokyo

Singapore

Hemingway's Suitcase

MacDonald Harris

c. 1

Simon and Schuster
Simon & Schuster Building
Rockefeller Center
1230 Avenue of the Americas
New York, New York 10020

SIMON AND SCHUSTER and colophon are registered trademarks of Simon & Schuster, Inc.

DESIGNED BY BARBARA M. BACHMAN

Manufactured in the United States of America

10 9 8 7 6 5 4 3 2 1

Library of Congress Cataloging-in-Publication data

Harris, MacDonald, date
    Hemingway's suitcase / MacDonald Harris.
        p.   cm.
    I. Title.
PS3558.E458H46   1990
813'.54—dc20   90–30235
                                                          CIP

ISBN 0-671-70082-0

For Gwyneth Cravens

"Right now I am making a *blague*."

A middle-aged American author "discovers" some stories written by Hemingway missing since 1922.

1 ▪ *The Trouble with People*

THERE WAS A CROWD at the Rotonde but they found a table inside looking out through the windows at the terrasse and the boulevard. It was five o'clock and already dark. It was cold outside but inside it was warm and the windows were steamy. Nick saw Helen looking around at the pictures. There were supposed to be three thousand of them on the walls of the Rotonde but he had never counted. Helen had not been there very often and was very impressed with everything including the people. Most of them were people who talked about art in cafés instead of doing it, Americans or English who had a little money so they could live in Paris without working. There were a couple of newspapermen he knew and he nodded to them before he sat down.

"There's a Dufy," said Helen.

Helen knew a lot about pictures and could recognize them all. There was only one Dufy and the rest of them were by the painters who sat around in the café and gave them to the proprietor.

"What are you going to have, Helen?"

"A café crème."

"Have some wine. A glass of Sancerre. A fine à l'eau for me. What do you want, Tito?"

"A demi-blonde."

The waiter went away and while they were waiting they

didn't talk very much. Helen said, "It is so nice going to a café. You never take me out."

"If Tito is going to drink beer we should have gone to Lipp's. At Lipp's they have a beer called a distingué. *A big glass mug that holds a liter."*

"I could not drink a liter of beer."

"Look at all the pretty girls, Tito. Most of them are fakes but some of them are pretty. Do you have a légitime, Tito?"

"A what?"

"A regular girl."

"I do not have a regular girl. I like all the girls."

"Helen is my légitime. *She's fake too. She is from Saint Louis, Missouri."*

"Mrs. Adams is a fine person. I admire her very much. It is an honor to know her."

The drinks came and Tito touched the beer carefully to his lips. He was a good dresser and careful in everything he did. He was wiry and brown, with small hands and a dark handsome face. He was as good-looking as a girl, and he dressed carefully in his Spanish shirt and suit that looked as though they might have come from a mail-order house in America.

"Légitime," said Nick, "is what you say to the poules *when they want you to go with them. You say, Thank you but I have a* légitime."

"I do not go with the poules," *said Tito.*

"Neither do I. I have a légitime."

Helen said, "Could we talk about something else besides poules? *Tell me about the pictures, Nick."*

"You can tell me about them. There is one Dufy, but most of them are by the so-called artists you see sitting around here. That woman over there dressed like a spaniel at a wedding is Nadia Booker. She is sitting right in front of her own picture, the gouache of the bathers in the Seine. She is hoping that someone will look at the picture and then notice her sitting in front of it."

"It's not such an awful picture. It's like Renoir."

"Mrs. Adams is a picture," said Tito. "You can look at the pictures but I will look at Mrs. Adams."

"You pay such nice compliments, Tito."

"It's because he is Spanish. Spaniards all have nice manners."

"In effect I am Catalan."

"They have nice manners too."

"Have you been writing any poems, Tito?" said Helen.

"I am always writing poems but they are not any good."

"I think some of them are very good," said Helen. "The ones in English at least. I can't understand the ones in Spanish."

"Mrs. Adams, my légitime, is not only an art critic but she is a very good literary critic."

"Mrs. Adams is a very talented person. I am a great admirer of Mrs. Adams. I am a great admirer of you too, Mr. Adams."

"That is why I buy you drinks," said Nick. "Because you admire me so much. Would you like another beer, Tito?"

"No."

"We could go to Lipp's and you could have a distingué."

"Thank you, Mr. Adams. It is fine here."

"Tito," said Nick, "is a Catalan and they do not understand irony. Spaniards understand irony."

He drank his brandy and soda and Helen her glass of white wine. It was beginning to rain a little now and there were dots of rain on the windows facing toward the boulevard. When someone opened the door to come in you could feel a little stir of cold air on your face, then it was warm again. While the door was open you could hear the swish of taxis going by on the boulevard.

"Those are some people we know," said Helen. "The ones who just came in. We could invite them to our table."

"They're wire service guys. They copy things out of the French papers and translate them into English. They are not really writers. All they have to know is how to translate French."

"I thought they were friends of yours."

"They are. That is Henry Boll sitting over there. The stocky man in the cap. He has already got a table so we can not invite him to ours. He is an English fighter and he stayed eight rounds with Georges Carpentier."

"I understand that Georges Carpentier is a very good pugilist," said Tito.

"Do you like boxing, Tito?"

"Oh, very much." He never liked to admit that he didn't know about something.

"Maybe we could go to the Stade Anastasie sometime. The boxers serve as waiters and the ring is in the garden. You can only go there in the summer. We could go to the Cirque d'Hiver. They have great twenty-round fights there."

"That would be nice."

"Helen could go with us. Would you like to go, Helen?"

"I don't care for your bloody blood sports."

"Boxing is not a blood sport. That is an English term and it means hunting."

"I don't bloody care for it."

"Helen," he explained to Tito, "picks up all these English terms from friends of ours. She thinks it makes her sound more intelligent."

"I think Helen is very nice. You know, I am afraid to call her Helen. I think of her as Mrs. Adams."

"You do think she is nice, don't you?"

"I am honored to be her friend."

After they left Tito they had dinner at the Pré aux Clercs, the good place in rue Jacob where you could get a prix fixe with wine for not very much, and then they went back to their apartment. It was still fairly early and they had nothing to do in the evening. Nick didn't feel like turning in yet but he didn't know what he wanted to do. Maybe he would go out again.

Helen said, "I like it when you take me to cafés. I know you don't like the Rotonde but I do. It doesn't matter whether the people are fakes. We had a nice drink and we talked. I *liked it when you showed me the woman who was sitting under her own picture."*

"I'm sorry we don't do more things. I go out and leave you every day. There's nothing for you to do here in the apartment."

"As long as you come home at night it's all right. There are things I can do. I can go to the market in Place Contrescarpe and I can walk in the park, and I can go to the Luxembourg and look at the pictures. Then when you come home at night everything will be all right."

"I'm getting tired of this town. It was all right in the summer but big towns are no good in the winter. You end up going to cafés. There are some people who go to cafés at eleven o'clock and spend the whole day there."

"They aren't real writers. You can't work here and so you have to go away to your room. I understand that."

"Do you like Tito?"

"He's all right. He's just a child really. He's very pretty. I don't really care for pretty men. I mean, I'm not attracted to them. A real woman is not. Everyone knows that."

"You love me because I am so ugly."

"That's right. My big ugly Puff. It is so nice when we have each other."

"It's funny, I like to have you when we're alone. I don't really like it when there are other people around."

"I do love you, Puff."

"We should get out of this town for a while. Where would you like to go?"

"I'd like to go wherever you would like to go."

"We could go back to Chamby. There's the good Swiss wine and the schnapps, and we could ski in the daytime. We could go all the way up on the funicular until it stops because of the snow, and then get off and ski down."

"And sleep at night under the feather comforter. Do you remember the duvet de plumes?"

"The water in the pitcher was frozen in the morning. You had to break the ice to wash your face."

"Do we have the money to go to Switzerland?"

"No."

"We can be poor and in love just as we are here."

"We will have to wait until a check comes."

"It's a good thing about the checks."

"Maybe," he said, *"after a while I will make enough so we don't need the checks."*

"Do you mind it because the checks are mine?"

"No. But if I make a little more we won't need them."

"Can we talk about something else? Not money."

"What will we talk about then?"

"About going to Chamby, and the good wine, and the feather comforter."

"And skiing. You forgot the skiing."

"Will we have the same room, Puff?"

"If you want to. We'll see if we can get the same room."

After they went to bed it had stopped raining and the moonlight came through the window. They left the shutters open so it would not be too dark in the room. Neither of them liked to sleep without some light in the room. A little after midnight she awakened, but he was facing the other way and pretended to be asleep.

From the café Nick and Tito went down the rue Cardinal Lemoine, across the rue des Écoles and past the square Langevin where the grass was brown now in the winter, and into the rue Pontoise that led down to the river. The gym was on the right just before you came to the quays. Tony came out of the locker room as they went in.

"Hello, Mr. Adams. We haven't seen you for a while. What did you think of the fight at the Cirque?"

"I didn't think the kid could do it and he couldn't."

"Belzies had the weight. He had seven pounds, and he's very experienced. But I thought the kid might stay the time."

"This is Tito."

"How do you do," said Tony.

A couple of people were sparring in the main ring. One of them was a Negro who looked very good. "Billy Cummings, a Jamaican," said Tony. "He can hit real good but he's no thinker. And he can't stay it when the going gets rough."

"What about the other one?"

"Oh, the Gypsy. Just a punching bag, Mr. Adams."

"Nobody is just a punching bag. He doesn't look too bad."

"I really got nobody to show you that would interest you, Mr. Adams. Come back in a week maybe and something better will turn up."

"Tito and I would like to spar a little in the second ring."

Tony looked at Tito. "Fine, Mr. Adams. The ring is free. Some people are going to use it about eleven but it's free now. Is your friend a boxer?"

"Tito is an all round athlete. He can do anything."

"You are a lot heavier than him, Mr. Adams."

"He is wiry and he has got a lot of reach. He has almost as much reach as I have."

"Did anybody ever train him, Mr. Adams?"

"He's pretty good. We're just going to spar around a little."

"Whatever you say, Mr. Adams."

They changed their shoes and Tony got the gloves. Nick's gloves were the ones he always used, not his own that he left in his suitcase in the apartment but the old Austrian Kempells with the leather labels that he had been using at Tony's for almost a year. Tony gave Tito some light French gloves that looked almost new. They left their street clothes on but took off their coats. Tito was wearing his white Spanish shirt without a tie and black pants. The gloves looked too large at the end of his wiry brown arms.

The second ring did not amount to much. There was no canvas and it was just a pad like a big mattress with a rope around it on four posts. You could knock over the posts with your hand. The main ring with its regulation ropes and canvas was for the professionals who could not afford to get hurt because it was their living. Nick and Tito went in and stood on the pad while Tony watched them. Nick said, "The thing *is, it all depends on your left." He showed Tito where to place the left, high up with the elbow bent, the thumb a little to the left of the nose, and the right behind it in front of the mouth. He reached in and tapped him lightly on the eye to show him how the left was used. Tony went away; he stood watching the Negro and the Gypsy sparring for a while and then he went back in the locker room.*

Tito was a quick learner. He had all the right instincts and his reflexes were very good. He was an athlete and he had been a dancer. They sparred lightly for a while and Tito would tap Nick on the head, then Nick would do the same to him.

"You see, Tito, your left is getting heavy. You see how it's drooping? You want to keep it up." To illustrate the point he got in a jab over the top of it and left a red mark on Tito's cheek.

Tito frowned and concentrated. He kept his left up but now he forgot what he was supposed to do with his right. Nick could get in easily under it and work him at the bottom of the ribs. They rested for a while and then they started in again.

"You're good, Tito. You're going to be good at it. I'll show you how to work the right now." He kept the left dancing in front of Tito's nose and then he brought the right over, suddenly and with force, getting him hard on the side of the head. Tito was busy trying to cover himself there and also lower down. He tried the right and tapped Nick on the shoulder, just as Nick had shown him.

Tito was pleased at having learned how to use his right and got Nick several more times on the shoulder and head with it. He was strong even though he was lightly built and Nick's head rang a little after the last one. Tito was very vigorous and he was not tiring at all. He was using both gloves now almost like a professional and his footwork was good too. It showed that he had been a dancer. He could be very good if somebody trained him.

Nick jabbed at him with the left a couple of times and then he gave him a hard uppercut that got his nose with the heel of the glove. He had not taught Tito to shorten his right and it kept stretching out so it was slow and you could easily get past it. Nick hit him with a couple more of the jabs to the face and then used the left which he had been ignoring for several minutes. Tito backed away a little and Nick switched to the right again. The uppercut caught Tito on the nose and Nick could feel it squash. The blood came almost immediately in a spurt that ran down his lip. While he was still surprised Nick caught him with a hard left on the side of the jaw. Tito's middle weakened and he went down in a sprawl. He did not fall violently, it was just as though he realized suddenly that he would be more comfortable sitting down. The blood from his nose ran down his shirt and when he noticed this he tried to wipe it away with his glove. Then he realized what he was doing and started to get up again.

"Take it easy, kid," said Tony.

He came up with a couple of gauze plugs and put them in Tito's nose. He had a bucket and he had Tito spit out some blood in that too. It wasn't very bad. The nose was not broken and it was just the ordinary kind of nosebleed that kids get when they are playing.

"You should leave him with me, Mr. Adams," said Tony. "We have got a fellow here that could train him. Just a couple of afternoons. Then he would know what he was doing."

"His timing is good. He doesn't look very strong but he's wiry. He could be a good fighter."

Tito had blood all over his Spanish shirt that looked as though it came from Montgomery Ward. They both washed down at the basin and toweled off and Nick put his coat back on. Tito carried his coat on his arm because of the blood on his shirt. He was fastidious about his clothes and the coat was the one to his good suit. He would have to put the coat on before he went out in the street because it was cold. He was a nice kid and it was hard to explain to him how things turned out sometimes. It was nothing special really. The same thing had happened to Nick the first time he had sparred in Chicago with Mike Dolan at the old Emperor Gym on Division. He *said to Tito, "You're pretty good. You ought to let them train you. You could talk to Tony." Tito didn't say anything and after they were outside he still carried his coat over his arm in spite of the cold.*

2 ■

NILS-FREDERIK SAT at the desk, pale and imperturbable, leaning back in the chair with his fingertips pressed together. Alan and Wolf were sitting at the table with the pages of the manuscript spread out before them. Wolf had a bottle of Jim Beam and a glass. He took a sip from the glass and looked thoughtful. Nils-Frederik smiled at them in a reserved complacent way that he had. It was a smile that Alan knew, a smile of inner amusement, at the expense of others who didn't know something he knew.

"Well, what do you think?"

"It's a story by Hemingway," said Alan.

"Have you ever read it before?"

"No, I don't think I have."

"There is no way you could have read it before," said Nils-Frederik.

Alan had not seen his father for several years and was curious to see if he had changed. He was exactly the same, in a gray checked suit and a maroon waistcoat, with a maroon handkerchief in the pocket of the jacket. His shoes were black wingtips and his socks were silk. His suits had to be made specially for him because of his size. He wore his hair long, with a duck-tail curve at the back of the neck. The white spots on his face were from small blemishes removed by a dermatologist.

The study too was exactly as Alan remembered it. It was a large room with a window looking out over the city at one end and the other three walls lined with books, mainly American and English fiction, some of them first editions or rare books. The furniture was modern Swedish, and the desk was teak with a white Formica top. Next to it was the table, with a map of Paris spread out on it and the sheets of the manuscript on top of the map. Nils-Frederik had acquired a word processor since Alan saw him last.

Nils-Frederik said, "Well, how do you like it? Is it any good?" He seemed to be addressing Wolf as well as Alan. He glanced from one of them to the other.

"I don't know, Father. It's a Hemingway story. They're all pretty much alike."

Nils-Frederik lit a cigarette from the box on the desk and got up to pace back and forth in front of the window. He still smoked the same kind, Sobranie Black Russians, with a tiny Czarist crest on each one. It had stopped raining now but the window was still dotted with raindrops. He drew at the cigarette and then exhaled so that the smoke hung in a veil around his head, rimmed in the light from the window as in a Dutch painting.

Wolf asked him, "Is it really a Hemingway story?"

"You've read it."

"An unpublished one? Is it authentic?"

"What do you think?"

"I don't think anything," said Wolf, who was a rare book dealer and an expert on old documents. "I'd have to see the evidence. Is there an original manuscript?"

"There is what I've just shown you."

"That was done on your word processor."

Nils-Frederik smiled at him indulgently, as though these were the comments of a clever child. He turned to Alan. "Do you think it's a Hemingway story?"

"I said it was. I was the first one who spoke."

"Bravo for you, Alan."

"Well, is it, Father? Now that Wolf has raised the question. Is it an authentic unpublished story by Hemingway? And if it is, how do you happen to have it?"

Nils-Frederik took a last drag on the cigarette, held the smoke as long as he could, and exhaled reluctantly. "Is it really an authentic unpublished story, you ask me." He came to the desk and crushed out the cigarette in the ashtray. "This is the last one. I'm giving them up. The box is empty." He found the box on the desk and threw it into the wastebasket. The box too was black, with a gold stripe and a crest on it.

Wolf said, "That's a terrible habit, Nils. Sensible people have given it up years ago. And that's not your only vice."

Nils-Frederik glanced at Wolf's glass and bottle, with a private little smile for Alan. "Our vices are the only things that make life worth living, Wolfgang. If we were left with nothing but our virtues, we might as well hang ourselves." He seemed to be in the best of humor. He paced about the room beaming with good nature, stopping now and then to look out the window. "Isn't it a beautiful view of the city in this way after a rain! I myself find life full of good things. I've been out of the country for a month. It was good to go away and it's good to come back. Life is good, that's the fact of it, Wolfgang, you old pessimist! And you too, Alan."

"Where did you go, Father?"

"As you know, I often go to France, or to Belgium or Switzerland. It's nice to go somewhere where you speak the language."

As long as Alan could remember his father had been reluctant to answer a direct question, although he sometimes seemed to have answered it, as he had just now. He felt a twinge of the annoyance with Nils-Frederik that had dogged him all through his childhood.

The door opened and Charmian, a blond woman in a flowered print dress, came in with the coffee and pastries. The pastries were the same kind she used to serve in the old days when Alan and Wolf came to the house on Sunday afternoons, crisp sugary *palmiers* from the French bakery on North Vermont.

"Ah, our afternoon coffee!" said Nils-Frederik with a smile. "Our charming custom, gentlemen. Just as in the old days."

Charmian left the tray on the table and went away without a word. They pulled up their chairs and poured themselves coffee. There were two thermos pots, regular and decaf, and Nils-Frederik took decaf. Wolf put cream in his coffee and set the glass of bourbon next to it, precisely, as though they were chess pieces. He ate his *palmier* and took a second, holding his hand under it to catch the crumbs. Even in his fifties, middle-aged like Nils-Frederik, he had the appetite for sweets of a small child. He was thin as a rail and he always seemed hungry.

"Charmian is very good at making coffee," said Nils-Frederik. "That is what we have her for."

He himself didn't have a *palmier*, and he took his decaf without cream or sugar, but he sipped it with the leisurely savor of an epicure, in the way he smoked a cigarette, in the way he did everything. Alan imagined him in bed with Charmian. It is always difficult to imagine our parents in the act of sexual intercourse, although nothing could be more certain than that they have done it. Of course, Nils-Frederik had conceived him with Maggie, not with Charmian. That was even more difficult for him to visualize. His mother was a small pert woman with blond hair and dark eyes, who dressed cleverly and spent a great deal of money on her makeup and hair. It was impossible to imagine her under large and gray, faintly damp, overweight Nils-Frederik. Alan's conception took place exactly thirty-four years ago. He had never been quite sure why his parents had divorced; they hadn't confided in him. Maggie now lived in Manhattan and ran an art gallery.

Wolf finished his coffee and sipped at his bourbon. "If you wrote that story yourself, Nils, you're very clever."

"Do you think I wrote it?"

"I don't know whether you did or not. If you did you're very clever."

"Where did the story come from?" Alan asked.

Nils-Frederik felt around on the table for the black cardboard box, couldn't find it, and realized he had thrown it into the wastebasket.

3 ∎

"IN THE WINTER of 1922," he began in a slow offhand voice, like a professor giving a lecture, "Hemingway was living with his first wife, Hadley, in Paris. Their address was 74, rue du Cardinal Lemoine. Hemingway often left Hadley alone in the apartment while he went off on various trips. At this particular time, just before Christmas of 1922, he was in Lausanne to cover an international conference. He had arranged for Hadley to meet him in Lausanne, and then they were going to go skiing at Chamby above Montreux."

"How do you know all this?"

"I know everything about Hemingway. Do you want to know where he was married? In Horton Bay, Michigan, on September third, 1921."

"The story you just showed us talks about Chamby and also about the rue Cardinal Lemoine."

"Yes, it does. When Hadley left Paris for Lausanne, she decided to surprise Hemingway by taking along all of his manuscripts, so he could work on them in the evenings during their ski trip. She packed everything he had written up to that time in a small suitcase. The longhand originals, the typescripts, and the carbon copies of the transcripts. At the Gare de Lyon she had the porter put her baggage into a compartment on the train. She put her big bag up out of the way and left the smaller suitcase on the seat. She got out to talk to some newspapermen she knew on the platform, and when she came back the suitcase with the manuscripts was missing from the compartment. She searched through several other compartments and asked her newspaper friends what to do, but the suitcase was gone. It has never been found. When she got to Lausanne she could hardly bring herself to tell Hemingway what had happened. He came right back to Paris on the train to see if she was mistaken and perhaps she had left at least the carbon copies in the apartment. But it was all gone."

"Everything he wrote up to that time was lost?"

"Yes. Twenty or more stories, a part of a novel, and some sketches. A couple of things were saved. One story happened to be mailed out to a magazine, and another had fallen behind the sofa in the apartment and Hadley didn't notice it when she packed the suitcase. But the rest of it never turned up."

He stopped. He seemed to be waiting to see if either of them had a comment on this, but they didn't say anything.

"This is the lurking fear of every writer, at a certain stage when he's only got one copy of the material, that he's going to lose it somehow. That his house is going to burn down, that a burglar is going to steal it, that his jealous wife is going to destroy it. It doesn't happen very often; it's just a kind of neurotic fear. But sometimes it does, and it's the worst thing that can happen. People think you can recover it again from memory, but you can't. It can only come out of you once. Making writing is a libido expression. You can no more write the same story twice than you can have the same orgasm twice. Writers take all kinds of precautions to be sure this doesn't happen. They photocopy the material and put the copies away in the safe deposit box at the bank. They make carbons of every day's work and mail them to a university library. Some of them keep two copies, one in one place and one in another. If you have a processor, you print out your work and put the floppy disk in the box at the bank. It's better to have two disks. If you don't know how to use a word processor, you can make a mistake and erase one of them."

He was up to something dubious again, Alan was sure of that. He was evading the point, maundering on about word processors and writers' fears of losing their manuscripts instead of telling them where he had got the Hemingway story. "What do you do, Father?"

As usual he didn't answer, or answered only obliquely. "I might make two disks and keep one in the bank. No one knows," he went on, "what happened to that suitcase. Most people believe it ended up in the hands of a very disappointed thief. All that was in it was paper. Probably he threw it away, or maybe he burned up the papers and kept the suitcase. It was a nice small traveling bag and it had hardly been used. Hadley bought it in St. Louis when she knew she was going to be married to Hemingway. It was green leather with metal reinforcements on the corners, and it had a green leather handle. There were two brass latches at the top that could be locked with a key. That was sixty-five years ago. If the suitcase were going to come to light it would have long ago. If anybody had been keeping it all these years he would have realized in time that these were manuscripts by a famous American author and they were worth money. Money, Alan!" He chuckled. "And they would be of great interest. But the suitcase didn't turn up. All the people concerned are dead now and they can't tell us any more about the suitcase than we know now. We can only conjecture what was in it."

He paused as if to collect his breath. Alan found himself looking at the manuscript on the table before them. It was immaculately typed on Nils-Frederik's processor; the paper was new and crisp.

"But," he went on. "Suppose the suitcase still did exist. Suppose some person, a tourist, a bibliophile, an American, an amateur collector of rare documents, was traveling around in Europe and he heard a rumor that someone had something very special, something his informant couldn't tell him about, but that he could see for himself if he went to a certain place. Say it was, well, it could be anywhere, a remote farm in Belgium in the Scheldt Valley. Suppose this traveler, say he was an American, knew what this material was as soon as he saw it but realized the farmer didn't know how valuable it was. He only thought it was some papers in English that might interest the American. Suppose the American bought it for not much, a few hundred dollars, and brought it back to America. Hemingway's missing manuscripts—a whole suitcase full of them, twenty or more stories and parts of an unfinished novel! All the original notebooks with the stories in longhand, the typescripts of the stories, and the carbon copies of the typescripts. And suppose you found that Hadley's diary was also in it, and her sewing kit, and a book with her name in it, to show that it was the right suitcase."

"Did that happen, Father?"

"It's just a story I'm telling you. Suppose I did find that suitcase. I've got it now, here in America. No one in the world knows I have it. What could I do with it? What do you think, Alan? And what do you think, Wolfgang?"

When Alan said nothing Nils-Frederik turned to Wolf with his fixed little smile. It was so quiet in the room that you could hear the sound of traffic on Los Feliz Boulevard below the hill. Wolf seemed uneasy. He cleared his throat and said, "Why are you asking us?"

"It's just a game. A story we're telling ourselves. The two of you can help me write the story." He stopped and looked at them, smiling. He still seemed to be in an excellent humor. "If they existed, the contents of that suitcase would be immensely valuable. Twenty unpublished stories, and twenty-seven pages of a novel that no one has ever seen before. It would be like finding buried treasure! It would be like digging up an old Spanish galleon full of gold pieces. These stories would interest anybody who is interested in Hemingway, and that's hundreds of millions of people! When *Life* magazine published *The Old Man and the Sea* in its entirety in one issue, they printed five million copies and sold them all in two days. Hemingway's publisher is Scribners, but the rights to any unpublished work would be owned by the Hemingway Estate. I don't know who that is. Hemingway's wife is dead but his sons are still around. Probably the Estate is handled by some law firm. They would be very happy to get their hands on that suitcase. It would bring in a lot of money for the Estate if they could publish those stories. Maybe you could hold them for ransom. But that would be illegal, wouldn't it?" Nils-Frederik laughed, his wily Dutch-uncle chuckle.

"You're darned right it would be illegal." Alan was exasperated with his father. "It's a crime. They wouldn't stand for it. They'd ask you to come in and deliver the suitcase and get your money, and the police would be waiting in the closet. You'd go to prison for it."

"No one in his right mind would do that anyhow," said Nils-Frederik, still smiling. "Suppose you didn't take it to the Estate. Suppose you decided to publish the stories yourself."

"That would be illegal too. You'd be infringing on the rights of the Estate. They would sue you."

"But suppose we didn't claim that Hemingway wrote them."

Alan noticed that imperceptibly, perhaps without noticing it himself, he had shifted from a story about a conjectural "somebody" who had found the suitcase to a "we" which included himself and the two of them.

"That Hemingway didn't write them? I don't quite follow you."

"Suppose you published the stories and made no claim at all about who wrote them. You just said here are some stories, I don't know where they came from, they may interest some people. They would look like Hemingway stories and everybody would see that immediately. The two of you saw right off that what I showed you was a Hemingway story, even though I told you nothing about it. You wouldn't have to mention the business about the stolen suitcase. The reviewers would point that out. Such a book might sell even better than a new book of Hemingway stories that were guaranteed to be authentic, because it would create a controversy."

"That would probably be illegal too. I'm not sure. In any case it's highly dubious."

Wolf said, "Of course, if anybody could prove you had the missing suitcase with the originals, then the materials you were publishing would be authentic, and they could sue you."

"That's right," said Nils-Frederik. "Maybe even prosecute me for theft."

Alan finished off the last of the lukewarm coffee in his mug and got more from the thermos on the tray, studying Nils-Frederik skeptically out of the corner of his eye. He still had that pleased, not to say fatuous, smile on his face, like a cat (Alan had thought when he was a child) that knew where there was a canary he could go and swallow whenever he wanted. Alan didn't know what to think about this new business. Probably his father was only playing a game with them, one of the elaborate canards he sometimes devised to amuse people, or to amuse himself at their expense. He was up to his old tricks and he, Alan, didn't have much patience with them. He asked him bluntly, "Where did this story that you showed us come from, Father?"

"I typed it up myself, a couple of hours before you got here."

"Are there any more?"

"I just got back from Europe a few days ago. This is the first one of them that I've typed up."

"Where are the originals, Father?"

"If anybody had them, and he was smart, he would keep them in a safe deposit box at the bank."

Alan looked around the room. The drawers of the desk could be locked, and there were some fireproof steel file cabinets at the back of the room, also fitted with locks and keys. There was no sign anywhere in the room of a green suitcase with metal reinforcements.

Wolf finished off his Jim Beam. He said mildly, "Well, this is a queer business, Nils. I don't know why you fool around typing these things up and showing them to us. Perhaps as you say it's a game you're playing. If you're not careful, you could land yourself in jail without very much trouble at all."

"I'd like to avoid that," said Nils-Frederik. He caught Alan's eye and grinned. It was all a game of Monopoly, Alan thought, with pretend Belgian farmhouses and pretend suitcases. But, as he thought about it, he saw that it was not that simple. It was typical of Nils-Frederik to play games with people and pretend that he had a secret when he didn't. But if he had found something valuable, it would also be typical of him to make a game of it and only offer these playful hints and innuendoes.

4 ▪

UNTIL THE TELEPHONE CALL on Friday, Alan and his father had not been on good terms for some time. It was about five years ago that Nils-Frederik had finished his novel *The Mastermind*. He showed it to Alan; in fact Alan and Wolf had seen weekly installments of it on their Sunday afternoons at the house. Alan saw that it was unpublishable by any of the major trade houses in New York; it was too special, too self-indulgent, too unclear and obscure, too literary in its imitation of Henry James and its references to hundreds of other novels, poems, and obscure works of French surrealism. But there were flashes of brilliance in it, and it demonstrated, if nothing else, that Nils-Frederik had a talent that might break out later in some form and result in the writing of a really successful book. In the case of this novel, Alan told him that he thought the only way he could publish it was with a small press. There were hundreds of these, most of them paying almost nothing in royalties, and in some cases even demanding subsidies from their authors, but they often put out attractive and nicely edited books. To Alan's surprise he agreed, and Alan arranged for the publication of the book with Salamander Press in Santa Monica. Its editor, Myron Case, was an old friend of Alan's from his student days at Johns Hopkins. A few months later Nils-Frederik held in his hands a book he had written, a thing he had always wanted.

Then he got another idea; he decided that he wanted to write off his typewriter and all of his travel costs as tax expenses. He went to Europe frequently to gather material for his writing, and his novel and a good many of his stories were set in Europe. The trouble was that he didn't really make any money as a writer; in fact publishing the novel with Salamander had left him several thousand dollars out of pocket. The IRS rule on declaring your costs as tax deductions was that you had to make a profit in three years out of five, otherwise your writing was just a hobby.

At this point, he proposed a plan to Alan. He would actually deliver to Alan the manuscripts of some stories and a second novel he was working on, and Alan could keep them in his office. Then Alan could pretend to have sold the stories and the novel, and make some paper payments to him for them, so that he could report these payments to the IRS as income from his writing. Then he would be a real writer and could claim his travel costs as business expenses. In another tax year, he would return this money to Alan "in some other way," for example as a gift from father to son, which was privileged in some way under tax law. He presented this idea to Alan in such a complicated way that it was some time before he, a professional literary agent, saw that it was tax fraud. The whole thing went on for a year. By this time Nils-Frederik had actually filed a tax return showing the paper income from Alan's agency, and it took the services of a good tax lawyer to get them both out of this predicament by claiming an accounting error and filing an amended tax return. It was a near thing that they didn't both end up going to jail. Yet Nils-Frederik was not really dishonest or even devious; he invented these schemes, plans, and stories, pure phantoms of his imagination, and then reflected on them, added to them and embroidered them until they became so solid in his mind that he himself began to believe they were real, and even convinced others they were real.

Alan and his father had a bitter quarrel over this business. Alan stopped going to the house entirely, and only spoke to him on the telephone rarely, on some piece of necessary business. Then on Friday, two days ago, he called Alan up and invited him to come for coffee on Sunday afternoon, as if nothing had happened. Wolf would be there, and he wanted to get their advice on something. His voice on the phone was cheerful and amiable, with only a trace of the irony that was a part of his personality and never entirely disappeared in his manner. Alan decided to go, even though Lily begged him not to. She had never trusted Nils-Frederik, even before she and Alan were married. Her antipathy was so deep that Alan wondered if there was some kind of sexual thing in it. He didn't understand women very well but he had an enormous respect for their complexity.

Alan had been married to Lily for ten years. He had met her when they were both students at Johns Hopkins, she majoring in psychology, he in English. The fact that she had accepted him still seemed to him a minor miracle. At Hopkins, English was a prestige subject, with a department full of celebrity professors. Alan studied literary theory and also took some creative writing courses. When they met, Lily was impressed with the poems he had written, and he realized that the reason he had written the poems was that he had known subconsciously that she was going to come into his life, and he wrote them in advance to impress her. They somewhat resembled the poems of Rilke, except that they were all addressed to a pale, dark-eyed, cool Levantine princess, the beloved of his imagination, an image that Lily exactly fitted when she appeared. Her dark exotic beauty (her father was an art dealer named Horvitz, her mother a pianist) exactly balanced his own pale and white-eyebrowed Swedish blondness. He really couldn't account for his obsession with pale-skinned dark-eyed women; it was a kind of *Drang nach Suden*, a craving for the mysterious sensuality of the Mediterranean, a form, perhaps, of slight mental illness.

After he won Lily, Alan's poems stopped coming. They had performed their function and found him his Jungian *anima*. When he graduated he saw clearly that he couldn't make a living as a poet, and if he wanted to teach he would have to get a Ph.D., and he was too impatient for that. He came back to Los Angeles, and Nils-Frederik put up a small amount of money for him to start a literary agency. On the strength of this he wrote to Lily, and she came out and met Nils-Frederik and the rest of his family, and they were married in a wedding chapel in Glendale. Lily quickly found a job in a school for the mentally retarded, where she had worked ever since. No more poems from Alan. Sometimes, in his office with nothing to do, he composed obscene limericks, which he threw away. They were clever enough, as a matter of fact.

5 ■

AFTER WOLF had gone Alan stopped in the kitchen to say a word to Charmian and Nana. The house was laid out in a peculiar way, nestled into a cove in the hill, with the kitchen in the front and the living room and study upstairs. For this reason, when you came to the house the kitchen was the first room you entered. The living room upstairs was almost never used. Nils-Frederik didn't entertain very much and spent his evenings, when he was home, in his study with the door shut.

Nana, an old woman in a shapeless cotton smock, over-weight and almost blind, was sitting at the kitchen table as she always did in the daytime, as far back as Alan could remember. It was six now and Charmian was busy fixing dinner. She was an excellent cook but she ate little herself, only dabbling at the elaborate dishes she prepared with so much care. Nana paid little attention to what she was eating. It was all for Nils-Frederik, an epicure who ate even a roll and butter with a leisurely savor, the way he smoked, the way he talked, the way he did everything. His main complaint about Maggie had been that she was not a very good cook, or more precisely that she didn't spend enough time in the kitchen.

Now that Wolf had left, Nils-Frederik abandoned his mysterious mannerisms and became easygoing and genial. He caressed the nape of Charmian's neck as she worked at the stove, and he ran his hand over the kitchen counter, the butcher block, the blond-wood table, and the whole kitchen as though it was a creature he was affectionate toward. He came back to the stove, set his hand on Charmian's bottom, and looked over her shoulder.

"And what is the delicious thing we have for tonight?"

"A salmon soufflé with capers. Don't jiggle me or it will fall."

Alan did not know Charmian very well. After Nils-Frederik was divorced, he had met Charmian in Belgium on one of his European trips. Alan didn't even know what her last name was. She was a young blond woman whose main qualities were her patience and her inconspicuousness. Her face was unmemorable. It was difficult or impossible to remember what she looked like when she was not there. She had the rounded body of a Rubens model, a nice figure, and a good complexion. Although she was much younger than Nils-Frederik, she didn't appeal to Alan, because of his obsession with the oriental houri type; he was put off by healthy pink faces and blond hair. Charmian was a pleasant enough person and he had no objection to the fact that she had replaced his mother in the house where he had grown up.

Nils-Frederik smiled at Alan. "Charmian is so good to me. What would I do without her? I would have to subsist on television dinners or things from the delicatessen. You know I can't turn a hand in the kitchen." He also couldn't drive a car, he had never learned and said it was impossible for him. He had arranged his life so that other people did these things for him.

Charmian was perspiring and tucked up a lock of hair that had fallen down. "Just stand out of the way if you want your dinner."

"How long will it be?"

"A half an hour."

"You're putting it in the oven now?"

"Yes."

"In the meantime, Sweetheart, will you do something for me? Go down to Savory's on Beverly and get me some Sobranie Black Russians. Just one box. I'm giving them up. It won't take you ten minutes, and you'll be back before the dinner is done."

He always kept the keys in the pocket of his jacket; that way he knew where the car was. He handed them to her, and she took them without a word and left. Through the wall they heard the sound of the car starting up in the garage adjoining the house.

They were alone with Nana, whose face had followed Nils-Frederik like a slow and lazy searchlight as he talked.

He grinned. "Ah, Nana. Dear old Nana. You are always sitting there at that table with nothing to do. I'm afraid you must be lonely." He bent to kiss her, in the roguish manner of a stage actor kissing an old lady, cocking an eye at Alan to see if he was watching. Nana looked straight ahead out of her white filmy eyes. "Well, we're all a little lonely, Nana. It's the human condition. Each of us is isolated in the great throng of humanity. I'm alone all day too, working like a dog. We have our arrangement. You took care of me for so many years, and now I'm taking care of you. The wall held up the vine when it was young, and now the vine holds up the old and crumbling wall." He chuckled at this literary aperçu. "We want you to be happy. Anything you want, you can have. You know that, don't you?"

Nana turned her head as though she had noticed for the first time that there was someone else in the room.

"Who is that with you there, Nils? Is it Alan?"

"You know very well it is, Nana. You can see better than that. Your hearing is excellent too." He smiled and winked at Alan. "We are going to try to persuade Alan to stay to dinner, but he is very uxorious. He slights us in favor of his family. For Alan, everything is his family. We don't count. We're just his progenitors, the people who brought him into being, unimportant creatures you cast aside once they've produced you. Alan hasn't been here to the house for a long time. And the times I've been to his house you can count on Captain Hook's fingers."

"I know all that, Nils." She turned her glaucous eyes in Alan's direction. "Come over here, Alan. Let me feel you."

He went over and stood by the kitchen table. "Sit down in the chair." He sat down, and she held out her hands and ran them over his shoulders, then around his chest and up onto his face, tracing the contours of his cheekbones and jaws. She used to do this even when he was a child; she was in her eighties now and she had been blind since she was sixty.

Even more strange to him than the idea that his father engaged in sexual intercourse was the idea that Nils-Frederik had a mother, and that it was this overweight blind old woman he had known all his life. She sat at the table in the shapeless food-stained smock that she had worn as long as he could remember. Her hair, iron gray like Nils-Frederik's but mixed with strands of white, was greasy and uncombed; no one took care of her and with her poor eyesight she didn't take care of herself. But it was her money; she inherited it from Nils-Frederik's father Klaus, who invented the container ships that now carried most of the cargo on the seven seas all over the world. Klaus began as a sea captain in his native Sweden, but he was far too clever for that. Alan was born too late to know him but he had seen pictures of him in an album—a heavy suspicious tight-jawed man with a small nose and eyes like gimlets. Probably Nana had been very glad to get rid of him and have the money for herself. Now she dispensed it freely to Nils-Frederik, since she had no need of it for her own purposes. Nana had been pretty in her day. In the pictures in the album she was a tall young woman a little broad in the hips, and with a somewhat freckled face, but with large beautiful eyes and a look of cutting intelligence, an intelligence that must have been disconcerting to the average man.

She said, "Why did they call you Alan? Couldn't they find a Swedish name for you—Lars or Olof or Dag?"

"His name is Lars, Nana," said Nils-Frederik with the special smile he reserved for her. "He changed it for professional reasons. The Alan Glas Agency. No one wants to go to an agent called Lars. It sounds like a rustic."

"Alan Glas sounds like a person in Hollywood with a false name."

Nils-Frederik laughed. "Well, he does have a false name. And his office is not far from Hollywood."

"My office is nowhere near Hollywood. It's at Pico and La Cienega," said Alan, irritated. He got up from the chair, and Nana released him with a final caress, or exploratory slide of her hand, that came perilously close to his genital region.

"You're a good boy, Alan. A good Swedish boy."

"He's not much of a literary agent," said Nils-Frederik. "How many clients do you have now, Alan?"

"A dozen or so."

"And none of them are novelists. They're people who write self-help books, a former stunt man who is writing his memoirs, and a second-rate ghost writer. Isn't that right, Alan?"

"I do have one novelist. Lucius Plum."

"Ah yes. The octogenarian who is writing his Civil War novel. Is he still working on that? It's been years."

"He'll finish it some day. It has the potential of being a bestseller."

"Ha ha! You've got a great sense of humor, Alan."

"I need it to be around you. Can't you say something nice about someone sometime?"

"I do say nice things about people. I said that Charmian was a great cook."

"You're always putting her down for being dumb."

"Well she is. She's a nice enough person. Just not very smart, that's all."

Nana said, "Alan, whatever happened to that other woman? Your mother."

Nils-Frederik detected a jab at him. He was amused. He smiled broadly. "Don't play dumb, Nana. We've been divorced for years. Maggie lives in New York now."

"I liked her better than this one you've got now."

"She was smarter. This one is a better cook."

There was the rumbling of the car from the garage, then the sound stopped and the kitchen door opened. Charmian gave Nils-Frederik back the car keys and threw the cigarettes onto the kitchen counter. Nils-Frederik, no longer jovial but intent on the cigarettes, opened the box and lit one. Charmian hurried to the stove and opened the oven door to check on the soufflé.

Nils-Frederik said, "You still haven't told me what you think, Alan."

"About what?"

"About that matter we were discussing upstairs. That fellow's suitcase." He made a side-glance at Charmian, then turned back to Alan with a subdued conspiratorial smile. He pulled at his cigarette.

"I advise you to do nothing. The whole thing is crazy."

"Life is crazy, Alan. And especially this business of trying to make a living as a writer. It's the craziest business there is."

"For you it's not a business. It's a hobby. You don't need the money."

"Don't kid me about this, Alan. It's serious."

"Why is it that you're allowed to be serious about your own affairs when you kid everybody else about theirs?"

"Royal privilege, Alan. The divine right of kings." He laughed, and Alan smiled too in spite of himself. "Alan, I'm thinking about having a party."

"A party?"

"Yes, a party. You know what a party is. We'll have some people in for drinks, conversation, something to eat, then everybody goes home."

"Well, that's nice. I don't remember your ever having a party. Who would come to it?"

"My friends. Who else do you ask to a party? Maybe some of your friends too."

"My friends?"

"Yes, your literary friends. I think of it as a kind of literary party—writers, editors, book reviewers. Agents like yourself."

"You could ask Lucius Plum, the well-known historical novelist."

"Ha! That's it." He grinned broadly at this idea. "You come

and bring all your literary friends. Lily will come too, of course."

"Well, I don't know."

"Lily will come."

"Stand out of the way," said Charmian. "The soufflé is coming out of the oven."

"I've got to be going," said Alan.

He got his helmet from the coathook in the hall, and Nils-Frederik followed him out to the street where he had left the Beast at the curb. The big Honda was wet from the rain and he got out a rag from the carrier and wiped off the seat. It was almost dark now and the streetlights had come on. Nils-Frederik, in his checked suit with the maroon handkerchief in his pocket, looked out of place in the suburban neighborhood. Alan was in his usual black leather jacket, jeans, and moccasins.

He mounted the Beast and put his helmet on. A fine rain was beginning to fall again and the drops on the plastic visor obscured his vision. "You'd better go back in, Father. Charmian's soufflé will fall."

Nils-Frederik still held the cigarette, shielding it from the rain in his bent hand. As Alan was buckling the helmet he came up to him and put his arm around him without a word. Unexpectedly, with the human touch, the warm pressure of the embrace in the rainy twilight, Alan felt the old fierce pull of blood, a burst of emotion that almost made tears well. It all came back, the love he had felt for him as a child, in the times when he wasn't being angry with him. He had remembered the anger but he had forgotten the love. The thing he felt at this casual embrace came from a place so deep that he couldn't even reach it with his thoughts. For the first time in years he felt the emotion of a son toward a father, unspoken and embarrassed, a wave of feeling as strong as a sexual impulse, yet chaste, as though it were religious, an act of communion. As long as he is alive, some instinct told him, I will be all right. When he is gone, then I will be the next. He knew in that moment what a father meant. Nils-Frederik was a wall for him against mortality, against the night, the unknown, the cold and lonely. When he was a child he had felt this without understanding it. Now he knew why this brief touch of flesh made his eyes wet, even though he fought fiercely against this weakness in himself. He had no idea what Nils-Frederik felt. In the poor light he couldn't see his expression, but probably he was wearing the same tolerant smile that he wore when he was teasing Nana, superior, mock-serious, and ironic.

"You know, sometimes I think you ride this thing so you can't take me home with you. How are Lily and Kilda anyhow? I hunger after your family. I want to see them; I want to have them around me."

"You know Lily. She's a special kind of person and she has her own special needs. She doesn't want to share Kilda with anyone."

"A man wants someone to carry on after him. A child isn't enough; a man wants a grandchild too. If he goes on living, he wants a grandchild. He wants to see them go on coming into the world, his progeny, his children and grandchildren."

"You have progeny."

"Yes, but I don't have them if I can't feel them and embrace them." He smiled ruefully, examined his cigarette, and sighed.

"I'll be seeing you, Father. You'd better go back in. You'll get wet."

"Wet? I would swim the English Channel," he said, "to hold Kilda in my arms."

Nils-Frederik had never before shown any particular interest in Kilda. He had been in her presence only a half-dozen times in his life. He had sent her presents at Christmas and on her birthday, and asked Alan about her in a perfunctory way when Alan came to the house, but he seemed to be lacking in any normal impulses of a grandfather. He wants something from me, Alan thought, and he thinks he can get it through Kilda. He is as devious as an old gray fox in the woods. And yet the love he had felt for him in that moment beside the motorcycle was still there. He was helpless against it; it was as though he had been touched by a girl.

6 ▪

THE WOLVES lived in a small house in the Echo Park district, a bungalow dating from the turn of the century, with an old-fashioned screened porch on the front, supported by pillars made of stream-rounded stones. Inside, after you passed through the screened porch, was the combined living room and dining room, with the kitchen at one side. Most of the walls were covered with bookcases, and there were more books piled on the floor. An aquarium bubbled at one end of the room, and there was a sagging sofa with a knitted orange shawl flung over it. On the sofa were two pillows; one said "Aloha" on it and the other "Waikiki." A Tiffany chandelier hung in the middle of the room. Under its yellow circle of light Wolf and Myra were seated at the table finishing their dinner. Myra was in her fifties, a pale and thin, somewhat sallow woman with dark hair and dark expressive eyes. Wolf was passionately attached to her and had been since the first day he caught sight of her. That was over twenty years ago.

She said, "You were at Nils-Frederik's?"

"Yes. Alan was there. I was surprised to see him. He hasn't been there for years."

"They quarreled about something, didn't they?"

"Yes. It was over money, I think. Or something to do with Nils's writing. I was never clear on the details."

"I've always liked Alan, and Lily too. They seem like us, somehow, only younger."

"I think Nils wants to make it up with them. He was very cordial to Alan today. Insofar as it's possible for Nils to be cordial. There's always a vein of irony in everything he does. He's lonely I think, living in that big house with nobody to talk to but those two women."

"Two women?"

"His mother and Charmian."

"I always forget the mother. She hardly seems to count. I don't think I've spoken a word to her in my life."

"She doesn't talk to anyone. She just sits there at the kitchen table. But it's all her money, you know."

"How can she take care of the money if she's blind?"

"Oh, I imagine Nils manages it for her. Nils is never too clear on family matters of that kind. In fact, he's never too clear on anything. He likes to make his life mysterious; it's a game he plays."

"What did you talk about today?"

"Oh, the usual nonsense. He always has some harebrained scheme in his head. Now he's brought something back from Europe . . ."

She stopped eating and looked at him. "What?"

Wolf took a forkful of Sachertorte and pushed the rest of it around on his plate. He was reluctant to reply. He was torn between his love for Myra, the long years of intimacy in which he had told her everything, and his holy awe of Nils-Frederik and his secrets. "I don't think he wants me to tell you very much about it. He's very secretive. He hardly wanted to tell us about it. Maybe he's only playing anyhow. Maybe there's nothing to it. He wants us . . ."

"Wolf—"

He threw down his napkin angrily. "I know. Myra, believe me, I'm not going to have anything to do with it. I swore that from the moment he started telling us about it. I can't tell you what it is, but the whole scheme is dubious. It's crazy. He thinks that—well, I told you I can't tell you anything about it."

"I don't know what to think about Nils-Frederik. He's so crazy. He thinks of these extravagant things. But you've always enjoyed the Sunday afternoons. It's a way for you to get out of the house. It's almost the only pleasure you have, I think. Except sitting here at home with me."

He smiled at her with sad affection, set his hand tentatively on her knee, and removed it. "Yes. And he spends a lot of money on books. When I first started the store, he bought a lot of rare books from me, some very expensive. Without that, I might not have made it. And since then he's been my best customer. I owe the existence of the store to him. That's why he thinks he can count on me to—well." He stopped in the middle of the sentence.

Myra poured out the espresso into two tiny striped cups. He saw that she was studying him reflectively. He felt naked under her glance. She knew him intimately and knew what he was thinking at any time. Their eyes met, and he got up and went to sit on the sofa with its orange shawl and its two Hawaiian pillows. She brought the two espressos to the table in front of the sofa, then she went for the bottle of Jim Beam and the glass and set them on the end table by his elbow.

He was a worrier, a man of scruples, a small-scale philosopher, a failure in his own eyes if not in hers. She was a person of elegance, thin, urbane, sophisticated, ironic, witty. He was not worthy of her, but without her support he would be lost. She always brought the bottle and set it by his elbow when they sat on the sofa after dinner. She herself never touched the whiskey, although she took a little wine with her meals. She was an abstemious sensualist, he was a dissolute puritan. Sometimes he thought that the reason he married her was to atone for what his people, the Austrians, had done to her race. That would account for the powerful and irrational grip that his love for her had on him, and for the admixture of guilt that somehow always lay at the bottom of it. If he did anything wrong, it was to Myra that he would have to account for it. She was the Universal Mother, all-seeing and compassionate, and yet the ultimate judge of good and wrong. He took a long sip of the bourbon and held the glass cradled at the point of his groin.

"Nils is an extraordinary man. He has many of the qualities of a genius. I have known him for many years, I have lived under his sway, and yet I know him only imperfectly, the way a German might have known Hitler, or a Catholic the Pope. He is more than a friend, Myra. He calls to a side of myself that I cannot ignore. Every Sunday I go to see him, the way another person might go to church. He is not a good man, but he is not evil either; there is no wickedness in him. He is Loki, the Universal Trickster, the playful antagonist of God. Others who follow him, who share in his mischief, may do evil things. That's because they don't share in his magic, his mana, his invulnerability. And he is an excellent writer. He is a writer of genius. If he is not successful, it is because of his playfulness, his daimonic playfulness, which makes it impossible for him to take anything seriously. Yet this time," he told her, after another sip from the glass, "I believe he may be serious."

"Serious about what?"

He sipped from the glass and was silent for a while. Then he told her, "He has stolen something from someone else. He has stolen from a dead man. And he wishes to offer what he has stolen as something that belongs to him. Or," he said, pondering into his almost empty glass, "he has made a very clever counterfeit of something, and he wishes us to believe it is real. I don't know which."

"You speak in mysteries and riddles. It's not like you, Wolf. You get that from him."

"No doubt. He influences me in many things."

"If he is counterfeiting something, isn't that illegal?"

"That's what he wanted to ask us. That's why he invited us to the house today. Alan as an agent, me as a documents expert. He wants our advice. He wants to play some kind of game, and he wants us to help him."

"A game? What kind of a game?"

"It's just an idea. Words. A play of language. Nothing important in the cosmic scale of things. The thing is," he said after a pause, "there might be some money in it. Quite a lot of it."

"Nils is your friend. If we have this house it's because he has bought so many books from you. But if what he asks you to do is not right, you shouldn't do it."

"I don't know what to do. I can't make up my mind."

"Don't think about it now. It's nine o'clock." Deftly, almost without his noticing, she poured a little more in his glass for him. "Drink, dear, and then you can go to bed early. Tomorrow is Monday, you'll be back at the store, and you can think about it then."

"Will you come to bed too?"

She smiled. "You're quite a man for your age, do you know that? You're my lover. My curly-haired Austrian boy. My *Wienerknabe*."

She moved next to him on the sofa and they put their arms around each other. Wolf finished the whiskey in his glass. "The idea he has," he told Myra, "is so crazy that it is divine." He was afraid to tell her what it was, for fear that she would say no.

7 ∎

WHEN CHARMIAN finished with the kitchen and came to bed Nils-Frederik was already in the bedroom, in his pajamas, dressing gown, and burgundy leather slippers, sitting in the armchair smoking a Havana. The lights were low. The room was filled with the smell of the expensive cigar, and the smoke coiled around Nils-Frederik's head and drifted slowly over the bed before it dissolved in the pinkish haze of the lighting. The windows were closed, the room was hermetically sealed, and there were no drafts. The motion of the door, when Charmian entered, made the coil of smoke start up and move slightly, then it settled back into fixity. The room was silent except for the faint murmur of the traffic on the boulevard.

"So you went to the Film Artz?"

"Yes. The matinee was from two to four, then I came home and fixed your coffee, then I started dinner."

"Did you like the movie?"

"It was all right."

"Susan Langley in *The Yacht Narcissus*."

"That's right."

"A René Arnold film from 1930. One of his early sound pictures. Did you observe her closely? Did you see how she did it?"

"Yes."

"Are you sure you have the right one? She wears a large hat and speaks in a breathless way."

"Oh yes. There are only two women in the movie. The wife is a silly blond thing and the husband doesn't love her."

"Did you notice the way she walks? Classic, statuesque, dignified. She keeps her knees together and puts one foot exactly in front of the other. When she stops, she turns one foot slightly out."

Charmian shrugged. All these things were easy.

Nils-Frederik tapped the long gray ash from his cigar onto the carpet. He believed that cigar ash was good for carpets, and he also knew that this habit annoyed her. She showed no sign that she noticed it now. She would vacuum it up tomorrow, after he had gone to work in his study.

"Show me," he said.

Their eyes met for an instant, then she turned and disappeared through the curtain. There was a dark space here between the curtain and the room behind it. She felt for the door and opened it, switching on the light. The room that she entered was fitted up as a closet at one end and a bathroom at the other. She took off her blunt brown shoes, her flowered print dress, her slip, and her underwear. The dress she hung carefully in the closet; the underwear and slip she threw into the laundry hamper. She never wore stockings in the daytime. She set the shoes on the floor of the closet, ready to put on the next morning.

She went to the other end of the room and urinated standing up, a trick she had learned as a girl in Belgium, when she was poor and the facilities available in public places were primitive. She was always careful to close the door so that Nils-Frederik wouldn't notice the noise. There were two bathrooms off the master bedroom, and she never used Nils-Frederik's; she entered it only to clean it.

In her own bathroom, in addition to the toilet there was a bidet, a washbasin, and an oversized triangular bathtub with a device that shot swirls of hot water around the body of the bather. Next to the bathtub was a dressing table with a circle of bare bulbs around the mirror. She turned on the lights and sat down.

Remembering the movie, she first put up her hair with a chignon at the back of her head, fastening it with a narrow mauve ribbon. Then, scrutinizing the reflection in the mirror carefully, she applied her makeup, beginning with the foundation and adding the rest with a professional deftness. Her square bovine face gradually assumed a svelte elegance, with dark violet eye-shadows and hollow cheeks. The wine-colored lipstick, almost purple, she applied in a way that narrowed her mouth, with a touch of tragic drooping at the ends. She dabbed scent behind her ears, on her shoulder blades, at the point between her breasts, and on the back of her neck, a place that Nils-Frederik always took a special interest in. Then she went back to the closet. It was really a large walk-in wardrobe with several rows of garment racks and a number of cabinets. From a drawer she took a black lace teddy, mauve stockings, a pair of garters, and a thin rayon blouse. She put on the teddy and the stockings, rolling the garters up into place with her blunt fingertips. It was difficult to keep stockings smooth with old-fashioned garters; if you sat down they bagged at the knees and you had to pull them tight again. To find such things you had to go to specialty shops. But Nils-Frederik preferred them.

She turned to the rack of clothes and took down a dark tailored suit with a white collar that she had not worn for some time. Holding it on its hanger, she smelled it quickly. It ought to be cleaned, but it could be worn for another time or two. She put on the skirt and jacket and glanced into the mirror. Then she selected a pair of spike-heeled pumps and sat down on the gilded chair to put them on, remembering to smooth her stockings again when she stood up. Finally, from the collection of hats on the shelf, she took a straw picture hat with a broad brim and a violet ribbon that hung down the back. Turning off the lights, she went out the door.

Before her was the curtain, heavy and opaque; the darkened space where she was standing was like the stage of a miniature theater. She felt for the switch at one side. With a faint electrical hum the curtain drew apart. At the same time, soft floodlights went on over her head.

Nils-Frederik was still sitting in the armchair; he had almost finished his cigar. From long experience she knew that the time she took to make herself up and dress was exactly the same as the time it took him to smoke a cigar. She stood for a moment until the curtain had disappeared into the columns at the sides and the humming stopped. Then she moved forward, keeping her knees together and setting one foot exactly in front of the other. Before the armchair she stopped and turned her right foot out slightly in the gesture of a ballet dancer or a model. He smoked his cigar and looked at her.

She turned away with a smile. In a low and breathy voice, the voice of a woman whose throat has been scarred by some corrosive, she said, "I've never been on a yacht. I don't know what to do. Will I have to scrub the decks? I can't tie knots." Still smiling in a suggestive way, she said, "There is only one thing I know how to do. I don't know why you invited me. You must explain all this to me." Her accent was Philadelphia Main Line, which she had never heard before she went to the movie. She was a clever mimic of voices; she could pick them up effortlessly. With a different kind of luck she might have been an actress.

Nils-Frederik stood up, still holding the stub of the Havana. When he approached her she took it from him and drew on it, expelling the smoke through her nostrils. Then she crushed it out in a saucer on the dresser, not an ashtray but a plate that held pins. In her breathy voice she said, "Your cigar is delicious. There are so many good things that men keep for themselves and don't share with women. Smoking cigars is one of them. Do you have many others? You must tell me about them."

Nils-Frederik murmured, "Susan Langley in *The Yacht Narcissus.*"

He circled around behind her, took her by the arms, and kissed the nape of her neck. Turning her around, he unbuttoned the jacket of the tailored suit. His hands ripped open the blouse and pushed the black teddy from her breasts. Clutched together, they fell onto the bed; her hat toppled off and her lightly pinned hair came down. His hand slipped up the water-smooth stocking until it encountered the garter. There it stopped, the fingers creeping tentatively toward the bare skin higher on the leg. "We are far out at sea," he said in a low voice. "There is no one else on board. Only the crew. And they have their orders."

8 ∎

WHEN SHE was sure he was asleep she pushed herself up for a moment to listen to his breathing, then she got out of bed without a sound. Groping in the dark, she found the black lace teddy and put it on. Then she crept out of the room, with a glance behind her at the sleeping man in the bed. He always slept soundly afterwards. In her bare feet she moved noiselessly through the house, closing doors behind her. When she came to the foot of the stairs she felt under the blue vase in the alcove for the key to the study. Nils-Frederik kept it there so she could clean the study when he was out of the house. She was always careful not to disturb his things. At the top of the stairs, without turning on the light, she fitted the key into the door and opened it. Only when the door was closed did she turn on the lamp on the desk.

The manuscript was still on the table where the three men had left it, on top of the map. She brought it over to the desk and set it in the circle of light under the lamp. She read through it, skipping a page now and then, as though she were reading it in her sleep, or as though she were a stage actress pretending to read a manuscript. Since there were no pockets in the teddy she held the key to the study in her teeth. After she finished the manuscript she sat thinking for a while. She felt a vague and inchoate desire to possess the words on the paper. She did not appreciate them as fiction, but she felt in some way that they were valuable, that they would be useful to her, that she had a deep need to possess them. She was impressed by the incantatory, the necromantic power of words, especially written words, especially words written by someone she knew, someone close to her; to possess words written by such a person was like possessing his picture, his fingernail clippings, the exhalation of his breath. It would be like stealing a small part of his soul; it would give her a power over him. She began going through the drawers of the desk, not sure what she was looking for, until she came across a pack of blank three-by-five file cards. There was a row of neatly sharpened pencils at the side of the desk, by the processor with its darkened screen. With the manuscript in front of her she took one of the cards and began writing. She had forgotten the key in her teeth; she took it out and set it on the desk.

There was a crowd at the Rotonde but they found a table inside looking out through the windows at the terrasse *and the boulevard. It was five o'clock and already dark. It was cold outside but inside it was warm and the windows were steamy. Nick saw Helen looking around at the pictures. There were supposed to be three thousand of them on the walls of the Rotonde but he had never counted. Helen had not been there very often and was very impressed with everything . . .*

When she had covered the card in her fine European calligraphy she took another card and went on. It took her almost two hours to copy the story, writing slowly and carefully. She had to go back into the desk drawer for another pack of file cards, but there were still several more packs left. When she was done she had dulled all six of the pencils. She took them to the sharpener, inserted them one by one, and turned the crank slowly, making only a little noise. Then she put the sharpened pencils back where she had found them and replaced the manuscript on the table. She picked up the key, turned out the lamp, and left with the file cards, locking the door of the study behind her.

She had no difficulty going down the stairs in the dark; she often walked around the house like this in the night. In total darkness she put the key away in its hiding place under the vase. Neither did she need to grope in the kitchen; she knew it as a blind person would know it, as Nana would know it. (What was her opinion of the blind crazy old Swedish lady? It was very complex and not entirely negative.) She felt for the box which she kept on top of the cupboard and took it down. It was an old-fashioned recipe box made of dark polished wood. It was almost dark here in the kitchen too, with only a faint light from the windows. Opening the box, she felt for the tabs that divided the collection of recipes. The third tab, she knew, was "Salads," and there were not very many cards in this section, because Nils-Frederik didn't care for salads. Here she slipped the bundle of cards she had brought from upstairs, tapping them down so they were even with the others. All these things she did in total darkness except for the grayish starlight that came through the kitchen windows.

In her bare feet, moving soundlessly, she stole back into the bedroom. Nils-Frederik was still asleep, making a sound like the slow-moving waterwheel of a Belgian mill. On his side of the bed she bent to look at him. He lay on his back with his mouth open, blowing back the edge of the sheet with each breath. She watched him for a minute or two, then she went around to her side of the bed and got into it in the black lace teddy. But the garment was a cheap one, bought in a novelty clothing shop on Hollywood Boulevard, and the scratchy lace irritated her body. She got out of bed and took it off, crumpling it up with the other garments on the bed. Then she got back into bed naked and fell asleep, dreaming of a white yacht drifting to a stop in a coral lagoon, while the links of the anchor chain fell into the water one by one like the pearls of a necklace.

9 ∎

ALAN AND LILY had dinner at Biedemeyer's in Beverly Hills. When they went out in the evening they used Lily's car, an almost-new Toyota, and Alan drove it. They left the car in a parking structure and walked down the street to the restaurant. The rain had stopped now and there was a glowing loom of clouds over the city, with patches of dark sky between. Lily, pale as a Kabuki actress with dark crepuscular eyes, wore a white plastic raincoat and a cranberry-colored rain hat. When she took these off in the restaurant she was in a blouse and narrow gray silk trousers, with silver jewelry. He had a scotch and water while they were waiting for their orders to come and Lily had a mineral water.

She twisted her napkin and said, "I had hoped you had given up on Nils-Frederik. I wish you wouldn't start going back there. What did he want anyhow?"

"It was nothing much. Wolf was there. We had coffee and talked as we used to in the old days. I think he gets lonely there in the house with nobody to talk to. Since he doesn't drive he can't go anywhere unless Charmian takes him."

"He's not exactly housebound. He goes to Europe all the time."

"He just got back, as a matter of fact."

"What does he do in Europe exactly? All by himself."

"Stop fooling with your napkin. You're making me nervous too. He looks for rare books and other things. Maybe he picks up women. That's the way he found Charmian, after all."

"He has her now. He doesn't need to pick up any more women."

He wondered how much to tell her about the Hemingway story that Nils-Frederik had showed them. It was such a crazy business that he didn't really understand it himself, and Lily would probably find something to disapprove in it.

"He's been doing some research in Europe. He's brought back some stuff—some manuscripts."

"What kind of manuscripts?"

"He didn't tell us much about it."

"Us?"

"Yes, I told you Wolf was there too."

"Then Charmian wasn't there?"

"No. She stays in the kitchen. We talk upstairs in the study."

"How about your grandmother?"

"She stays downstairs too."

"Nils-Frederik is a Leo, you know. They're attracted to women but they're not kind to them. Also, they travel a lot. Charmian is a Pisces, passive and wishy-washy but intuitive. They're an ideal couple."

He had heard this sort of thing so much that he hardly paid attention to it. Listening idly to the flow of her voice, he found his eyes fixed on the top of her blouse where it curved along her breasts, with a tiny canyon between them. Even though he had been married to her for ten years he fell into his usual habit and began disrobing her in his mind: first the blouse came off, then the small black shoes, the narrow pants, the underwear, and finally the silver jewelry, the bracelets, necklace, and earrings. He said, "I'm sorry you don't get along better with Nils-Frederik. He likes you and he'd like to see you more often."

"I didn't like him from the first and I don't like him now," she said, attacking her seafood cocktail with a small fork as though she were angry at it. "I'm fed up with the whole gang of them. Large-breasted Charmian, quaint doddering blind old Nana, fat charismatic Nils-Frederik—the whole Swedish menagerie."

"Charmian is Belgian."

"They're all characters out of Strindberg—*The Dream Play*," she went on as though she hadn't heard him. "Do you remember that woman who pastes and pastes paper over all the cracks in the house until everybody is stifling? That's Charmian. I can't bear to go near the place."

"You don't know anything at all about Charmian. You'd like her if you got to know her a little better. She's the one who goes out and does things, all the shopping and the errands, while Nils-Frederik stays shut up in the house."

"What does he do? Is he still writing?"

"I think he's working on a book. I'm not sure."

"You've never showed me any of his writing. I don't think you want me to read it. It might give me an insight into that fascinating and brilliant mind that you don't want me to see."

"You can read it if you want. I didn't think you'd be interested. His novel doesn't amount to much. It's an imitation of Henry James. He's very clever at parody. He's like one of those clever painters of fakes who can imitate the styles of all the masters."

"He's a parody himself. It's because he has no real originality that he imitates other writers."

"You don't know that. I'm not sure on that point myself."

"I can see he's worked his wiles on you as usual."

"Don't tell me what a pain in the ass he is. I know it. God, how I know it. I've known it since I was a small child. He's difficult, secretive, an egomaniac, whatever you like. But I do feel a certain affection for him. I realized that this afternoon as I was saying goodbye to him. He is my father after all. There's something to be said for blood. No matter who your father is, he's still your father."

"Yes, look at Abraham and Isaac."

"Oh, spare me your Middle-Eastern folktales. Besides Abraham didn't actually sacrifice Isaac. Jehovah substituted a ram at the last moment."

"Still it wasn't a great day to be a son. There's nothing magic about parents. They're not sacrosanct. They're not divinely appointed to run our lives for us. They have their own interests, and they may not be our interests. I know that from my own parents. Watch out for Nils-Frederik, I say."

Their attention was distracted by a commotion at the next table, behind Lily and to her right. As if ordered by an invisible

stage manager to reflect their argument, it was a parable of
parents and children. The hostess was nervously moving chairs
out of the way, and a couple in their forties were wheeling up
an old lady in a wheelchair. Following after, a busboy moved
the chairs back to their proper places. The old lady was installed
at a table almost at Lily's elbow. The busboy rearranged the
place settings on the table, and the couple, evidently the
daughter and son-in-law of the old lady, took their places.
While this was going on everything came to a stop in the
restaurant and all heads were turned. The old lady could not
sit upright and was crumpled into the chair in the shape of a
question mark. Her right hand was clawlike, but her left arm
and hand were far worse; the hand was bent over at right angles
to the wrist, and her fingers dangled like ineffectual stiff ten-
tacles that got in her way when she tried to move her arm.
Her wheelchair was so close to the table where Alan and Lily
were sitting that it was difficult for them to talk without being
heard.

Lowering his voice a little, Alan said, "Nils-Frederik is going
to have a party. You ought to make an effort and come with
me."

"When?"

"In a couple of weeks. He didn't say precisely. I know you
don't like him, but we haven't been there together for a long
time. It's a nice house. If you don't want to talk to him you
can just wander around and look at things."

"Oh, I know. The fake Rouault. The Klimt prints. The
Degas bronze from the Metropolitan Museum shop."

"What's the difference? From across the room you can't tell
it from a real Degas."

"What you've just said is a good description of Nils-Frederik.
From across the room you can't tell him from a real writer."

"There's a difference. A statuette is just a statuette. You can
tell whether a writer is real because a real writer produces
something."

"Well, he hasn't produced anything, from what you say."

"Not much yet."

The waiter came with their entrees: venison with bacon for Alan and carpaccio for Lily.

She said, "Do you know why you order things like bacon in public? Just to show that you're not Jewish, even though you're married to me."

"Oh, Lily."

"In your subconscious, of course. You don't really realize that's your reason. Virgos are very good at concealing their motives from themselves."

"I'm glad I'm good at something."

"Oh, you're very good at some things. You're a wonderful lover."

"You might drop your voice just a little. We're in a public restaurant."

At the next table the couple with the old lady in the wheelchair had ordered steaks with fries, although Biedemeyer's had an excellent continental cuisine. The old lady herself had ordered French onion soup gratinée, or her daughter had ordered it for her. It was evidently some kind of family celebration, a birthday or an anniversary, otherwise these people would not have taken the trouble to come to such a pretentious restaurant, with all the bother that it entailed and the disturbance to other people. Perhaps the old lady had expressed a desire for French onion soup or a regret that she never had it anymore. As you got older, you were no doubt stricken with all sorts of thoughts that you were never again going to do this or that or the other thing again. For instance, did the old lady look around at the lovers in the restaurant, or at Alan and Lily themselves, and realize that she was never going to make love again? Alan imagined her thoughts: people running, divers diving into the sea, jugglers in shopping malls keeping seven balls in the air with agile hands. Nevermore! I may have done these things but they are not for me now. Nevertheless, I can still try, at least, to eat French onion soup. It was a terrible choice. She couldn't sit upright, she could only lie coiled back in her wheelchair, and she could eat only with one hand. The cheese on top of the soup was like warm chewing gum. Each spoonful stretched out into a rubbery string, connected at one end to the bowl and at the other end to the spoon. The broth dripped off onto her flowered silk dress. The younger couple wished they had never thought of this idea of taking her out to dinner in a restaurant. They ignored her as much as possible, eating their own dinners and talking in low tones. At one point the daughter took a table knife and tried to sever a long string of cheese that was sinking toward the old lady's lap, but this was impossible, it would have taken a pair of scissors to do the trick, and the daughter had to seize the cheese in one hand and cut it off with the other. She tucked the end of it into her mother's mouth. The old lady looked grimly at the table in front of her. Alan heard her muttering "Messy" to herself. She gave up on the soup and began gnawing at the hard French roll that came with it.

Alan found himself fascinated with this painful spectacle at the next table, forgetting that he was with Lily and had been talking to her. Finally he managed to turn his eyes away from it and regain the thread of his discourse. "The fact is, Lily, that I may be going to see Nils-Frederik more in the future. I enjoyed going there today. He's an interesting person, in spite of his various obnoxious qualities." He was astonished to hear himself saying this; at the time he had been rather irritated by Nils-Frederik. "He has a fertile mind and he has interesting things to say, even though a lot of it is sham. And I'm fond of Nana. After all she's my grandmother."

"A very odd one. Does Nils-Frederik still have his dog?"

"His dog?"

"At one time, do you remember, he brought back some rare kind of dog from Europe."

"A Shih Tzu. That was years ago. It lived only for a few weeks. He didn't take proper care of it."

"And Charmian is another one of these *souvenirs de voyage*. And the Peugeot car. Every time he goes he brings back something. This time you said he brought back some manuscripts. Tell me about them."

"Oh, it's nothing much. Undiscovered works by an old author. That kind of thing."

"What's he going to do with them? Is he going to publish them?"

"I don't know. He didn't say much about it."

"Alan, I know you very well, do you know that? You're my main hobby, watching you and trying to decide what you're thinking and what you're up to. Now I can tell that you're lying. You and Nils-Frederik are getting together on something, and Wolf is probably in it too. I wish you wouldn't do it, whatever it is. Just for me. It's something about publishing. You already told me that."

He didn't remember telling her anything about publishing. Either he had let something slip and then forgotten it, or she had guessed it in some way.

"Don't get involved with him again. Just promise me that. Remember that business with the IRS," she went on, turning over her entree with her fork as though she were suspicious of it.

"Please, let's talk about something else. It's not serious. Nils-Frederik is not going to do anything. In any case, whatever he does, I'm not going to get mixed up in it myself. This is a pleasant restaurant and the food is good so let's enjoy ourselves. Is your carpaccio all right?"

"I don't know why I ordered it. I'd forgotten that it was raw. I don't eat raw meat. In fact I don't really eat meat at all. Those lovely creatures you see when you're driving in the country."

"Do you want to order something else?"

"No, no, it's lovely. Once you forget what it is."

He was anxious not to quarrel with Lily because he had plans for what they were going to do later in the evening, after they got home from the restaurant. In order to carry all this out it was important not to get her upset over Nils-Frederik and his affairs, always a sore subject with her. Lily was so special and difficult, so complexly neurotic, that making love to her was like trying to balance a fine gold watch on the end of your nose.

"I'm sorry that . . ."

"Everything's lovely, Alan. I like Biedemeyer's. Thank you for bringing me."

At the next table the drama of the old lady and her onion soup continued. She was evidently declaring (because of her affliction she couldn't speak very well except for words like "messy" and "no") that she wanted no more of the soup, that the soup was a horrible idea, a botch, and a fiasco, and that she would be perfectly content with her hard French roll if somebody would just put a little butter on it for her. But the daughter insisted that her mother had wanted the onion soup and it wasn't any trouble at all to help her eat it. She helped her in this way at home, and it was silly for her to object to it just because they were out to dinner in a restaurant; all the other diners (here the daughter caught Alan's eye) understood and sympathized. Moving her chair closer to her mother's wheelchair, she herself took the spoon and a knife and began arranging workable portions of the soup, dipping the spoon into the bowl and then cutting off the cheese around the edge of the spoon, as though she were edging a tiny pie. It was more difficult than she thought, however, to serve somebody else soup with a spoon, and the broth spilled again onto the old lady's flowered dress. She grimaced, pressed her mouth shut, and turned her head from side to side like a baby that doesn't want to be fed.

"Let's get out of here," Alan said.

He signaled the waiter and got the check. He had planned to pay with his credit card, but he got the cash out of his wallet and managed to make up the proper sum with only a little too much for the tip.

"But I haven't finished my coffee."

"Let's go, I say."

He led the way out of the restaurant with Lily following after him through the tables. Outside the pavements were still wet and there was a leftover smell of rain; he felt refreshed and all the unpleasantness of the restaurant was washed away. He sensed Lily's disapproval. "I'm sorry, but I couldn't sit there looking at that woman for another moment. I'm ashamed of myself, but there you are. I appreciate the plight of all the handicapped and hungering and disenfranchised of the world, I will make out endless checks to charities for them, but I simply cannot sit eating my dinner while watching that unfortunate woman spilling soup onto her dress. Couldn't they have taken her somewhere else? Couldn't they have ordered something a little less asinine for her to eat?"

Lily had snatched her white raincoat and her cranberry-colored hat from the coatrack in their hurried exit from the restaurant, and she put them back on now. Under the brim of the hat there was only a cave with the white gleams of her eyes showing. She worked with retarded children every day of her life and she was very angry. "You have no compassion, Alan. You're a Virgo. If ever I saw a typical Virgo it's you. You want everything in your life just right, everything arranged neatly on shelves. Everybody else has to be exactly like you; you're critical of anyone who isn't as neat as you are. That poor woman couldn't help herself. She probably doesn't go out to restaurants very much and she's entitled to enjoy herself as best she can."

They often quarreled like this. Alan had noticed that, after they made it up, it acted like an aphrodisiac on both of them. He felt more optimistic now about the later part of the evening, and began anticipating it in his mind's eye. "She wasn't enjoying herself. I do have compassion, Lily. I don't know whether Virgos have compassion or not, but I was full of compassion for her, and that's why I couldn't go on sitting there looking at her. I'm not a saint, Lily, I'm not a licker of lepers. I'm ready to help the unfortunate of the world in any way I can, but I just can't look at them. I couldn't ever be a doctor or a coroner or an ambulance driver. But I do have compassion, Lily. I'm full of love for the whole world and I'm full of love for you. Isn't it a wonderful evening? The smell the rain leaves behind." He put his arm around the white raincoat and she responded, slipping her arm around him and resting her hand on the crook of his hip. They went on together down the damp sidewalk toward the parking structure in the next block.

10 ∎

MRS. QUON, in her Sears housedress without a belt and her fleece-lined carpet slippers, gathered her sewing, her police whistle which she always carried in case somebody attacked her, and her book on how to speak English from the night school she attended on Monday, Wednesday, and Friday so that Alan and Lily couldn't go out on those nights, and Alan put her into the car, while Lily went into the house to see what Kilda was doing. It was a long way to the other side of town where Mrs. Quon lived. She sat in the front seat beside him and gazed out placidly at the tacky strip malls and auto repair shops on Crenshaw. As he turned onto Pico she opened her mouth and said with a thread of a voice, "Your Kilda is almost ripe." Or perhaps it was "right," or "rife." She couldn't have said that Kilda was almost ripe; Kilda was only nine years old. But perhaps to Mrs. Quon's Asian eye she really was on the brink of womanhood. Mrs. Quon herself had almost nothing in the way of breasts and no doubt she didn't see why you had to have any to be a woman. But why would Mrs. Quon, entirely out of the blue, after twenty minutes' silence, tell him while he was turning onto Pico Boulevard that Kilda was almost ripe? Was it a warning that someone might pick her from the branch? Or did she imagine that Alan and other Americans were uninformed about the phenomenon of the menarche, that this was a special piece of wisdom that only persons of her race and ancient civilization possessed, and she wished to put him on his guard against this mysterious, magical, and unpleasant event that was to take place shortly?

"She is still very young. She is just a child," he told her, realizing that because of the language difficulty he was speaking to her as if she too were a child, which she obviously was not. "It's for that, Mrs. Quon, that we have you come to take care of her. If she were not a child, she could take care of herself."

Mrs. Quon seemed to understand this perfectly; she did not even have to consult her book on how to speak English. She was silent for a while longer, and then she said, "She is very ripe for a child. When I speak to her she understand everything. She can take care of herself. Take clothes from floor and put in closet. She is like a grown person."

Ripe was only her word for mature then, something she had picked up in the slightly distorted linguistic ambience of the night school. It was true that Kilda was ripe beyond her years in the ways of the world, in her confidence, in her enigmatic mastery not only of her own culture, the culture of nine-year-olds, but of the culture of adults who thought they were so much smarter and knew so much more.

"Do you have children, Mrs. Quon?"

"Not now."

"Not now?"

"I don't have now. One die of fever, a man, and the other marry, a woman."

"I am sorry about your son."

"He was nine, same as Kilda. He die of fever in Saigon city."

Mrs. Quon, as he understood it, was an ethnic Chinese from Vietnam. He didn't know exactly why she had come to America. Perhaps because her son died and her daughter got married. He stopped the car in front of her house, a very nice one with geraniums on the ledge of the wooden porch, and said, "How much do I owe you?"

"Twenty dollar and sixty cent exactly."

He gave her twenty-five, because of her son who had died of a fever in Saigon, although it was really an offering to the gods so that something like this shouldn't happen to Kilda, who was exactly the same age.

11 ∎

IT WAS about eleven when Alan got home. He and Lily lived
in an apartment on Bagley Avenue, just off the freeway in
Palms. They had been lucky to find the place; it wasn't ideal,
and it cost more than they could afford, but it was large enough
for the three of them until Kilda got older. It was true there
were some bizarre people in the neighborhood who had large
parties and dealt in drugs, and a couple of years ago some kids
from Watts had come up in their car and just started shooting
people in the street. It was only an accident that they were
black; they were just kids. There were some other bad elements
in the neighborhood too, a gang on the other side of Robertson
that terrorized people, but for the time being they stayed on
their side of the boulevard. It was important not to panic; it
was not really such a bad neighborhood. Still Alan had a secret
dream of moving to a better place, in Beverly Hills or Hancock
Park, where they could have a house with a green lawn in the
front and a recreation room where Kilda could entertain her
friends. Getting out of the car in the basement garage, he had
a pain as he thought of half-ripe Kilda having her own friends
and bringing them home, pubescent teenagers with smirks,
total strangers to him. But she would be better off having them
in the recreation room in Beverly Hills than roaming around
the streets of West L.A. with people dealing dope, and sex
shops on the corner. And in Beverly Hills she could go to a
superior high school where she could learn French and com-
pose poems in a creative writing class, and be taught by teachers
who had been to Europe.

In the kitchen he got a glass of water from the sink; he was
thirsty from the dinner with wine and the long drive across
the city. He looked down the hall to the bedroom. Lily started
at the school at eight o'clock in the morning and she had to

be up early. He was afraid she might already have gone to sleep. The bedroom door was open; through it he could see the subdued light of the lamp and the covers turned back on the bed. The light was on in the bathroom. It would be some time before she came out. He set the glass down on the sink and went to look at Kilda.

The light from the opening door invaded the darkness of the bedroom, crawling slowly over the floor and jumping across the bed, but Kilda didn't stir. Her rear was thrust up under the covers, a babyish way she had of lying, and her head was half hidden under the pillow. It was a miracle that she could breathe under there with only one ear showing. One hand was outspread on the pillow, the small fingers and thumb splayed out like the paw of a gecko. He had the impression of a small vulnerable person who was in terrible peril, simply the peril of the world itself, but was serenely indifferent to this and confident of her own power to survive, even to make off with a little more than the others had and clutch it to herself secretly, gnaw at it in private, sustain herself in her own half-safe corner of the world, and escape unscathed from the kids from across town with guns, the dope dealers, the porno shops, the high school boys with hard-ons, the colas that rotted your teeth, the bad words sprayed on walls, the teachers who would explain to her the structure of the family and the repressive influence of parents on idealistic and rebellious youth. This invulnerable quality of hers, this air of self-possession and charmed indifference, scared him a little. He had never felt like that as a child and he didn't know what it meant. He didn't know what kind of human being would grow from a nine-year-old girl who could pass through fire like an angel and not be singed, and who had, as far as he could tell, no eliminative processes at all; he had never in his life seen her head for the bathroom, go into it, and shut the door. Perhaps she did it when he was away at work, or got up in the middle of the night when he and Lily were asleep.

She read books she got from the library or brought home from school, but he never succeeded in getting his hands on one and finding out what it was. She did not chew gum as all other children of her age did. She did not listen to music but she occasionally sang to herself, a monotonous incantation in sounds unknown to English, a chant to accompany a prayer wheel. For her only companion, as far as he could tell—she didn't have much to do with the other kids at school or on the street—she had a tarantula which Lily bought her at a pet store, and which came in its own plastic container with a handle on it like a small valise. "It's what she wanted," Lily told him. "I suggested a gerbil or a tropical fish, I said, You'll have to take care of it and get up in the middle of the night when it has a stomachache, but she insisted." She showed no affection to this creature, and after all how could you, and it had no stomachaches in the middle of the night, but she did take care of it and feed it dead flies, and once she even took it to school, but he had no idea what she did with it there; he couldn't imagine her prattling away to the class about it in the usual cheerful and fatuous show-and-tell style. Probably she just carried it around with her all day and said nothing to anyone about it. The tarantula had a name; he was called Dr. Freud, on account of the whiskers on his legs.

It was possible that she had a secret friend and had taken the tarantula to school to show it to her, but she had never mentioned a friend if she had one. She had the motions and gestures of a clever and self-assured animal, a solitary one that did not roam in packs. Once, a couple of weeks ago, Alan had gone out at dusk to look for her and found her where he thought she would be, at the golf course a half a mile away. She was with some other children, but she was not *with* them, she was lurking around their periphery. Even from a distance he recognized her instantly, a skinny little thing in a dirty white dress that came to her knees, with toothpick arms like a survivor of a death camp, and a bristle of black hair cut short so that it stuck out around her head like a chimney-sweep's brush; but more than any of these things it was her stance that he knew her by from a hundred yards away, the bend of her body, the furtive but confident lope as she circled the group

of other kids, watching them sideways but making no effort to
join them, skipping a little now and then in her solemn en-
joyment of the world in the twilight, but making the skip into
something hieratic, something not at all childish but a part of
the mysterious dance by which she dominated the world, a
Tibetan incantation of her white dirty ankles in their babyish
shoes. At that point one of the children turned and noticed
her and said something, some infantile jeer or menace, a
warning to go away and stop bothering them, or to stop acting
so goofy, and abruptly she fell to the ground on the coarse
grass of the fairway and began crawling skillfully toward a
nearby group of trees. Her knees slithered along acquiring grass
stains, her arms made the motions of swimming, her bottom
squirmed up and down in an innocent imitation of coitus, her
small head stuck up alert, fixed like a searchlight in the direction of the other kids who were now ignoring her. As she
undulated over the grass she gave the impression of a small
exotic animal for whom this means of locomotion was natural,
a harmless weasel from a children's book, a miniature Loch
Ness serpent sticking her head above the surface to show the
world that the legend was true, that there really was a Nessie
but they would never capture her or photograph her, that their
sonar was powerless to detect her shape in the depths of the
Loch, that she manifested herself only at times of her choice
and to a chosen elect, the queer and mysterious self-sufficient
ones of the world. And then it struck him that she was very
much like Nils-Frederik. She reached the clump of trees and
disappeared entirely except for the gleam of her eye as it caught
the light of the city.

12 ■

THE LONE WOLF Bookstore was on Melrose west of La Cienega. It was small in front, only wide enough for a glass door
and a show-window, and larger in the rear where Wolf had

his office and stockroom. A girl named Steve Ann worked in the front shop, selling current books, novels, and classics in publishers' series, along with a few books in Spanish and French. It was eight o'clock in the morning, a cool clear day with the sky washed clean by the recent rain. The store wouldn't open for an hour yet. Wolf parked in the alley, but instead of going in through the rear door he walked around to the front to look at the store from the sidewalk, as though he were a customer or someone else who was seeing it for the first time. The front resembled a bookshop in a small English town; it was white enameled wood, with a sign out over the sidewalk on an arm, and the window was divided into small diamond panes. The window was full of current books, even though the sign said "Rare Books and Documents." Wolf looked through the window for a while as though he were still pretending to be a customer. One of the most pleasant sensations of life, he thought, is to stand out in the perilous world, outside of some place that is yours, a burrow or a fortress, knowing that you can go into this cosy and safe place whenever you want. He unlocked the door and went in, locking it again behind him.

Steve Ann would not arrive until a little before nine. He deliberately came early because he enjoyed this forty-five minutes of solitude in the store, in the early morning before it opened. Ordinarily he spent this time in the back room, cataloguing his rare books or examining new purchases that had come in the mail. In this room, with two dusty windows facing the alley, there were glass-fronted bookcases for rare books and a locked steel cabinet for documents, letters, and loose pages from old books. Wolf did a good business selling these to people who wanted to frame them. There was also a vault like that of a bank but in miniature, large enough to hold only one person at a time. In the middle of the room was a long wooden table with an electric typewriter on it. The worn cord of the typewriter drooped from the table and ran across the floor to an outlet in the wall. Wolf stood for a few minutes looking at these things with a pleasant sense of ownership. Most of the books were in foreign languages which he loved, especially in their archaic forms. He thought how lucky he was; he had always wanted to spend his life among books, with the smell of fine leather and glue, the feeling of old paper under his fingers, and now this contentment was his.

He opened the door of the vault, took out a stack of books which had arrived the week before, and carried them over to the table. He took the one from the top and examined it more carefully than he had when he unpacked it, savoring its odor, the fragile crispness of the yellowed pages, the crudeness of the antique type as exquisite as the footprints of a fawn, the hand-sewn binding with its corded ridges, the gilded decorations and title on the spine. He peered between the pages with a magnifying glass to examine the condition of the stitches, and he leafed through the book, without opening it fully, to look for ink marks or marginalia. Propping it on the reading stand and holding it open carefully with a pair of soft rubber bands, he began writing out a catalogue description on the typewriter.

"Gesta Romanorum, ed. Ulrici Zell. Zurich, 1520. Quarto, ½ calf; boards. Frontispiece engraving; title. Colophon *term*. Paper oxidized. Rubbed; one corner slightly foxed. 2A."

He had paid six hundred dollars for it; he would be lucky to sell it for that, but meanwhile it was his possession and he could take it from the vault and run his hands over it whenever he wanted. He would almost be sorry if someone noticed it in the catalogue and bought it. It took him about an hour to write the catalogue descriptions of these five books, including long intervals for examining them page by page in search of flaws. By that time Steve Ann had arrived for work; he heard her moving about in the front shop, setting out the paperback display in the doorway and opening the cash register to put in the change. He typed a couple of letters, one to a dealer and one to a customer, and he wrote out a bill for another customer who had bought a book through the mail.

Tiring of these trivial tasks, he looked around on the table for another book that had come through the mail from a dealer in New York. With a glance at the front shop, where Steve Ann had just dealt with a customer and was sitting back down at her desk, he unwrapped it carefully. It was a Swiss book showing unclad youths in athletic and balletic poses in a setting of Alps and forests. It was a rare edition, published by Greefen in 1926 and bound in velvet paper. He was just starting to leaf through it when Alan came through the door, followed by Nils-Frederik carrying a cardboard box of the kind that comes with a ream of paper. He slipped the book into the drawer of the table.

Alan said, "Hello, Wolf." Nils-Frederik set the cardboard box down on the table and smiled. He was wearing a corduroy jacket with patches on the elbows, a leather waistcoat, beige slacks, and woven Italian shoes of honey-colored leather.

"What were you looking at when we came in?"

He came around the table, opened the drawer, and slipped out the Swiss picture book. He smiled broadly, first at Alan and then at Wolf. "Very fine! You surprise me sometimes, Wolfgang. You have unexpectedly refined tastes."

"It's something I bought for a customer. A Greefen Verlag book from the twenties." He felt himself reddening.

Nils-Frederik put the book away and shut the drawer. "What else have you got that's nice to show me today, Wolfgang?"

Wolf went to the glass case across the room, unlocked it, and took out a book. "This might interest you. Mint condition. It's never been broken open, really. It's like a new book."

It was A *Farewell to Arms* in the Scribner first edition of 1929, in black cloth with gold labels on the front and spine. The gold was as shiny and new as the gold on Nils-Frederik's cigarette box. Nils-Frederik passed it to Alan. He handled it carefully, afraid of soiling it with his fingers, and passed it back to his father without opening it. Nils-Frederik broke it open at a point near the end and glanced at it only for a second, then he handed it back to Wolf. He recited, "*I ate the ham and eggs and drank the beer. The ham and eggs were in a round dish—the ham underneath and the eggs on top. It was very hot and at the first mouthful I had to take a drink of beer to cool my mouth.*" He went on reciting the long passage to the bottom of the page, finishing with "*through the rain to the hospital.*"

"You can open that book anywhere. Read me a few words, and I'll go on with the rest of the passage."

Wolf found a place earlier in the novel. Without showing the book to Nils-Frederik he read, "*I was in under the canvas with guns.*"

"Canvas with guns. Oh, he's on the freight train escaping from the retreat at Caporetto. *I was in under the canvas with guns. They smelled cleanly of oil and grease. I lay and listened to the rain on the canvas and the clicking of the car over the rails. There was a little light came through and I lay and looked at the guns.*"

Wolf chuckled. "Do you know all of his work by heart?"

"I know that one. And some of the stories."

"In Homeric times there were rhapsodes who could recite the whole *Iliad* and *Odyssey* from memory. Twenty-four volumes of poetry."

"Not too difficult, if you made it your profession."

Alan had not said anything during this demonstration. Nils-Frederik's showing off in this way always irritated him. Now he said, "You don't have to be very bright to memorize a book. It can be done by an idiot savant. There are very simple people who have memorized the whole Bible."

"I am very bright," said Nils-Frederik. He was serious; although he was still in a good humor he hadn't smiled all the way through the demonstration. "I am not an idiot savant. I don't read the Bible. How much is the *Farewell to Arms*, Wolfgang?"

"Two thousand. A friendly discount to you."

"I'll think about it."

"What have you got in the box, Nils? Sit down, both of you. There are plenty of chairs."

They sat down at the table. To clear a space Wolf stacked up the rare books he had been cataloguing and took them away to the vault, which he left with the door open.

Nils-Frederik untied the string from the box, opened it, and took out eight typescripts which he set on the table. "My creative writing," he said. They were not long, ten pages or so each, and they were fastened with shiny jumbo paper clips.

They were all impeccably typed on Nils-Frederik's word processor, with a large typeface for the titles. One of them was the story he had shown them in his study, "The Trouble with People." Wolf glanced at the rest of them and read the titles, while Alan looked over his shoulder. "Down from Schruns." "The Lady with the Dog." "It's Marvelous, She Said." "Snatch." "Your Face Gets Very Cold." "The Real Thing." "A Broken Doll."

Wolf passed half of them to Alan and they set to work reading them. Nils-Frederik still had his hat on, a Tyrolean with a narrow brim and a feather, and he took it off and set it on the table. He sat watching them for a while, then he got up and wandered around the room, looking absently at the books in the glass bookcases. Wolf saw him feel in his pockets for the cigarettes but he didn't take them out yet. It was as though he wanted to reassure himself that they were still there.

It took them an hour to go through the seven stories they hadn't read yet. Two of them were skiing stories, "Down from Schruns" and "Your Face Gets Very Cold." They were set in Austria and the skiers were Nick and Helen, the same as the characters in "The Trouble with People." The others all seemed to be Nick Adams stories too. In one of them he was in Milan during the War. "The Lady with the Dog" and "It's Marvelous, She Said" were Montparnasse stories very similar to "The Trouble with People." "It's Marvelous, She Said" was about a flirtation that Nick carried out in a café, right before the eyes of Helen, and how she had hysterics about it afterwards in their apartment in rue Cardinal Lemoine. It ended, *It would be the same again. He was sure of that. It would be the same again after a while.*

"The heck it would," said Alan. "Nick doesn't sound as though he knows very much about women." Nils-Frederik, across the room, glanced at him with a smile.

"You claim you do?" Wolf asked him.

"What do you think about 'The Lady with the Dog'?" It was a portrait of a mysterious Russian woman in Paris. "Listen to this." Alan read aloud.

"A *new person, someone that nobody knew, had appeared in the cafés on the boulevard Montparnasse. I didn't see her myself, at first, although everyone was talking about her, and then I happened to encounter her in the Rotonde when I was with a lot of other people.*"

"How does that grab you?"

"It sounds like a story by Chekhov."

"There's a story by Chekhov with the same title, and it begins the same way. There's no reason why a writer shouldn't imitate Chekhov at a certain stage in his career. In both of these stories Nick is playing around with other women when he's married to Helen. This really must have happened to Hemingway and Hadley, since he wrote about it so much."

Alan sounded more and more as though he was buying these stories as authentic Hemingway. Wolf said, "He might have just imagined playing around with other women. Just because he wrote about it in stories doesn't mean he did it."

"What about 'Snatch'?"

Wolf shook his head. It was a rather nasty story which described the female genitalia in detail. It began *Nick didn't like to think about it.* "He really hated women, do you know that? He was attracted to them but he hated them at the same time. This story would certainly have been unpublishable in 1922."

Nils-Frederik said, "It's probably unpublishable now. Except in some specialty magazine. Maybe you know one that would do it, Wolfgang. You have all these racy books in your drawer."

"Only one. Do you know what I think, Nils? I think you made these stories up. It's like one of your tricks."

Alan asked him flatly, "Did you find the Suitcase, Father?"

"Heavens, so many questions. I can't respond to all of them at once."

"Let's start with the easy one," said Wolf. "Do you plan to try to publish this stuff?"

"I might. I'd like to get your opinion."

"Very difficult. We told you that before. Somebody else owns the rights."

Nils-Frederik smiled. Wolf saw his hand go into his coat pocket again where the cigarettes were and then come out. He was sitting at the table now, leaning back comfortably with his feet stretched out in front of him.

"Let's tell ourselves a story about it. Suppose that I heard about Hemingway's Suitcase, and while I was on a trip to Europe I had a reverie—just a reverie, you know, the kind we all have—about what a person might do if he were lucky enough to find that Suitcase. Suppose I *didn't* find it—it was destroyed years ago, thrown away or burned up, or it would have turned up by this time. Suppose I had the reverie that I found it, but instead of coming true, this reverie turned into a story in my own mind." He corrected himself. "It turned into stories in my own mind. Suppose I said to myself, The stories in the Suitcase are gone forever. Nobody will ever find them. But they existed once. Can we imagine what those lost stories were like? We're free to imagine, because the real stories will never be found. No one can say to us, Those aren't the right Suitcase stories. We're just going to say, Here are some stories, and people can decide for themselves what they are."

"So you wrote the eight stories yourself."

"Let's not talk about just eight. Suppose there were enough of them to make a whole book. And suppose you published them without any attribution. Without an author. Just simply *Twenty Stories*, edited by Nils-Frederik Glas."

"Why would anybody want to read a book like that?"

"Because, rightly or wrongly, they would guess where the stories came from. They would take them for Hemingway stories. The experts would begin disputing as to whether the stories were authentic or not, and people would want to read the book *because* of the controversy, and because they wanted to see for themselves. In the end it doesn't matter whether the stories are authentic or not. Everybody is going to read this book, just as everybody wanted to read the Hitler Diaries, and newspapers paid big money for them, when most experts thought from the beginning that they were fake. People will flock to a museum to see a Matisse that an expert has identified as fake when they wouldn't go to see a real Matisse. Because they want to decide for themselves whether it's fake, although they don't have the first tiny notion about such things. You see, although we will never claim that the stories are genuine, we'll never admit that they're fake either. We'll just say that we got them somewhere and we've retyped them and here they are."

"You're crazy, Nils," said Wolf.

"There are a lot of people interested in Hemingway." He slumped in the chair, smiled to himself, and seemed lost in his own thoughts for a while. Then he said, "How much does an author make for each copy of a book, Alan?"

"It depends on the royalty rate and the price of the book. In general, about two dollars a copy of a hardcover book."

"*Life* published five million copies of *The Old Man and The Sea*." There was a silence. He looked at them for a long moment before he spoke. "I'm proposing that the three of us do this thing and split the proceeds. Or put it another way, I'll pay you commissions, ten percent for each."

Alan looked thoughtfully at the manuscripts on the table before them. He touched one with his hand, looked at it briefly, and pushed it away. "Why do you want to do this, Father?"

"It would be a nice joke on the publishing establishment. On the critics, those who go for it and believe it's authentic; not all of them will. And on the public. The great dumb brute public, that won't buy anything and won't read anything unless it's by a big-name writer, and they'll read anything by that big-name author even though it's junk."

"I hear the cry of agony of a novelist who had to publish with a vanity press."

"Salamander is not a vanity press, Wolfgang. It's true they

accept subsidies from authors, but they have very high standards. They don't take just every book. If this book is published, it will not be with Salamander."

"Who would publish it?"

"That's your specialty, Alan. I'll leave that to you."

"I don't want anything to do with it."

"What do you think, Wolfgang?"

"As I said, this idea is crazy and you're crazy, Nils."

"That may be. I'd have to be a crazy genius to write stories that are so much like Hemingway's that you can't tell them apart. But if I'm crazy, so was Andy Warhol. He began making exact replicas of Campbell's soup cans, and got better and better at it until finally you couldn't tell them from the real ones. He sold them for hundreds of dollars each."

"He never claimed there was soup in them."

"No, and he never said there wasn't. We're not talking about soup. We're talking about these eight stories, and some more that I can type up without any very great effort."

"You wrote all these after you got back from Europe? You've only been back for a couple of weeks."

"Hemingway once wrote two of his best stories in one morning. He was staying in a Spanish hotel. He came downstairs and told the proprietor, who was a friend of his, and the proprietor said, 'It's still only eleven o'clock. Why don't you go up and write another one?' "

"That chap didn't understand writing," said Wolf with a gloomy grin.

Nils-Frederik got the box of Sobranie Black Russians out of his pocket, extracted a cigarette, and lit it, pulling at it with deep satisfaction. His genial manner had disappeared; he looked not at them but across the room at the blank wall, reflective and serious.

"I'm going to leave these manuscripts here, Wolfgang. So you and Alan can work on them."

"Work on them?"

"Just tidy them up. A little editing work. I'll tell you later what to do."

"Could I take that one away with me?" asked Alan. "'The Lady with the Dog.' I'd like to look at it more carefully."

"Sure." He picked it up and tossed it into Alan's lap. He wasn't concerned now about the manuscripts getting lost. It was clear that he had other copies of them, perhaps on his floppy disk in the bank vault. Alan folded the story and put it into the back pocket of his jeans. He did this like an automaton, as though he were Nils-Frederik's puppet. An odd feeling spread through him, a resentment, a rebellion that was at the same time a kind of pleasure. He couldn't imagine why he had asked him if he could take the story away with him. The way his father manipulated him was a kind of evil magic. He remembered Lily's remark about Abraham and Isaac, and he wondered if Nils-Frederik was planning to sacrifice him to his own god, art, as Abraham had sacrificed Isaac to Jehovah. If so, there would be no ram appearing at the end to save him.

13 ∎

ALAN SAT in his office, pretending to work. The office was in the courtyard of a rather tacky one-story building on Pico near La Cienega, along with a chiropractor, a check-cashing agency, and a business that offered to grow hair on bald men. In the front, separated from Alan by a glass partition, sat Corinne, his secretary-receptionist, a middle-aged woman with a beehive hairdo and glasses encrusted with something like coral. When she looked up she could see everything Alan was doing behind the glass.

He looked at the two letters that had come in the mail— one an ad, the other from a high school girl in San Fernando Valley who had got his name out of a writer's magazine and wanted him to read her stories—and dropped them in the wastebasket. There were times when he wished he smoked, like Nils-Frederik. It would give him something to do when he ran out of work and didn't have anything to do with his hands. He sat doing nothing for a while. Corinne was typing away at the memoirs of the former stunt man. The stunt man couldn't type himself, and he said he couldn't afford a typist, so Alan was having Corinne do it for him. He could charge him against the royalties, if the book ever came out, which was not likely. Corinne looked up through the glass, found Alan loafing, and went back to typing.

Alan got a sheet of paper out of the drawer with the idea of writing a limerick, which would at least give Corinne the impression that he was doing something, although as the years went on he grew less and less confident of his ability to fool women about anything. He wrote, *There was a young man of Ben Loch*, then tore up the sheet and threw it in the wastebasket. It occurred to him for the first time in years that he might write a serious poem; in fact he found that the poem was lurking there in the bottom of his mind, just below the level of the conscious. He would have to pull it out with infinite care, like a fish on a fragile hook. He wrote:

> *Caged, he knows only bars;*
> *He paces left, right, left, right,*
> *His world is the cage and the bars,*
> *The half-gnawed bone in the corner,*
> *The heap of indifferent excrement . . .*

But the meter was all wrong, the lines too short, the pace jerky. He started over:

> *His frame of vision shows him only bars;*
> *He paces left and right, left and right . . .*

This was better. He had seen the caged panther in a science film on TV. It was a film on mental illness, explaining that all caged animals are insane and making conjectures about the causes of mental illness in humans. He sat with his pencil poised trying to write the next line, which would be about a bewildered mind bound in a dance, and then he realized that what he was trying to write was a poem by Rilke that he had studied in a class at Johns Hopkins. After the passage about the bewildered mind bound in a dance, it ended:

> *Yet now and then the curtain of the pupil*
> *silently parts: a picture goes inside,*
> *slips through the tightened limbs, and in the heart*
> *stops, like something that has died.*

He crumpled up this second piece of paper and threw it away too. Rilke was a hell of a lot better poet than he was. He would do better to give it up and stick to writing limericks. It occurred to him for the first time that it was Nils-Frederik who had bribed him not to be a poet by giving him the money to start up the literary agency when he got out of college.

For some reason this thought was not entirely unpleasant. Now, in his lazy and indolent state, his chain of thought was: my talent, which doesn't amount to much; Nils-Frederik's talent, which is fake; the Hemingway story in his pocket. Glancing at Corinne to see if she was watching, he felt in his jeans for the manuscript and took it out. He had folded it in thirds to put it in his pocket, and now he carefully pressed out the creases. He spread it on the desk and began reading it, for the third or fourth time.

The Lady with the Dog

A NEW PERSON, *someone that nobody knew, had appeared in the cafés on the boulevard Montparnasse. I didn't see her myself, at first, although everyone was talking about her, and then I happened to encounter her in the Rotonde when I was with a lot of other people. She was not a young woman but she was quite good-looking. She wore a mauve dress with a kind of mauve gauze scarf around her shoulders, and she had* purple enamel earrings of the kind they sell to tourists in Greece. No one knew where she had come from. She spoke French with a Russian accent. Someone said he had heard her speaking Russian, but this person didn't know Russian himself, so it didn't mean much. She was slender, with a profile like a Greek coin, and a good bone structure. I thought she was someone I would like to know, but I didn't do anything about it because the wife I had at that time was sitting at the table with us. The Russian lady's dog was a Skye terrier. It sat under the table and panted, looking up now and then to see if the lady was still there.

People also saw her at Patrick's, at the Dôme, and at the small restaurant in rue Jacob where she took her meals alone. Evidently she lived in a hotel, but if she did no one ever found out where it was. I was in the Luxembourg Gardens one day that summer and found her walking by herself, with the Skye terrier trailing her on a leash.

I said, "You have a joli chien. Is it purebred?"

"Yes, it is, and so am I."

We both smiled. There were a lot of people who tried to pass themselves off as Russian nobility in Paris, every taxi driver claimed to have been a count, and I was skeptical. We talked for a while, walking by the pond and along the Allée to the Medici Fountain. I was getting along very well with her. She even told me her name, Madame Khlestakov. I congratulated myself that I was going to have an adventure. She didn't give me her address, however, and when she left me she went off down the rue de Tournon without looking back.

The wife that I had at that time was waiting for me when I got home, lying on the bed reading. She asked me where I had been. I told her I had been walking with the Russian lady in the park; her name was Madame Khlestakov.

"You've been gone an awfully long time. I thought we were going to go to Auteuil this afternoon to see the horses run."

"I'd like to see the horses run. We can still go if you want. It's only four. They run until six."

"I only go because you want to go. I like to do things with you."

"You like the horses too."

"I like the horses but I don't like it when we lose all that money."

"We don't lose a lot of money. Sometimes we do but sometimes we win a little."

"It's too late to go to the track now. We could go some other time. What would you like to do?"

"We could go to Saint-Martin and watch the canal boats going through the locks. You've never seen that."

"Let's go then. I hate this apartment. I'm alone here all day long."

"Oh, let's not talk about that."

We took the Métro to the Gare de l'Est and walked over to the canal. It was a working-class quarter and I always felt good there. I liked the people and I liked watching the boats in the canal. The long narrow ones were called péniches. They carried coal or wine from the provinces into Paris; you could go all the way to the Midi on the system of canals. The middle part of the péniches was like that of an ordinary cargo boat, plain and serviceable, but the small cabins on the stern were as neat as a yacht. There were curtains in the windows and some of them had flowerpots with carnations. They had oil engines, and you steered them from the end with a long tiller made from a piece of pipe.

"I like the boats. This is better than going to see the horses."

"Some of them have been fitted up as pleasure boats." I showed her one. It was no different from the others except that the cargo hold had been converted into a cabin with windows along the top like a railroad carriage. Through the windows you could see that lights were on down in the cabin. There was a stovepipe with a hood like a priest's hat for the galley.

"If we had some money we could hire a péniche and leave by the Porte de Pantin, and go onto the Marne and the Ourcq and all the way to Flanders. There's a whole network

of canals. We could go to Holland if we had the time."

"That would be nice." She didn't sound as though she thought it was going to happen.

We watched the péniches going through the locks for a while and then we had dinner in a bistro on the quay. We had white beans with ham, fresh peas, and salad. The wine was the pinot that everybody else was drinking. It was a good dinner and I thought that I ought to remember this bistro and come back to it again. It was a working-class place and it was full of people who worked on the canal boats. "This is a nice part of Paris," I told her. "There are people here who never leave this quarter. Everything is for the canal boats. There are marine hardware stores and places that sell them supplies. It's like a miniature piece of Holland in the middle of Paris."

"I'd like to go to Holland," she said.

We didn't go to Holland that summer because we didn't have the money and besides I had work to do. I had some pieces for the Star to write, and I had a new idea that I might write a piece about the Canal Saint-Martin, the bistro where you ate white beans with pinot, and the people who gathered to watch the boats go through the locks. My wife found a new author, W. H. Hudson, and she sat in the park reading Green Mansions. I thought it was a rotten book and I told her so, but she said there was nothing else to read in the American library. I told her to read a French book, but she said that was too intellectually demanding.

I saw quite a lot of George that summer. He had a good job working for a wire service, with nothing to do but translate stories from the French newspapers and send them to New York. Occasionally he went out on a story, but he picked places that were pleasant, like Deauville or the château country. I sometimes had a reverie in which George was run over by a taxi and I got his job. He was a pleasant chap and I liked being around him. He was better-looking than I was and I tried to grow a mustache like his, but it was not a success. I was in better shape than George, though, and now and then I would get him to do something physical, like running through the park or Indian wrestling. Then I could beat him. It made up for the mustache. He was a great hand with the women, and had a lot of success at it. He would work all day and then spend half the night in the Montmartre clubs with the people he went around with. I didn't go out in the evening as much as he did and I didn't know as many girls. Partly that was because I was married and he wasn't.

George met Madame Khlestakov in the same way I did, in the Luxembourg Gardens. Evidently she spent a lot of time there walking her dog. I was drinking with him at the Closerie des Lilas and he said, "You know that Russian woman who wears mauve? I've found out her name. It's Madame Khlestakov."

I told him I already knew that. "What more can you tell me about her?"

"She's related to the Romanoffs. She's lived pretty much everywhere in the world, Athens and Constantinople. She's not married."

"You sound like a press release. Can't you tell me anything more personal about her?"

"I'll let you know. I'm still working on it."

A lot of other people were too. Madame Khlestakov was very popular in the Montparnasse set that we knew, although no one knew very much about her. She became a popular topic of conversation in the cafés on the boulevard. Someone told me that she liked women too. In fact, she liked them better than men. I didn't believe this because the one who told it to me was a man who liked men better than women. Anyhow I thought I could detect such things, and Madame Khlestakov gave out powerful signals that she preferred the company of men to that of women. If she liked both that wasn't important. I asked the one who told me she preferred women to men, "Do you like her?" He said, "There's something sinister about her." I just laughed and bought him a

drink. He was a nice enough chap, even though ordinarily
I don't care much for them.

Madame Khlestakov was seen in the cafés with a number
of people that we knew. One of them was an Englishman
that everybody called Germy. His name was really Jeremy.
He had a lot of money and wore good clothes, and some
people were impressed by his accent. Another was a Greek
who sold automobiles and wanted to be a painter. When
Madame Khlestakov was seen with such people it was always
just the two of them. She never joined the crowd, and when
Germy or the Greek was sitting with her they wouldn't speak
to other people or even catch their eye. It was as though
they had captured something they wanted to keep for themselves.

I could understand this impulse because I had it just the
same as the rest of them. When she was sitting in a café
by herself I would walk by the table to see if she would
catch my eye, but she always kept her eyes fixed on her
hands holding the coffee cup. I didn't feel I could intrude
if she didn't want to meet people. If she had so much as
moved an eyebrow, I would have spoken to her, but she
never did.

I did have one date with her. I met her again in the
Luxembourg; this seemed to be the place where she went
when she was looking for company. It was about six o'clock
and people were leaving the gardens. She was sitting on an
iron chair near the marionette theater with her dog, and
when the old woman came by to make her buy a ticket for
the chair she got up and walked away down the path toward
the terrasse. I was coming the other way and I was just about
to speak to her, but the dog lifted its leg and wetted a bush.
I didn't think that was the right moment. I followed her on
until she stopped on the terrasse. She looked around as
though she was looking for another chair to sit down on.

I said, "Bonjour, Madame Khlestakov. Are you looking
for a chair? The old woman will come along any minute
to sell you a ticket. It will cost you ten centimes."

She said in her French with a Russian accent, "I don't know what you are getting at."

"We could go to some place where the chairs are free."

I got her into a taxi in place Rostand just outside the gardens. I could hardly believe my good luck. We went down the Boul' Mich' and across the river on the bridge while the small dog on the floor of the taxi licked my hand.

We had Pernods at the Café Américain and then I took her to dinner at Maxim's. It was a warm evening and we had a table on the terrasse outside. She was wearing her mauve dress with the gauze around her shoulders so that her pale skin showed through. I wanted her very badly. She ordered her dinner without looking at the carte. She had ris de veau à la Maréchale, and she fed sweetbreads with her hand to the dog under the table. Afterwards she rinsed her hand in her water glass. I had a steak, and we had a good wine, a Chambelle-Musigny. The wine itself was as much as five dinners at the bistro on the canal. When the bill came I got out my billfold to see if I could cover it. I took out a couple of hundred-franc notes and there was not much left. I could see that she was looking into the billfold too. I sent the waiter off with the two hundred francs and put the billfold in my pocket. It was about nine o'clock. I asked her if she wanted to go somewhere for a drink, but she said she had another engagement. It was just as well because I didn't have the money to buy her a drink.

The wife that I had then was good in bed, but she was a bore in the daytime because she talked too much and always wanted things we couldn't have. She thought that I should look for a better job, so that we could go to the Midi at Christmas and go to Holland in a péniche. I would have been glad to trade places with George and have his job, but in that case, she wouldn't have fitted into the program. I didn't explain this to her. I didn't see as much of George for several weeks, because he was out of town on assignments, or so I thought.

Then I saw him at the Lilas. I was sitting at a table with my notebook, writing something down now and then but mainly looking at the people. He was with some people I didn't know and he looked thinner than usual. There were lines in his face that I hadn't noticed before; he looked older than I remembered. Perhaps it was just the lighting. I motioned to him and he came over to my table.

"Who are those people?"

"Just some people. Friends from the States. He's a stockbroker. She's just his wife."

"What have you been doing with yourself?"

"I've been out of town. And I've spent some time in the clinic."

"You were sick?"

"You might say that."

"I don't see you around with the old gang any more."

"No, I've given them up."

"Why?"

"It's not fun any more. Not doing the same old things. I've had all that. It's not any fun."

"Have you seen Madame Khlestakov?"

"Have you?"

"I took her to dinner at Maxim's."

"When was that?"

"Oh, some time ago. I don't remember exactly."

"The incubation period is twenty-one days."

"What do you mean?"

"Germy has it too, and also the Greek. Just about everybody in the gang is the same. The crowd that hangs around at the Rotonde."

I didn't know what to say. "How are you?"

"The treatment is no fun. It makes you sick. They say I'll probably have it all my life. Five minutes with Venus and the rest of your life with Mercury, they say."

I think he resented my not getting it too. I told him I tried my best but I couldn't make it. He shrugged and went back to his friends, the stockbroker and his wife. It didn't seem like the old

*George. He didn't smile very much and he didn't seem to want
to have much to do with me or the rest of his friends. After that
I saw him only now and then, and in the fall he went back to
the States and worked for the wire service in New York.*

*Whether everybody in Montparnasse was in the same trou-
ble as George, everybody knew about it. They talked about it
in the cafés, and finally my wife found out about it. Of course
her first concern was to find out if I was involved. I was sorry
that I had told her about the time I met Madame Khlestakov
in the Luxembourg. I never had told her about the second
time when I took her to Maxim's. I told her that I had only
talked to the lady about her dog, and never had anything more
to do with her, but I'm not sure she believed me. She didn't
have anything to do with me in bed for a long while after that.*

*I told her, "I think she did it deliberately. She's getting
revenge on somebody for something. There are people like
that. She'd probably destroy the whole male sex if she could
do it."*

"Why do you blame her? She got it from some man."

*"A man wouldn't set out to make a whole lot of women
sick. Not deliberately. Only a woman would do that."*

"You don't know that she did that."

"It's not too hard to figure out."

*"Oh, you're so clever. You're so omniscient. You always
know all about everything. How canal boats work. Which
horses to bet on. And especially about women."*

*"Oh, I know a lot more than that. Hunting and fishing.
Military strategy. The psychology of cats. I've got the whole
Paris Métro system in my head." I was hoping to turn it into
a joke but she was too sore.*

*"Couldn't we get out of town? I'm fed up with everything.
I'm so bored I could scream. All I do is sit in the park and
read. You're right about W. H. Hudson. He's an awful writer.
I tried* The Purple Land *but I couldn't finish it."*

*I was sorry that being with me didn't make her happy. I had
thought she would enjoy living in Paris and all the things you
could do there. But she came from the Middle West and she*

never got rid of that part of her. I knew that the way I had treated her was rotten but I couldn't do anything about it. She didn't like my friends, except for George, and he had gone back to America now. I didn't really know what she liked to do. I never found out.

Later I met an intern from the Hôtel-Dieu who told me that Madame Khlestakov had infected over thirty males that summer, and that included only the ones that sought medical help. It was a particularly virulent form of the disease that came from the Middle East. It was widespread in Constantinople but it had never appeared in a European city until now. As for Madame Khlestakov, she disappeared from town about the same time that George did. The things that happened that summer didn't affect me very much. It even gave you a bond of some kind with the others, to realize that everybody suffered but they suffered in different ways. For a long time I resented the fact that I had been in the war and a lot of other people hadn't. That was a bad time, but after the war I had a lot of good times too. I didn't know what I was thinking this way for, as if my life were over. I was still young and there would be other good things to do. Even when I was old I could live in my memories as they say in books. I could remember that I had talked to Madame Khlestakov in the Luxembourg, that I took her to dinner at Maxim's, and that I didn't have the money to take her to a hotel. That was the only good luck I had with women that summer.

It was unmistakably a Hemingway story, Alan thought. He was sure of that now. Some of the language. A *profile like a Greek coin.* And the line *I wanted her very badly.* Short, direct, understated. Typical of the authentic stories. The final dialogue with George. George's simple statement *The incubation period is twenty-one days.* The narrator's blunt misunderstanding of what is wrong with his wife, when the reader can see it clearly. He buys beans for his wife and sweetbreads for the Russian lady. The significance of the fact that he never calls his wife by her name. She is not a person to him, only someone who fills his bed and is difficult to understand. You could see why Hemingway had four wives. They were all just receptacles to him. He didn't understand them and he treated them like dirt, when he wasn't taking them to Maxim's. They were dirt to him, all sex was dirt. It was a dirt he was highly attracted to, but it was still dirt.

Other touches. When the lady tells him she is purebred like her dog, it suggests her animal nature which is to come out only later in the story. Her rinsing her hand in the water glass. His sentimentality; he doesn't want to talk to her while her dog is peeing. It was a marvel that the reader could understand him so well when he didn't understand himself.

That was the only good luck I had with women that summer. He went back and read that again. He felt a rare thing for a person like him who had wanted to be a writer too, an admiration without jealousy. It was as though he was carrying around in his pocket some small and secret treasure, like the relic of a saint. It didn't matter that Hemingway was a bastard about women. The important thing was that he could write.

14 ∎

CARRYING HIS HELMET and a bundle of papers, Alan came out of his office into the courtyard of the building, a dusty enclosure with tropical plants sitting around in tubs. Facing onto it were the other three offices, the chiropractor, the check-cashing agency, and the baldness clinic. A narrow shady passageway led out to the sidewalk. It ran between the two stores facing the boulevard, a boutique that sold New Age clothes and an oriental herb store.

The Beast was parked on the sidewalk in front of the boutique, next to a planter full of straggly azaleas. He put the papers into the carrier of the bike and was about to get on it when something caught his eye in the window of the boutique.

MACDONALD HARRIS 89

It was a mask of some nacreous substance, gilded in patches and painted in a spiral pattern of pinstripes and curlicues. There were seashells on the brow, and feathers of various colors on the temples. The eyes were mysteriously blank, like the eyes of all masks. There was no string or band to it; it was designed to be fixed to the face with some secret mucilage, or held on by magic.

As soon as he saw it he thought of Lily, of her Nilotic eyes that would fit into the mysterious ovals like a pair of pictures into frames, of her face that was itself a mask, concealing her thoughts and yet offering to the world a flamboyance that was a kind of mockery or parody of the dark tumult beneath it. The seashells and the feathers, the fine spirals, were a clever portrait of her thought processes.

Christmas was still two months away, but he went in the place and bought it. It cost more than he expected, a hundred and fifty dollars. The girl in the shop was wearing raspberry-colored jodhpurs and a man's shirt with one long sleeve and the other cut off at the elbow. A huge jade mandala hung around her neck on a chain.

"Would this mask be right for a Libra?"

"It would be perfect for a Libra. It's an air sign. Its ruler is Venus. Venusians like to display their love power in visual form. Is the person you're buying it for an artist or a musician?"

"Sort of."

"It's the right time of the year for it too, the autumnal equinox."

While she was putting the mask in a box he wondered why he had paid so much money for it when he couldn't afford it. Was he feeling guilty toward Lily about something? Maybe it was the business about Nils-Frederik and the manuscripts. He had not yet told her about it, and he knew she would disapprove. It wasn't really that, he decided. Lily was an attractive woman, he was still in love with her after all these years, and he wanted to please her. He wanted to see her face, hear her surprised laugh of pleasure, when she opened the box and found the mask: "*Oh Alan. How crazy. It's mine, somehow. It's me.*"

. . .

He left the boutique with the box in a framboise-colored
paper bag, feeling pleased with himself. He was starting to get
on the Beast when a car pulled up to the curb and stopped.
It was a green coupe decorated with darker green pinstripes
like jungle vines, culminating in a swirl of palm leaves on the
trunk. As Alan watched a pale man in a safari jacket got out
of the car. He had milky skin, reddish hair, and freckled hands.
His eyes were a pale blue, magnified like sea creatures by his
glasses with their heavy frames. The car door closed with a
soft complex cluck. The pale man came across the sidewalk,
smiled at Alan like a movie villain, and said, "Hallo, Mr.
Glas. I'm Klipspringer."

"What do you want?"

"Mr. Glas, can I have a word with you?"

"What about? I'm in a hurry. I'm on my way to an appointment." In reality his work was done for the day and he
had no place to go except home. He was looking forward to
a kiss from Lily, a drink before dinner, and a half an hour in
the patio with a volume of Chekhov stories in his lap and the
smell of good cooking wafting to him from the kitchen.

"It's about a matter of some manuscripts."

Alan felt a twinge of panic. He had known from the moment
he saw this milky red-headed man get out of his car that this
was what he would say. It was like a bad dream in which you
woke up and found that everything you had dreamed was
absolutely true. The manuscript of "The Lady with the Dog"
was no more than three feet from where they were standing,
in the bullet-shaped carrier of the Beast. It was unlocked and
anyone could come up to it, flip the catch, and open it. Forcing
himself to appear calm, he studied Klipspringer. His pale blue
glance had nothing human in it at all. It might have been the
look of a cleverly made wax figure. His eyes, which were fixed
steadily on Alan, flickered at intervals behind the glasses.

"Why don't we go into my office and have a talk?"

As he said this it occurred to him that, if they did this, he would have to take the manuscript out of the carrier under the eyes of Klipspringer, or leave it in the carrier which anyone walking by on the sidewalk could open.

"To tell you the truth, Mr. Glas, there are some things I'd like to discuss with you outside the earshot of your secretary. It's a very small office. Almost anything you say in the back, she can hear you in the front."

"How do you know what my office is like?"

"Oh, it's a small place. If you come and stand in the courtyard you can see right into it."

He handed Alan a card, offering a verbal explanation in case he couldn't read it for himself. "Klipspringer and Fineman. We do confidential services for clients. I considerably admire your machine."

"My machine?"

"The bike." His pale spectacled eyes ran over the array of instruments, the polished ebony womb of the gas tank, the streamlined black-and-silver carrier on the back. "A Honda 1200 cc. four-cylinder, isn't it? Plenty of power. Twinned ignition. Hydraulic shift. You call it the Animal, don't you?"

"The Beast."

"Ah yes, the Beast. A beautiful machine. You must be fond of it."

"Is that what you wanted to talk to me about?"

Through the window of the boutique he saw the girl with the jade mandala looking out to see who was talking on the sidewalk. Klipspringer saw her too and smiled disturbingly at her. "No. As I told you, it's about the manuscripts."

"I don't know what manuscripts you're talking about."

"Mr. Nils-Frederik Glas, who I believe is an associate of yours—"

"My father."

"Yes. He has in his possession some manuscripts of doubtful provenance. My client hopes he is not going to take any unwise action in respect to these manuscripts. My client is urgently concerned with the ethical, and even, I might say, the legal aspects of what an unwise use of these manuscripts might entail."

"Unwise use?" Alan felt a little calmer now. This display of clumsy legalese lent a slight admixture of the comical to his antagonist. He seemed now not so much like Peter Lorre as like a clever person at a party doing a Peter Lorre imitation. "Listen, I can't go on talking to you on the sidewalk like this. If you don't want to come to my office, make an appointment with me and we can meet somewhere else and talk about it."

"Ah, then you admit your father has the manuscripts?"

"I don't admit anything. I don't even know who you are. This card doesn't mean a thing. Anybody can have a card printed up."

"My identity is defined by my information, Mr. Glas. If I'm nobody, how is it that I know about the manuscripts?"

"I'm not sure you know about them."

Klipspringer became more genial. Now everything in his manner radiated a synthetic friendship and good will. "Ah, you speak in paradoxes. Delightful. I know that in doing business with you I have to deal with a man of culture and intelligence. You mean, I know about the manuscripts, but in what sense? There are many ways of knowing. The ordinary or vernacular use of the term, the sense of to believe with conviction, the sense of being acquainted with an individual, the Biblical sense, and so on. Mr. Glas, we think it would be better if your father didn't attempt to publish these manuscripts. We think it would be better if he returned them to their rightful owner."

"Who's we?"

"My client and I. And my partner, Mr. Fineman, concurs."

"Ah, Fineman has knowledge too. Who is your client? Are you claiming that your client holds the rights to these manuscripts you claim that you know about?"

"I am not prepared to define the legal position of my client at the present time. Neither can I identify my client, either by name or by status, that is, whether an individual or an institution of some kind, such as a corporation or a government agency. My client is defined by the position assumed. My client stands for honesty, truth, and the creativity of the artist.

My client is not interested in epistemology or metaphysics, but only in concretes."

"What is it that you're proposing we do?"

"Who's we?"

"My father and I."

"You don't include Mr. Wolf?"

"His name is Wolf Ober. Everybody calls him Wolf. My father calls him Wolfgang."

"Ah, now that I didn't know. My client is proposing that the three of you surrender to him any unpublished manuscripts that you have for which you don't hold the copyright, and that you sign an agreement not to publish any copies that you may have made of them."

"Do you understand that I am Mr. Nils-Frederik Glas's agent?"

"Of course."

"What you're saying is ridiculous. You're asking us to sign an agreement not to publish certain unspecified materials, and you're offering nothing in return. No quid pro quo."

"The inducements are negative."

"What do you mean?"

He made his Klipspringer smile. It was a smile that made an unconvincing effort to be human, the smile of a guppy, or of a rubber face with levers inside it. "You're a good person," he said. "An honest, upstanding man. You wouldn't want to get involved with anything substandard. Think of the harm it might do to your little family."

"My family?"

"Your wife, Lily, and your little daughter, Kildy."

Something dark arose in Alan and almost obscured his vision; he saw Klipspringer as through a thin black veil. After his initial panic, he had felt that he was getting the best of the encounter with this curiously inept antagonist whose behavior hovered just on the edge of comedy. He was almost beginning to enjoy it; it was part of the game that he, Nils-Frederik, and Wolf were playing. Now the thought that Klipspringer might seek out Lily and tell her about Nils-Frederik's conspiracy to commit fraud filled him with dread. This was immediately replaced by another thought, which involved Kilda, Klipspringer with his glasses and his mechanical intentness, and his low-slung pinstriped car which stood at the curb.

"Are you threatening me with something or other?"

Through the black veil, which made vision difficult, he heard a fruity melodious voice, different from Klipspringer's only a moment before. "Oh, dear no. Mr. Glas! How could you think such a thing? I just remark, as an item of conversation, that when a young married man embarks into a substandard venture, he ought to consider the possible effects on those near and dear to him."

"How did you find out what my wife's and child's names are?"

"You are good at being a literary agent, Mr. Glas." (Was this an irony?) "I am good at what I do."

Another disquieting thought struck Alan. "Have you been there bothering my family?"

"Where, Mr. Glas?"

"At the place where they live."

"At 1013 Bagley, Mr. Glas. That wasn't necessary."

"See here. Klipspringer. If that's your name."

"But you have an appointment, Mr. Glas, as you said, and I also have my own work to do."

The conversation seemed at an end. Klipspringer made a tentative movement of his shoulders, and Alan was afraid he was going to offer his hand to shake. Instead he turned away toward his car, rotating his head like a dancer so that his pale blue eyes remained fixed on Alan. Only when the door of the car was shut did he turn his attention to the task of driving. Alan noticed now that the car was facing the wrong way at the curb. Klipspringer pulled out and made a wide U-turn, and the jungle-green car slithered away into the traffic on Pico. Alan was left standing on the sidewalk holding the bag with the mask, which he had completely forgotten about. The girl in the shop was watching him through the window.

15 ■

THE HOUSE in Los Feliz was crammed full of people; the guests filled it both upstairs in the living room and downstairs in the kitchen, where they stood elbow to elbow. Other people were sitting on the stairs with their drinks, so that it was hard to get from one floor of the house to the other. There was a self-service bar in the living room and another in the kitchen, with every possible kind of liquor and a number of wines, along with a bottle of aquavit frozen into a block of ice. Charmian, in her printed house dress, was baking piroshki in the oven.

The Glasses (as they were called, just as Wolf and Myra were called the Wolves) came with Lucius Plum, but as soon as they were in the door Lucius disappeared and was lost in the throng. Alan and Lily themselves couldn't penetrate any farther than the kitchen, where they fell in with Wolf and Myra. Lily was sorry now that she had let Alan talk her into coming to this party. She didn't know any of these people except for the Wolves, and she didn't think she was going to like them. Too many of them wore metallicized stretch pants and sandals. There were a couple of middle-aged gays who looked very superior about themselves, and a silly woman in a tweed coat and a tarboosh.

Alan caught Wolf's eye and raised his eyebrow. "Quite a gala affair, eh? I didn't expect this."

"Our friend seems to have gone to a casting office and rented himself a party."

"And a costume agency. Some of the clothes are bizarre," said Myra. She herself was dressed in her usual slightly too dramatic way, in a long black sleeveless dress, clashing bracelets, and a turquoise scarf for a belt. "Who are all these people anyhow? I didn't know he had so many friends."

"He doesn't. That's Lucius Plum over there. He came with

us. I don't know who the rest of them are. Olga Hilliard is here. She's a food writer for the *Times*."

"It's such a crush," said Lily. Alan had got her a drink but she set it on the floor. "Somebody is pressing up against my back. I don't dare turn to see who it is."

"It's just Charmian. She's taking something out of the oven."

"Look at those two women all in white, with white veils."

"They're Sikhs. They always dress like that."

"They don't look Indian."

"Oh, they're not. They're probably American. Real Sikhs in India don't dress anything like that."

"And I saw two young men in shorts and tank tops. Is that the thing to wear to a party?"

"Well, in certain circles."

Lily said, "Alan, here comes Nils-Frederik. If he tries to hug me I'm going to kick him."

"I don't think he will."

Nils-Frederik breasted through the crowd leading several people after him. He was presiding over the party with the geniality of a born host. He was friendly, winsome, and witty, with a personal word and a joke for each guest. Lily remembered again how he could charm people, how nice he could be when he wanted. He was wearing green velveteen pants and a smoking jacket with leather facings.

"Hello, Alan. And Lily! How nice to see you, Lily. How lovely. Lily is a lovely woman, don't you think, everybody?" He hugged her and she smiled palely. "Lily is Alan's wife, and Alan is my son. He's an agent, you know—he's going to handle my book."

"Your book?" Myra was curious.

"Well, I don't like to talk about it much. It's still in the preliminary stages. This is Dr. Ermiane, everyone. He's my dermatologist. I think you all know who Olga Hilliard is. The food writer for the *Times*." This was the silly woman in the tarboosh. "And these are the Thorntons, Burton and Emily. Burton owns the insurance machines at the airport." He didn't explain this joke, if that was what it was. "And over there is Homer Hobart, the art critic for the *Times*, and with him is Will Alpen, who writes for the *L.A. Weekly*." These were the two people that Lily had taken for middle-aged gays, and perhaps that was what they were.

Myra said, "Oh, the *Weekly*. The paper with those wicked personal ads."

"Will doesn't have anything to do with those. He writes about art and books. And over there is Lucius Plum, the historical novelist. Come over here, Lucius."

"You don't have to introduce us," said Alan. "We brought him."

Lucius Plum came up to the group, shouldering his way through the crowd. He was in his eighties and had a shock of vibrant white hair. He was dressed in a tweed suit with shoulder straps and patch pockets, and he carried a leather shoulder bag like a woman's purse.

"This is Lucius Plum, everybody. How's your book coming, Lucius?"

"I'm almost up to Appomattox. I'm getting toward the end."

Nils-Frederik asked him slyly, with a glance at the others, "How long have you been working on it?"

"About nine years."

"Nine years. Ha ha! You know, God made the whole world in a week."

"Rome wasn't built in a day."

Olga Hilliard said, "Is that a sample of your style, Mr. Plum? Is the book to be all clichés?"

Nils-Frederik broke in to deflect the incipient quarrel. "Try the piroshkis, everybody. They're delicious. Has everybody got drinks?"

Alan went with Olga Hilliard to the table with the food. In addition to the piroshkis there were miniature pizzas the size of coins, guacamole dip with raw vegetables, fried wonton, dim sum dumplings, tempura shrimp, quails' eggs with hollandaise, Brie with chutney on water biscuits, assorted sushi, and spring rolls with Hoisin sauce. Olga took nothing but a piece of raw broccoli and a single fried wonton. As a professional food writer she probably made it a point not to eat at parties. She said, "Our hostess has assembled every food cliché of the smart contemporary party. She got it all out of the *Times*. I know, because I wrote most of it."

"Her name is Charmian."

"Is she his wife?"

"No, just a friend."

"Is Nils-Frederik really a writer?"

"Oh yes."

"What's he written?"

"A novel, and a lot of stories."

"I understand the book he's working on is going to be tremendous."

"Who told you that?"

"He did."

"What did he say about it?"

"Well, he was rather mysterious. At one point it sounded like a novel, and at another point he seemed to be saying he was editing a book by somebody else."

"I don't know much about it."

"I thought you were his agent."

"Me? I'm his son."

"He *said* you were his agent."

"I might handle the book, if he writes it. Look, Olga." He counterattacked abruptly, to change the subject. "I used to be your agent too. What happened? You have a new book coming out and I'm not handling it."

"It's being handled by William Morris. You see, Alan, *Festive Dining* is my magnum opus. It has the capability of being a really big success, so I thought I'd better have a real agent, one with an office in New York."

"I see. Olga, how do you happen to know Nils-Frederik anyhow?"

"I don't. He called me up at the *Times* and told me he was

giving a party for some writers and people in publishing, and it might be interesting for me to report in my column. I don't do a party column, but I decided to come anyhow. He asked me to bring other interesting people and I brought Homer and Will."

This was what Alan had wanted to know. He left Olga and went back to the others, carrying his plate. He recommended the food to everybody, and Lily, Wolf, and Myra headed for the table. He was left with Dr. Ermiane and the Thorntons. Dr. Ermiane was a crashing bore. He was giving a lecture about melanoma; he said they should all inspect their backsides every day with a mirror. As Dr. Ermiane was talking Alan caught sight of somebody across the kitchen that he knew, but he couldn't figure out at first who it was. It was a pale man with red hair and glasses with heavy frames. He was wearing a safari jacket, knitted stretch pants, and lemon-colored loafers. He wasn't talking to anybody; he was prowling around carrying an empty glass. Alan saw that it was Klipspringer. He felt another wave of panic, even worse than the one he had felt on the sidewalk in front of his office when Klipspringer had shown such a keen interest in his family. Up to this point he had been enjoying the party, even though it was rather silly, or precisely because it was rather silly. Nils-Frederik was up to his usual antics, and nobody took him seriously, and Olga in her tarboosh, Lucius Plum, and Dr. Ermiane were all part of the fun. The entry of Klipspringer onto the scene changed everything. Alan had the premonition that suddenly the party might turn into something dark and ominous. He watched Klipspringer threading his way through the crowd in the kitchen, still holding his empty glass which he made no effort to fill. Alan stared at him but he seemed to be avoiding eye contact. Alan didn't really want to catch his eye anyhow and be looked at through those thick lenses. He turned over the possibilities. He was a policeman of some sort, for example an FBI agent. But he had said he was a private investigator and showed Alan his card. He was a detective hired by the Hemingway Estate, or by Scribners. He was a quite private blackmailer who had somehow found out what he, Nils-Frederik, and Wolf were up to. He was an amateur philosopher interested in talking about epistemology and the various senses of the word "know," a harmless lunatic. He might be the person that Nils-Frederik bought the manuscripts from. Alan followed him with his eyes. He wondered whether he should tell Nils-Frederik about him, but decided not to.

Nils-Frederik unlocked the door of the study and he and Lucius Plum entered. Everything was exactly as it had been on the Sunday when Alan and Wolf drank coffee here and looked at the story manuscript, except that the table was bare now. There was a stack of blank paper on the desk next to the printer. Lucius Plum was still carrying his leather shoulder bag, which he clutched with one hand as though he was afraid someone would take it away from him. Nils-Frederik was ge-nial. He held a glass with some Perrier and ice in it, and Lucius Plum had a gin and water.

"This is where I work. You see, I'm a writer. Just like you."

"What do you write?"

"Oh, fiction and other things. Nothing important. It's really just a hobby. Not serious like your Civil War novel."

"You said you had some rare manuscripts to show me."

"I did? Oh, so I did. That's why we came here, isn't it?"

He took a key from his pocket and unlocked a file cabinet. In the drawer were folders with manuscripts in them. He extracted some of the manuscripts and spread them out on the table fanwise, like a dealer displaying cards. Lucius Plum picked up one of the stories and began reading it.

"This reads like . . ."

"Yes, it does, doesn't it? I've been making copies from the originals. I do it on the processor you see here."

Lucius Plum looked briefly at the others. "'Down from Schruns.' 'It's Marvelous, She Said.' There's no question that they—yes, yes, it's clear from the style. You say you have the originals?"

"You have the copies in your hand. I could hardly have written them myself, could I?"

"But where did you get them?"

"Suppose I went to Cuba, and somebody in a bar showed them to me. He thought they might be valuable and offered to sell them to me for a few hundred dollars. Everybody is short of dollars in Cuba."

"Cuba?"

"He lived there, you know. Probably he left a lot of stuff behind."

"What are you going to do with them?"

"Hold them for ransom. Ha ha! I'm going to ask the Hemingway Estate how much they'll pay for them."

"You're joking."

"Yes, I am. I'm always joking. Sometimes the jokes are real and sometimes I make them up. It's up to you to decide which it is."

"'An Incantation Against Dying.' This is a long thing. It sounds like that Italian story he wrote. An early one."

"'A Natural History of the Dead.' Did you ever hear about his suitcase?"

"His suitcase?"

"All his manuscripts were in it. It was stolen in 1922 and it's never turned up."

"Was this in Italy?"

"In Paris."

"I thought you said you bought them in a bar in Cuba."

"I said just suppose that. If you're done looking at them now I'll put them away."

"I'm by no means done looking at them. Why, these things are immensely valuable."

"If they're real."

He took the folders away from Lucius Plum and put them back into the file cabinet. Still genial, he propelled him toward the door with a hand around his shoulder. On the landing he locked the door and put the key back in his pocket. The landing was crowded with people and there were more sitting on the stairs, some of them embracing and starting to take each other's clothes off. Instead of going down the stairs he led him across the landing into the living room.

"I thought you'd appreciate those things. A man of fine literary culture like you. And he's a writer of your generation, you know. You must be about his age."

"Not exactly. He was born in ninety-nine. I was born in nineteen ought six."

"How's your drink?" said Nils-Frederik. "Let me freshen it up for you." He went to the bar and added a generous dollop of gin to Lucius Plum's glass.

Klipspringer seemed to have disappeared. He was not in the kitchen, unless he was lying on the floor under people's legs, and he was not in the dining room next to it, which hadn't caught on as one of the venues of the party and was still almost empty. Alan opened the door to the hall, glanced cautiously through it, and ventured on. Finding that Klipspringer had evaporated, he almost succeeded in putting him out of his mind. A residue of dread still clung at the bottom of his chest, like an old wound, but he ignored it and tried to recover his earlier mood in which the party had been a harmless entertainment, a clown show put on by Nils-Frederik, an amateurish publicity stunt for his book. There was nothing he could do about Klipspringer anyhow, and if he ignored him, if he pretended he wasn't there, perhaps he would disappear as fatefully as he had on the sidewalk in front of Alan's office. Alan decided to treat Klipspringer as a harmless hallucination, as something that was only in his mind, as something that hadn't happened.

He was standing in the dark hall with the sounds of the party behind him. Out of impulse he decided to go on a tour of the house, the one in which he had grown up, although now it seemed oddly defamiliarized to him, a place in which his own presence was that of an intruder, a revenant.

In this guise he set off to explore it. On his recent Sunday visit he had seen only the kitchen and the study, and he was curious to see what the rest of it looked like after so long a time.

The house was far too large for Nils-Frederik and the two women. There were a dozen or more rooms off the downstairs hall and more upstairs. Some of them were empty, and others were full of Nils-Frederik's books or unused furniture. Maggie used to call it the Gattopardo house, after the mysterious old castle in the novel of Tomasi di Lampedusa, full of empty rooms, family secrets, and forgotten scandals. He went down the hall and opened the door of the master bedroom. The furniture was different and he hardly recognized the room. Everything was in modern Swedish wood and black enamel. There was a king-size bed with a teak headboard, and the rest of the furniture was teak and black leather. Alan noticed a lingering odor of cigar smoke in the room. He had never known his father to smoke cigars. Of course he had never known him to wear green velveteen pants and a smoking jacket with leather facings either.

It was not only the furniture; the bedroom had been remodeled completely since he had last seen it. To the left the bathroom door was where it had always been. Next to it were a pair of corinthian columns and a curtain with a pastoral scene embroidered on it; nymphs, shepherds, and piled-up cumulus clouds. He pushed through the curtain and found himself in the dark; it was some time before he found the door in the wall at the other side. He entered, groped for a light, and turned it on.

Before him was a dressing table with a circle of bare bulbs around the mirror. On the dressing table was a collection of perfumes and cosmetics; there was a gilded chair before the table. The end of the room was fitted out like a theatrical wardrobe, with hundreds of costumes hanging on racks. Shoes were lined neatly on shelves, and there were mannequin heads for hats and wigs. The drawers of the cabinets were full of underwear, lingerie, and hosiery. There was a heavy odor of face powder and perfume; it made him giddy and he wanted to get out of this confining space.

He went out through the door he had come in, leaving the light on so he could see what was in the space behind the curtain. The curtain was thick and smelled musty; from the back you could see the underside stitching of the embroidery. On one of the columns he found a switch and pushed it. The curtain glided open with a hum and soft pink lights went on overhead. He found himself looking directly at the large bed across the room.

He turned off all the lights, closed the door to the combined closet and bathroom, and pushed the switch to close the curtain again. The pink lights overhead went off. He was puzzled about where the space for these new arrangements had come from. Evidently the small room next to the master bedroom had been eliminated completely and converted to the new bathroom and dressing room. Out in the hall, he found that the door to this former room had been removed completely; there was only a blank wall.

He opened another room and found a small desk and a chair in it, some papers, an old-fashioned sewing machine worked by a treadle, sewing materials, some dog-eared Belgian magazines, and an old gramophone with a tulip horn. This room was evidently Charmian's workroom or retreat, the one place in the house that belonged to her. For some reason he found these things unpleasant. The house seemed alien to him, altered and unreal, a stage set. He left the room and shut the door carefully.

The last room at the end of the hall was the one that had been his when he was a boy. He opened the door slowly and entered. It was dark; the only light came through the door from the hall behind him. The bed was the same narrow one he had slept in as a child. It was neatly made up with the spread pulled over the pillow. As his eyes adjusted he made out Nana sitting by the bed in a teak chair like the ones in the master bedroom. Her white eyes caught the light from the open door. On her lap was a small radio with earphones to fit over her ears. She had not put on the earphones; they were lying in her lap next to the radio. He now made out the rest of the furniture in the room: a dresser, a kneehole desk and chair, and a standing lamp, all in the same modern Scandinavian style.

"It's Alan, isn't it?"

When he didn't answer she said, "I don't like that noise. Shut the door."

The sounds from the party at the other end of the house were almost inaudible. He turned on the lamp and shut the door. Now he could see her more clearly; she was wearing her usual colorless smock with spots of food and grease on it.

"Is this your room, Nana?"

"Yes."

"Why have they put you here? It's a room for a child. It used to be mine when I was little."

She made no reply. It was the least desirable room in the house, windowless and reduced to an awkward L-shape by the linen closet in the hall outside. The furniture, except for his old bed, was modern and impersonal; it might have been in a television commercial or the showroom of a store. Alan realized now that Nana's room when he lived in the house had been the one that had now been eliminated in the remodeling of the master bedroom.

"What are you doing in here, Nana? Are you listening to your radio?"

"There's nothing on it. It's all American. I've asked Nils for a Swedish radio but he says there aren't any."

"This is America, Nana. Don't talk foolishness. Why don't you listen to the American radio?"

She smiled craftily, a peasant smile. He couldn't help feeling that she was watching him with her milky eyes. It was possible that her eyesight was better than she let on.

"If you don't listen to the radio, Nana, what do you do?"

She sat for a moment as though she was thinking of the answer to this question. Then she said, "I travel a lot, you know, Alan."

"What do you mean, Nana?"

"Now that I can't see so well I travel all the time. You see, I can go anywhere I want. I can find a road, a long narrow road with a row of poplars on each side, and I can go down it as far as I like. It stretches on and on; as far as I walk there is still more road. On one side," she went on in a singsong tone as though she was repeating things that she herself knew well, "there's a town, and on the other side a cliff and a river. The road goes down along the side of the cliff and follows the river for a while. Then it comes to another town, a pretty one where the houses are white and have green shutters. If I want I can stop by the side of the river and take my shoes off and walk in the water, holding up my skirt. I can be a young girl again if I want."

"I hope I have as many memories when I'm your age."

"It isn't memories, Alan. Don't talk to me as though I were a foolish old woman. You know I'm not. Come closer to me, Alan. Sit on the bed."

He sat down on the bed without taking his eyes from her face; he felt her hand come out and explore his body like a snake. The hand drew him closer, with a gesture rather than with real force, and he slid over toward the chair so that his knees were almost touching her. While she talked she left her hand resting lightly on his waist.

"I'm glad you're listening to me, Alan. Nils doesn't like it when I talk about these things. After a long while, on this road along the river, I come to the outskirts of a city. First there's a crossroads with a gas station on one corner and a little grocery on the other. I can go in the grocery and look at the things. Then as I go on there are more stores, and the streetcar track begins and goes the rest of the way into the city. I can get on the streetcar but I don't have to pay. No one can see me, no one knows that I'm there. The streetcar goes on past houses with gardens, and the library and the park. I can go wherever I want in the city. When I'm done seeing all the shops and stores, and the museum and the gardens, I don't have to go back home where I came from; I can go further on down the road out of the city and find a hotel to stay in, by the riverbank with windows opening on the water so I can hear it as I go to sleep. Or by a lake with water rippling, and ducks and geese. And in the hotel too no one can see me; I can push open the door and go into my room, and turn back the covers and get into bed with clean sheets, and go to sleep listening to the sound of water outside the window."

The sounds of the party penetrated dimly through the walls, a distant buzz like bees, with occasional peals of laughter. "And when you wake up you're back here in your room."

"It's not a dream, Alan. I'm telling you about places I can go. My life in this room is not real. It's darkness and silence. I have everything I want, Alan. Nils gives me everything I want. I lack for nothing."

"How old are you, Nana?"

Her voice fell into a playful tone, a kind of lilt. It was clear that many people asked her this question, and she had found an answer to it that amused her or gave her pleasure. "I don't know. I may be eighty or ninety. Eighty or ninety," she repeated in her singsong tone. "I was born on the island of Kymmendö in the Stockholm skerries, Alan." He didn't know this; he knew only that she and her sea-captain husband came from Stockholm. "It's a beautiful place with water all around. There are many rocky islands with pines, in a black sea, and white villages. Stormy bays backed by the boundless ocean," she went on as though she was reciting a poem. "You can go there on a boat, it takes a half a day. And do you know, I was born the same night that my grandfather died. Nobody paid any attention to my mother because they were too busy taking care of my grandfather who had a lot of money. They told me later that I was born a half an hour after he died, and in between it was midnight. And do you know, Alan, he died in the other century and I was born at the beginning of this century," she told him in a voice that trailed off into a little quaver of satisfaction.

He smiled. "I can't believe that, Nana. It's too neat a story. You just made that up."

"Then you tell me how old I am, Alan," she said craftily. "You tell me where I was born."

"Maybe someone could take down your stories and they could be published in a book."

"I don't need a book. I can go wherever I want. I can go to all the places where there is water, and kneel down and it will flow through my hands. And do you know, Alan, all the rivers flow to the sea, but the sea is not full."

"That's from the Bible, Nana."

"I don't care for the Bible. It's nothing but stories by old men. I am telling you about all the places where I can go. You ask me what I am doing here alone in the dark. But I am not listening to this stupid radio."

"It only gets American stations. Maybe I could find you a shortwave radio that would get Sweden."

"All these things are toys, Alan." She said abruptly, "Alan, are you thinking of taking a trip?"

"A trip? Not particularly."

"I thought you might be going to New York to see Nils's other wife."

"Maggie. My mother." She knew perfectly well who the two women were.

"If you go, maybe you could use a nice suitcase. Why don't you borrow one of Nils's? He has a lot of them in the closet in his bedroom."

"I don't think so. It's full of Charmian's clothes."

"Oh, not that closet." She smiled as though he had made a childish mistake. "His own closet. The one that's always been there. I'm sure you'd find a nice suitcase in it."

He felt something like a small electric shock. She watched him with her peasant craftiness as he left the room and shut the door behind him, leaving her in darkness.

• • •

The hallway was still deserted. No one at the party would have any reason to come to this part of the house; there was a bathroom off the kitchen and another one upstairs. Nils-Frederik was busy playing the host and was unlikely to leave his guests. He opened the door noiselessly and slipped back into the master bedroom.

Nils-Frederik's own closet, the one that Nana had spoken about, was at the other end of the room from Charmian's. He opened it, groped for the dangling string, and turned on the light. It too was a large room, although not as large as Charmian's closet. Nils-Frederik's clothes filled the racks; dozens of suits, jackets, dressing gowns, slacks, and shirts. The shoes with shoe trees in them were neatly arranged on shelves. There were built-in cabinets for underwear and other small clothing. A hundred or more neckties hung from patent racks. There was a black leather vest of the kind worn by rock musicians, a garment he couldn't imagine his father wearing. Under the clothes, in the corner of the closet, was a bulky shape covered with a Navajo rug that had been in the house since he was a child. He removed it and found a stack of cardboard cartons and something green showing below them. With his heart pounding he lifted the cartons and set them on the floor; they were heavy and seemed to be full of crockery or kitchen appliances. At the bottom was the Suitcase.

It was a small traveling case in green leather, spotted with oil stains and scratched and battered. The brass corner reinforcements were green with verdigris. The handle had come loose and had been repaired with a piece of wire. It looked very old.

He pulled it out into the center of the closet where the light was better. It was moderately heavy as though there was something inside it. There were a couple of small green stickers on it from U.S. customs inspections. The brass clasps at the top were covered with verdigris like the corner reinforcements. They showed signs they had recently been opened; they felt greasy as though someone had oiled them to free up the corrosion. Now they were locked, and they were solid metal fittings not easy to force. He looked around; there was no sign of a key.

At that moment he heard a noise in the hallway outside the bedroom, an intermittent bump as though someone were sweeping. He was conscious of the beating of his heart and of a light sweat under his clothing. He lifted the Suitcase, turned it upside down, and shook it. Whatever was inside was moderately heavy and made a dull sound as it fell. It could very well have been bundles of paper. He hurriedly put the Suitcase back in its place in the corner, stacked the cartons on top of it, and replaced the Navajo rug.

In the kitchen the crowd had thinned out a little; some people had already left, and others had gone upstairs to the living room. Most of the people downstairs were clustered around the food table or the bar. At the end of the kitchen, near the stove, Charmian was with Klipspringer, who had materialized through the door from the garage and begun talking to her as though he were a door-to-door vacuum-cleaner salesman. He was a queer-looking duck but engaging; she had always admired safari suits, the uniform of adventurers, and she was attracted to men with pale skins and freckles. Thick eyeglasses, to her mind, were a sign of learning. She told him, "I don't know why you should take an interest in me."

"You're the hostess of the party. It's only polite to pay my respects."

"Nobody else has."

"They're overlooking something. Besides, you have something valuable that I want."

"What is it?"

He said waggishly, "It might be hidden under your clothing. May I search?"

"No, you may not." She smiled in spite of herself. "At least not here. What do you think I am?"

"A charming lady." His eyes fell over her print dress and her pale bare arms. "You're Belgian, aren't you?"

"Yes, I came from Ghent."

"You know, I'm Belgian too."

"You? You couldn't be. Say something in Flemish."

"Well, I wasn't exactly a Flemish Belgian."

"Were you a Walloon then? Say something in French."

"Languages were never my forte. To tell you the truth, I don't remember what language I spoke when I was in Belgium. I was only a child."

"You know," she said coquettishly, "I hardly believe anything you're saying to me."

"Mistrustful charmer! I assure you it's all true. Are you going to give me this valuable thing that I covet?"

"If I gave it away, I wouldn't have it anymore. It would be gone forever." Charmian felt that she had strayed into one of the romances she read as a girl, or a popular song of a bygone era.

"But you would have instead my infinite and inestimable gratitude."

"What would Nils say?"

"He need never know about it. Besides, it would serve him right for all these bad things he's done to you."

"Bad things? I don't know what you're talking about."

"Surely you do. Can you really say he's treated you kindly?"

"Yes, I can. He's brought me to America. I have a nice kitchen, better things to eat, my own bathroom. I could never have had that in Belgium."

"And your costume collection. Nils-Frederik has some strange ways."

"What do you know about that?"

"My business is knowing about things. Tell me more about Nils-Frederik. Is he really as important a writer as they say?"

"I don't know. He writes every morning. He's got file cabinets full of the stuff he's written."

"I understand you've got your own little collection too."

"Collection of what?"

"Of Nils-Frederik's writing. It's a perfectly understandable impulse. One is curious about what such a talented person is up to. I myself would be extremely interested in getting a glimpse of it."

"Is this what you meant by saying I had something valuable you coveted?"

"How clever you are! Most women would have taken my remark as purely romantic."

"I took it both ways."

"That shows what a complex person you are. The ability to maintain two contradictory ideas in mind at the same time is a mark of high intelligence. Then I can assume that you will give me the thing I covet, or at least," he added, heavy with innuendo, "show me a glimpse of it?"

"You're very bad!" She laughed. "What would I get out of it?"

"My eternal friendship. And a bit of *Schadenfreude.*"

"Then you know German."

"Yes, I remember now, it was German I spoke in Belgium."

"Do you think that I might take joy in someone else's misfortunes?"

"I'm just guessing."

"Well, I'm afraid you're mistaken. I'm just a kind person, really. I enjoy doing things for others. I like to cook. Did you try my piroshkis? The quails' eggs with hollandaise? The dim sum?"

"I've already tried them. They're delicious."

"Are you interested in cooking?"

"Oh, yes."

"I could show you some of my recipes."

"That would be nice."

She reached for the recipe box on top of the cupboard and took it down. Searching through it with her fingers, she came to the tab marked "Salads" and took out the cards behind it. Instead of showing them to him she handed them to him without a word. She was moved by malice, as Klipspringer had suggested she might be, but also by a spirit of romance, a faith in life as a storybook, that was always hidden just under the surface in her mind. Now she knew why she had copied the story so painstakingly onto the cards. He smiled and slipped them into his pocket without looking at them.

Upstairs in the living room someone was playing the piano and people were singing. Alan pushed his way to the window with the idea of standing there quietly by himself sipping his drink and looking out at the city, but he found that people were standing with their backs to the window so that he couldn't get to it, and also that the glass was steamed up and it was impossible to see anything through it. He turned and found himself in a circle of people including the Thorntons, Olga Hilliard, and a couple he hadn't been introduced to, a lean bearded man and his wife in a dress with zigzags like a camouflaged destroyer. He was a photographer and she was an attorney, or perhaps she only worked in an attorney's office; she talked very knowledgeably about the law. Their names were Kevin and Margaret. It was hard to follow what people were saying over the hum of conversation and music from the piano. Alan absentmindedly tried to keep track of it all while he sipped his vermouth and looked around the living room. There was a large Rouault reproduction on the wall facing the window. It was in an elaborate gilt and ochre frame and it was done in a process that even simulated the impasto, so that for a person not knowledgeable about art it might be taken for an original. On the other wall were the Gustav Klimt prints, and in a lighted alcove at the end of the room was the small bronze Degas dancer, the statuette that he and Lily had quarreled over at dinner in the restaurant.

There was no sign of Klipspringer either downstairs or upstairs; he had disappeared just as Alan had hoped he magically might. He had come up here to the living room only after he had carefully searched the rest of the house for him. It was years since Alan had been in this room. He looked around at it, seeing it now in a new guise. The Rouault was a clever fake, the

Klimts were only prints, the Degas was a museum facsimile. And the objects in Charmian's room, the sewing machine, the old-fashioned gramophone, and the magazines, had been brought from Europe to make a place in the house that would serve as a nest or frame for the Charmian that Nils-Frederik imagined, the Charmian he wished her to be, a Belgian peasant with old-fashioned ideas. His life was a facsimile. He was not a gentleman, he was not a bibliophile and a collector of old books, he was not a person of superior and refined taste. He didn't really understand clothes; he thought green pants and a smoking jacket were the thing to wear at a party.

And the party itself was fake; Alan had seen this the moment he came in the door with Lily and Lucius Plum. Nils-Frederik was writing certain fictions which he hoped might be taken for stories by a famous and celebrated author, or (at times Alan himself almost forgot which it was) he was copying some stories by a famous author which he hoped might be taken for his own. He gave this party to hint to people about what he was doing, so that the word would spread through the underground, preparing the way for the book when it appeared. He didn't really have this many friends; he didn't have any friends at all except Wolf. He had invited his insurance agent, his attorney and her husband, his doctor, and some names he got out of the newspaper. Each of the guests imagined that the others were friends of Nils-Frederik, but he had collected these people out of the phone book. The party was an elaborately staged drama, and in it Nils-Frederik was playing himself, the self he wished people to believe in.

But the Suitcase was real, Alan reminded himself. In the bedroom of the house, its most intimate retreat, one that was itself a theater, he had found the one object among Nils-Frederik's possessions that was unmistakably authentic. The stories were real, and they were stolen. He wished to conceal this, and he had enlisted Alan and Wolf in a scheme to suggest that he had written the stories himself. That persevering pest Klipspringer could penetrate the house, and he would eventually discover the Suitcase in the closet if somebody didn't prevent him, and then the whole thing would blow up and they would all be arrested for theft. Alan was confused and uncertain and didn't know what he wanted to do. He had an idea that whatever he did in the end would be not what he wanted to do but what Nils-Frederik decided he would do.

Lucius Plum was standing by the bar talking to Homer Hobart and Will Alpen. He wasn't sure who they were, except that they were newspapermen and writers. He suspected that they might be the kind of men who went around together and didn't care for women. He was drawn to them because of that; he too had always felt himself to be an outsider and a person regarded as queer because he was creative. He himself wasn't queer in that way, of course, but he still got along perfectly well with such people and was attracted to them. As a matter of fact, Lucius Plum had never been to bed with a woman, but he had a powerful imagination and some scenes that happened in his head were at least as vivid to him as things that took place in the outside world. He described sexual intercourse at several places in his novel and he was confident that people would find it convincing.

He had a gin and water in his hand; his fourth or fifth, he hadn't been counting. There was the one he started with in the kitchen, the refill that Nils-Frederik had given him upstairs in the living room, another he had garnered for himself at the same upstairs bar, and the one he now held in his hand, which had probably come from the bar he was now standing in front of. (In front of which he was now standing, he corrected himself; he was a classicist in style and did not believe in ending a sentence with a preposition.) He had felt a little woozy earlier, when he was talking to Nils-Frederik in his study, but that was probably because of his several trips up and down the stairs. Lucius Plum did not take kindly to stairs. He always carried a few nitro tablets in his pocket in case of chest pains. What he felt upstairs was not a chest pain but a slight wooziness. He liked this word, along with other words and expressions that were typical of rural American culture: all around Robin Hood's barn, sitting in the catbird seat, as queer as Dick's hatband. It was partly because of this that he was writing his Civil War novel; he could give free rein to his penchant for these salty old-fashioned locutions. But Homer and Will were saying something to him.

"Freshen up your drink?"

"Oh, thanks." He surrendered the glass and watched it fill up with gin. "That's enough; a little water please. Our host has already plied me generously with his alcoholic largesse."

"Do you know Nils-Frederik well?"

"Oh, not well. I know him a little." As a matter of fact he had met him only this evening, and the conversation in the study was the first time he had talked to him. Of course he knew Alan well; he was his agent. Alan had often spoken to him about his father.

"What kind of a chap is he?"

"Oh, he's a splendid person. Friendly, generous, witty, well-read. He doesn't have an awful lot of creative talent, though. He's written one novel, but it didn't amount to much."

"Have you read it?"

"No. I don't think anyone else has either. That's what I mean by saying it didn't amount to much."

"I understand it's an imitation of Henry James."

"I wouldn't know."

"That's what Olga says."

Lucius Plum had no idea who Olga was. She must be that woman in the Turkish fez who had twitted him about his style in the kitchen. He didn't care for her. He didn't regard food writers as arbiters of prose style, or of anything else for that matter. To his mind an excessive preoccupation with what you ate was one of the most foolish concerns in the world. It was all just calories; you put it in your mouth and ate it and it all turned into the same thing. He knew the word for this too and had put it into his novel several times. Readers liked such things. Of course he always attributed such language to enlisted men and not officers. Readers liked their officers to be gentlemen, even though they might engage in sexual misconduct. Lucius Plum thought of a new thing that General Lee might do in his novel. It involved an innkeeper named Appassionata Duvalier that he had already established as a flamboyant character. He wished he had a pencil and a scrap of paper; he felt surreptitiously in his pockets.

"It seems he's working on a book."

"Who? Oh, our host. I wouldn't know about that. You know, he has some extraordinary things in his study. He has some unpublished things by a famous writer. All his manuscripts were stolen in Paris in 1922. Now it seems they've turned up."

Will looked at Homer. "Paris? 1922?"

"It's Balzac," said Homer.

Lucius Plum colored. They seemed to be pulling his leg. He was about to reveal the true name of the author but changed his mind. "Balzac was not alive in 1922. His manuscripts might have been stolen in that year, but not from him."

"It was from the Bibliothèque Nationale," said Homer. "A famous case."

The guests all left at the same time, a little after midnight, in a kind of mass panic, a flight of gazelles from the watering hole. It was as though all of them, taken in at first by Nils-Frederik's geniality and plausibility, by the luxury of the house with its view of the city, had detected at the same moment the hint of the spurious in the elaborately contrived setting, and had taken fright and fled lest they be trapped forever in this skein of illusion and reality. Or, less fantastically, Alan told himself, they had all drunk too much and were behaving like a herd of animals. He and Lily took Lucius Plum home to his apartment on North Whitley in Hollywood.

In the car afterwards Lily said, "I'm glad I went to the party, actually. It gives me some notion what you're up to at the agency."

"What do you mean, what I'm up to at the agency?"

"Nothing in particular. You go away to your job every day and you don't tell me what you do there. I saw you talking to that food writer. She's your client, isn't she?"

"She used to be. She's with William Morris now."

"She's a very attractive woman. She's a Capricorn, of course. Capricorns appear reserved and cool, but actually they're eager and passionate. They have artistic ability, but they use it to advance their ambitions instead of creating true works of art. An interest in food can be a form of artistic expression."

"How do you know she's a Capricorn?"

"Oh, you can see that easily enough. Your work with your clients is very intimate, I can see that now. It isn't like a tax accountant with his clients or a dentist with his patients. You work with them more personally."

"Dentistry is much more intimate than my work. I've never had my hand inside Olga's mouth. Besides, as I told you, she's not my client anymore. She has a book that may make real money so she left me."

"I never suggested that you had your hand in her mouth. All I said was that she's a very attractive person and I understand a little better now what your work is like at the agency. It just seems strange that she's supposed to be one of your clients, and then she turns up at this party which is a purely social affair having nothing to do with your agency."

"It was Nils-Frederik who invited her to the party."

"I know that. That's part of what I'm talking about. Nils-Frederik probably has some deep reason for wanting to bring you and Olga together. Leos are manipulative and like to control other people's sex lives. First he invited her to the party, then he works his will on you so that the two of you are across the room with your heads together. God knows what he has in mind but I'm sure it's something. I do not trust Nils-Frederik, Alan. I don't trust you either, of course, but I trust Nils-Frederik even less. He is powerful, Alan." Her voice dropped almost to a whisper. "He is a very powerful man. He can do what he wants."

"That's nonsense. He has a little money, that's all. He has no particular power that anybody else doesn't have."

"Those two women are his slaves, Alan, Nana and Charmian. And he has you in his power. He can do whatever he wants with you. After all those bad things that happened with the IRS, after you swore you wouldn't have anything to do with him anymore, all he has to do is make one telephone call and you fly right back to him."

"I didn't fly right back to him. I went to see him and we talked, he and I and Wolf. Nils-Frederik is a very talented person. He has some crazy ideas, but there is also a kind of genius to him. I'm not going to do anything that will hurt me or us, Lily." (*Think of the harm you might do your little family,* said Klipspringer.) "I'm not a child," he blurted on to her. Look, Lily. Where am I getting in my life? I've had this agency for ten years and it's barely paying the rent on the office. My present life is not acceptable to me. I'm not satisfied with myself. Something has got to change in my life. In our lives," he corrected.

"You say something has got to change. What would it be, Alan? We're the way we are. You can't change yourself and neither can I."

Alan had a new idea now. No more Beverly Hills, green plot of lawn, and recreation room. "I've thought about our moving to New York. I could be a real agent there, and not just a provincial agent who deals with people like Lucius Plum and the stunt man who is writing his memoirs."

"That's ridiculous, Alan. You couldn't have your motorcycle in New York. I couldn't even have a car. It's a totally different kind of life. It isn't safe on the streets and the schools are bad. It's impossible to find an apartment."

"It just takes money. If I went into a certain venture with Nils-Frederik, just for a year, we might make enough money so we could rent an apartment in New York. Then we would leave Nils-Frederik behind. Maggie moved to New York to get out of Nils-Frederik's influence, Lily. I like Maggie. She's my mother, after all. If we lived in New York we could see a lot of her. She would be our family instead of Nils-Frederik. Kilda could go to a private school. And I would be a real agent, not the fake that I am now."

"What's this certain venture? I don't like the sound of that. He said he was writing a book."

"Yes, what's wrong with that? Maybe I'll help him get it published."

"His writing has never made any money. His novel was published by a vanity press. What's this all about, Alan? I wish you wouldn't get involved with him."

"Lily, you know very well how the agent business works. I don't risk anything except a little time and energy. If the book makes money, I get a commission."

"Things are never that simple with Nils-Frederik. Whatever it is that the three of you are planning, don't do it. We're getting along all right as we are."

Alan said, "You're the Female Principle in the family, wanting not to take risks and to preserve things as they are. I'm the Male Principle, thinking up new things to make our life better. If women had their way we would still be living in a cave wearing skins. Hey, look at this round thing I've invented. I call it a wheel. Don't have anything to do with it, the women would tell him. It will just cause trouble. They were right, of course. Look at all the trouble wheels have caused."

"Oh, don't talk such shit, Alan!" she said, exasperated. "You always drivel on like this; you think you're so clever, and so malicious. You get that from Nils-Frederik."

16 ▪

CHARMIAN WAS sitting in the Parnassus, an art film theater on Wilshire, watching a movie she had never seen before. She always enjoyed this; she knew the old ones so well that they bored her. People around her were eating popcorn and candy bars and sipping sodas from paper cups, but she had not bought anything in the lobby. She scorned these plebeian pleasures and preferred to postpone her self-indulgence until after the movie. This was a particularly nice movie, with two couples, one vulgar and one sophisticated. The photography was sharply focused and glowed with a silvery effulgence. She watched a scene in a newspaper office, another in a rich mansion, a dinner party with the men in tuxedos, a trout-fishing scene where the suave hero fell in the water, and a titillating encounter on an ocean liner. In only a few minutes she had associated herself totally with the heroine, the one in the ermine cape. She was distant, cool, full of innuendoes and sideways glances, and he was smooth and duplicitous with a small mustache. He was a reporter but he concealed this from her. He was also her blackmailer, but even when she discovered this it didn't bring an end to their arch flirtations. She was the richest girl in the world, and she could deal with this as smoothly as she did the other minor problems of her life. It was easy when you had lots of money. She was smart and dangerous. He was in love and she was not, at least not at this stage. She wore a white organdy dress sparkling with sequins, a knee-length ermine cape, and a jeweled bracelet. Her complexion was pale and her dark hair was marcelled in the style of the thirties. They danced; she spoke with cryptic mystery; she knew who he was; he smiled.

Charmian lost herself completely in this world of furs, jewels, and wealth. Not only had she herself become the woman in the ermine cape, but the world around her, the tacky theater and the vulgar people with their popcorn, had vanished entirely to be replaced by ocean liners and mansions. She felt drugged and slightly drowsy, and at the same time keenly aware of everything that was happening. In her ordinary life, her life outside the theater, she did not feel things nearly so sharply and vividly. In the movie there were no dirty clothes or dishes to wash. There were bedrooms but they had single beds. People touched and embraced, they kissed, but they kept their clothes on and one foot on the floor. She knew that after the movie

ended the suave man would take the pale lady into his bed and
do certain things to her, and she would submit to them, just as
she, Charmian (with an effort she separated the two identities)
submitted when they were done to her. That was the way life
was. You could not change that, even in movies, although in
the movies these things took place after the end so that they
were not seen. This seemed to Charmian to be an eminently
civilized way to arrange matters. She had no objections to
housework, dirty clothes, or animal couplings; she simply preferred to look at other things when she went out to enjoy herself. The movie turned out about as she expected, both for the
classy couple and the mug couple. The lady in the ermine cape
got her way, even though in a complicated and unexpected
fashion. The last scene faded, the lights came on, and the popcorn eaters stood up and gazed about them, bewildered.

  In the street outside Charmian paused to savor her exact
sensations. The opulence of the movie had disappeared as
though at the turning of a switch. It was three o'clock in the
afternoon on Wilshire Boulevard. A grayish light that was at
the same time curiously intense fell from the overcast sky.
Things were shabby, ordinary, lacking in mystery but at the
same time solid and opaque, concealing some secret in their
mass and hardness, their bright impenetrable colors, their real-
ness. Everything was very spacious; the real world was larger
than the world of the movie. It was slightly too cool; she
shivered. There was dirt everywhere; she had forgotten about
dirt while she was in the movie. The sidewalk was grimy, the
buildings had a thin layer of soot on them, and there were
candy wrappers and paper cups in the gutter.
  She was still wearing her flowered print dress and round-
toed brown shoes, without stockings. She had added a round
straw hat with a wooden cherry on one side, and she carried
an imitation gold-mesh bag on a long gold chain. Her car was
across the street in the parking lot. Negotiating the crosswalk
with care on the light, she got into it, paid for the parking at

the gate, and drove off west toward a better part of Wilshire that beckoned her.

It was not really her car, of course; it was Nils-Frederik's Peugeot. For him the car was a joke; he loved to pronounce its name in a French accent, rounding his lips exaggeratedly and sticking them out: *Puh-ZHO*. Charmian took cars seriously and thought she was lucky to have it. It *was* her car for all purposes; Nils-Frederik couldn't go out in it unless she was at the wheel, or unless Alan drove him. She appreciated its shiny ebony finish, its discreet interior, its smoothly clicking efficiency. In it she felt herself to be a true citizen of this city which was really only a collection of streets and freeways, in which people's identities were merged with their cars. It was she who was really the American, she thought. It was Nils-Frederik who was the European, in his tastes and temperament and in the life he led. She did not know anyone else like Nils-Frederik in America; however, she had encountered other people like him in Europe. Slowing for a light at La Brea, she shifted dexterously into third and accelerated around a bus. The cherry on her hat bobbed.

At Beverly Center she drove to the valet station and got out. A young man in a tuxedo with a frilled shirt and running shoes gave her a ticket, and she turned her back on the car and went into the center. She loved being alone in a crowd of strangers. She much preferred it to being with people she knew. She went to several stores, seeming to glance idly at things but having an exact idea in her mind of what she wanted. When she needed to do things with two hands, such as taking a garment from a rack, she hung the gold bag around her neck so that it rested on her stomach. She bought some expensive perfume, after sampling several. She tried them on both wrists, and then on both elbows. The clerk said, "I don't see how you can smell it on your elbow." Charmian told her, "We have a saying, your elbow is near but try to kiss it." The clerk tittered. "Who's we?" "I'm from Belgium." "Oh well," said the clerk, "I guess you have lots of wonderful perfumes in Europe."

After a while she sat down and had an ice cream in a specialty shop, a confection with three different-colored balls in it, along with some crème de menthe, a dab of Swiss chocolate, and some crushed macadamia nuts. It came with a tiny Japanese umbrella which she took off and put in her purse. Then she got up and went through some more stores. There must be hundreds of them in the center, she thought; she had never explored them all. In a fake fur shop she found a cape that would do. It was not as long as the one in the movie, it came only to her hips, but the plastic fur glistened with a snowy phosphorescence sharper than real life. In some way they had made it smell like leather, a sharp feral scent. She paid for it with her card and left the shop carrying a huge bag.

With the gold handbag banging softly against her hip, she looked in several more places for a white organdy dress. She didn't find it, but she bought a silver bracelet glittering with gems, and an arrangement consisting of a pair of stockings with old-fashioned garters sewed to them and a garter belt to match; she had never before seen such a thing. This was in a shop that sold novelty lingerie. She was tired after being on her feet for so long, and she sat down again and had a pastry with a cappuccino royale. The pastry was a Napoleon, and the cappuccino had coffee, chocolate, and brandy in it, with a froth of whipped cream on top. She took her time with them, turning from one to the other, and she savored them in two ways, as a secret sensualist and as a cook who might try to make both the coffee and the pastry herself sometime.

When she left the pastry shop she bought a box of expensive cigarettes, smoked only one, and threw the rest away. Then she stopped once more, to buy some Godiva chocolates which she put into her purse and nibbled on now and then as she shopped. All these things she paid for with her card, which was gold and had a hologram on it that changed pictures when you wiggled it, a thing that amused her greatly. The dress she finally found was not quite like the one in the movie, although Nils-Frederik would probably not notice. It was white organdy with sequins, lacy and frilled, clinging close to the body and then flaring out above the knee in a way that was perfect for dancing. A silver belt came with it. She tried it on in the dressing room, taking off her hat and print dress but leaving on her shoes. After she put on her clothes again she took the white dress out and set it by the register with her card.

The clerk, glancing at her print dress and the hat with the cherry, said, "Is it the right size, dear?"

"A little too full around the hips. I can take it in."

"I can hardly believe that; it's a twelve."

"I'm not as large as I look," said Charmian. She went off with all her packages.

At the valet station she handed in her ticket and waited until the car came. It was ten dollars, and she paid for this too with her card. On the whole it had been a very satisfactory afternoon. Turning back onto Wilshire, she checked the clock in the dash of the Peugeot. It was a little after six. Nils-Frederik would be restive, but she could tell him that she had gone to a movie and then shopping, all of which was perfectly true. She reached for the last of the chocolates and ate them as she drove.

17 ▪

ALAN GOT to the house early and then had to wait while Nils-Frederik changed his clothes to go out. He spent the time talking to Nana. Charmian was out in the garden weeding. The old woman rambled on in her usual way. He had to sit close to her at the kitchen table to understand her. Staring past his ear with her white eyes, she murmured fragmentary recollections of her childhood in Sweden, interlarding them with cryptic remarks about human relations, remarks that, although hard to follow, were evidently aimed at his own relationship with Nils-Frederik. In spite of her poor eyesight and her rambling speech it was clear that she knew perfectly well who he was. She heard Nils-Frederik coming down the hall and whispered, "Don't tell him that we were talking about money. That will make him angry."

Nils-Frederik appeared in his checked suit, maroon waistcoat, and wingtip shoes. Since he was going out he had added a gray fedora with a snap brim, a gangster's hat. He smiled broadly when he saw Alan and Nana at the table. "Well, well, what are you two conspiring over? Up to some mischief, I imagine. Nana, you old dear." He patted her head as though she were a favorite spaniel. "You always did have a taste for younger men. And Alan's your favorite, that's clear."

"Alan is a good boy," said Nana.

"We're all good boys. Alan's a good boy and I'm a good boy. And you love us both, don't you?" He caught Alan's glance, with his knowing smile, and gave Nana's head a final pat. "Your two big boys. Nils and Alan. I'll bet that sometimes you forget which is which. And Klaus, your husband? Which one of us is Klaus? And which one is Nils, and Alan?"

"You're Klaus," said the old woman grumpily.

Nils-Frederik laughed. "Let's go, Alan." He took the car keys from his pocket and tossed them to him.

Alan backed the Peugeot out of the garage. It was a nice car and he enjoyed driving it. It hadn't been driven very much and still had a new-car smell inside it, a thing that always gave him pleasure.

"What were you and Nana talking about?"

"We were talking about money," he said, simply out of malice, to see what would happen. He suspected that Nils-Frederik sometimes had difficulty with Nana about money, since she still controlled it (or so Alan imagined; he had no precise information on this point), and probably he was continually at her for more of it.

"That surprises me a great deal," he said. "She doesn't know the first thing about it. I handle all that for her." Alan smiled to himself. "Don't drive quite so fast," said Nils-Frederik. "It makes me nervous. We have plenty of time. Let's go by Savory's first."

At Savory's he got out and Alan waited in the car at the

curb. Through the window he saw the tired-looking clerk, a small pinched man in shirtsleeves and a bow tie, reach behind him on the shelf for the Sobranies and set them on the counter without a word. Money changed hands, Nils-Frederik pocketed the cigarettes and left, all without a word on either side. It was as though it were some kind of surreptitious transaction, a sale of illegal drugs or an exchange of ransom in a kidnapping. Nils-Frederik got back into the car, opened the small black-and-gold box, and lit a cigarette with the lighter on the dash. He never bought more than one pack at a time.

"I really am going to give these things up, Alan. It's important for me to give them up. But it's important for me to smoke them too. Do you know that there are special receptors in the body for nicotine and for opium derivatives? In the brain there are tiny microscopic cells, almost invisible. They have very complicated shapes, and these shapes are made so that the shapes of nicotine molecules, which are also very complicated, fit exactly into them. When that happens the pleasure centers in the brain are stimulated. Over millions of years the human body evolved until it produced these tiny jigsaw pieces, waiting for the other pieces that we call nicotine to be fitted into them. Why do you think that is, Alan? What did evolution have in mind?"

"I have no idea," said Alan cautiously.

"I have. Somebody up there had planned this all out, and I'm not sure He's on our side. It may be just his idea of a joke. Deus ludens, the playful God. He slays us for his sport. First He invented vices for us, and then He gave us cells in the brain that make it impossible for us to resist those vices. We'd be doing fine without Him. Of course, we wouldn't have any vices and we'd be bored to death." He drew on the cigarette, held the smoke in his lungs, and then slowly released it. A bluish haze filled the car. "It's very nice. It's like a tiny little sexual intercourse. One that you carry around with you in your pocket. It calms you the same way."

Alan felt himself only reluctantly drawn into this conversation that was a good deal more intimate than he would have chosen. Even when he was a child his father had talked to him in the same way, as though he were an adult, a fellow male, the two of them bawdy and jocular together. He hadn't liked it then and he didn't like it now. He felt as though he were a child unwillingly being made to listen to an adult conversation.

"Does sexual intercourse calm you?"

"It excites you, then it calms you. Cigarettes, in addition to their portability, have the advantage that you don't have to get excited first so you can get calm afterwards. Another difference, of course, is that sexual intercourse isn't bad for you like cigarettes. It's good for you."

"It is?"

"It reduces the blood pressure. Improves the circulation. Stimulates hormone production. And it's very calming to the nerves. It makes your hair grow. Did you know that, Alan? Fucking makes your hair grow."

Alan's own hair was thinning at the temples; Nils-Frederik's was iron gray, thick, and bushy. Alan said, "I didn't know that."

"I don't drink, as you know. Drinking blunts the edges of the nerves. Drinking is for people who are afraid of the world. When they drink it gets blurry and it doesn't bother them anymore. I love the world. I want it sharp and in focus. Smoking sharpens up the world so I can see things more clearly. I become more aware. Smoking is first of all smell. It doesn't dull your sense of smell as people say. It enhances it. It's funny to imagine losing your sense of smell. It could happen through an accident to your head, you know. Or through surgery. You could fall off that motorcycle of yours and you wouldn't be able to smell anymore. No smells! It's an awful idea. If it happened to me I probably couldn't go on living. It's like a man who is fond of women, who has to have women, one after another. He lives for that. Ask him what he'd do if he became impotent."

"You're fond of women too."

"Everybody is, Alan. I wanted women when I was ten years

old. I didn't know what I wanted, and even if I had known I wouldn't have been able to do it. But that was what I wanted. Now I know what I want, and I'm living with Charmian and I can have it every night. Every time it's different. She's very versatile." He laughed outright. "What a glory! To think that we've been given such a thing. There are all kinds of other ways that nature could have solved this problem. I mean the problem of reproduction. But we've been given this."

"By the same God who gave us the tobacco receptors in our brain."

"That's right." He chuckled at this. Then he was thoughtful for a while, and said, "You know, for me women will always be Maggie. I don't say that just because you're her son. I tell everybody. I even tell Charmian. She doesn't mind; she knows she can be sure of me now. Do you ever see Maggie, by the way?"

"Once in a while when I'm in New York."

"And how is she?"

"Just the same. Her whole life is the gallery. That's all she talks about, the artists she knows and the other people in her gallery life. She finally found something she wants to do."

"I guess so. It wasn't being married to me. We lived together for twenty years, and then she fled out of my hands like a bird. She was a wonderful person! She still is, probably. She had flair. She knew how to wear clothes, how to hold herself, how to enter a room. I always admire that, because it's something I don't have. I'm just a nicotine-stained old bum. I have many other wonderful qualities."

"Such as?"

"Oh, I'm just such a lovable person," said Nils-Fredrik, laughing out loud. "My keen human insight. My honesty and candor. My generosity, my selflessness. My physical beauty, clad in rags as I am. Oh, I'm just so lovable all around."

"Your modesty. You forgot your modesty."

"Yes, I'm humble as a saint," he said still laughing. He always thought it was fun to make jokes about his bad character. He did it himself and he enjoyed it when other people did it. It was his chief subject of amusement, in fact. He didn't have much of a sense of humor about other things.

"And don't forget my chivalry toward women. And my lack of small vices like smoking."

"You're not nearly as wicked as you'd like people to think, Father. You have a romantic view of your own temperament."

"Byronesque. The Doomed Poet. The God-driven soul wandering through the landscape of the night." He began laughing again, then he gripped Alan by the shoulder, almost pulling his hands off the steering wheel. "I can't talk to anybody else like I talk to you, Alan. Imagine talking this way to Charmian."

18 ▪

ALONE IN the back room of the bookstore, Wolf was cataloguing the four volumes of a Renaissance book of manners, expensively bound in antique leather, each volume with a tiny clasp that locked with a key. Some gentleman of Valladolid had kept them in his private closet and read them now and then on cold winter evenings by the light of a candle. These books had arrived by express the day before from a dealer in New York. Books of manners were common in Italy and England, but there were only a few known examples from Spain. The volumes were small, in octavo format, and they were in excellent condition. They seemed to him even finer books than the Zell Gesta Romanorum that had excited him so much a few weeks before. He held the books to the lamp to examine the watermark, then he put rubber bands around the first volume to hold it open, propped it on the table in front of him, and began writing out a description.

"Espejo de Principes y Cavalleros. Tomo I–IV. Anon., impr. Gonzales Mojena, Valladolid, 1583. 8vo, full calf, boards. Title; colophon. Flax paper, WM armorial bearing.

Clavis; brass latches. Vols. III, IV rubbed on spine. Unmarked. 1C."

He went on working in this way for a half an hour, forgetting time. Steve Ann was taking care of things in the front of the store. He catalogued another book or two and then took up the *Espejo de Principes y Cavalleros* again from the table, looking into the second volume. He read the Renaissance Spanish with ease, although occasionally a word was unfamiliar to him. He consulted a dictionary and made some notes about the archaic vocabulary. He almost regretted it when he heard the door of the store open and the voices of Alan and Nils-Frederik out in front talking to Steve Ann. He closed the Spanish book and put the four volumes back in the vault, along with the other books he had been cataloguing.

The Swiss picture book was no longer in the drawer of the table; it was in the vault. Years ago, before he was married, Wolf had felt himself lightly attracted to boys. It was probably a normal stage that many young men went through. The wonderful encounter with Myra had cured him of all that. He didn't feel a touch of it now, although possibly there was still a residuum of it hidden inside him. And if so, possibly Nils had detected it, although he never mentioned it except for a sort of light raillery which might have been all in Wolf's mind. Still, he had put the picture book away in the vault. It gave Nils a power over him to know his sexual secrets when he didn't know Nils's sexual secrets. Or rather, Nils had no sexual secrets at all; he told everybody about everything of that side of his life. Once he had confided to Wolf the secret of the Magic Theater. Wolf thought it was disgusting and said so, and Nils had never referred to it again. He respected Wolf's peculiar *pudeurs*. Still, he had smiled when he found the picture book in the drawer.

The voices of Nils-Frederik and Alan moved from the front of the store into the room where he was sitting. Nils-Frederik had a hat on that he had never seen before, the kind worn by George Raft in movies. He took this off and set it on the table. "Get the stuff, Wolfgang," he said.

Wolf went to the vault for the stories and set them on the table, and Alan took the story he had borrowed out of the pocket of his jeans, smoothing out the wrinkles before he laid it with the others. Alan sat down, but Nils-Frederik wandered around the room, stopping now and then to look at the books in the glass cases.

"Now we come to the delightful parts of this little prank of ours," he said.

Wolf fixed on the word prank. Put this way, what they were doing seemed perfectly innocent, a game of schoolboys, a trick to make fun of their masters. He looked at the story Alan had taken away with him, "The Lady with the Dog." He now remembered it only imperfectly, but it left an unpleasant impression in his mind because of its references to venereal disease. Of course, schoolboys were always talking about clap and syph.

"You see," said Nils-Frederik, "we have these copies, made on my processor. But if we want people to take these stories as authentic, we're going to have to go to work and create the documents. The original manuscripts of which these are only copies."

"Why?" said Alan.

"In case somebody wants to see them. In case somebody insists on seeing them. You see, we're not just writing imitation Hemingway stories. We're *creating* a body of writing, complete with documents."

"Imitation Hemingway stories?" Wolf saw Alan stare curiously at Nils-Frederik as if he were trying to make sense out of what he was saying. It all seemed perfectly sensible to him.

Nils-Frederik smiled. "It's a game. Life is a game. Without games to play, life is very boring."

"You're telling us the original manuscripts don't exist?" Alan persisted. "That you never found the Suitcase?"

"Did I tell you that? I don't believe I told you that."

"Why did you go to Europe, Father?"

"I went to Europe because I like to play games, and if I'm

going to play games I need the counters. The pieces to move around on the Monopoly board. I might have gone to all kinds of places that Hemingway talks about in his writing to see what they look like now. Rue Cardinal Lemoine, where he and Hadley lived in 1922. The gym in rue Pontoise. It's not there anymore. There's an electronics store at that address. The places where he went to fights, the Cirque d'Hiver and the Stade Anastasie. The restaurant in rue Jacob where the Hemingways used to go, the Pré aux Clercs. It's still there. There's a shop near place des Vosges that has old postcards of Paris showing what the streets looked like in those days. In the bookstalls along the Seine you can find things like old Baedekers that have maps, the names of restaurants, the prices of everything, even the bus lines. I might go around to the Rotonde in Montparnasse to see if it was still the same as it was in those days, full of tourists and phonies. Maybe I went to Belgium to see if there are any remote farmhouses in the Scheldt Valley. Any eccentric old farmers with interesting things in their cellars. I might want to investigate what the problems are in getting a suitcase full of old manuscripts through customs without anyone taking too great an interest in them. There are all kinds of reasons why I might want to go to Europe."

"Did you do any of these things, Father?"

"Oh, lay off, Alan, he's not going to tell you. Let's just assume that he wrote the stories and go on from there."

"I was hoping you would both want to join in the game. Don't you want to hear about the fun?"

"All right."

"Hemingway's typewriter," said Nils-Frederik.

Alan and Wolf exchanged a glance. "What about Hemingway's typewriter, Father?"

"It was a 1921 Corona portable. Hadley bought it in St. Louis when she knew they were going to be married, and she gave it to him on his birthday, July twenty-first. They were married in September. By the winter of 1922 it had a hell of a lot of wear on it. He had written a lot of journalism on it, and that whole suitcase full of stories. All Corona portables made in the twenties have the same type face."

"You couldn't just type these things on some paper you bought at the store," said Wolf. "You'd have to have the right paper. Old paper. Have you thought of that?"

"You're right, it will be hard to get the paper. It would be hard to get the paper," he corrected himself. "I'm counting on you for that, Wolfgang. Hemingway wasn't rich in those days and he probably couldn't afford very good paper. The chances are that he used newsprint to type his stories on. He could have gone around to printing plants and bought the old pieces left over from their press runs and cut them to size."

"He might have. Did he?"

"Nobody knows. The biographies don't say anything about what kind of paper."

"It would be very hard to get the paper."

"Wolfgang, you know all about old paper and you have nothing else to do with yourself but hang around the back of this bookstore looking at Swiss picture books." With his oblique smile, glancing at Wolf and then at Alan, he said, "I've saved the best thing for last."

He removed an immaculately folded handkerchief from the pocket of his jacket, groped for what was under it, and came out with a handful of paperclips. There was a large mass of them, twenty-five or thirty, and he spread them around on the polished surface of the table.

They all looked at them in silence for a moment or two. Then Alan said, "Those are French paperclips."

"Or European of some kind," said Wolf.

They were badly rusted and some of them were broken. The shape was different from that of American paperclips; they were wider and shorter, and instead of being rounded they had points like arrowheads.

"They're very old."

"Yes, they are."

"Where did you get them?"

"I might have found them in the flea market in Paris. A French friend might have given them to me. He might have been saving them in an old tin can."

"You might have found them in the cellar of an old farmhouse in the Scheldt Valley."

"That's right, if I had gone to the Scheldt Valley. Suppose you did want to recreate those missing Hemingway manuscripts. How would you hold them together? You couldn't use modern paperclips. You couldn't staple them. You couldn't even leave them loose in folders. Somebody might say, Funny, why did he leave them loose that way? Any author, when he finished a story, would put a paperclip on it."

"What size would the paper be?"

"Twenty-one by twenty-nine-and-a-half centimeters. That's about eight and a half by twelve. It's the standard French size typing paper."

"How can you tell if paper is old?" said Alan.

"Older paper would be oxidized. That is, it would have brown spots on it, freckles. You're the expert on paper, Wolfgang. Maybe you could oxidize it artificially by spraying something on it—lemon juice, say—with an atomizer."

"It would smell like lemon juice from then on."

"Something else then. The paper would be very badly dried out. It would look as though it had been parched in an oven. Maybe you could put it in an oven and parch it. All this," he said, "you would do after you had typed on the pages with a 1921 Corona portable, so the typing would be aged in the same way as the paper. An expert could tell whether the typing had been done before or after the paper was aged. The ink from the ribbon would oxidize too in time, so it wouldn't be as dark as it was originally. Sort of grayish."

"We've all seen old manuscripts," said Wolf.

"Isn't this fraud?"

"Is it fraud to make a facsimile? Is it fraud for a body shop to make a facsimile of a 1926 Bugatti Royale?"

"It would be if they tried to sell it as genuine."

"They'd be crazy to do that," said Nils-Frederik. "But a lot

of people would like to buy a facsimile Bugatti for fun." He
seemed satisfied with himself. When Alan and Wolf didn't
say anything he leaned back in the chair and groped in his
pocket for the black-and-gold box. He lit the cigarette and
drew on it deeply, while they watched him. Wolf saw that
Alan, without thinking about it, had slipped the small pile of
rusted paperclips into the pocket of his leather jacket.

19 ■

WHEN THEY were gone Wolf sat thinking for a while, then he
spread the manuscripts out on the table and began looking at
them. He glanced at the front shop in a vaguely guilty way to
be sure Steve Ann was still busy with her customers. She knew
nothing about what was going on with Alan and Nils-Frederik
and the manuscripts in the vault. It was the first time he had
concealed anything about his business from her, although of
course there had never been anything to conceal before. Without intending to he seemed to be drifting into a life of deceit
and dissembling, one that he almost managed to conceal from
himself.

"The Trouble with People." "The Lady with the Dog."
"Snatch." That was a nasty one. He would just as soon they
didn't have anything to do with it and didn't include it in the
book. He suspected that his revulsion for this story came from
the fact that, like Nils, he thought the female genitalia were
disgusting. He avoided looking at them if he could. "It's Marvelous, She Said." All the Paris stories had a glib, knowing,
superior quality to them. Nick was so cocksure of himself.
Then there were the skiing stories, and the one set in Milan,
"A Broken Doll." Wolf had never been in Milan, although
he and Myra had been to Paris several times. Still he had a
strong and clear impression of the city from this story: the
Galleria, the strolling wartime crowds in the Corso, the smoky
air. Nevertheless, he thought, still pondering, he liked the

Paris ones better. He had read them too hurriedly when Nils
had first showed them to him and Alan here in the store, and
he took one off the pile again and examined it more carefully.
He glanced once more at the open door to the front shop. He
ought to close the door, but Steve Ann would wonder why he
had done that. If she came into the back room unexpectedly,
as she sometimes did, he would simply have to tell her that
he was reading a manuscript. It was none of her business.
Something that Nils-Frederik was writing. That was the for-
mula. He was glad he had thought of that. He settled back
into the chair and began reading.

The Real Thing

THAT SUMMER *Nick and Harvey Greer were on good terms
with a girl named Marie-Georges who worked in a café where
they used to go on the Île Saint-Louis. She was just an
ordinary café girl except for her odd name. The French had
some funny names; there was a nobleman before the Rev-
olution who was called Anne. Maybe it was aristocratic for
a girl to be called Marie-Georges. She came from Tours and
she had worked in Paris since she was seventeen. Now she
was about thirty. She was a nice decent girl and both Nick
and Harvey liked her.*

*It was at the café on the Île, while they were standing at
the zinc counter watching Marie-Georges work the coffee machine, that Harvey told Nick about the Doughertys. They were
old friends of his from South Carolina. At least Mrs. Dougherty
was; Dougherty was a business man that Mrs. Dougherty had
married. He came from a tobacco family and he had plenty
of money, Harvey said. Harvey was in need of money because
he wanted to start up a magazine. He felt that he could rev-
olutionize literature in our time if he could just get his hands
on twenty thousand francs. He knew a printer in Lyons who
could do the work cheap, and he had many friends who were*

*talented writers. Harvey was one of several dozen Americans
who wanted to start up a magazine in Paris. Most of them
failed, but a couple of them discovered real new writers and
became a part of literary history. Harvey wasn't one of these.*

*Marie-Georges said, "Mr. Greer, it is not your friend's hus-
band but your friend herself that you should try to get the
money from." English was difficult for her and she could not
pronounce Dougherty, so she referred to them in this way.*

"Why?"

*"Because it is women who are the patrons of the arts. Look
at Madame Récamier."*

"It's different in America," said Harvey.

*Nick said, "I think Marie-Georges is right. If you want some
money from them, you should talk to Mrs. Dougherty about
it."*

*"They're arriving tomorrow at Saint-Lazare. I'm going to
take them to their hotel. They're staying at the Crillon."*

"Naturally they're staying at the Crillon."

"What are they going to do in Paris?"

*"I am going to show them around. Mr. Dougherty wrote
me from America. He wants to see something special in Paris,
he said. He doesn't want to do the usual tourist things."*

"He wants to have an adventure," said Marie-Georges.

*"I'm meeting the boat train at eleven. I'll take them to their
hotel and then I'll find out what they want to do."*

*"I can imagine very well what he wants to do," said Marie-
Georges.*

*After he met the Doughertys and took them to their hotel,
Harvey met Nick for dinner and told him the plan he had
worked out. Mr. Dougherty, he said, did not want to spend
all his time in Paris with Mrs. Dougherty. Harvey decided that
he and Mr. Dougherty should go around and see some things
together, the sort of things that wouldn't interest Mrs. Dougherty. Harvey had to think of something else for Mrs. Dougherty
to do. She could go shopping with someone, or she could visit*

the Eiffel Tower and the sewers of Paris as described by Victor Hugo. Harvey probably didn't mean it about the sewers. He had a literary background and was given to flamboyant language. Probably he meant the Louvre.

"You've got to help me out, Nick." He explained that he was going to have lunch at the Closerie des Lilas with the Doughertys, and that Nick could go along. After lunch they could separate, and Nick could do something with Mrs. Dougherty.

"You make me sound like a gigolo. Am I going to get paid for this?"

"Please don't joke, Nick. She is a very nice person, a cultivated woman. She comes from a very good family in Charleston. Her people are the cream of society. You will enjoy her. It is very important to me that Samuel and I spend the day together." By this time he was referring to Mr. Dougherty by his first name. "Marie-Georges is going to help."

"How?" Nick didn't like the sound of that. Marie-Georges was not a Parisian. She was a decent girl from the Touraine and Nick was fond of her. He didn't like the idea of her going around with some tobacco millionaire that Harvey was trying to get some money out of. It seemed that in Harvey's mind Nick was a gigolo and Marie-Georges was a tart.

"Samuel and I will do something in the afternoon. Then we're going to Montmartre in the evening. We'll meet Marie-Georges there by accident."

"There are plenty of other girls in Montmartre. You don't have to involve Marie-Georges."

"I can count on Marie-Georges," said Harvey.

When Nick got to the Lilas the Doughertys and Harvey were already there. Mr. Dougherty was a middle-aged man a little heavy around the middle. He was wearing a dark suit and a bowler he had bought in London. It made him look like an Irish alderman. Mrs. Dougherty was about the same age, with a good deal of paint on her face, and she was dressed

*all wrong, in a fur cape and a printed silk dress. They sat down
and ordered drinks. Mrs. Dougherty had champagne, and Nick
had some too when she insisted.*

*"It costs only a little more and it's so much nicer. I'm so
fond of it. I have it whenever I can. At home, they drink
elderberry wine out of tiny little glasses. I'm so glad to be in
Paris."*

"Don't drink too much of it, Estelle," said Mr. Dougherty.

"What are you going to have to eat, Nick?" said Harvey.

*Harvey was paying for the lunch. Nick ordered the steak au
poivre, the most expensive thing they had at the Lilas. Mrs.
Dougherty said, "I'd like that too if Mr. Adams is going to
have it." Mr. Dougherty and Harvey had the côtelette de veau.
The veal was better in France, Harvey explained to Mr.
Dougherty. You could not get veal like this in America. Mrs.
Dougherty said that at home they called it a Dreaded Veal
Cutlet. Harvey and Mr. Dougherty had a Graves with their
veal, and Nick had a claret with the steak. Mrs. Dougherty
insisted on going on with the champagne. The waiters brought
up another bottle and put it in the bucket, and they had more
ready at the buffet, where they stood watching her eating her
steak and drinking champagne. She ate the steak neatly, cutting
it into small pieces as she had been trained to do as a well
brought up girl in Charleston. Like all Americans, she held
her fork in her left hand and then transferred it to her right
as she ate each piece of steak.*

*After lunch Harvey and Mr. Dougherty went off in a taxi,
and Nick took Mrs. Dougherty for a walk. It was one of his
favorite walks, starting at the statue of Marshall Ney on the
corner by the Lilas and going on down the avenue de l'Ob-
servatoire to the Luxembourg. Mrs. Dougherty said the trees
in the avenue were like Charleston, but the Luxembourg was
like nothing she had ever seen before. She said it was a child's
dream of a park. She said that a part of her had always remained
a child and she had dreamed of a park like this, with a palace*

at one side and a round pond where children could float boats.
She had had quite a bit of champagne and she did most of
the talking.

"Did you have a happy childhood, Mrs. Dougherty?"

"Call me Estelle. I am having a happy childhood right now.
Never mind about the other one."

"What do you want to do for the rest of the afternoon?"

"What do you think Harvey and Samuel are doing?"

"He will probably take him to some tough bars around the
Halles, where he will show him some apaches."

"What are apaches?"

"They are people who wear jerseys and talk with their cigarettes in their mouths."

"Do they have girls?"

"Oh yes, they have their tarts. That's how they earn their
money. They live off their girls."

"Are they really tough?"

"Not as tough as people think. They're just trying to earn
their living."

"Why don't we go and look at some tough bars?"

"We might run into Harvey and Samuel. How would you
like to go to the races? There's a steeplechase at Auteuil. It's
a nice place and they have trees like those in Charleston."

"Do they have champagne there?"

"Yes."

"Would I be able to make a small bet?"

"Of course."

"Let's go to the races."

Nick had a pleasant afternoon with Estelle at the track. They
went straight to the buffet and Nick bought a bottle of champagne and two glasses, and they sat in the stands and looked
at the racing paper. They carried their champagne with them
when they went down to the paddock to look at the horses.
Estelle was interested in everything, the jumpers with their
docked tails and the white wrappings on their ankles, the way

they stepped delicately in the soft dirt like cats, the touts in
their striped business suits who were sizing up the horses. Nick
pointed out a couple of good jumpers.

"Look at their forelegs and their chests. That's what they
jump with."

"I would think it would be the hindquarters."

"You'd think so, but it's the forelegs that lift them into the
air. If the front end of the horse goes over the hedge, the rear
end will follow it."

"Which one should I bet on?"

"One with good forelegs. And a nervous one, one with a
light in his eye."

"I like Bon Maréchal. He has a light in his eye. And I like
the silks, mint green and purple."

"The horse can't see the colors. He just jumps the hedge.
If he has good forequarters, he'll get over it."

"Could I bet a hundred francs on Bon Maréchal?"

"Of course."

They both lost on the first race, and they sat in the stands
drinking their champagne. She said, "You know, Harvey wants
Samuel to give him some money to start a magazine."

"Do you think he will?"

"He will if I tell him to. Do you think I should?"

"I don't know. Ask yourself what Madame Récamier would
do."

"What do you think she would do?"

"I think she would give him the money, but the magazine
wouldn't amount to much."

"That's probably what will happen."

"Does it bother you that Samuel has gone off with Harvey?"

"Oh no. We have an arrangement. We get along very well.
You see, he has money and I have family, so it works out
nicely. Of course, my family didn't approve when I married
an Irishman. But it's worked out very well. Where do you
think that they will go in the evening?"

"To Montmartre."
"What is there in Montmartre?"
"Places like the Moulin de la Galette. Girl shows."
"Well, a little cancan will probably do Samuel good."
In the next race, for two-year-olds, he put a hundred francs
on a filly named Joyeuse and she came in at eight to one.
Estelle was bringing him luck. She lost again, but she didn't
seem to mind. Nick went to the buffet for another bottle of
champagne and they watched the next race together without
betting on it. She enjoyed everything, the jockeys standing in
the stirrups in their tight white pants that fitted their bottoms
as though they were painted on, their yells and the slaps of
leather as they went by, the solid thud-thud of hooves on the
grass. A horse and rider went down in the water right in front
of them. The jockey got up and walked away, but the horse
flopped and couldn't get up, splashing water on the people
who were trying to help.
Estelle said, *"That horse had poor forequarters."*
"The jockey made a mistake."
"Will they shoot the horse?"
*"I don't know. It depends on whether she can get up and
walk."*
The filly in the water finally staggered up and shook herself.
She danced a few steps sideways, and the groom caught her
and checked her.
"I'm so glad. I was afraid they would shoot her."
"They should shoot the jockey."
*"I liked it when they fell, though. That was exciting. Do
you think there will be more falls in the other races?"*
"Probably. Do you want to bet on the next race?"
*"No. Let's just sit and watch them. You could get some
more champagne though."*
She was a nice old trout and pleasant enough in spite of coming from such a good family. After all, you couldn't hold that
against her. Nick didn't even mind if she had married an Irishman. He enjoyed himself at the track and he had won eight
hundred francs. When they left she asked him to buy her an-

other bottle of champagne to take with her in the taxi. She even brought her glass which she held carefully on her knees in order not to spill it. Everything seemed fuzzy and pleasant to Nick and he didn't drink in the taxi. She said, "Oh, I've had so much fun. It's so much nicer than going to tough bars."

"Does Samuel drink?"

"Not very much. He has other vices. Oh I see, you're saying that I drink too much, is that it?"

"Not as far as I'm concerned. You can drink as much as you want."

"Oh, it's so much nicer than Charleston."

He left her at the Crillon; she didn't invite him in to finish off the rest of the bottle, and she declined his invitation to go out to dinner. She would be all right; the Crillon was full of champagne. He ate by himself at his usual place in the rue Vavin; he had roast chicken, mashed potatoes, and new peas, with tarte tatin *to finish. He thought of her eating alone in the hotel.*

The next day he went around to the café on the Île to see what had happened to Harvey and Samuel. Harvey wasn't there but Marie-Georges was at the zinc serving a customer. He was a porter from the Halles and he lingered over his glass of wine for a long time. Nick couldn't talk to Marie-Georges as long as he was there. The patron was in the back making out his accounts and he was paying no attention to the front of the café. Nick watched while Marie-Georges cleaned the counter with a rag and then began polishing the steam pressure coffee machine. She was a handsome country girl with large strong arms and Nick liked her a lot. Finally the porter left.

"Has Harvey been in?"

"Not yet, Mr. Adams."

"Did you see him last night?"

"Oh yes."

"Did you meet his friend Mr. Dougherty?"

"I can't pronounce that name. I call him Samuel. I met

them in a boîte in Montmartre. I just happened to be there,
wearing silk stockings and a red dress like a cocotte. Harvey
came over and brought me back to their table and introduced
me to Samuel. It was easy for me to behave like a cocotte.
There is a little of that in every woman. Samuel liked me very
much, and he bought me several drinks. Then we went to the
Moulin de la Galette and saw the show, and then we went to
another bar. Harvey went to the rear to use the convenience,
and while he was gone Samuel persuaded me to leave the bar
with him. We went in a taxi to a hotel. Samuel does not speak
French and I know very little English, so we did everything
by sign language. Samuel indicated by sign language that he
loved me very much. At the hotel, he had difficulty demonstrating this but finally he succeeded. He had drunk quite a
bit and after that he fell asleep."

"It doesn't sound as though it was very agreeable for you."

"It was very agreeable for me, Mr. Adams. I had a chance
to wear my red dress and go to some nice places in Montmartre.
I like to go out in the evening. I seldom have a chance. As
for his demonstrating his love for me, that is a thing that
women learn to put up with."

"Did he pay you anything?"

"No. He didn't think of that because he was sound asleep.
However, when I left I took his money. His pants were over
the chair and he had two thousand francs in the pocket."

"Do you think he will go to the police?"

"No. You see, he wanted to have an adventure in Paris.
That is all a part of it. If he had an adventure in Paris, it is
natural that the cocotte would steal his money. If I hadn't, he
would have been almost disappointed. According to Harvey,
he has plenty of money. Believe me, Mr. Adams, I know
Americans. He won't complain."

"Mr. Dougherty is a romantic."

"You see, in the Touraine we are realists. If other people
are romantics, we are willing to be paid by them to help them
act out their fantasies. The best thing, Mr. Adams, is to be a
realist in a world of romantics."

The patron came out from the rear and asked what all the talking was about. Another customer came in and Marie-Georges served him his glass of wine at the zinc counter. Nick talked to the patron a little and then he left. He had pretty much heard the whole story anyhow. Marie-Georges was a nice girl and she didn't have an easy life of it. Nick remained on friendly terms with her until the end of the year when he went back to America.

In the end, Samuel did give Harvey the money he wanted, but the magazine failed anyhow. There were too many Americans starting up magazines in Paris that year. Harvey published too many stories by his friends who were untalented, and also he tried to publish his own poems in the magazine. He was another romantic, like Samuel.

Wolf sat musing. After a while it occurred to him that there was no Helen in this story. No hint of a wife at all. A writer could make her disappear when he didn't need her. There was no need for a wife in the plot, so Nick isn't married. If only life were that simple. Maybe, he thought, Nick was intimate with the café girl, Marie-Georges. According to the story he and Harvey were on good terms with her. On the other hand, she called him Mr. Adams and she called Harvey Mr. Greer. But perhaps that was only in the café. It was a professional nomenclature that she used when the *patron* was listening. Samuel too got rid of his wife when he wanted to have a little adventure. Of course, Hemingway behaved much like this with women in real life. He got rid of them as soon as they weren't needed. Like poor Hadley. Well, she wasn't the hero of the story and she had to go to make the plot work. How had he, Wolf, got so cynical all of a sudden? He loved Myra and he had no need for her to vanish so he could have adventures with other women. He had picked up that kind of attitude from the story. Literature could be a bad influence on the young, and the old too. Flaubert said that no young girl was ever ruined by a book, but that wasn't so.

Then it struck him that this story had the same title as a story by Henry James. "The Real Thing." And they were both about the same thing. In the James story, a couple of actors are better at posing for aristocratic paintings than real aristocrats. In this story, Marie-Georges is better than a real *cocotte*, because Harvey can "count on her," and because she's a nice girl and not likely to give Samuel some disease. Of course, she does steal his money from him. But that's what Samuel really wants; she's an actress playing her part to perfection. Wolf was stunned by this parallel. He felt like a graduate student who has stumbled across an idea for a thesis. *The Influence of Henry James on Hemingway*. Nobody had done that yet, as far as he knew.

The next time he saw Alan, he showed him this story again and they talked about the James business. Alan said, "Hemingway couldn't stand James. He said he was an old maid. Of course, that didn't mean that he wouldn't steal a story from him. He was just about as unscrupulous as most authors. He stole another title from Chekhov. 'The Lady with the Dog.' People think of Hemingway as a man of action who only wrote about what he knew, but he had read a lot of books."

Wolf thought about this for a while. It seemed to him that if Hemingway thought James was an old maid he wouldn't be likely to read very many of his books. He wasn't the sort to read his way through a very difficult author he didn't like. But then he remembered that Nils-Frederik did know James. His novel, *The Mastermind*, was an imitation of James. To Wolf's mind, this was just another proof that Nils had written the stories. Alan thought that they were real Hemingway stories. But Nils had dropped enough heavy hints to make it perfectly certain that he had written them himself. Alan was hostile to Nils in all kinds of ways and couldn't believe that he had enough talent to write the stories. But he had. The fact that he wanted them to make the fake originals was proof of that. The Suitcase didn't exist. If it did, Nils could have produced the originals from it, instead of having them go through all this trouble of manufacturing the fakes.

20 ■

ALAN AND LILY spent Christmas day at home with Kilda. Their only close friends were Wolf and Myra. Since Myra was Jewish, the Wolves didn't celebrate Christmas. Alan had no idea what Nils-Frederik did on Christmas day; he probably stayed at home and wrote as he did every other day of the year. Of course Lily was Jewish too, so in deference to her race there was no Christmas tree, just a kind of mobile, an arrangement of painted wooden sticks with a half-dozen very expensive ornaments on it. They had discussed and rejected the idea of a Hanukkah bush. They called the thing the Tree, and spoke of decorating the Tree, so they managed to pretend at least in this respect that they were a normal family. Of course, decorating the thing took ten minutes.

And here is what the presents were. Alan gave Lily the mask from the boutique next to his office, in an elegant gold box with pine cones and a tiny Swiss house attached to the bow. She unfolded the tissue, there was a pause of about three seconds, and she said, "Oh Alan, how lovely." He desperately wanted her to like it, but he could see she didn't. He watched her face closely. She was acting as well as she could the part of a wife opening a very special present from her husband which surprises and delights her. She stuck the mask on her face and turned it toward him, then toward Kilda. Kilda gave a mock shriek. Against Lily's face the gilt and enamel, the pinstriped curlicues, the seashells, the feathers, were just as he imagined they would be, a kind of dream-Lily, a Lily of another phantom world where things were distorted and surrealistic, where watches bent and lions strode among classic ruins, watched by figures with Cyclops eyes. Inside the holes he could see the moving whites of her eyes. He felt a desire for her and realized that it was only nine o'clock in the morning. It would be at least twelve hours before Kilda was in bed and they were alone together. His mind raced improbably. Perhaps in the afternoon they could have Mrs. Quon come over and he and Lily could go to a motel. But the motels probably weren't open on Christmas, and anyhow Mrs. Quon was no doubt celebrating Tet or whatever persons of her background did on this occasion. The sight of Lily in the mask really incited an insane degree of lust in him, as he had guessed it might when he saw it in the boutique.

She said, "It's very nice. You must have been thinking exactly of me."

He said nothing to this. After she took it off he didn't know whether to look at the mask or at her. Neither she nor the mask, when looked on separately, had any particular effect on him. He seemed to have inoculated himself with a powerful fetish, the first sexual deviation he had ever noticed in himself. It wasn't a particularly good feeling.

On to the other presents. Lily gave Alan a picture frame full of sand and oil, enclosed between two sheets of glass. There were two kinds of sand, fine white and coarse black, and when you turned the frame upside down the black sand and white sand drifted slowly downward, coiling and turning into patterns that resembled a Japanese brush painting, a black arctic mountain with glaciers, or a Walpurgis Night from an opera. He really did like it, although he was uncertain what he ought to say about it. He said it was interesting, it was wonderful, how original it was, where did you ever find it, but he didn't say it was what he had always wanted. He did sit looking at it for half an hour, turning it up and down, bored as people are on Christmas, and he found that it passed the time.

Nils-Frederik had sent a box of expensive chocolates for Kilda, with a Santa Claus and holly on the box. Chocolates were not really good for her and they would have to ration them out. Alan's present to Kilda was a stuffed animal of a special kind, representing a dead cat. It looked exactly as though it had been run over by a car; it was flat and limp and one eye had popped out. She carried it around by one leg and seemed quite fond of it. Lily gave her several presents: *The Wind in the Willows*, a barrette in the hope she would put it in her hair and not go around like a Zulu princess, and a makeup kit for little girls, with moisturizer cream, cheek blush, black stuff to put on her eyes, and a tiny lipstick. Alan's gift, he felt, was for the real Kilda, a crazy kid who wandered alone around the city and attached her affection to unsuitable objects, and Lily's three gifts were an effort to civilize her and make her more like everybody else, reading *The Wind in the Willows*, keeping her hair neat, and putting on cosmetics, eye shadow, and lipstick. "Of course it's only a toy," said Lily to the air, neither to Alan nor to Kilda. Kilda gave Lily a bracelet she bought at the drugstore with her allowance. It was very nice, pewter with a red glass jewel, but if kept polished it might be taken for silver and ruby. The present was exactly Lily. Alan's present from Kilda was a picture she made in school, labeled "A gent" or "Agent" and showing a middle-aged gentleman in a high silk hat and covered with spangles which she had made by outlining the figure with glue and then sprinkling on tiny bits of silver, gold, crimson, and blue tinsel. It was in a frame which she had made from balsa wood, also decorated with primary colors and glued-on spangles. He didn't know what to make of this portrait. Insofar as it was supposed to represent him it seemed off the mark; maybe it only reflected the teacher's aesthetic ideas or some art technique she had picked up in teacher's college. He hugged Kilda and thanked her, and she went off carrying her dead cat, which she had named Larry.

While she was out of the room the phone rang and Alan heard her answering it in her flat monosyllabic tone. The phone was in the hall. He didn't know who could be calling her; it must be one of her friends. He and Lily knew now that she had friends but she would never tell them anything about them. She said on the phone, "Oh, okay. What did you get?" A pause. "A dead cat and some stuff to put on my face." Another pause. "My Dad. He's funny." Alan had never heard

her use this word before. She always called him You, or just
didn't refer to him at all. It felt funny to think that he was a
Dad. Was Lily a Mom? Forget the whole thing. Kilda said,
"I might. Why don't you come over here sometime?" Then
she hung up.

Lily was trying on her bracelet. Alan took the mask from
the table and held it up to her face. His ideas about the mask
were solidifying, and now he saw it as something from an
Offenbach opera, Tales of Hoffmann. He tried to remember
the plot, but it seemed to him that there were three plots and
he couldn't get them straight in his head. One of them, he
thought, was about Venice, and that was the one the mask
reminded him of. He remembered more of it as he thought.
It was about the beautiful courtesan Giulietta, who was under
the sway of the magician Dappertutto, and it was about stealing
people's reflections. He wondered if he could get out the record
and induce Lily to leave the mask on, or even dance around
the room, while he played it. She fitted the mask briefly onto
her face again, with a blank expression underneath, and then
set it back on the table.

"Don't you like it?"

She twisted her mouth around for a moment and then she
said, "You bought me a mask, Alan. Of all the things you
could have got me, you bought me a mask. To cover up my
face. You wouldn't have done that ten years ago."

"You're far too subtle, Lily. I didn't buy it to cover up your
face. I bought it because it is your face. It's exotic and mysterious and magical, and it's like a you I might see in a dream.
Every time you put it on, it makes me want to go to bed with
you."

"Fine, I'll leave the mask on in bed."

"Lily, that was not what I meant." He started to tell her
about the opera and the plot involving people stealing each
other's reflections, but he had to go for the Oxford Dictionary
of Opera to look it up, and when he came back with the book
she had the television on and was watching it, turning the

bracelet that Kilda had given her back and forth on her wrist. At the end of the opera, he found, Giulietta drifts away in a gondola with a dwarf.

The television show was a Christmas program for children, and they had another quarrel about that. Kilda wasn't in the apartment anymore, as a matter of fact; she had gone outside taking her dead cat, with the barrette clamped to one leg of it and an incompetent smear of crimson on her lips. Alan and Lily sat for a while watching the program, which was about Santa's workshop at the North Pole. He said, "This is silly. There's no such thing as Mrs. Santa. There is only Santa Claus and his elves."

"Alan, think what you are saying. Just think. The whole thing is a fiction. Christmas is just a fiction. And if it's a fiction, then there could be a Mrs. Santa."

"There is no Mrs. Santa. The story of Santa Claus is a fiction, right. But we know what the fiction is. It's established. It's all in the poem 'The Night Before Christmas.' That is what Christmas is to us. If it isn't in the poem, then it's not true."

"What on earth can you mean by true?"

"Fiction is true. After it's established it becomes a kind of truth, parallel to but not the same as the real world. And after that it's unchangeable. I learned this at Johns Hopkins, in a course I took from Hugh Kenner."

"Oh, don't pull your education on me. I went to Hopkins too."

"Yes, but you didn't take this course from Kenner. A work of fiction has a life of its own. All you have to go on is the text, and you can only talk about the text. Shakespeare doesn't tell us whether Lady Macbeth has children, so we just don't know whether she did and it's futile to discuss it."

"But she does. A male baby. She says she'd pluck her nipple from his boneless gums and dash his brains out." Lily smiled obliquely. She seemed pleased with her skill as a Shakespeare scholar.

"Okay, but Emma Bovary did not have a brother. If anybody says she had a brother, or writes a TV show in which we see Emma Bovary's brother, that's just not true. The same thing goes for Mrs. Santa."

"Oh, Alan." She was exasperated. "Recent research has shown that Emma Bovary did have two brothers. Both older. We can write any fictions we want. There is a Mrs. Santa in this program because girls have to have some role model."

"Is that what you want Kilda to grow up into? A fat moron with a simper who bakes cookies for elves?"

"I don't think you understand feminism, Alan."

"How could I understand feminism? I don't understand women."

At this point the doorbell rang. It was the Wolves. They shut off the TV.

The Wolves came in trailed by Kilda, who was still carrying Larry with the barrette on his leg. "What a surprise," Alan told them. "Please come in."

They were laden with presents. Wolf said, "Having no children, we like to find some child to give things to."

Kilda was showing Myra her present. "What is it, dear? Oh, I see, a dead cat. How fantastic. You must just love it. And what's this on its leg? It looks like a cat trap. That's probably how it died." Kilda nodded. Myra, a sorceress, had guessed why the barrette was on the cat's leg.

The Wolves had presents for all three of them. Alan said, "Gee, how nice. I'm sorry that we haven't got anything to give you."

"Don't mention it."

"Lily, for God's sake, don't we have something to give these kind people, a bottle of booze or a Christmas tree ornament or something?"

Myra said, "Where is Lily, anyhow?"

She was across the room in the doorway, looking at them and holding the mask in front of her face.

"Oh Lily, how fabulous. I wish I had something like that. Wolf has no imagination. He always gives me underwear, or a nightgown."

"They make me hot, that's why."

"Alan says the mask makes him hot."

"Oh, you queer old Alan."

Wolf said, "You put the mask on, Lily, and dance around the room and make Alan hot. We ought to have some music. What kind of music should it be?"

"The Barcarolle from *Tales of Hoffmann*," Alan said. "I'll put it on."

The Wolves' presents for them were: for Kilda an antique toy of pressed tin, a little Negro boy who when wound up pushed his wheelbarrow across the floor with a clack; for Lily, an Armagnac cake from Neiman-Marcus; and for Alan a copy of the *Ancren Riwle*, a medieval manual of conduct for hermitesses. Kilda said that the Negro boy was called Garvey.

21 ∎

CHARMIAN CAME out of the dressing room and pushed the switch, the curtain opened, and the pink lights went on over her head. She was wearing a white organdy dress with sequins, a jeweled bracelet, and a long ermine cape. Nils-Frederik was sitting in the chair by the bed with his cigar. In the background there was the sound of music, a string ensemble playing "Dancing in the Dark." It was three o'clock in the afternoon on Christmas day, and the shutters of the bedroom were tightly shut.

He sat looking at her for a moment. "It's Christmas. I expect something special."

"Myrna Loy in *Libeled Lady*."

"With William Powell, Jean Harlow, and Spencer Tracy. Where did you see it?"

"At the Parnassus. Last week when I went out shopping."

"Are you sure the dress is right?"

"Perfectly right."

He stood up and took her in his arms, and they danced. Behind her back he held the cigar carefully in his right hand. "I thought she wore a coronet in it."

"No, she's not a princess. She's just the richest girl in the world."

"William Powell is a reporter, but she doesn't know this. He's been assigned by his paper to compromise her reputation. It's a matter of a lawsuit. Lots of innuendo."

"If there's anything I dislike it's a reporter. They're a nuisance. Probing into people's lives."

"I dislike them too. Didn't I save you from those photographers?"

"That's how we met. I still don't know who you are."

He whirled her, making the ermine cape flare out. He removed the hand from behind her back to draw on the cigar, and replaced it. Over the background music, as discreet and bland as Muzak, he said, "I'm afraid dancing isn't exactly my line."

"I should say it was part of your line."

"H'mm? Well, may I be frank too?"

"Why not?"

"You dance superbly." He stumbled. "I wasn't concentrating." Then he added, "It was your eyes."

"Beautiful, aren't they?"

"We ought to go back and join your father now."

"We can stay for just a while longer. I adore dancing."

"I adore you."

"*You* wouldn't by any chance be a reporter for a newspaper, Mr. Chandler?"

"I? Ha ha. The farthest thing in the world from it."

"What *do* you do?"

"I follow you around the world adoring you."

"The music is coming to an end. I'll change it."

"Don't bother." His hands felt under the cape, and it slipped off her shoulders and fell to the floor. When she knelt to pick it up he was on top of her in an instant.

"Right here. On the cape. Right now."

"The bed is right here."

"I want to feel the cape under me."

"It's not real ermine."

"It doesn't matter."

She straightened her legs and he penetrated her with the organdy dress pushed up around her hips.

22 ■

KLIPSPRINGER WAS working in his office in Santa Monica. He had taken off his safari jacket, revealing burgundy suspenders with gazelles on them. The building was deserted and there was also no traffic in the street outside. On his desk was a small dime-store imitation Christmas tree, no more than a foot high. He typed with two fingers on a manual typewriter, like an old-fashioned reporter.

On 14 December, per information that a social function was to take place that evening, Operator attended event at 2418 Los Encantos Way. Subject was serving as host. Operator arrived at 8:20 P.M., left 11:02 P.M. Entry gained through unlocked front door of premises. Operator's presence unnoticed in large throng of guests. Subject's son A.G. was among guests. Following movements of A.G., Operator investigated master bedroom closet and found in it one piece of green leather luggage, used, concealed under household goods. Item corresponds to object mentioned in Operator's instructions from Client. Item (suitcase) was left undisturbed. In surveillance of guests, conversations overheard touching on possible literary activities of Subject. Belief was expressed that Subject was writing a book, and also that he was editing some documents. Subject himself freely admitted this activity to guests. Operator made acquaintance of Charmian Berghe, housekeeper of Subject. Her confidence gained through sexual overtures. After discussion, she provided Operator with confidential materials bearing on case. Subject was not aware of transfer of materials to Operator. Upon examination, materials were found to consist of 37 (thirty-seven) unnumbered 3 × 5 file cards containing a short fiction in presumed style of Author as determined by library investigation. There is no specific data available about the authorship of materials. A transcript is attached. (Exhibit B).

Klipspringer stopped, opened the drawer of the desk, and took out a Smith Brothers cough drop. He put it in his mouth and sucked it while he gazed reflectively at the report in his typewriter. Then he pulled the paper out, making a noise like an angry wasp, and put in a fresh sheet. Arranging the file cards on the desk in front of him, he began copying them on the typewriter with his two-fingered stabs as though he were killing ants with his forefingers.

Exhibit B.

The Trouble with People

There was a crowd at the Rotonde but they found a table inside looking out through the windows at the terrasse and the boulevard. It was five o'clock and already dark. It was cold outside but inside it was warm and the windows were steamy.

Klipspringer went on typing for some time, occasionally making a mistake and going back to X it out. When the cough drop was gone he reached into the drawer of the desk for another. The tinsel on the tiny Christmas tree caught the light from the street. Below on the sidewalk a drunk went by singing. Klipspringer was not interested in either music or holidays. All days were the same to him. His life was centered on his work. This particular case he found neither more nor less interesting than the others. He did not know anything about Montparnasse, boxing, or what the Rotonde was. According to the fiction, it was an establishment where alcoholic beverages were served.

Klipspringer was an educated man. He had attended two years of university in a certain country. He knew that certain facts in books were true and that others were non-existent, that is to say, fictions. For his purposes it made very little difference. He was capable of going to the library, holding a book open and comparing it to the file cards, and determining that the file cards and the stories in the book reported similar (nonexistent) facts and were in much the same English. With a pocket calculator he had done a study of the length of sentences and found they were short in the cases of both book and file cards. The average length of sentences in a story from the book was 13 words, on the cards 12.8 words. An adjective count showed that there were fewer adjectives than in normal printed books. There were 3.1 (cards) or 3.2 (story in book) adjectives per one hundred words, whereas in a printed book by another author nearby on the shelf, *Jude the Obscure* by Thomas Hardy, there were 7.2 adjectives per one hundred words. All of this investigation at the library had been reduced to five words in the report, "in presumed style of Author."

Klipspringer understood very well the human soul. It held no mysteries for him. He was not surprised at what anybody did, however strange or inexplicable. And it usually turned out not to be inexplicable when you had all the facts. Klipspringer understood the behavior of Subject in this case, although nobody had explained it to him. It was his business to know such things. Klipspringer had no opinions about who had written the story on the thirty-seven cards or whether it was worth saving for posterity. He felt that, if the story had been real, it would have been wrong for the fellow to hit the Spanish kid and make his nose bleed, but on the other hand the Spanish kid brought it on himself. He should not have fooled around with the fellow's wife. Klipspringer was not a literary critic and had no ambitions to be one. He had only read one work of fiction in his life and that was a book by Stephen King. It was about a Saint Bernard that ate people in a small town. The facts related were not pretty, which, along with their non-reality, was another reason for not reading them. It seemed to Klipspringer that people who wrote fictions, and people who read them, were mildly deranged but in a harmless way. However that was not the opinion that Client held. Client intimated that the writing, or the possession, of fictions could be an evil act punishable by law. Client was willing to pay Klipspringer & Fineman a considerable sum of money to investigate the qualities, provenance, and ownership of these fictions. Other people were willing to pay sums of money to investigate the totally fictitious misbehavior of their wives. It made them feel better to pay the money. If they paid out money to investigate it, then their wives must really be misbehaving, and their concern over it was not mistaken or the result of mental illness. Likewise the materials on these cards. Client and Subject seemed to attach a great importance to the provenance and ownership of these materials. Constantly in Klipspringer's mind was the vision that Client and Subject were one person; the Hunter and the Prey merged. In this lay Klipspringer's power and the citadel of his safety. Nothing bad could happen to him, Klipspringer, as long as he was in possession of this paradox. Maybe Author was part of the same person too; it might be a three-headed Hydra. It was even possible, Klipspringer thought, that all other persons in the world except himself were one person.

23 ∎

ALAN DECIDED he would take Nils-Frederik out to lunch on his birthday. He was born just after Christmas, so that when Alan was living in the house he and Maggie had always given him his two presents at the same time, one for Christmas and the other for his birthday. Unlike most grown men, he always took a great interest in his birthdays and the presents he got for them. He would tell everybody what people had given him, and if a present was anything to wear, or show, he would take it out and show it to everybody he met for several days afterwards.

Alan didn't know what to get his father for a present; he had everything he could possibly need. Maybe he could get him a mask; that had been such a success with Lily. Or the first edition of A *Farewell to Arms* that Wolf had in his store, but that would be two thousand dollars even with the friendly discount and he couldn't afford it.

In the end what he got him was a kind of a joke: a miniature traveling kit for writers. It looked like an ordinary toilet kit about the size of a book, and when you opened it there was everything a writer was supposed to need: a pen, a pencil, a small pad of paper, a miniature stapler with miniature staples, paper clips, a tiny pair of scissors, and so on. Everything, including the scissors, was black in an elegant black leather case.

At the novelty store where he bought it they didn't gift-wrap, so he wrapped it himself in his office in some green paper and silver ribbon he got at the drugstore. In the process of wrapping it he got into a philosophical dilemma. You need something for the outside of something, but this thing is on the inside of your outside and can't be in both places at the same time. All this happened under the ironic eye of Corinne. At the point where he was holding the ribbon down with his finger and trying to fasten it with his other hand he realized that he needed some transparent tape. He was damned if he was going to ask Corinne for hers. He had some around somewhere and, still holding down the ribbon with one finger, he looked around the office trying to figure out where it was. He knew he had seen it just a few minutes before. Then he remembered: it was in the writer's kit itself, the contents of which he had examined before he started to wrap it. He could open the wrapping and use this tape to seal the package, but then it would be outside the package he had sealed with it, and there would be no way to get it back inside.

The solution came to him after some thought. He unwrapped the green paper, zipped open the leather kit, took out the roll of transparent tape in its black plastic holder, and dispensed a piece of it about an inch long, which he stuck carefully onto the corner of his desk. Then he put the tape back in its place, zipped up the case, and wrapped the green paper around it again, careful to fold the paper at exactly the same places. This time when he got his finger into position on the ribbon, he was able to reach down to the end of the desk, take the scrap of plastic tape, and stick down the ribbon to hold it into place. With the last of the silver ribbon he made an incompetent bow of which Kilda might be proud. He put the wrapped present into his attaché case. Corinne, who did not seem to have been watching, said, "I have some transparent tape right here on my desk, Alan."

At the last minute he persuaded Lily to go along to the lunch. He needed to use her car, because he didn't want to drive Nils-Frederik in his own Peugeot. In that case he would not really be taking him out to lunch but only chauffeuring him in his own car. Alan wanted to take charge and see to all the details himself. He went to the school where Lily worked near the USC campus and left the Beast in the parking lot there, and they drove in her Toyota to Los Feliz to get Nils-Frederik. Lily would never drive the car when Alan was in it, even though it was her car. She said she didn't feel comfortable driving with a man in the right-hand seat. He told her it was the last vestige in her of the old-fashioned woman, that is, the woman who liked to be taken care of by men. As a matter of fact, he had to admit that he too was reactionary in the same way, and enjoyed driving women in cars, opening doors for them, buying them presents, complimenting them on their clothes, and explaining the more difficult parts of the universe to them. Nowadays men weren't allowed to do this. In time, he hoped, the fashion would come full circle and they would be allowed to open car doors for them again. He really felt that they liked it. Perhaps he was wrong.

At the house he went in to get Nils-Frederik, as though he were a high school boy calling for his date. When he brought him out there was a French comedy about who was going to sit where in the car. Nils-Frederik obviously wanted to sit in the front, the most important place, and a place where he could talk to the driver. So did Lily. It was her car and she couldn't see why she should take the back seat—an eloquent phrase in our language—to somebody just because he was Alan's father. All this of course was unspoken, a hidden agenda. Alan would have preferred for Nils-Frederik to sit in the front seat, if only because he was used to Lily being annoyed but he didn't want to annoy Nils-Frederik on this occasion. The Birthday Boy, he thought, should sit in his favorite place.

What happened was that, as soon as Nils-Frederik appeared, Lily sprang out of the car like a figure in a Swiss clock and held the door open for him. He spread his arms generously and expansively (*Come to my arms, don't be shy, I know I'm big and ugly but I'm lovable*), with a smile and an expression of pained disavowal. He said, "But no, of course, dear Lily, you should sit in the front with Alan, I'll just ride along in back and chat with both of you from the rear." "Oh, no no . . ." (Lily never knew what to call him, Nils-Frederik was too formal and intricate and she thought it was pretentious to use the two names; she wasn't intimate enough with him to call him Nils as Wolf and Nana did, and she certainly wasn't going to call him Father, so she only called him You, or left a little silence, a space with three dots, as she did now)—"You sit up in front with Alan, that way the two of you can talk, and sitting in the back will be something new for me, would you believe it, it's my own car and I've never sat in the back seat." "Ah, but no, dear Lily, my very charming daughter, how lucky Alan is to have you, if he ever mislays you and you don't know where to go, please let me know, ha ha!—you please sit up in front"— he spread his arms again in a gesture of expansive gallantry— "and it will be a pleasure for me simply looking at the back of your head"—was this sarcasm? Possibly. And Lily: "But . . ." (again the little silence, in which she did not say either Nils or Nils-Frederik) "I wouldn't dream of it, please get in, it's so much more comfortable in the front"—here she raised a hand with the palm flat and—did not push him into the seat—but held the hand an inch from his arm and moved it in his direction, as though she were propelling him into the car with some kind of magnetic force that didn't require her to touch him. He got in, and as she closed the door she said with a smile, "You see, there you are . . . Nils-Frederik," this last as though it were wrung out of her by torturers. Then she got into the back seat and they drove away. It was only about five minutes to the restaurant.

They went to Nils-Frederik's idea of a good restaurant, the Montagnola on North Vermont, which was reputed to have crime connections; or, if the owners themselves didn't have crime connections, a lot of criminals hung around there. Or at least so people said. Maybe that was why Nils-Frederik liked it. It was a little drama to go there, and perhaps he thought that he himself might be taken for a criminal with his flashy clothes and his Al Capone hat. Alan was in his usual jeans and black leather jacket, since he had gone by to get Lily on the Beast, and he was incongruously carrying the attaché case, the symbolic burden of a young executive. Lily had on a pair of tapered white pants and an oversized framboise-colored sweater, so large that it came down over her hips and she wouldn't have needed to wear anything else. She didn't wear clashing bracelets but she managed to make a slave bracelet out of her wristwatch, simply by her way of holding her wrist. The young Chicano headwaiter gave her a long look as he seated them at the table. Then he took away Nils-Frederik's gangster hat to hang it up on the hat rack.

They ordered the usual specialties of the place, the things that Lily always called (but not now, since it was Nils-Frederik's favorite restaurant) Italian gangster cuisine, the Italian food of thirty years ago, before it was transformed by haute cuisine. Everything had red tomato sauce on it and tasted much the

same. Nils-Frederik ordered a bottle of Chianti and quizzed
the wine waiter as to why the bottle was not wrapped in straw.
The wine waiter, eager to entertain them, told them a long
story about some little old ladies in Tuscany who had painstakingly woven straw around the bottles, taking an hour to do
each one, but now they had died and their children were
unwilling to continue this tedious and unremunerative task.
"It's too bad, traditions are dying out everywhere." He un-
corked it and poured out a little for Nils-Frederik, who pushed
the glass to Alan to taste. It was really not so bad. Alan wasn't
a wine expert himself. When Nils-Frederik's glass was filled
he only touched it to his lips, like a priest going through the
motions at a Mass, and ignored it for the rest of the meal.
Lily had a Vittel, since she was teaching in the afternoon.

When they finished their entrees Alan reached down for the
attaché case at his feet and took out the green and silver package. Nils-Frederik feigned elaborate surprise; he held up both
hands like a robbery victim and waggled them while he smiled
broadly. *(You shouldn't have, but I give up, I surrender, you
can give it to me.)* The headwaiter came across the room to
watch him open it. Nils-Frederik said, "Ah, a toilet kit. Just the
thing for traveling in Europe." He couldn't grasp at first why a
toilet kit had transparent tape, a stapler, and a staple remover in
it. Alan had to explain, "It's a traveling kit for writers, Father."
The headwaiter caught his eye and nodded. This was evidently
the thing that writers gave each other on their birthday. Nils-
Frederik said, "That's very nice, Alan. It will be very useful."
Alan could see that he didn't understand that it was a joke, that
he thought that Alan thought the writer's kit would be very useful, and even though he thought it was a silly idea he was being
polite about it, or his version of polite, a stiff little smile which
he turned in Alan's direction and then showed around to the
others. There was a miniature knife in the writer's kit for cutting the pages of old-fashioned books, or French books. Alan
thought he would like that. When the waiter came with their
zabaglione and espresso Nils-Frederik pretended to cut his
wrists with the knife and told him, "This is all my son gave me

for my birthday." He smiled broadly and the waiter smiled too. Alan had intended for the writer's kit to be a joke. But in the end Nils-Frederik made it his joke, not Alan's.

They sat for some time over their espresso, although Lily wanted to go. Alan could see her fidgeting. She was supposed to be back at work at one-thirty. Alan tried to catch the waiter's attention to have him bring the check. Nils-Frederik seemed to be in no hurry to leave. He leaned back in his chair and lit a Sobranie Black Russian; he was expansive, genial, and totally at his ease. He smiled at the busboy who came to take away the plates from the zabaglione and the waiter who set an ashtray by his elbow. He smiled at Alan over his cigarette and told him, "I have four more stories for you."

"Four? You've been working hard."

"With a good processor it's no trick to type four stories in two weeks." This was another little joke; he twinkled through the bluish-gray smoke wreathing his head. Alan saw now that they were sitting in the no-smoking section of the restaurant, but nobody mentioned this to Nils-Frederik, an important gangster.

Alan asked him, "Did you work on Christmas day?" He was curious to find out just what his father had done on Christmas. He felt a little guilty. He hadn't asked him to come to their place, for obvious reasons, and he hadn't even sent him a present.

"Oh, if you're a serious writer of course you write on Christmas day," he said jovially. "You write every day of your life, if only for an hour."

Lily asked him pointedly, "Did you have guests for Christmas?"

Nils-Frederik drew at the cigarette and exhaled. The cloud of smoke coiled about him in slow motion. It was very still in the room. It was past the hour for lunch and almost all the other guests had left. The waiters watched them from their post against the wall. He told her genially, "Oh, my dear, I often have guests. I like people around me. Fundamentally I

am a lonely man, although no one believes me when I say
so. My domestic establishment"—here he lifted his eyebrows
to indicate that Nana and Charmian were not really a source
of adequate companionship for him—"is . . . you know what.
The tasks of the household, shall I say, are taken care of."
Another motion of the eyebrows and a faint smile suggested
that some of the tasks of the household took place in bed.
"And so one is left with one's reveries. Quite impossible to
achieve. If only because younger and more attractive persons
are already occupying the place one covets." Here he smiled
roguishly and removed his hand from under the tablecloth.
Alan thought he was going to reach out and touch Lily, perhaps
chuck her under the chin. But he only sighed, with a mock-
rueful smile, and dropped his hand to the table. A slightly
different Nils-Frederik emerged when he was with a woman
not his own; winsome, genial, gallant, full of playful innuendoes. Alan glanced covertly at Lily and found on her face a
combination of disapproval and amusement. Nils-Frederik was
working his wiles on her, and not entirely without success.

The waiter set the check by Alan's elbow. He ignored it.
He wanted to hear the rest of Nils-Frederik's speech to Lily.

"But my dear," he went on perfectly blandly, "what sad-
dened my Christmas was the thought that, on this day of all
days, my family was not with me. What I would have given
to have your charming presence, and that of little Kilda, my
favorite child in the whole world, around our Christmas tree."
He had said not one word about their coming there for Christmas. "But I understand that you and Alan wish to keep your
happiness to yourselves. And so I wrote a little in the morning,"
he concluded, "and in the afternoon Charmian and I were
together."

"What are you writing, Nils-Frederik?"

Alan noticed that she had finally managed to address him
by his name. He smiled and, to all appearances, ignored her
totally. He turned to Alan and said, "You know, I told you
and Wolfgang that what I am writing is just a game. It's not
just a game, Alan." He drew on his cigarette, sighed, and set

it in the ashtray. "I am a writer, Alan. My very nature is that of the creative artist. If I cannot create, something withers at the center of me, and I die a little. If I ceased to create entirely, then I would cease to live. Oh, I'm not saying that I would actually expire and have to be taken to an undertaking establishment, nor am I threatening to take my life if my writing doesn't go well. But it is very fundamental to me, Alan. Very necessary. Very crucial. It is at the center of my being. A writer of fiction becomes God in his work, Alan. He creates a world and peoples it with living, sensate, feeling and thinking beings. This fictional world becomes more real to him than the real world, so-called, that he inhabits with other so-called real people. He lives in it day and night. He takes a divine pleasure in it. Even in his sleep he lives in this fictional world he is creating. And when he has created it, he feels a satisfaction that no other satisfaction can equal."

"And on the seventh day he rests," said Lily.

He continued to ignore her. He paid no attention to women when he was talking seriously. "Not even sex. Not even sex," he said, as though this was his final and overwhelming argument, "can equal the satisfaction of creating that fictional world." He took up the cigarette and drew on it again. Then he said, "It's important to me, Alan."

"I imagine it's important to every writer."

"Maybe. All I can report is what I feel. And you see, Alan"— he pulled again at the cigarette, as though he were going to say something important—"until now, because of the commercialism and indifference of the New York publishing world, I've been frustrated at every turn. I can't get my writing published and I have to turn to a small press. Now this is my chance. It doesn't matter that my name will not be on the book. Everyone will know that I've done it, and that's enough for me. It will be more than enough. I will know it in my own mind."

Lily frowned. "What is this all about?"

Crushing out his cigarette, he relaxed and became his old self again, devious, playful, and a little teasing. "What about it, Alan? In regard to our little prank. Is Lily to be one of the conspirators?"

"I don't know. I don't think so."

He hardly dared to glance at Lily. He met her eye only for a second. He saw that for some reason Nils-Frederik wanted to draw her into his secret. He couldn't imagine why he wanted to do this. Did he regard her as an ally he had decided to enlist in his cause, or as an enemy he wanted to disarm with a joking smoke screen? Alan knew him well enough to know that he was never merely spontaneous or impulsive. Of course, all this talk about his creativity was hot air, garbage. Alan knew that he was faking, that none of what he said was true, that the Suitcase was still there hidden away at the bottom of the closet in the house, and he could go there and get it and confront Nils-Frederik with it whenever he wanted. If Nils-Frederik let Lily into the prank, and intimated to her that he had written the stories, should he, Alan, tell her about the Suitcase and the true source of the stories? He didn't feel like getting involved in such an elaborate web of deceit and misinformation.

He was curious to see whether Nils-Frederik would tell her more about the Suitcase and the stolen stories. It would be better, he thought, if he didn't. He wondered whether he should try to deflect the conversation away from the subject. But in the end, Nils-Frederik did this himself.

Setting his hand lightly on Alan's arm—shyly, as though he were afraid he wouldn't accept the gesture—he said, "You know, Alan, I was jealous of you when you were eight years old. You wrote stories in your class at school and your teachers praised you for it. A couple of them even appeared in the school paper. I had a theory at the time that only one person in the family could be creative, either the father or the son." His expression, with a suppressed smile playing at the corners of his mouth, indicated that this was only a joke. "So if you were the creator, if you were the writer, then I couldn't be. At midnight, after you were asleep, I would burn your stories over a candle, with a leer. This lasted until the time when you left college and became an agent and not a writer. Then

I was reassured and became fond of you again."

Alan smiled too. His father's candor was disarming; it was hard to resent a person who confessed his hostility to you so openly, especially when he claimed it was all over and a thing of the past. And when it was only a joke. Of course, it wasn't really pleasant to be told by someone that he loved you because you weren't creative. That thought occurred to Alan about a second after the first one.

"I'm sure you loved me all along."

"Oh, I did. In some ways. But not in that way. I didn't love you for the stories you wrote in school."

Lily said, "Alan, you never told me you wrote stories in school. I knew you wrote some poems at Johns Hopkins. That's how you wooed me."

"Everybody writes poems in college. It was in a creative writing class." Alan didn't mention the limericks, or the failed attempt to write a Rilke poem in his office. "They were not bad," he said.

"I'm ready to overlook the poems," said Nils-Frederik genially. "It doesn't represent a threat to me, since I don't write poems myself."

"I might be a poet today if you hadn't bought me the agency," said Alan with an ill-disguised truculence.

"Yes, isn't it lucky? You would have been a rotten poet. See how much I've done for you." He laughed outright. He was in an excellent humor, in spite of the birthday present he didn't like.

When they got into the car after taking Nils-Frederik back to the house, it was after two. Lily would be late for work. He drove down Vermont through the traffic, feeling good to be out of the gloomy Italian restaurant with its smell of spaghetti and stale beer, and to be alone in the car with Lily, if only for a few minutes. He felt as though he were a kid on a date with a wonderful girl, as he always did when he was alone in the car with her.

She said, "Alan, this bothers me. You promised you wouldn't get involved with him again. What's it all about? A prank. Conspirators. He must create or die. He is going to astonish everybody with something. He will have his revenge on the publishing world. What's he going to do, plant a bomb on Madison Avenue?"

"It's nothing. Relax, Lily. Nils-Frederik has written some stories. He's going to publish them. They're similar to Hemingway's stories and he's hoping that people will say they're as good as Hemingway's." He was astonished to hear himself telling her this. Even from a distance Nils-Frederik had drawn him into his net of concealments and fabrications, causing him to lie to his own wife when he was alone in the car with her.

"But he said something about not signing them."

In order to gain time for a moment to think what to tell her he glanced at her briefly, as though he hadn't understood.

She said, "He said his name wouldn't be on the book."

"His name will be on the book, although perhaps not as author. Still it will be obvious that he's written the stories. People will know it anyhow. He won't have to sign the book."

"Alan, don't be shifty. What in the world are you talking about? When a person writes a book he signs it with his name."

"There are reasons why he doesn't want to. Modesty, shall we say." He could see that the more he went on trying to explain this to her the more lies he was going to tell. He cast about for some way to change the subject.

She said, "I don't trust him and I never have. And the reason I don't trust him—would you like to know the reason I don't trust him, Alan?" Without waiting for him to say whether he wanted to know this she went on. "The reason I don't trust him is that he is a very charismatic person and I'm afraid of falling under his influence. If he were only some dishonest car salesman, or a shabby preacher trying to convert us, we would both see through him and we would not be in any danger from him. But when I am with him, Alan"—here her voice dropped and she looked at him fixedly—"I find myself almost persuaded by him. He has an energy that radiates like electricity. He can look at a woman and simply say nothing, or say stupid and banal things that would be ridiculous if another man said them, and a woman feels the marrow of her bones softening. Even his mother. He has that power over her. And of course Charmian. He is a Leo, and Leo is a sign of fire. Leo is a kingly lion. He claims the limelight; he seeks the center of attention. He is creative and other people are the clay with which he creates. He molds them to suit his will. You shouldn't have asked me to come to lunch with him, Alan. And especially not today. On January fifth, the Moon enters Leo."

"You mean he was born as the Moon entered his sign?"

"Yes. He's a Leo, but one with a lunar temperament. He is dominant and leonine, but mysterious."

"I think you invent your astrology to suit what you already know about Nils-Frederik's temperament, or what you think it is."

She shrugged and said, "And there is my own sign."

"Your own sign?"

"I'm a Libra. It's an air sign. Fire is inimical to it. Air is necessary to fire, but fire consumes it. Libra falls at the equinox, when day and night are equal. Its sign is the Balance. A Libra is a compromiser. Her ruler is Venus, but she's a compromiser, so her sign also represents the artist and musician, someone who compromises art and love, who brings them together. Someone with an elegant aesthetic sensibility."

"How do Virgos get along with Libras? You and me."

"Very well, if they behave themselves. They're both autumnal signs. Virgo is a critic and healer. It's an earth sign. Earth and air together make fertility."

"With a little water."

"That's Kilda. She's an Aquarius."

They had arrived at Lily's school. It was two-thirty; she was an hour late. In the car in the parking lot he entwined her in his arms and kissed her.

24 ▪

WOLF WAS sitting at the table in the back room of the bookstore with the Book Review section of the *Los Angeles Times* spread out before him, reading a piece on the last page. He had read it at breakfast, concealing it from Myra, and now he had brought it to the store to read again. Dewitt Thomas was a journalist who wrote a weekly column about events in the Los Angeles literary world, if there was such a thing. Wolf read the short paragraph again.

A colleague at the Times *has passed along to me a tip that I'll just report without commenting on it. A certain L.A. writer is in possession of some unpublished stories by a famous, and dead, author. He'd like to publish them if he can find a way to do it without getting into trouble with the copyright holders. Who is the famous author? He's a Nobel Laureate, and he's famous for his short blunt sentences. The rest is* nada y pues nada y pues nada.

He heard the door to the street opening, then someone talking to Steve Ann in the front shop. He put the newspaper away in the drawer of the table. Alan entered, silently but with a little smile.

"What's that you've got in your hand?"

"What do you think?" said Alan.

"It looks like an old typewriter. Maybe it's a 1921 Corona portable."

"That's right."

"Where did you find it?"

"It wasn't easy. I ran across a couple of others that were in rotten condition and wouldn't work, and then I found this one in a pawnshop on West Olympic, almost out to the beach." He set it on the table. The case was covered in black imitation

leather, worn around the edges so that you could see it was
made of wood, like a cigar box. He fumbled for the latch and
removed the case. The typewriter itself was small and spindly.
The word Corona on the front in old-fashioned cursive script
was almost worn away. There were traces of yellow pinstriping
on the black enameled metal.

"And it works?"

"After a fashion."

"What about ribbons?"

"You can't get ribbons for it anymore. The one on the
machine was worn out. I bought some ribbon for another
typewriter and wound it onto the spools."

"It sounds as though you've been busy."

"I've done more than that. I've been to the UCLA library
and looked at the materials in their Hemingway collection.
Letters, manuscripts, journals. They're very interesting. I had
no idea what Hemingway's original manuscripts looked like.
I had copies made of some of the materials at UCLA."

He also had his attaché case with him. Wolf didn't see how
he could carry all these things on the motorcycle. He set down
his helmet, opened the case, took out a thin sheaf of photocopies, and spread them around on the table.

"These are the manuscripts of the stories in Hemingway's
first book *In Our Time*. Actually they're copies of copies. The
originals are in the Kennedy Library in Boston. There are
other Hemingway manuscript collections at Princeton, Yale,
and Texas. UCLA has copies of them all."

Wolf looked at the photocopies in silence for a while, picking
up a couple of sheets to examine them more carefully. "He
was a rotten typist."

"They're full of typing errors. And he tended to make the
same mistakes over and over. For example, he often wrote *the*
as *teh*. Those are just typos. But he also didn't know how to
spell certain words."

In the pages on the table he pointed out words he had
underlined with a red pencil: *optomistic, apoligize, columne,
necessery.*

Alan said, "You'll notice that there are a few corrections in pencil, made by the editor at Boni and Liveright who published the book. They're hard to make out."

"Graphite oxidizes in time. Penciled corrections are very hard to read on old manuscripts."

Alan fidgeted with the Corona on the table. "Can I go to work? You said I could do the typing in the stockroom."

"All right. I'll get the stories for you."

"What about the paper, Wolf? We need some old paper."

Wolf had put the paper in the vault so Steve Ann wouldn't notice it and ask what it was. He went to get it. From inside the vault he said, "Did you see the piece in the *Times?* In Dewitt Thomas's column?"

"Yep. It was Homer Hobart who picked that up at the party. Or Olga. They both work for the *Times.*"

"Do you think it's going to be a problem?"

"Nope. Nils-Frederik is planting that stuff deliberately to build up interest in the book. That's why he had the party."

Wolf came out of the vault with the story manuscripts and several reams of paper, and stacked the paper on the table. It was a pale watery gray in color and had little brown dots on it like flyspecks.

"I had a hell of a time finding this too, if you think it was trouble finding your typewriter. I got it finally from a dealer in San Diego. It's only about forty years old. It dates from the period just after the Second World War when they were printing books on this stuff. It's been sitting in a warehouse ever since. The dealer has about four tons of it, in case you want more. There's no reason why someone wouldn't have found paper like this in Paris in the twenties by going around to printers and buying up their leftovers. I cut it myself to twenty-one by twenty-nine and a half centimeters, right here in the stockroom."

Alan picked up a piece of the paper, felt it, and held it up to the light. "Are you sure this is going to do it? Will it fool the world?"

"After you type the stories I can spray a little diluted hydrochloric acid on the paper. Most of it evaporates. Then I can take the whole bundle of papers home and put it in the oven and parch it for a couple of hours. It will get brittle and turn nicely brown around the edges."

"Wolf, I thought you said you were not going to have anything to do with this."

Wolf went to the bookshelf, moved the three volumes of Proust in the Pléiade edition, and took the bottle of Jim Beam and the glass from behind them. He sat down at the table and poured the glass a quarter full.

"Do you know, Alan, I was raised in an orphanage in Vienna and I was trained to be scrupulously honest by the Sisters. I am not a believer but the training is a thing that stays with you. Several times in this store I have handled books that were fakes, and customers were ready to pay large sums of money for them. In one case, the customer wouldn't believe me when I told him the book was a fake. He finally paid me the very low price I asked for it, thinking he was cheating me and getting a valuable book for a bargain."

He took a sip from the glass. "I never even told lies as a boy in Vienna. Once, I remember, I went with some other boys to the Konditorei that was down the street from the orphanage. The proprietor of the store was a rather foolish old man with a white beard; we used to call him Father Christmas. He left for a moment to go to the rear of the store because his wife had called him, and the other boys immediately began filling their pockets from the jar of chocolate kisses on the counter, trying to be quiet about it but all of them punching the others to make them giggle. I was the only one who didn't take any. When Father Christmas came back into the shop, everyone's pockets were bulging but mine. The boys were all tittering, and he was suspicious, but we bought our ten *groschen* worth of candy and we left. Back in the orphanage, they all hid their chocolate in various places, and they had enough of it that it lasted them for days. In those days I was very thin and I was always hungry. But I never asked for any of the stolen chocolate, and I never told anybody about what had happened, even when Father Christmas found that his jar of kisses was empty and the Sisters asked us all if we knew anything about it. Even today I can remember the hunger I felt for those stolen chocolates. But I never tasted them."

"And now?"

"Now," he said, "I have decided that I made a mistake at the orphanage. And I have decided to help Nils steal these chocolates. It's only a schoolboy prank after all. And Nils is the leader of the boys, so if we are caught, he will take the blame."

"Right," said Alan. "Just a schoolboy prank. The stories are real, or the stories are not real, and the experts will go gaga trying to figure it out. It's an amusing canard, nothing more. *Épater le bourgeois*. Revenge on the publishing world. Which shell is the pea under? You guess." He made the mock leer of a conspirator. "And hidden from the world, in our secret hideout, we rub our hands and cackle."

All this was coming out in a kind of mad sarcasm, as though Alan had gone off his rocker, or was trying to be funny in a way that didn't succeed. Wolf wondered if he were cracking under the strain.

"What do you think about the stories, Alan? Did Hemingway write them or did Nils?"

Alan didn't answer this question. He stared at Wolf with a little smile. "You know, Wolf, there are people in the universities, Hemingway experts, who have the answer to that question. They know every line he ever wrote. Those are the people we've got to convince. I did something else yesterday when I was at UCLA getting the facsimiles copied. There's a Hemingway scholar there on the faculty named Peter Columbine. I know him slightly because for a number of years he's had an idea for a book on the Paris of the twenties and he wants me to handle it. He hasn't written the book yet. I went by to see him and told him about this whole business. Not all of it; I just told him that I'd come into possession of some interesting manuscripts and I'd like his opinion of them. I left him copies of some of the stuff that Nils-Frederik has given us. He said he would read it, and I'm going back in a week or two and find out what he thinks."

"He's probably already read the piece in the *Times*. He can guess what we're up to."

Alan, who was behaving very mysteriously, just stared back at him.

"Did you tell Nils you were going to do this?"

"No, I didn't. But people like Columbine will read the stuff anyhow when it's published. I think Columbine will say that they're real Hemingway stories."

"This is very risky, Alan. Will this Columbine keep his mouth shut about this?"

"He said he would. I swore him to secrecy."

"Well, Alan, I wish you had talked to me before you did this."

"What would you have said?"

"I would have probably told you to go ahead. It will be interesting to see what this wise fellow, this expert, has to say."

"This famous Suitcase is assuming metaphysical qualities," said Alan in a mocking, fake-portentous voice. "It may end by becoming one of the great symbols of our time, like Pandora's box, or Faust's pact with the Devil. They're about good and evil, of course. This one is about real and false."

"It's about good and evil too," Wolf said. "It will be hard to explain to Myra what I'm doing."

"It's hard to explain to Lily what I'm doing."

Wolf was left with the thought that he and Alan belonged to the secret league of men who felt guilt toward their wives. Nils did not. For Wolf and Alan, all women were mothers, who loved you but chided you when you did something wrong. For Nils they were children, to be petted and indulged but not taken seriously.

25 ■

ALAN WAS glad to be alone at last, in the stockroom with the old Corona and the stack of grayish paper. Wolf was very shrewd. Alan had difficulty concealing from him the fact that he knew the Suitcase existed and was hidden in Nils-Frederik's closet. He was pretty sure—he was certain—that Columbine would say the stories were authentic. Columbine was just a harmless charade for the benefit of Wolf.

Alan sat down at the table. The small windowless room also contained two chairs, some stationery in cardboard boxes, a paper-cutter, and materials for wrapping books for mailing. He cleared a space on the table and took the case off the old Corona. There was something about its archaic simplicity, its obsoleteness, its childlike size, that pleased him. He arranged the stack of grayish paper on the right-hand side of the type-writer and Nils-Frederik's first story on the left. It was "The Trouble with People." He fed a piece of paper into the machine and typed the title. Then he indented to begin the first paragraph of the story.

There was a crowd at the Rotonde but they found a table inside looking out through teh windows at the terrasse and the boulevard.

Looking at what he had written, he noticed the misspelled *teh* and decided to leave it. He made several more errors of this kind on the first pages, but after a while he got used to the action of the old typewriter and found himself doing better. It was still a tedious process if you were used to an electric typewriter. He had to keep pushing back the return lever by hand, and his fingers began to get cramped from the long plunge of the keys. It took him a little over an hour to type this first story, about eleven pages. He lined up the pages and felt into the attaché case for one of the rusty European paper-clips that Nils-Frederik had given him. It immediately left a rust mark on the paper, he noticed.

He put the finished story away in the attaché case and took out the next. It was "The Lady with the Dog," one of his favorites. He typed the title and began on the text.

A new person, someone that nobody knew, had appeared in the cafés on the boulevard Montparnasse. I didn't see her myself, at first, although everyone was talking about her, and then I happened to encounter her in the Rotonde when I was with a lot of other people.

He began to enjoy the work now. In typing the stories he had the odd sensation that he had *become* Hemingway in some way, that he was feeling exactly what it would have been like to be Hemingway and to have typed these stories on an identical typewriter in Paris in 1922. A funny idea occurred to him: what if this really *was* Hemingway's typewriter? There must have been millions of Coronas of this model made. Still it wasn't impossible; *something* must have happened to Hemingway's old typewriter, people after all didn't just throw such things away, and it was conceivable that it had somehow found its way to a pawnshop on West Olympic Boulevard. There was nothing on the case to identify it except the remains of a hotel sticker which, as he now examined it more closely, seemed to have come from a hotel in Athens called the Xenia. And Hemingway had been to Greece; he had reported on the Greco-Turkish War in the fall of 1922. It took him over an hour also to type "The Lady with the Dog," but it was a little longer than the first one. He was getting better at the job. He looked at his watch. He had to be away by twelve because he had a luncheon engagement.

The next one was "It's Marvelous, She Said." He began typing it and found himself not paying attention to his typing because he was caught up in the story and its easy flowing style.

It seemed natural to ask her to their table. Helen didn't say anything although he could see she didn't care for the idea. The girl came over and sat down with them, bringing her cup of tea with her. She was very thin, with the pinched face of an undernourished Greek child, and she had very large eyes. She looked like something in a magazine illustration. She spoke in a low voice and she always hesitated for a moment and smiled before she spoke. There was an odor to her that he couldn't identify. It was not a body odor or anything unpleasant and

*it was not a perfume. It seemed to remind him of something
exotic and yet ordinary, something he knew very well and identified with a small simple pleasure he had enjoyed many times.
Then he realized that it was the infusion of lime tea that she
had brought with her from the other table. He smiled at her
too and let the aroma from the* tilleul *sink into his mind.*

Alan could almost smell the lime tea too; it reminded him
of Paris. That "sink into his mind" was odd; it was more subtle
and feminine than the way Hemingway usually wrote. He
went on typing, glancing back and forth from Nils-Frederik's
typescript to the words forming on the Corona. It was not the
correct way to type; you were supposed to keep your eyes on
what you were copying and not on the words coming out of
the typewriter. But the process of the words and sentences
forming on the old-fashioned machine, some letters out of
line and others blurred, fascinated him as though he were
seeing come into existence a new and brilliantly interesting
work of literature.

*He and Helen were having roast chicken with new peas and
mashed potatoes, and he found it was not necessery to look at
the girl with her cup of lime tea, because the smell of it was
still in his mind and that was all he needed to know that she
was there and exactly what she was like.*

He looked at the misspelling, *necessery.* He had never made
this mistake before in his life, but it was one of the half-dozen
mistakes that Hemingway frequently made. He checked with
the typescript he was copying from; Nils-Frederik had spelled
it correctly. He felt an odd sensation, and it was a pleasurable
one. He felt that his own personality was slipping away from
him and he was becoming another person, a cocky, irascible,
athletic, egocentric young man with a short temper, one who
was a hell of a good writer and knew it. He had the sensation
that the features of the photograph in Hemingway's biography
were growing onto his face: the dark clipped mustache, the
even teeth showing in the tough boxer's smile, the slightly
pompous wrinkle of seriousness on the forehead. The stockroom of the bookstore became the room of an apartment in

rue Cardinal Lemoine, and he could almost smell the French coffee from the café downstairs.

They finished teh chicken and the bottle of good pinot and Nick ordered Tarte Tatin for himself and Helen. The girl would not take anything to eat although she looked very hungry. She had not told them her name yet and he was very curious to know what it was.

He was misspelling *the* about every other time, he noticed, even though he was not particularly trying to. He too was very curious about the girl with the Greek eyes. He wanted to know her better and get her away from Helen if possible. Perhaps he could meet her in the Luxembourg for a walk, and afterwards they could go for *distingués* at Lipp's. *I could not drink a liter of beer*, he heard her saying with her smile, and after a while he saw those words coming out of the typewriter.

The door of the stockroom opened and Lucius Plum came in, timid but smiling. He was wearing his usual garb, the tweed suit with the patch pockets and a white shirt with a tartan necktie. He had his leather bag over his shoulder on its strap.

"What are you doing here, Lucius? I thought we were going to have lunch together. We were going to meet in my office."

"Well, I came by here to bring something for you. We can still go to lunch together. It's about eleven-thirty."

"What did you bring me?"

Lucius slipped the bag from his shoulder and opened it on the table. "Nils-Frederik sent over a couple more stories. These are the latest he's typed up."

"Stories? What are you talking about, Lucius?"

"He knew you'd be working on them this morning, so he thought you'd like to have these too."

Nils-Frederik must have gone out of his head. To give the manuscripts to this foolish garrulous old man was tantamount to putting them on the bulletin board at the police station, or in the office of the lawyers in New York. "What did he say they were?"

"Why, they're the stories from the Suitcase. You know, the one that was stolen from Hemingway in Paris. Nils-Frederik is typing them up, and then you're going to do the facsimiles."

"Facsimiles?"

"The fake originals. Why, look at that typewriter! It's the living image of the one Hemingway wrote on. Was that in the Suitcase too?"

"Let's see the stories, Lucius."

Lucius handed them over with a pleased look. He sat down in the chair opposite Alan at the table.

Alan looked at them. One was called "This Is Me, Dr. Schultz" and the other "A Sad Thing to Happen." The first was an initiation story about a young Nick Adams in Michigan, similar to the later stories in *In Our Time*. This was a little odd, since all of the other stories that Nils had given him took place after the war. Alan read through it with a fascinated interest, while Lucius waited with his smile. He only glanced at "A Sad Thing to Happen." It consisted almost entirely of laconic dialogue like that in "Hills Like White Elephants," one of Hemingway's most famous stories.

"What have you got to do with this business, Lucius?"

"Oh, nothing in particular. I'm a friend of Nils-Frederik, and I just brought the stories over for you."

As far as he knew, Lucius had never met Nils-Frederik until the night of the party, and that was only a few weeks ago. "Lucius, you've got to keep your mouth shut about this."

"Oh, I will. I'm the soul of discretion."

Alan now began to wonder if Lucius Plum wasn't the source of the leak to the *Times*, and not Homer Hobart or Olga. "How much more of this stuff has he showed you?"

"Oh, I read some of the stories in his study, the night of the party."

"I'll bet."

"And he showed me 'It's Marvelous, She Said' just this morning. He printed it out from his disk so I could read it. It's fascinating to see the words coming out of the printer before your very eyes. It's almost like writing it yourself."

Alan smiled at him blandly. It was exactly what he himself had thought an hour ago as he was typing this same story.

"Did he give you the copy?"

"Oh yes. I've got it here in my bag. I asked him if I could have it for a souvenir. You know how he is. So generous, so friendly. He can never say no to anyone."

Alan tried not to laugh at this. "Let's go to lunch, Lucius."

Alan left the old typewriter on the table, but he gathered up the manuscripts and put them in his attaché case, both Nils-Frederik's versions and the copies he was making on the Corona. He also put in the two new stories that Lucius Plum had brought.

"We're going out to lunch," he told Wolf in the back room. "Lucius brought over a couple of new stories that Nils-Frederik has typed."

"Yes, so he told me," said Wolf placidly. Alan remembered Wolf saying, only a couple of hours ago, that if the Suitcase was a symbol it was about good and evil, like Pandora's box. Evidently he had committed himself to the schoolboy prank with enthusiasm and was ready to eat the chocolates with the other culprits. As for Alan, he felt as innocent as a babe. He was buoyed up by the morning's work of typing the stories on the old paper. He felt like calling all the women Daughter and asking the men if they wanted to spar a round. Maybe he could get Lucius Plum into the ring and bloody his nose the way Nick had Tito's.

"You'll have to ride on the Beast."

"What? Oh, splendid," said Lucius Plum, catching sight of it on the sidewalk. "It'll be an adventure."

"Life is an adventure. Living dangerously. Ours is the age of Nietzschean uncertainty." He put on his helmet and mounted the Beast.

Lucius Plum climbed up behind him, holding his bag with a firm hand. "Do you think that people will think that Nils-Frederik wrote these stories?"

"That's what Wolf thinks right now."

For lunch they went to Chopstix, a dim sum place on

Melrose that Alan liked. He had forgotten how crowded it would be; the tiny tables were jammed together and the other patrons could hear everything they were saying.

Lucius Plum said, "Splendid news about my novel *Strife and Charade*. Salamander Press is going to publish it, you know."

"They are?" Alan was thunderstruck by this piece of news.

"Yes. Nils-Frederik spoke a word to them for me. They published his novel, you know."

"Lucius, I'm your agent. Why didn't you tell me about this? Salamander is a vanity press. They'll ask you for some money to publish it."

"Oh, Nils-Frederik is taking care of that. He has plenty of it, as I understand."

"I could have placed it for you with a publisher in New York," said Alan irritably. "You would get an advance, and I'd get a commission."

"How much would the advance have been?"

"Say twenty thousand."

"My, my. Well, it's too late now. I'm sure Salamander will do a good job on it."

"Have you been seeing a lot of Nils-Frederik lately?"

"Quite a lot," said Lucius Plum. "I've got to know Nana quite well. Do you know what her name really is? It's Birgit."

"I think I knew that once but I'd forgotten it."

26 ■

CHARMIAN AND NILS-FREDERIK left the Parnassus to walk to their car. It was about ten o'clock; the sidewalk was deserted except for other moviegoers leaving the theater. In the lot she unlocked the car and they got in. Nils-Frederik was in a cheerful but calm and thoughtful mood. In the car he said very little. He lit a Sobranie from the lighter, then he sat quietly looking out the window at the lights of Wilshire Boulevard.

She said, "You've seen it a thousand times."

"I always like it."

"It's your favorite."

"Yes, I suppose it is. It not only has a role for you, but it has a role for me too."

Charmian really liked her role. She associated herself strongly with this plain, mentally retarded, poetic, sly, and yet loyal mistress of an unfeeling and brutal man who broke chains with his chest. She had seen the movie many times with Nils-Frederik, and she had gone back to see it alone until she knew all the lines by heart. She said, "I like it too. Only I wish you wouldn't—you know."

"That's part of the fun."

Charmian drove out Wilshire to the beach, turned onto the Coast Highway, and continued along in the direction of Malibu. There was almost no traffic. Nils-Frederik sat beside her speaking only a word now and then. "A little cool tonight." He gazed out the window at the fog over the sea.

"The movie starts in the winter. On the beach."

He nodded. "For people like them winter is hard." He finished his cigarette and threw it out the window without crushing it in the ashtray. In the mirror Charmian saw a shower of sparks dwindle away behind the car like a tiny firework. In Malibu she turned off on the road that led to the small beach hamlet. Lights were on in only a few of the houses; most of them were dark. She parked the car at the edge of the sand. You could hear the surf growling in the darkness only a few yards away. A sallow light fell over the beach from the houses in the distance.

She got out, went around the car, and opened the trunk. Nils-Frederik stayed where he was in the car. A light went on in the trunk when it was opened. Charmian propped up a mirror at one side of the trunk, then she took off her flowered print dress and her shoes. Standing in her slip on the pavement, she took her costume out of the trunk and put it on: a red-and-white jersey with black sleeves, a loose skirt that came to her knees, and shoes like a soldier's. Then she turned her attention to her makeup. The tiny light in the trunk illuminated her face. She glanced at the mirror now and then. She put on clown eyebrows, sunburst lines around her eyes, a red spot on her nose, and a cupid-bow mouth. To the costume she added a long cloak that tied around the neck and a soft derby like a magician's hat. From the trunk she took a marching drum, which she hung around her neck on its strap, and two drumsticks. Then she went around to the front of the car.

"*Sono pronta.*"

Nils-Frederik got out and went around to the rear of the car, where the trunk was still open. He took off his jacket and shirt and laid them carefully in the trunk. Naked to the waist, he put on a wide studded belt and studded leather wristlets. In the trunk he felt for a length of false-bronze chain and a switch cut from a willow tree. He draped the chain around his neck and came around the car to join her, holding the switch in his hand. They walked a little way out onto the beach. The light from the houses illuminated them dimly.

She stood ready with her drumsticks poised, looking solemn and prim in spite of the clown costume. She was pleased with herself.

He said slowly, as in an incantation, "A beach on the Adriatic. Giulietta Masina in *La Strada*. You're Gelsomina. I bought you from your mother on the beach."

She smiled impishly.

"You'll do anything I want. You love me, even though you don't understand what love is. You're like a child. To fuck you is like fucking a child."

He always said exactly this.

"Say it! You're announcing me to the crowd. *È arrivato Zampanò!* Beat your drum."

She rattled a tattoo on the drum. "*È arrivato Zampanò!*" In her mind little white letters appeared at her ankles, giving the dialogue in English.

"Louder! Shout it! I'm the strongest man in the world! È arrivato Zampanò!"

There were three stages with the drum: first she beat it timidly, then, as he threatened her, moderately, then very loudly. "È arrivato Zampanò!"

Without warning he struck her on the legs with the switch. She cried "Ouch!" and backed away.

"Come here."

He pointed with his switch to the sand and she came back to the spot where she had been.

"Try again." He held the switch ready.

She played a furious drumroll and cried at the top of her voice, "È ARRIVATO ZAMPANÒ!"

Staring at her, he dropped the switch and wrapped the chain around his bare chest. It was a piece of hardware for a hanging lamp made of brass-plated pot metal. Straining and grunting, baring his teeth, he tensed his muscles against the chain. His breasts were pendulous, almost feminine, and there was only a tuft of hair on the chest between them. Gelsomina played another drumroll and shouted, "Ecco! Ecco! L'uomo forte! L'uomo più forte del mondo! È arrivato Zampanò!"

The links of the chain opened and it burst from his chest. "Ecco!" cried Gelsomina again. "L'uomo forte!" He dropped the chain and seized her, pulling off the drum and throwing it onto the sand. The drumsticks fell from her hands. She was on her back and he was fumbling with the loose skirt and the cloak. Gelsomina said out loud, "I'm fed up. Io me ne frego. Not from the work. I like the work. I like being an artiste. It's you I don't like."

27 ▪

Lucius Plum parked his old Chevrolet on the street in front of the house, careful not to block the driveway. It was a cool crisp morning with a layer of fog lower down over the city.

Here in the hills it was clear and the sun was out. He knew by this time how to enter the house without a key: you lifted the garage door, then inside the garage there was an unlocked door that led to the kitchen. He had his bag over his shoulder as usual. He was in the best of spirits and his arthritis was hardly bothering him at all. It was all in the mind, he thought, like a great many other physical ailments.

In the kitchen Charmian was sitting at the table reading the *Times*, with a mug of coffee in front of her, and Nana was standing at the sink washing the cup, saucer, and dish from her own breakfast. It was a reversal of the usual scene in the kitchen. The two women had changed places; Charmian was sitting at the table and Nana was where Charmian usually was, standing at the sink working, even though her work was only the minor ritual of rinsing the cup and saucer and putting them away in the cupboard, which she did by blind feel. She looked even smaller when she was standing up, hardly the size of a child. She didn't turn her head when Lucius came in. Charmian lowered her paper and said, "Did you come to see Nils? He's still asleep."

"Still asleep?"

"He was out late last night."

This was strange. He told Lucius that he always worked on his writing in the morning and was done by ten or eleven.

"Did he go out by himself?"

"He and I went to the movies. Then we drove out to the beach and didn't get back until midnight. Now he's sleeping it off."

Lucius said, "Consider the possibility that I came to see you. And Nana."

"Maybe I could read you the funnies out of the paper. Children like that."

The whole house was different today. Nils-Frederik was in bed at nine-thirty in the morning. Nana was standing at the sink. Charmian was sitting down at the table, reading the paper and making jokes. He had never seen any sign before that she had a sense of humor.

"Are they funny?"

"Here's one. A man is in hell and he's standing before two doors. One of them says, 'Damned if you do' and the other says 'Damned if you don't.' A devil is prodding him to choose one."

"Which would you take?"

"Nils would take Damned if you do. I would take Damned if you don't."

Definitely it was a new Charmian. It would have been interesting to talk to her and see what else came out, but she laid the paper down, got up from the table without a word, and went away to the bathroom off the kitchen. This reminded him of something he had meant to do before he left his apartment and had forgotten. Charmian was now in the downstairs bathroom, so he went to use the one upstairs in the study. Nils-Frederik had shown him where the key to the study was hidden, under the blue vase at the bottom of the stairs. He unlocked the door and went through the study directly to the bathroom. This bathroom was only for Nils-Frederik's personal use when he was working on his writing in the morning. It was not the bathroom where he shaved and bathed. That was the bathroom downstairs off the master bedroom. All these details Nils-Frederik had confided to him in his friendly and candid way. Lucius had not yet seen the master bedroom, although Nils-Frederik had told him with a sideways smile that it was "tastefully furnished."

After Lucius had performed a structurally perfect bowel movement he washed his hands, dried them on the guest towel, and went out into the study. In his haste he had not looked around carefully as he had passed through it on his way to the bathroom. Through the big window at the end of the room there was a nice view of the city under its layer of fog, with the Palos Verdes hills sticking up out of it to the south. The desk where Nils-Frederik worked was almost bare. Beside the printer was a stack of manuscripts. Looking at them, he found there were two stories he hadn't seen yet, one of them unfinished. The unfinished story had no title. The opening words were *That summer we wanted to go to Spain, but we didn't have any money. Finally we decided to go whether we had the money or not. We could go to the Fiesta at Pamplona.* It sounded like an early sketch for *The Sun Also Rises.* Lucius looked around for the originals that Nils-Frederik was typing these stories from. They were nowhere in sight. Of course, they were valuable and he probably kept them locked up. For example, in the desk. Lucius would not have dreamed of tampering with someone's desk when he was not present. He cautiously tried the drawer of the desk. It was locked. Likewise the file cabinet. He ran his fingers over the printer and looked under the keyboard of the word processor. He imagined what the things he was looking for would look like: bundles of grayish paper with typing on them, fastened at the top with rusty paperclips. They would be exactly like the facsimiles that Alan was making in the back room of the bookstore. If he found them, how could he tell which they were? He looked again at the Spanish story. The funny thing was that, as far as he knew, Hemingway had not been to Spain in 1922. He couldn't tell whether the people in the story actually went to Spain because there were only about three pages of it.

He tidied up the stack of stories and put them back exactly where they had been. In a part of his mind he was listening for sounds from the kitchen or some other part of the house. As he set the stories down he heard someone coming up the stairs—slow creaks, the sound of breathing, a hand sliding on the banister. If it was Nils-Frederik he was coming very slowly, perhaps in the hope of catching him at something he wasn't supposed to be doing. Of course, he wasn't supposed to be in the study at all. He had never before been in it when Nils-Frederik wasn't there. He prepared his response: *I just came up to use the bathroom. Charmian was using the one downstairs.* If Nils-Frederik went into the bathroom, he would notice the odor. That would be a convincing proof. Lucius felt confident about his defense against a charge of snooping.

Presently Nana appeared in the doorway, towing herself along by pulling at the frame of the door. She turned her head straight toward him in that disconcerting way she had as though she were seeing him. Her cotton smock was freshly laundered and pressed. He had thought she always wore the same one but evidently she had more than one of them. Someone had fixed up her hair too. It was neatly brushed and held with a tortoise comb in the back. He could see that she had been a great beauty when she was young. She still looked quite small, like a child dressed up as an old woman for a school pageant. She sat down in the chair with her face still turned directly toward him.

"What are you doing here?"

"I . . ." In an instant he abandoned his unsavory alibi. "Nils-Frederik asked me for my opinion of some manuscripts he's working on. I came up to look at them."

"I want to tell you about my boat, Alan."

"I'm not Alan. I'm Lucius."

"You can be anybody I want. I have a boat now. It's new and I just thought of it. My boat comes with a skipper. He is a young man named Frank. He is tall and has broad shoulders. His hair is long and he has a beard. He looks like Jesus, but he is very strong and knows about boats. He is a sailor. The boat has high bows for breasting the rough seas, and it has a little cabin with a steering wheel and a stool and a place for a cup of coffee. We leave the wharf and go through the harbor, among the ships, some of them from Africa or America. Frank points out the flags and tells me which countries they come from. There are also tugboats, barges, and small navy ships in the harbor. The navy ships are sleek and gray and the sailors in white uniforms wave to us as we pass. Then we are out of the harbor and in the open sea, with islands in the distance. The islands are black on the dark sea, and there are white towns on them. There is a wind and there are whitecaps on the sea. The boat pitches but it is snug inside the cabin and Frank makes me coffee and gives it to me in a mug. He is kind to me because I pay him good wages for being the skipper of the boat, and he wants to keep the job."

"I can see a picture of your boat in my mind."

"After a while we pass several islands, small ones, with children waving to us from the rocks, and fishermen drying nets. These are the Skerries. I can stop at any of the islands that I want, and talk to the children, or buy smoked fish from the fishermen and have it on black bread when we drink our coffee in the boat. Sometimes the people on the islands invite us to stay for dinner, but Frank eats with the servants, even though he is the skipper of the boat. I can stay out in the Skerries as long as I want. There are no inns or hotels, but I can stay overnight with the fishing folk, or with my wealthy friends who have a summer house on an island. If it's winter, then they tell their servants and I stay overnight in the house anyhow, with a tiny little heater in my room, and everything I need is provided by the servants. In the house of my rich friends Frank sleeps in the kitchen. In my room I can look out the window in the night and see the black sea, the black rocks of the islands, and the white stones of the towns on the islands."

"That is a very fine picture. You describe the sea very well."

"I need to be near the water. I love water. You see, I was born in the Skerries, Alan, and I married Klaus because he was a man of the sea. He carried me away to many foreign lands, and then he brought me to America. But there is no sea in America."

"Yes there is, Birgit. I could take you to the beach sometime. I have a car. Doesn't Nils-Frederik take you to the beach?"

"No. He goes to the beach with that woman. His wife."

"Her name is Charmian. You know that. Would you like to go to the beach in my car?"

She said slyly, "We could go on my boat."

"I'd be jealous of Frank. I want to be your only lover."

She never smiled, but a spiderweb of wrinkles formed at the corners of her mouth, as if she was deliberately holding it firm. Then she turned serious again. "After Nils is no more, the money will be all mine again. I can do anything I want. I can go back to Sweden again and live in the Skerries."

"After Nils is no more?" He studied her face to see if she was still joking, but it was a pallid moon, unreadable. "Why should Nils be no more?"

"He is not real. And this house. These people, this whole city. It's not real. Haven't you noticed that?"

He thumped the desk and the printer, and switched the lamp on and off to show her how well the electricity worked. "It's all solid enough."

The spiderwebs appeared at the corners of her mouth again. "It's not real. And you are not Alan, you are not real. Alan I can feel." After a moment she said, "Would you like to be my lover? You could be the skipper of my boat. You could be Frank. Of course, you would have to eat with the servants."

Now it was Lucius Plum's turn to smile.

28 ■

PETER COLUMBINE sat in his office at UCLA reading the stories that Alan Glas had left with him. He had gone through them several times and he was still not sure what to make of them. He took out a pouch of tobacco from the drawer of his desk, filled his pipe, and tamped it down with a little silver device he had. The pipe was modern and chromium, and so was his office furniture. His own chair was upholstered in royal purple and the two chairs for visitors in chartreuse. The desk was metal with a white Formica top. Columbine was a modernist in most of his tastes. Everything in the office was piled high with books, student papers, and scholarly journals. Columbine had a somewhat forbidding manner and students didn't visit him often in his office. He preferred it that way. In his opinion the University would be a very fine place to work if it were not cluttered up with students, endless waves of them, year after year, needing to have it explained to them all over again that the First World War took place before the Second World War, and that T. S. Eliot was American and Isherwood was English even though they lived in each other's countries. Columbine gave them all straight A's so they wouldn't come into

his office to complain. He lit his pipe and sucked it until it
began emitting smoke like a tiny factory.

He gave the five stories another quick look. "The Real
Thing." That was a queer one. An American businessman
committed adultery with a café girl, while Nick Adams fooled
around with his old lady. That didn't seem like the Nick that
everybody knew. It was in the classic Hemingway style,
though. *Nick watched while Marie-Georges cleaned the counter
with a rag and then began polishing the steam pressure coffee
machine.* It sounded like "A Clean, Well-Lighted Place" with
a girl in it.

The one that really intrigued him, though, was "A Friend
from Detroit." It had a dialogue style exactly like the later stories, the ones that made Hemingway famous. Minimal char-
acterization, minimal scene-setting. The dialogue was
untagged. No he saids and she saids. He was supposed to have
invented this dialogue style later, but these stories were written
in 1921 when he was just beginning as a writer. He wondered
if Alan Glas knew what he had stumbled across here. A beautiful book could be written on these manuscripts and their im-
plications for criticism. No, he thought, first an article, a long,
carefully thought-out bombshell that would blast previous
Hemingway criticism to smithereens. Then a book. He already
had the title. *Nick Adams in Paris.* By Peter Columbine, Ph.D.
Harvard University Press, 1992.

No one had done dialogue as well as he had. Later they
all imitated him, but they didn't quite have the touch. It was
easy to write an imitation. All you had to do was pick up on the
little tricks, the lack of tags, the short lines, the repetitions
and bounces. But he had invented it, as Picasso invented cub-
ism and Schoenberg invented atonality. When he did it you
could see the hand of the master. The authentic stuff was in-
imitable. Columbine was pleased with this word and thought
he might use it in his article. He wrote it down on a slip of paper. *Inimitable.*

He looked at "A Friend from Detroit" again for the tenth
time. Alan had said he wanted the manuscripts back when he

came to talk about them. Of course he could photocopy them. But Columbine wanted to enter at least this story into his computer, so he could do a serious study of it and analyze its structure and style. Ordinarily he would have this done by a research assistant or by a department typist. He didn't want to do that now, because the fewer people that knew about this thing the better. There was already that hint in Dewitt Thomas's column in the *Times*. If the word got around that he had these stories, everyone would be coming into his office to look over his shoulder as he worked on them. His article had to be the first one to appear. Likewise his book. He had better get to work.

He set up the program on the computer, put the manuscript on the reading stand in front of him, and began tapping the white plastic keys. A FREND FROM. He backed up to extinguish the tiny green letters on the screen, then started the line over. The computer made a soft patter like rabbit feet, a sound he enjoyed. His pipe went out and he relit it. It was the real Hemingway all right; he was sure of that as he typed away on it entering it on the disk. What a stroke of luck that Alan had brought it to him.

A Friend from Detroit

NICK LIKED *to hang around the Halles early in the morning watching them unload vegetables and sides of beef and crates of fish coming in from the country. The big Renault camions with their shovel noses and their solid tires would start coming into the market about four. The porters would carry the sides of beef into the market with their aprons all bloody and dripping blood on the pavement. After you watched them unloading the camions you could get onion soup at a stall or you could have breakfast at one of the working-class restaurants. Nick liked to go to a bar in rue du Cygne just behind the market. You could get black coffee and good croissants, made*

in the Saint-Honoré quarter. According to the patron of the
bar, every quarter of Paris had its own kind of croissants, and
those from Saint-Honoré were the best.

"You appreciate such things, Mr. Adams. The others are
content with the ones from La Chapelle, or from the Sixteenth
Arrondissement. They are not as good."

"You can't get these in America."

"Is that so?"

"Even the ones from the Sixteenth Arrondissement are better than anything you can get in America."

"Where is your friend Mr. George, Mr. Adams? I haven't
seen him for some time."

"Mr. Elliot. George is his first name."

"Ah. I see."

"George Elliot. Actually he is a female novelist wearing
men's clothes."

"I don't believe you, Mr. Adams."

"Why not?"

"You have a rich sense of humor."

"A lot of people have that."

"It is not easy to tell when you are speaking veridically and
when you are making a blague."

"Right now I am making a blague. His name is Mr. George
Elliot, but he is not a female novelist."

"Americans have a rich sense of humor."

"Are you an expert on Americans?"

"Yes, I am."

"How many do you know?"

"I know you and Mr. Elliot."

"George and I are not typical."

"I have a sister who married an American soldier and now
lives in Cambridge, America."

"Cambridge, Maryland or Cambridge, Massachusetts?"

"In Cambridge, America. It is a city by the coast. Her
husband works in a factory of canned fish."

"That could be either Cambridge, Maryland or Cambridge,
Massachusetts."

"It's by the sea. The sea is necessary as a supplier of fish."

"I understand."

"Also, I have another of your compatriots who is renting a room over the bar."

"I didn't know you had rooms."

"I have three. His name is Mr. Biagi."

"Is he Italian?"

"He is an Italian who lives in America. He lives in Detroit." He pronounced it as if it were a French word, leaving off the T at the end.

George came in, looked around to see if the place was empty, and took a seat at the bar. The patron was polishing glasses. He had a row of six in front of him. "Ah, here is Mr. Elliot now." He seemed pleased that he had learned his correct name. He drew a cup of coffee and passed it to him before George had said anything.

Nick said, "Where the hell have you been?"

"I've been working on a story."

"Is it about the Halles?"

"It's about French gangsters. There are a lot of them in the Halles."

"I'll bet it's about girls too."

"Gangsters do have girls. Haven't you seen them in the movies?"

"Mr. Biagi has lots of girls. He is very popular with the ladies."

"Who is Mr. Biagi?"

"C'est mon locataire. My tenant. He was very popular with the ladies in America, and he is very popular with them here."

"An Italian?"

"We've already gone through that, George. He's a Wop from Detroit."

"What's he doing here?"

"He's living in the room upstairs."

"At the present time he is without employment. He is looking for something in the entertainment business."

"We're all in the entertainment business."

"What do you mean?"
"You and me, and this guy with his bar."
"Could you put that in French, Mr. Elliot?"
"He says that in running this bar you are in the entertainment business."
"Oh, absolutely."

Nick later made the acquaintance of the American who lived in the room over the bar. His name was Sam Biagi and he had just got out of the penitentiary in Michigan. That was why he had come to Paris, to forget his past troubles. Biagi seemed glad to meet Nick and George. He didn't know any Americans in Paris and he wanted to make some friends. The three of them sat in the bar drinking fines.
"Why were you in the penitentiary in Michigan?"
"They didn't like the way I ran my business."
"What was your business?"
"I ran a string of girls."
"Did you make any money?"
"Quite a lot, before they came down on me."
"Gentlemen, could you say this in French?"
They all shifted to French for the benefit of the patron. George's French was good but not fluent. Biagi's French was non-existent.
"Mr. Biagi was a prominent maquereau *in America. He had a string of* poules.*"*
George did not know words like maquereau and poule. It had to be explained to him that poules were tarts and maquereaux were pimps. You would think that these were words that would be known to an expert on gangsters. Biagi had already learned both words, even though his French was poor.
"I thought I might go into the same line here in Paris."
"A risky business. But one capable of much profit."
"Do you know any Frenchmen in the business?"
"No, but I know some girls. That's all you need."
"That and a couple of rooms. And a lot of luck."

"Mr. Diamant has offered to rent me the rooms." The name of the patron was Mr. Diamant. That was the first that Nick and George had heard of it.

"There are some Frenchmen in the same business, right here in the quarter. I'd be careful if I were you."

"I intend to be very careful."

Later that month Nick and George went to shoot grouse on the Marne. It was a thing they had planned for some time. It was swell country for shooting in the Marais de Saint-Gond and Nick had been there before. You took the train to Epernay and then you got a local taxi to take you to Vert-Toulon on the edge of the marsh. It was late fall now and the ground was so hard that it rang under their feet like iron. There were shards of ice around the edges of the marsh. Nick had his light Mancini and George had the twelve-gauge over-and-under Remington he had brought from America. The Remington was too heavy for birds and when it went off it spooked them for a mile around. They would fly away and circle over the marsh and it would be a half an hour before they came back. Nick started up a couple of grouse and knocked them down cleanly, and George got a quail but it was spoiled by the big magnum waterfowl shot.

"That gun would be good for shooting elephants."

"It does bring them down, though."

"Doesn't it kick an awful lot?"

"My shoulder is sore a lot. The gun and I have a relationship. When it kicks I kick back."

"Do you like this country?"

"I've never seen anything like it."

"It's like the country around Petoskey."

"Is it always this cold here?"

"I like it cold. It makes good shooting."

"You came from Michigan."

"Illinois. I used to shoot in Michigan."

George himself was a Californian. He didn't care much for

the cold. By eleven o'clock Nick had a half dozen birds and George had a few himself, and they sat down and ate the sandwiches they had bought at the station in Epernay. They also had a bottle of the local rouge. *Nick opened the wine with the corkscrew on his knife.*

"Is it all right to pee on the ground?"

"Not in the marsh. Go off in the bushes."

George went off in the bushes and came back. He didn't wash his hands before he ate his sandwich, probably because the water was so cold with needles of ice in it. George was a good friend but Nick was glad he wasn't a woman and married to him. He could imagine all kinds of George's habits you would find out about if you were married to him.

"This is where Gallieni stopped the Boches with his taxi-cabs."

"Who was he?"

"He was the general in charge of defending Paris. Instead of waiting for them to come to him, he commandeered all the taxis in Paris and put troops in them. They came out here and won the Battle of the Marne. The Boches hadn't expected them to come so quickly in taxis."

"Was this Gallieni a Wop?"

"He was a French general. He was also a Parisian. He was a chic *type."*

"Only a Parisian would think of using the taxis."

"That was an example of chic.*"*

"It's funny that a French general would have an Italian name."

"What do you think about Biagi?"

"I think he is a loser. He got in trouble in Michigan and he is going to get in trouble here."

"What will happen to him?"

"He will get his string of girls and run them for a week or two and then he'll be arrested. The local Frenchmen who are in the same business won't stand for it. They will tip off the cops on the Quai des Orfèvres. They never arrest Frenchmen, only foreigners. It's a form of national monopoly. Only

Frenchmen understand sex, so only Frenchmen should be in this business."

"Do you know any of the Frenchmen in the business?"

"Oh yes. They're all my friends. That's how I get my material."

"Do the police know about them?"

"Of course."

"Do they pay the police?"

"Sometimes. They don't have to. The police leave them alone anyhow, out of patriotism. The Paris police are very patriotic."

"Maybe Biagi is patriotic too."

"He may be patriotic in Michigan. Here he's a foreigner."

When they got back to Paris Biagi didn't show up for a couple of days. Nick went on eating breakfast in the bar in rue du Cygne, and he and the patron talked about bicycle racing and about the history of Paris.

"Why is this street called the Street of the Swan?"

"There used to be swans here in the river. The river was nearer in those days. That was before they built the quays."

"When was that?"

"In the time of Francis the First. He was the one who built the quays. Before that it was marshy along the river and you could catch fish in it. The fish liked to breed in the reeds in the marsh. Now that there are the quays, there are no more fish."

"There are many people fishing in the Seine."

"They are imbeciles. They do not catch any fish. The only ones who benefit are the sporting goods stores on quai Mégisserie who sell them their rods."

Imbecile was one of the favorite words of the patron. He thought a great many people were imbeciles. Anyone who did not speak French well was an imbecile, and so were the customers of poules, all South Americans, and the men who thought you could catch fish in the Seine.

"Where is Mr. Biagi these days?"

"Mr. Biagi, the American. Unfortunately he is in a cell at the Palace of Justice. He will have his procès-verbal in a few days."

"How did this happen?"

"The people who are already in business in the quarter found out about him. There was no need for them to be upset. There are plenty of customers for everybody. Those imbeciles."

"How did people find out about Mr. Biagi?"

"Mr. Elliot told them."

"I can't believe that."

"The police came to arrest Mr. Biagi. They told me that Mr. Elliot had passed the word in the quarter, and people were upset with Mr. Biagi. I am on very good terms with the police too. They come here to drink a blanc now and then and to see if they can get any information from me, but I don't tell them anything. Now I no longer have my tenant Mr. Biagi, and I no longer have the rent from the other two rooms he was using. It is a severe blow. I blame it all on Mr. Elliot."

"I'm sorry this happened."

"He is an imbecile, Mr. Adams. A moral imbecile. The worst kind."

George didn't show up after that in the bar in rue du Cygne. He probably knew he was not on good terms with the patron. A week or so later Nick ran into him by accident on the quay near Saint-Michel. George seemed to be his old self. They walked up the Left Bank toward Nick's place in rue Cardinal Lemoine.

"Did you write your story?"

"I cabled it last night. It's pretty good, I think."

"It's too bad about Biagi."

"Don't worry about him. They'll just send him back to America. They don't really lock up Americans. They say, after all, remember General Pershing."

"He's the one who sent the taxis to the Marne."

"No, that was some Wop, you told me."

"Yes, a Wop like Biagi."

"You're sore, aren't you, Nick?"

"I think it was a rotten thing to do."

"I had to for my story. It was too good to miss. The business about the police who leave them alone if they're French but arrest foreigners. If this thing didn't happen to Biagi, I wouldn't have any story. It would just be hypothetical. People would ask me if it really happened."

"Everything for the story, is that it?"

"That's right. It's the entertainment business. You have to keep them entertained."

"Diamant said you were a moral imbecile."

"Who? Oh, the patron. He's an imbecile himself. He's a sentimentalist. He's supposed to be in the entertainment business, and all he talks about is the history of Paris."

"He's interested in bike racing too."

"I don't care for bike racing."

"What do you do for exercise?"

"I run my beat."

"You chase poules and maquereaux."

"I chase the story."

"It's not a very muscular sport."

"Do you know what I'd like to do, Nick? I'd like to get a rod and fish here in the Seine. Like all these Frenchmen."

"Why?"

"It would be very relaxing and it would help with the grocery bill."

"You're still talking about the patron, aren't you?"

"What do you mean?"

"You're sore at him because he said you were an imbecile. He says that anyone who thinks there are fish in the Seine is an imbecile."

"Why does he say that? There are plenty of fish in the Seine. People catch them all the time."

"If Biagi goes to America, what will he do there?"

"Just what he did here. He's a loser," said George.

29 ∎

LILY SAID, "Kilda didn't come back for lunch."

It was a Saturday and she had torn out of the apartment after breakfast as she always did on weekends when she wasn't going to school. Alan had been at the bike shop on La Brea picking up the Beast after it had been repaired. He had to go on the bus and it was after three when he got home. He hadn't had any lunch either.

"She's never missed a meal before. I can't imagine where she is."

"Didn't she say anything when she left?"

"No. You know how she is. She just scooted out. Someone called her on the phone just after breakfast. I think she may have gone to some friend's house."

"What friend? Some kid from school?"

"I don't know. She never talks about her friends."

"She's probably at the golf course."

He couldn't banish from his mind the image of a long green car with pinstripes on it. He saw the door opening, the glasses flashing from inside, a voice asking if Kilda could help him find his lost puppy. He banished this from his thoughts as totally irrational. But the terrors that beset us in the world are not rational; they are in our emotions, and more real than the rational. He had never mentioned Klipspringer to Lily.

"Don't worry. I can find her," he told her. "The damned brat."

He went to the golf course on foot to look for her. It was a place where he had found her several times before. It was about a half a mile from the apartment, and the neighborhood around it was not very savory. In his mind he formed images of perverts in garages, a mutilated body, gangs of hoodlum kids. And he couldn't get the green car and the flashing eyeglasses out of his thoughts. In a case like this it was always a question when to call the police. If you called them too soon, the child was sure to be home and safe when they came to take the report. If you called them too late, people would say, Why didn't you call the police? Alan searched for a half an hour over the vast expanse of lawn scattered with Saturday golfers, but she wasn't there. It was all open fairway except for a few clumps of trees, and he checked those. When he got back it was after four.

"You're probably right. She's gone to some friend's house." He walked back and forth in the room in a physically painful state of anxiety. "When she comes home I'll slap her silly."

"No you won't."

"It's funny when kids are missing. It terrifies you, and at the same time you're so mad at them you could slap them."

"I keep thinking about that phone call."

"Did you hear the voice?"

"No, she got to it before I did. She's been doing that lately. She's just discovered the phone."

Alan remembered that other phone call on Christmas day. It was the first time Kilda had answered the phone and talked to someone and didn't tell them who it was. Whoever it was, they had talked about Christmas presents. Kilda had said, Why don't you ever come over here sometime? But the kid had never shown up.

An idea struck him with the shock of revelation. Why hadn't he thought of that? He rang the number and Charmian answered.

"This is Alan."

"Hello, Alan." She had never called him that before. She had never called him anything. It was strange to hear her speaking to him in this intimate way, as though they were friends.

"By any chance is Kilda there?"

"Who?"

"Our little girl."

"Oh yes, she's here. At least there's a little girl here."

"How did she get there?"

"I wouldn't know."

"Tell her to stay there, will you? I'm coming over."

"She's not going anywhere. Don't worry."

He hung up and told Lily, "She's at Nils-Frederik's."

"How on earth." Lily stared at him for a long moment, her expression puzzled. Alan was in a state of shock, but he felt better now that he knew where she was. His anger was now transferred to Nils-Frederik. He must have come over in the car with Charmian and kidnapped her off the street. He hadn't thought of asking Charmian that. No, Charmian had said she didn't know how she got there. He was getting confused. He tried to think reasonably.

"I'm going over and get her."

"Do you want me to come?"

"No, I'll probably have a fight with Nils-Frederik and you'd just make it worse."

"Don't be angry with him until you find out what really happened."

Lily was almost taking his side. Alan was astounded, but he had so many other emotions that this one was swallowed up in them. Taking his helmet, he went down and got on the newly repaired Beast, which was parked in the area behind the garage. He was a mile on his way, going up La Cienega through the Saturday traffic, before he realized that he should have taken Lily's car if he expected to bring Kilda back with him. It was because he had thought of it as some kind of rescue mission. He had imagined himself racing across the city on the Beast to save her from some obscure danger. He tried to calm himself, which was hard to do going at high speed through the traffic with the wind tearing past him. He waited for the left turn off Los Feliz with his foot on the ground, then went up the hill to the house.

In the kitchen, Charmian looked around from the stove and motioned with her head toward the rear of the house.

"Where are they?" He had an image of Nils-Frederik and Kilda together in one of the tiny bedrooms, or in the master bedroom with its queer equipment.

"Out in the garden." She turned back to the saucepan on the stove; she was skimming something off the top of it with a spoon. Nana was at her usual place at the kitchen table. Alan now saw that Lucius Plum was sitting there with her. So many new things were happening that this hardly affected him at all. He went out the door at the rear of the house into the garden. Because the house was built into the hill at the rear, the door opened into a kind of concrete tunnel, with steps leading up into the garden. It was nicely kept, with ficus trees, herbaceous borders, and annuals in flowerbeds. Nils-Frederik and Kilda were sitting in white enameled chairs under a striped umbrella, eating cookies.

"Have some lemonade," said Nils-Frederik.

Alan ignored him. "How did you get here?" he asked Kilda.

"I came on the bus."

"The bus?"

"You catch it on La Cienega, then you transfer at Santa Monica Boulevard, and get off the new bus at Los Feliz and Western."

"How did you know how to do that?"

"Grandpa told me how on the phone. It was easy. I talked to people on the bus. Some of them were crazy."

Alan's anger mounted. "Kilda, that was very bad. You could have got lost, or something else could have happened to you. Those are not nice people on the bus. Where did you get the money?"

"I have my school lunch money."

"Sit down, Alan. We're just having a little tea party. A lemonade party. Have a cookie. They're Charmian's walnut sugar squares. They're quite good."

It struck Alan now that Kilda had called him Grandpa. She had never used this term before in her life, but she had never had anything to do with Nils-Frederik before. The word was ludicrous applied to Nils-Frederik. Of course, he was behaving exactly like a Grandpa now, sitting with his granddaughter eating cookies and drinking lemonade. God knew what they were talking about.

"What were you talking about?"

"We were talking about literature," said Nils-Frederik.

"Grandpa was telling me about Dos. Dos. A Russian writer who loved children."

"Dostoevsky," said Nils-Frederik genially.

"He was a child molester."

Nils-Frederik laughed. "Oh, come now, Alan. Dostoevsky loved children. He wouldn't harm a hair of their heads."

"What's a child molester?"

Looking at her poker-faced and sly expression, Alan knew for a certainty that she knew. "One of the people on the bus."

"Some of them were nice. I talked to a lady."

"Why did you let her come on the bus?" Alan confronted his father. "If you wanted so badly to see her, you could have asked us, and maybe you could have come in the car with Charmian and brought her here."

"You wouldn't let me come near the place," said Nils-Frederik, still cheerful. "You know that."

"We were about to call the police."

"No need to do that."

"I've been telling Grandpa that he shouldn't smoke so much."

"Yes, she has." Nils-Frederik laughed again. "Maybe I'll stop."

"The cigarettes are Russian. Grandpa knows a lot about Russians."

"It'll be good for her geography class," said Nils-Frederik.

"Father, this was a sneaky thing for you to do."

"He's naughty," said Kilda. She was perfectly grave. She hadn't smiled at anything they were saying. "He's a very bad man. He smokes, and he says things that aren't true."

"Such as?"

"He said that the Russian writer liked children."

"He did like them, but in the wrong way."

"If you ate a cookie, Alan, then it would be a ritual breaking of bread between us, and we would make up our quarrel."

Alan didn't eat a cookie. He had no idea why the three of

them were here in Nils-Frederik's garden, conducting a conversation on pedophilia. Nils-Frederik was in control of the whole thing. He had made it all happen, including the fact that Alan would come across town to get her and the three of them would sit here in the garden talking. Alan hadn't sat down, though. He was still standing, holding his helmet in his hand and not smiling.

"Come on, Kilda."

"Take some cookies with you, Honey. Here, tuck one in your pocket."

"Charmian will give me a paper bag."

She knew who Charmian was too. Alan wondered now if she had been here before. She got up and Alan led her away by the hand. She carried a handful of cookies clutched against her body.

"Bye, Honey. Come again."

"Not on the bus," said Alan.

Nils-Frederik didn't get up. He watched them disappear into the house with an expression of ironic affection. In the kitchen Lucius Plum said, "Hello, Kilda. What a nice little girl you are." Nana turned her blind eyes in her direction without expression. Alan had the intuition that this was all somehow a plot, that Lucius Plum, Nana, and Charmian were all in on it. Everyone was behaving so perfectly naturally, as though they were a family and had all known one another for years. Kilda asked Charmian for a paper bag, and she handed it over without a word. No telling what Charmian thought about the whole business. Kilda put the cookies in it and they went out to the Beast parked at the curb.

"Oh, keen."

She had never been on the Beast before. It seemed too dangerous and Lily wouldn't allow it. First he put the bag of cookies into the carrier, while Kilda watched with interest. Then he put on his helmet and straddled the seat, and Kilda got on behind him. He showed her how to hang on with her arms around his waist. Then he thought better of it. If she were back there behind him, she could be whirled away by the wind and under a car in an instant. She needed to be where he could see her. He pushed himself back a few inches on the seat and installed her in front of him, in the place where he usually rode. There was nothing for her to hang on to, but she was enclosed by his legs and the rest of his body. He jumped savagely on the thing to start it, the exaggerated gesture that makes all motorcyclists, even intellectuals and mild postal clerks, look like violent strongmen. He put it in gear and they lurched off into the traffic on Los Feliz.

He himself never rode the Beast without a helmet. She shouldn't even be on the thing anyhow. He stopped at the bike shop on La Brea, where he had paid for the repairs on the Beast only a few hours before, and bought her a child's helmet. It was pink and white and had a picture of a cartoon rabbit on it. In it she looked like a cartoon herself, a skinny rabbit wearing a pink motorcycle helmet.

It struck him what an ingenious and diabolical machine a motorcycle was when it was carrying two riders in this posture. Through the clothing he could feel her small bifurcated bottom pressing against him. The black bike with its mechanical protuberances, its whirring flywheel, its silver mirror and its leather pad fitted into the legs of the two bodies, might have been an exotic torture machine out of a science fiction movie. Their posture also brought to his mind the subject of child molesting, the very subject that he himself, for some incredible reason, had brought up when they were talking in Nils-Frederik's garden. It was because he was so angry at Nils-Frederik and he wanted to say something extreme. He, Nils-Frederik, had behaved perfectly correctly to Kilda, like a grandpa, and Alan had led the conversation onto sexual perversion. He was some father. He longed for Kilda to make things right by calling him Dad, as she had done once on the telephone when she was talking to Nils-Frederik. "Hang on!" he yelled to her.

"Wow. It goes fast," she said in her usual flat tone, without excitement.

There was nothing for her to hang on to. He was really

going very slowly, about forty, although it probably seemed fast to her. She never turned her head; she stared straight forward at the traffic ahead like a searchlight. The pink helmet, at the level of his chest, bobbed as they raced over intersections. She was snug between his thighs, her back pressing into his chestbone, her body enclosed in his, an analogue of a mother carrying a baby in her womb, with the aid of this powerful obstetrical machine that gripped them both. The Beast was male and he was female. Between them they had given birth to this strange, wonderful, and disobedient child. Lily was not really in it. He felt that Lily really didn't understand Kilda, or had very conventional ideas about her. He longed for this motorcycle ride across town never to end.

30 ∎

ALAN WAS still typing the manuscripts on the old Corona at the bookstore. By this time Wolf had experimented with parching the finished stories in his oven at home, taking the opportunity of an evening when Myra went out to a movie with a friend. When Myra came home, she noticed the smell and asked him what it was, and he told her he was parching some paper in the oven. He was incapable of telling a lie to her. Myra, after giving him a queer look, dropped it there and didn't ask any more questions.

Before he gave the stories back to Alan, he put them into plastic document covers to protect them. They were very fragile after having been baked in the oven. The next day the two of them went to see Professor Columbine at UCLA. Alan was carrying his attaché case with the cooked manuscripts in them. They went in Wolf's car. Wolf was nervous; he was sure this expert would denounce the stories as forgeries. Columbine's office was in Rolfe, near the Research Library; they went down the hall and found his door open. He rose slightly to shake hands with Wolf. Alan he knew already.

Columbine was a large tapering man with a small head and small feet, and a Viking mustache too large for him. His blond hair was parted in the middle like a thatched roof. There was a chromium pipe on the desk in front of him, looking like an art object by a very modern artist.

Wolf, with European formality, said, "Professor . . . or do I call you Doctor?"

"Pete."

Wolf and Alan sat down. Wolf had to remove a heap of books from his chair and set them on the floor. Columbine said nothing for a moment and looked at them curiously. On the desk was a stack of Nils-Frederik's stories, with a shiny new paperclip on each one. They waited while he took out a pouch of tobacco from the desk, filled his pipe, and tamped it down. He didn't light the pipe now, though; he drew on it cold and set it back on the desk.

"If you'll pardon my saying so, I don't understand exactly why you came along with Alan, Mr. Wolf. Is it Mr. Wolf?"

"Wolf. If you can be Pete, why can't I be Wolf?"

"Wolf is just a friend," said Alan. "He has a bookstore on Melrose. He deals in rare books and manuscripts."

"Did these manuscripts come from Mr. Wolf?"

"No. I told you before that I couldn't tell you anything about where they came from. I got them from my father, Nils-Frederik Glas. He travels frequently in Europe."

Wolf could see Columbine putting these facts together in his mind to see what he could make of them. Not much, evidently.

"Well, Alan, we've made a deal. You said you had some materials to show me that were interesting, and I said I would keep it under my hat. Now I'm going to make you another offer. I'll agree to tell you what I think about them on one condition—that, if you publish them, you supply me with an advance copy of the book. I have an arrangement with *The New York Review of Books*. I'm on very good terms with their editors. One of them, I might say, is a very close friend of mine. They'll grab at the chance to be the first to publish a review of this book."

"We're a long way from publishing a book at this point."

"Yes, but you plan to, don't you? You told me when you left the stories off that there would be more to come. So that's my deal. I'll give you my opinion on these stories right now, and I won't say anything about it to anyone, provided you give me first crack at reviewing them when they're published."

Wolf said, "What will you say about them in your review?"

Columbine gave him a sharp look. He put the pipe back in his mouth, fitting it in carefully under his mustache. Then he got out a butane lighter and applied it to the pipe while he puffed and sucked. A large flame flared out from the bowl. He made Wolf nervous; he was afraid he was going to set fire to the office.

When the pipe was lighted he took it out and said, "How can I tell? I haven't seen them all yet. And I'm not going to tell you what I think about these five here until you agree to my deal. Look, you can't possibly lose. If the book comes out it's going to be reviewed anyhow. I want to be the first to review it. The review will be a sensational one."

"Sensational how?"

"Let's just say it will make eyes open. It's a deal, all right? You'll provide me with an advance copy of the book."

Alan and Wolf looked at each other. Alan said, "All right. Now tell us what you think about the stories."

Columbine puffed away at the pipe for some time, evidently having trouble keeping it going. Wolf always envied pipe-smokers for their ability to introduce significant pauses into their conversation through this simple expedient. Give yourself time to think. Suggest that your powerful brain is working on the problem. You could say more but right now you're sucking on your pipe.

He said, getting the pipe going, "What do I think of them. Well, where did you get these stories, Alan?"

"I already told you I couldn't tell you anything about that.

The person who is going to edit the book is my father, Nils-Frederik Glas. That's all I can tell you."

"I see." He took out his pipe, set it on the desk, and pondered. After a minute or so he picked up the story on top of the pile and balanced it on his knee. "They look like Hemingway stories," he said.

He waited to see if they had any response to this, but they didn't. After a while he went on.

"This first one, 'The Trouble with People,' is an awfully callous thing. His wife likes this Spanish kid, so he takes him to a gym and beats him up."

"That doesn't sound like Hemingway to you?"

"Oh yes. He was capable of it. It shows in his other writing. He's just never expressed his hostilities so openly."

"Maybe it's because they're early stories and he hadn't learned yet to be subtle."

"Are they early stories?"

"I couldn't say anything at all about that."

"They read like early stories to me. They read exactly like his earliest published stories, dating from 1922. There were some others from that period, but they were lost."

More pipe-puffing. Alan and Wolf remained silent.

"These are Nick Adams stories. There are other stories about Nick Adams, the Up in Michigan stories and some set in Italy. But this is the first time Nick Adams is put in Paris. And there's something else new. He's writing about Hadley. That is, Nick Adams and Helen are based on Hemingway and his wife. That's very interesting." He scratched his thatch. "Nick is tougher, less compassionate, more cynical here than either the Nick Adams of the Michigan stories or the stories set in Italy. But he still has feelings. He's sorry about beating up the Spanish kid."

"But he does beat him up."

"Yes, that scene is unique in all of Hemingway's work, I think. Hemingway himself liked boxing, and he liked to win, especially when he was boxing with people who weren't as good as he was. He beat the hell out of Ezra Pound once. But he doesn't attribute this kind of brutality to his autobiographical characters. In *The Sun Also Rises* it's Robert Cohn who hits people. He was based not on Hemingway himself but on a person that Hemingway didn't care much for, Harold Loeb."

Wolf said, "At least he's not anti-Semitic in these stories."

Columbine gave him another long look. Perhaps he took him for Jewish. It might be that after you lived with a Jewish wife for many years you started looking Jewish yourself, Wolf thought. Columbine said, "I don't think he was anti-Semitic. I think he just didn't like Harold Loeb."

"So you like the stories."

"I didn't say that. I said they look like Hemingway stories to me. Some of them are better than the others. The best one, to my mind, is 'A Friend from Detroit.' It has a Paris setting and a country setting. He handles the country setting well. The story has a strong ethical element. The dialogue is like that in 'The Killers' or 'A Clean, Well-Lighted Place.' Maybe it's better than the others because there are no women in it. As soon as Hemingway starts to write about women, he loses his temper and it's damaging to his style."

"You say they *look* like Hemingway stories. Are they?"

"I'd be a lot happier if I could see the originals, typed by Hemingway himself. But I don't suppose they exist."

This time the pregnant silence went on for thirty seconds, while Alan picked up the attaché case from the floor, set it on his lap, and opened it. He took out "A Friend from Detroit" and handed it to Columbine in its plastic document cover, hermetically sealed with tape. Columbine looked at him speculatively without speaking. He examined the plastic cover from the outside, then he opened it and slipped out the manuscript. A few scraps of fragile brown paper broke from the edges and fell onto his desk. He picked up one of these, examined it, and set it in his ashtray. Then he focused his attention on the manuscript.

"What have we got here anyhow?"

He removed the rusty paperclip, noticing the mark it had left on the old paper. After he took it off he handled the manuscript as though it were the relic of a saint. "You know, I've worked on Hemingway for twenty years, and I've never actually held an original manuscript in my hand. I've always worked from photocopies. That's all they'll let you see. The originals are too fragile to be handled."

He gently removed another crumbling brown scrap from the edge of a sheet and put it in the ashtray. With the manuscript on the desk in front of him he examined the sheets one by one. His pipe had gone out now and he set it on the desk. From time to time he made a comment.

"It's got all of Hemingway's usual misspellings in it. You wouldn't know about them, but I've examined the facsimile materials we have here in the UCLA library."

Alan said nothing. Columbine said, "I wonder where in the world you found this stuff, Alan. Do you realize it's valuable? After you publish, you could sell the manuscripts themselves for thousands of dollars. If you could prove you had a right to them."

He read some more and said, "You guys are doing something really risky, do you know that? If these manuscripts are authentic they belong to the Hemingway Estate. You have no more right to them than any burglar. You could do time in prison if anybody caught you with them."

He said, "Of course you swore me to secrecy and I'm not going to turn you in. Do you know very much about Hemingway's life?"

"Not very much."

"Well, I won't say more. There's a story about a suitcase but it's not important. Can you show me more of these original manuscripts?"

"No, I'm afraid not."

"Can I keep this one for a couple of days? I know someone in the Chemistry Department who does carbon 14 dating."

"These manuscripts are too valuable to let a chemist monkey around with them. Could I have that one back, please? Be careful putting it back in the cover. Also the typescripts of the

other five." Alan carefully took the scraps of brown paper from
the ashtray and put them into the attaché case too.

"I haven't seen a paperclip like that in years," said Columbine. "They're the kind they used in France years ago."

31 ▪

ALAN SENT copies of the manuscript to five publishers in New
York, and after he had given them a couple of weeks to look
at it he phoned and made appointments to talk to them while
he was in Manhattan. You couldn't exactly hold an auction
for a book by an unknown author like Nils-Frederik, but he
intended to play them off one against the other as best
he could. He was nervous about this stage in the business.
He was happy enough with the whole business up to now,
with the innocent prank of typing up the facsimile stories,
or with handling Columbine. Now he had to deal with the
law, with publishers he would try to persuade to pay money
for the stories, with the possibility of a suit or a criminal charge.
In the back of his mind was the fact that he wasn't a real New
York agent but a West Coast agent, and everybody knew West
Coast agents were a joke. Either they were film agents who
also handled books on the side, or they were hopeless amateurs.
After living with himself for all these years, Alan knew now
that he could never be a good agent because he was too irritable
and couldn't devote himself unselfishly to the concerns of other
people; he was an egotist like his father. Know thyself, said
some old Greek. It had taken him a long time.

He wasn't quite sure what he was supposed to be doing on
this trip to New York. Either he was selling some stories that
didn't belong to him, or he was selling some stories that pretended to be by a famous author and weren't. If someone got
their hands on those facsimile manuscripts and did a carbon
14 test on them, it would be clear they were forgeries. On the

other hand, Columbine thought the stories were real and he was no fool. Well, he was a fool, but he was also a Hemingway expert. Life was a gamble. Alan had always believed that the people who got ahead in the world were those who were willing to stake everything at a certain point; he had muffed it when he got out of college and decided not to be a poet, and this was his last chance to prove it. Behind him he felt the large, calm, and charismatic presence of Nils-Frederik, who would somehow make it come out all right.

When he started packing he couldn't decide what clothes to take with him. He was damned if he was going to conform to New York's idea of what a literary agent wore. At first he thought, defiantly, of going in his usual black leather and jeans of a trendy biker, but thought better of it and took a light summer suit. He could skip the necktie, or leave it at half mast to indicate his independence. Lily drove him to LAX and he flew to Kennedy tourist class. Back in first class or in handcuffs, he told himself. In his attaché case were the fake originals, typed on the old Corona. They were so parched that they would disintegrate to the touch, and he didn't intend to give anybody more than a glimpse of them. In Manhattan he checked in at the Elysée on East Fifty-fourth and got a good night's sleep, and the next morning he went to work.

The five publishers he had sent copies of the book to were Harper and Row, Simon and Schuster, Farrar Straus, Alliance Samuel Morgan, and Jasmine Tree. This last was a small firm that did high-quality books but wouldn't have much money for promotion, so it was last on his priority list. At each of the others he knew an editor who might be interested. Calvin Twining at Farrar Straus had published a book on long-distance yacht cruising that Alan had handled, and he hadn't lost money on it as far as Alan knew. As for the others, he knew them but he had never placed a book with them. His career as a literary agent had not been wildly successful. At least not yet.

Major editors had tight schedules, and his appointments were spread over a period of three days. He went first to see

Rawlins Casey at Harper's, then Bonner Blong at Simon and Schuster and Cal Twining at Farrar Straus. At each of these places he was looked at curiously and cautiously, as though he was a dangerous criminal but also possibly a bearer of rich treasure that might make the fortune of an editor who was lucky enough to snare it. This book was unlike anything that anybody had ever seen in the New York publishing world. It had no author, the origins of the material were unknown, and the right of Nils-Frederik to possess it and claim royalties from it was dubious. Rawlins Casey suggested that they show it to Hemingway's publisher, Scribners, to see whether they thought it was authentic. Alan didn't think an awful lot of that idea.

Bonner Blong, a man he had never met but had talked to several times on the phone, was an editor of blockbuster best-sellers and the memoirs of movie stars. He took Alan to lunch at a restaurant whose name was a byword to readers of gossip columns. He was very interested in the book and what Alan had to say about it. He smiled all the way through lunch. After they had split a bottle of excellent Vouvray, Alan showed him one of the fragile manuscripts in its plastic cover.

"You're carrying these around with you in your case? They should be in a bank vault."

"I know that. I brought them because I thought you'd be interested in looking at them."

"This is a multiple submission, right? You're showing it to other publishers too."

"That's right."

"Well, let them do it. It's very interesting. I wish you luck."

"What's the matter with it?"

"It's too risky. The Hemingway Estate could sue you, and sue me. They could bring criminal charges. It's as though you were trying to pass a lighted match to somebody, Alan. Nobody wants to take a chance, and you've got to get rid of it before it burns your own fingers."

He smiled and bought Alan a *pousse-café*, which he had heard about all his life but never actually seen. The various layers of brandy, liqueur, and cream were poured in so carefully that they remained separate and you could see them from the side of the glass, like dim geological strata in a cave.

Cal Twining, his friend at Farrar Straus, didn't take him to lunch but Alan had a very interesting conversation with him. They sat in his office on Union Square for over two hours while he went over the stories and commented on them. Cal was a Harvard graduate, good-looking and a careful dresser, highly intelligent, and he had read everything from the classics to the latest contemporary fiction. He was very good on the stories. He had read them carefully and he could cite incidents and the names of characters from them, or even quote short fragments from memory. He particularly liked the passage in "It's Marvelous, She Said" about the lime tea. *There was an odor to her that he couldn't identify, it was not a body odor or anything unpleasant, and it was not a perfume, it seemed to remind him of something exotic and yet ordinary, something he knew very well and identified with a small simple pleasure he had enjoyed many times, and then he realized it was the infusion of lime tea that she had brought with her from the other table.* This was one of the fragments he quoted from memory, halting only a couple of times. "Beautiful," he said.

"Are you going to make an offer?"

Cal looked at the manuscripts of the stories on the desk in front of him. "They would have to come out under your father's name. It would have to be clear that they're imitations. Parodies. Offered that way I think they'd have a considerable interest."

"How would you translate a considerable interest into an advance?"

"Ten thousand. Maybe fifteen."

"He wants far more than that."

He smiled and shrugged. "You want to offer them as authentic Hemingway stories? Take them to Scribners. They've published all his other work."

"Why do you think they're not authentic?"

"I didn't say I thought that. I just said that you could only publish them as imitations. Look, Alan. They're nicely done but it's not hard to do. And some of the details are not right. There's too much precision in the references to Paris streets and other locales. Much of it is straight autobiography. Hemingway did live in rue du Cardinal Lemoine, and there really was a gym in rue Pontoise. The restaurant mentioned several times, the Pré aux Clercs, is one where Ernest and Hadley often went to dinner in their early Paris days. This is not the way Hemingway wrote. He fictionalized things more. Somebody's been reading the biographies."

I could have brought the Suitcase with me, Alan thought. They could examine that all they wanted. It wasn't fake like the old manuscripts. Maybe he would have to show it to somebody sooner or later. But if it was the real Suitcase, that meant that it was stolen and so were the stories. His only chance lay in maintaining the ambiguity: the stories were real and they weren't.

Cal went on, "The dialogue is too clipped and finished, too smooth. If you go back and read the early Hemingway dialogue, you'll see that there's a crudeness about it for us today. Everybody has imitated this dialogue style, and when they imitate it it comes out sleeker and smoother. That's the way this stuff reads. There's a contest every year in which people are invited to submit parodies of Hemingway, and you'll see that there are hundreds of college students who can do it quite well."

He had stopped smiling now and he was telling Alan all this quite seriously, as though he were trying to help him with a problem he had.

"Do you want to publish them as imitations of Hemingway? With your father as author?"

"For fifteen thousand? No."

"It might be the best thing for you to do."

• • •

Alan had better luck at Alliance Samuel Morgan. The editor there was Deasy Parks, who specialized in literary fiction and had once published a Nobel laureate, although more recently he had lost him to another editor. Everyone called him Dizzy. He was considered a little crazy in the publishing world, an editor who acted out of impulse and sometimes made colossally bad decisions, but some of his books were very profitable for the firm, and he was the kind of editor who is given a free hand to do pretty much what he wants. Alliance Samuel Morgan was a British firm which had just launched into the American market a couple of years ago, so they hadn't built up much of a stable of authors. The British connection meant that any book they published would come out simultaneously in Britain.

Dizzy started right off by saying he liked the book. He would like to publish it. It would enhance the Alliance line and it would be a really distinguished book. It would also be highly controversial. He didn't seem to find this an objection. He left a pause of about ten seconds in the conversation, while he seemed to be thinking of something else, and then he said, "I imagine you're thinking about six figures."

"Seven," Alan laughed.

"We're a little short on that kind of money right now. We've just done the Disgraced Cabinet Secretary, I won't bother to mention his name, it's so boring, and that cost us a million and a half. We'll make it back, of course, but meanwhile it ties up our cash. We've just signed a contract with Nureyev—the Russian ballet dancer," he added, as though he were afraid somebody from out of town might not know this. "There are a number of other big books on the fall list. I don't know. I don't know. I do like literary books; I get so tired of this other trash." Here he drummed his pencil and cleared his throat, his only sign of bargaining. He had already practically agreed to take the book. "I imagine you're doing multiple submissions."

"That's right."

"Who else are you showing it to?"

"Harper's. Simon and Schuster. My friend Cal Twining at Farrar."

"H'mm. What would you say about seven hundred and fifty?"

"A cool million," Alan told him. He had to laugh again at this corny phrase.

"Well, we'd have to talk to the bank for that. I don't think there would be that many problems. Have you got any more good books out there on the Coast?"

"Not right now. I'll let you know if another one comes up."

Alliance was even more short of authors than Alan realized. Dizzy looked at the attaché case like a hungry man at a meal. "What have you got in the attaché?"

In the general air of euphoria and good will Alan got out a couple of the fakes and showed them to him, taking them carefully out of their plastic covers.

"My God, I've never had anything like this in my hands in my life. In fact I don't want to touch them. They look very fragile."

"They are."

He looked Alan straight in the face and said, "What are these things, Alan?"

"I can only tell you what I know. I'm acting as Nils-Frederik's agent. These manuscripts are in our possession. The texts are identical to the ones you have, except for a few misspellings."

"Can I keep them for a couple of days?"

"No, I'm sorry."

"Suppose I just take one sheet and have it photocopied. For example this first page of 'It's Wonderful, She Said.' Then we could use the facsimile on the jacket."

"All right."

"This is wonderful. I've never been so excited about a book in my life. This is going to whiz them off their perch."

He could scarcely contain himself. He seemed about to spring out of his chair. Alan could see why they called him Dizzy. They waited for the secretary to take the page off and photocopy it. When she came back Alan slipped it into the plastic cover and put it away in his attaché case. Dizzy watched him doing this with a fascinated curiosity.

"Are you busy for lunch?"

"It's four o'clock in the afternoon, Dizzy."

"My God, you're right. I didn't sleep well last night and I've been out of sync all day. Dinner then."

"Okay."

"We can talk about the title. What do you think about a title?"

"He wants to do it just as *Twenty Stories*, edited by Nils-Frederik Glas. That's the way it is on the manuscript."

"It's not very sexy. How about *Nick Adams in Paris?*"

"Some of the stories don't take place in Paris. One is in Italy and another up in Michigan."

"How about *Hemingway's Suitcase?*"

Neither of them had mentioned the Suitcase. Alan said cautiously, "Why would you call it that?"

"That's where these stories came from, didn't they?"

"I got them from my father, Nils-Frederik Glas. I'm serving as his agent. That's all I'm authorized to tell you."

A keen and thoughtful look came over him. "For the Hemingway Estate to claim copyright on the stories, they'd have to find the Suitcase. They'd have to produce it in court. Or the original manuscripts."

"That's right."

"And they can't do that."

Alan avoided discussion of the Suitcase. "I suppose they could subpoena the manuscripts. We could burn them before they got to that."

Dizzy narrowed his eyes and nodded. He was in on the plot now, along with the three of them. He said, "Leaving all that aside, how do you like the title *Hemingway's Suitcase?*"

"I like it," Alan told him. He wasn't sure he did. It seemed to make the whole venture far more perilous, but the barrel was headed over Niagara Falls now and he was past the place where he could stop. "It's a terrific title. I wonder why we didn't think of it before."

"I'll pick you up around seven, if that's all right. I think you said you're staying at the Elysée. We can have a couple of drinks at a place I know. For dinner, would Le Cirque be all right?"

"Fine," Alan said.

32 ■

THE NEXT MORNING Alan left the hotel early and decided to walk downtown, through Rockefeller Center and then down Fifth Avenue to the Village. It was a nice morning and after his success at selling the book to Dizzy Parks he felt omnipotent, as though he could leap over train viaducts, stop runaway horses, and rescue maidens from villains. Probably a half an hour with Maggie would knock this out of him. She had always viewed him with a certain irony, even though he was her son, or perhaps because he was her son.

On the Avenue somewhere south of Fourteenth Street he found himself keeping pace with a scattered group of people ahead of him. There was a pretty young woman in a tailored suit—Alan reflected how the female derriere is different according to the kind of clothes it is in, and is something quite special in a tailored suit—a pair of tourists in T-shirts, a black youth carrying a radio with two large speakers, and a man whose main characteristic was that he was wearing lime-green pants. After a while, lazily, only half thinking, Alan took in the safari jacket, then the lemon-colored loafers, and had a shock as though he had touched electricity. His first thought was that Klipspringer had come to New York to denounce the book as a forgery, or that he was going to follow him around New York and harass him as he had in Los Angeles. At the moment, however, Klipspringer gave no sign that he had noticed him. Perhaps the fact that the two of them were in town at the same time was only a coincidence. This wishful thought did little to alleviate the sense of dread Alan felt when he caught sight of him. He couldn't decide what to do—go on following Klipspringer, turn and flee back uptown on Fifth Avenue, or attempt to push him under a bus. The green pants ahead slowed as though their owner too were uncertain where he was going, or as if he wanted to survey this part of lower Fifth Avenue with more care. The girl in the tailored suit, the black youth, and the two tourists drew ahead and receded into the distance. Finding what he was looking for, Klipspringer turned off onto Eighth Street and went into a snack bar to use the phone.

From the other side of the street Alan saw his mouth moving, his hand gesticulating, his glasses flashing as he talked. He shook his head, then nodded. People on the phone often assume the mannerisms of the person they are talking to. From his gestures, from the expression on his face, from his solemn and deferential air, Alan had the absolute certainty that he was talking to Nils-Frederik. The conversation went on for a long time. When it was finally over Klipspringer opened the door of the snack bar, stuck his head out to look at the street, and emerged. Alan was in the doorway of a camera shop with several other people, out of the sunlight, and he was fairly sure that Klipspringer hadn't seen him. The thick glasses flashed only momentarily in his direction. Back on Fifth Avenue, Klipspringer crossed Waverly Place and entered Washington Square.

Alan was about to follow him, then changed his mind. He crossed the street to the snack bar and went in to the phone. He didn't know what he expected to find—some trace of Klipspringer's odor (cheap drugstore shave lotion and musky sweat) or a mark, a phone number which he might have written in pencil on the wall. Instead what he saw was a small black notebook on the shelf under the phone. It was an address book, arranged alphabetically. Tucked into a pocket in the front were three of Klipspringer's business cards. Alan put one in his pocket and replaced the others. Examining the book further, under the G's he found his own address and phone and Nils-Frederik's. Next to Nils-Frederik's name was the notation "760

LAX-JFK." By his own, "Lily" and "Kildy." He looked up Wolf in the W's. The word "Meira" was written next to the name, and the addresses of both Wolf's house and the bookstore. The bookstore address had two notes next to it, "Paper" and "Old typewriter." Back on the page of G's was something he hadn't noticed at first, the address of Maggie's gallery in a tiny hand at the bottom of the page.

Leafing through the book at random, he also found the addresses and phones of a lot of New York publishers, but not Alliance Samuel Morgan. He'd missed that one. He wasn't as omniscient as he seemed. Alan slipped the address book into his pocket and left the snack bar.

He was only a few minutes behind Klipspringer; he was pretty sure he could find him by walking on down the Avenue. Sure enough, he caught sight of him almost immediately; he was sitting on a bench in Washington Square reading an abandoned newspaper he had found there. Even from the rear his square head with the heavy glasses clamped on it was unmistakable.

As he approached the bench he saw that Klipspringer was reading the funnies. He walked up stealthily and sat down on the other end of the bench. Klipspringer didn't notice him. Alan sat there for some time, watching some children play with a new kind of Frisbee. Finally Klipspringer glanced up from his paper and saw him.

He showed no surprise. "Hello, Mr. Glas. What a coincidence that we should meet here in another city, far away from the one where we both live."

"Yes, isn't it."

"Are you here on business, Mr. Glas?"

"No, I'm here to visit my mother. She has a gallery in SoHo."

Lifting his chin in the way of short-sighted people, Klipspringer gazed at him through the whitish lenses of his glasses. "Eighty-eight Greene Street. The things there are very modern. I don't understand them."

"You have a great memory for addresses."

"Memory is a feat like any other. I never forget an address."

Alan slipped his hand into his coat pocket and brought out the address book. It was of a peculiar kind, tall and narrow, with a row of tiny rings binding it on one side. Klipspringer showed the only real emotion that Alan had ever seen on his face: surprise and alarm. He blanched and a muscle quivered in his face. In a reflex as human as breathing, he touched his own pocket and found it empty. With difficulty Alan restrained himself from grinning.

"Excuse me. I must have dropped that little memo book, Mr. Glas. Please give it back."

"You've got most of the major publishers in New York in it, but you missed one. I'll let you guess which it is."

"Mr. Glas, I'm surprised to find you engaging in this criminal behavior. A fine honest young man like you."

"Criminal behavior? I found it by the phone in a snack bar."

"Then give it back at once. I hope you weren't so unscrupulous as to look into it?"

"There are lots of addresses on the G page too. Why does it say '760 LAX-JFK' next to my father's name?"

"I wish you hadn't noticed that, Mr. Glas. It's really none of your business."

"But what does it mean?"

"That's the cost of a plane ticket from Los Angeles to New York."

"But why is it next to my father's name?"

"Because the trip to New York is in connection with your father's affairs, Mr. Glas. I would think that you could see that. Now please give the book back."

"How nice! Now you're saying please. I won't give it to you, but I'll put it somewhere where you can get it." Alan found himself exhilarated by his triumph over this shadowy adversary, who had turned all at once into a paper doll, while retaining the husk or shell of his clumsily menacing manners. "But first I have some questions for you. Who is your client, Klipspringer?"

"At Klipspringer and Fineman, we do not divulge clients."

"Would you say his name might begin with an N?"

"Certainly that, or some letter of the alphabet, Mr. Glas."

"Do you know who is the author of the manuscripts?"

"The manuscripts?" Klipspringer stared at him with a goggle-eyed vacuity, his best attempt at innocence.

"The famous manuscripts in question."

"Ah, the manuscripts. I would assume you and your father would be the best judges of that."

"Who told you that we have the manuscripts? Not that I admit we have any."

"I am not subject to being interrogated by you, Mr. Glas."

"Where exactly did you learn English? You never get it quite right."

"I learned English in school at an early age, Mr. Glas."

"What other languages do you know?"

"I can show you my résumé, Mr. Glas. Some other time."

"What would you do to get this address book back?" Alan brandished it playfully, attracting the attention of several passers-by. "Drink up eisel? Eat a crocodile?"

Klipspringer made a halfhearted attempt to snatch it from his hands. "Your language is very fanciful, Mr. Glas. I didn't finish the university. You have the advantage over me. You're an educated man."

Alan, filled with the spirit of fiendish play, got up from the bench abruptly, and Klipspringer followed him. "Before you leave, Mr. Glas, I'll trouble you for that little book." He raised his arm as though to seize Alan's arm, and at that moment they both saw a policeman. Klipspringer's hand dropped. Alan smiled winningly at the policeman and said, "We're from out of town." The policeman turned and stared, and Alan went off toward the nearest bus stop. Klipspringer followed at his elbow.

"My reading of you, Klipspringer, is that you lack imagination. You suffer severely from your failure to finish the university. I would suggest a course of reading in good fiction and poetry. Of course, you may point out that having an imagination leads to its own difficulties in life. Look at the predicament that my father and I are in now, for example. I wonder if you have pondered on just what it all means. Still, I'd rather be in our pickle, and have an imagination, than be looking at the pickle from the outside, like you, and have no imagination. Nils-Frederik and I may come out very well, or we may go down. But your kind, without imagination, are doomed to spend their lives looking dispassionately at the agonies and ecstasies of others, from the safe vantage point of the spectator. To my mind, that's not a life."

"I've often wondered why you call your father by his first name."

"It requires a little imagination to understand that. Sometimes I call him Father. It depends on how I'm feeling about him at the moment."

Klipspringer was panting a little. Alan was walking too fast for him. They arrived at the bus stop and Alan stopped.

"You could start with Keats," he said. "He has a vivid imagination. Shelley too is good on madness. Then you could work up through DeQuincey, E. T. A. Hoffmann, Swinburne, Gérard de Nerval, and Huysmans until you got to Kafka. I think you'd like Kafka. He has characters just like you, unreal and slightly comic."

"I don't have time for reading, Mr. Glas."

"You were reading a newspaper just now on the park bench. Believe me, Klipspringer, that's all dross and ephemera. It's of no importance. If you don't believe me, look at last week's newspaper."

"Mr. Glas, you possess an item of my property."

"I wonder too where you buy your clothes. Do you realize how conspicuous you are in that clown costume? Those green pants and yellow shoes?"

"Your personal remarks are uncalled for, Mr. Glas."

"Of course you were reading the funnies. That's a mark for you. It's the most imaginative part of the newspaper. It's surprising to me that a person like you, who reads the funnies, makes so many mistakes in life through lacking a perspective. Reading the funnies ought to make you able to laugh at yourself. That's the whole point of it. Although, I suppose you were reading the funnies only because they have something visual to offer, and are not intellectually demanding. I noticed you didn't pay for the newspaper. You found it on the bench, just as I found the address book in a phone booth."

"You're very observant, Mr. Glas."

"I was hoping you'd say that. You see, it isn't very difficult to do your kind of thing. It's just a matter of deciding to spend all your life on trivialities. You ought to return the newspaper to its rightful owner. You have no more right to it than I have to the address book."

"Sometimes I don't follow your turns of thought, Mr. Glas."

The bus appeared down the street and approached, looming larger, until it cast them into its shade. The door opened and three or four people who had been waiting on the sidewalk got in. The driver, with a typical New York expression of cynicism and patience on his face, looked at Alan and Klipspringer. Alan remained motionless. The driver shrugged and started the bus, and simultaneously the door began closing. At the last moment, Alan pitched the address book through the rapidly diminishing opening of the door. Klipspringer began running after the bus, hoping to catch it at its next stop.

33 ▪

THE GALLERY on Greene Street was simply called Maggie Glas. His mother had kept Nils-Frederik's name for the business because it was more striking than her own name, Hagstrom. It was only five minutes from Washington Square. The gallery had been enlarged since Alan saw it last. Maggie had taken over the store next door and knocked out part of the wall between them. She lived in an apartment over the gallery. It was a nice apartment, Alan remembered, cleverly decorated and full of pictures by good artists. She was busy with a customer and while he waited he looked around at things in the gallery. Everything was colorful and vivid against the gray of the soiled buildings outside. There was an electric smell in the air. New York was big and dirty and yet somehow younger, more vibrant, than his own lazy and somnolent L.A. He could live in this world, he thought. He would be a new Alan, a real literary agent with real writers for clients, and Lily and Kilda would be different too. He imagined their life in this huge, opulent, and callous city with its tree-lined avenues, its cynical cops, and its extravagant black hookers. It was true it wasn't safe to walk in Central Park, but there were other parts of town. They could make a down payment on a nice apartment with the money from the book. He looked out the window at the bright taxis and the girls passing, having already become, in his imagination, a New Yorker who was part of this garish and noisy scene.

Maggie joined him, in a white cotton sweater with a big band of red around it. She didn't ask him upstairs to the apartment, and she didn't offer him a cup of coffee. She was very businesslike and so was everything in the gallery. She had a partner now but she still didn't like to leave the place during business hours. The partner was a woman called Flore, tall and unsmiling, with a helmet of prematurely gray hair. She stared at them all the time they were talking. Alan wasn't sure Flore knew who he was; she was new since the last time he had come.

They walked around through the splashy pictures and Giacometti-like bronzes as they talked. Maggie, pushing the hair from her forehead, sized him up in small darting glances.

"What's Nils up to? Something, I know. Isn't that what you've come to tell me?"

"What do you mean?"

"People in Manhattan know about it. Not everybody, of course, but the 'in' bunch. Whenever I go to a party they say to me, 'Isn't he your ex?' Of course I still use his name."

"What do they say he's up to?"

"It's something about publishing. You probably won't tell me. I don't really care. They say it's something very odd, something that's going to be in all the papers and literary reviews."

"He's been working on a book. I've been here in New York trying to sell it."

"Is it any good?"

"His previous novel was published with a vanity press. He has a lot of talent."

"I know both those things. You're being devious, Alan, exactly like him. Oh, I know the manner so well."

"Do you know, he is very fond of you."

"I know that too. How is Charmian?"

"How do you know about her?"

"Oh, he tells me all about her, in the letters he writes from time to time. How good she is in bed and how she attends to his every want."

"He's joking."

"Nils never jokes. He laughs and says things, but he really means them."

"Do you answer his letters?"

"Yes. I don't want to be rude. I tell impersonal things, about my external life, how the gallery is going and so on."

"Do you feel anything for him now?"

"No. I feel that he's a person that I once knew, and a very interesting one. A person you can tell stories about at dinner parties. But I have no desire to see him anymore. It's as though he were someone I had once been in business with. The sexual part of our life together is something I never think about. It's as though it never happened."

Alan didn't know how to take this. He smiled awkwardly.

"And you are exactly his son. Except that you are lovable."

"I'm your son too."

"No," she said quite cheerfully, "you're your father's son, not mine. I'd like to agree that you're mine too, just to be conventional and not sound like some sort of unnatural mother, but I never really succeeded in thinking of you as mine. Of course, when a person is a tiny baby, he elicits all the usual maternal instincts, he coos and you coo back, and so forth. But that only lasted a certain time, until you began to talk, I think. As soon as you began to talk, you talked like him."

"I really don't know what you mean."

"You would never answer a direct question. If I asked you if you wanted some ice cream you would say you wanted your sweater off. That was a signal that you were hot and yes, you wanted some ice cream. But you wouldn't say so. If you had a rock in your shoe and I asked you why you were limping, you would say you had to go to the bathroom. Then, in the men's, you would take out the rock and never tell me about it."

"I can't believe you're talking about me."

"Oh, I did love you, even then. It's impossible not to love a child who refuses to tell you he has a rock in his shoe and locks himself in the bathroom to take it out."

Now Alan was beginning to recognize the portrait; it was exactly Kilda.

"When I say that I never thought of you as mine I don't mean that I didn't love you. The two things are quite separate. In fact," she said in another burst of candor, "I think I related to you in a quite special way, simply because you never seemed to me to be mine. More like a lover than a child. A young lover. What every middle-aged woman wants, even though they won't tell you so."

Alan glanced nervously at Flore, who was still following them with her glance wherever they moved, and was almost within earshot. He wondered if she and Maggie were lovers.

He told her, "Because the young lover will do whatever she wants. He has to obey her. He's more like a child, not a lover."

She smiled, almost laughed. "Yes. How unlike Nils. I do like you, you know, Alan."

"You say Nils-Frederik is like me. You must have liked him too."

"Oh, I did, in the beginning. I was in love with him or I wouldn't have married him. Then at a certain point—I think it must have been on our wedding night—I made the discovery of his terrific ego. He had somehow concealed this when he was courting me. It's an example of his deviousness. But very quickly I found out that what he needed me for was to convince him of his own grandness, to remind him at every turn that he was wise, talented, and manly. When we made love and he did some quite ordinary thing, what he wanted me to say was, How clever of you to know *that*."

Alan almost blushed. He glanced again at Flore.

"But I refused to play this game. And this was why we finally broke up. Not because I couldn't stand him anymore, but because he made it clear that if I wouldn't do these things he wanted, if I wouldn't admire him totally, flatter and play to his ego, without his giving anything at all in return, he didn't want me around. I had to compliment him on his clothes, his sexual prowess, his literary talent, his taste in the other women he flirted with; and all this without being crass or obvious, he wanted me to do it subtly, so it wouldn't be obvious on the surface that I was flattering him. He wanted me to be an actress. A talented actress. He wanted to write the script of his own life, in which I had a part. He didn't care whether I really meant it."

Alan wondered how much she knew about Charmian and the part she played in Nils-Frederik's life now. "We both love you. He still loves you and so do I."

"Did he tell you to tell me that?"

"No."

Flore called to her, "Mr. Abel Wenniger is on the phone, Maggie."

"I'll have to go. An important customer. Nils did tell you to tell me that. If he didn't tell you to, he wanted you to. No, Alan, go back to him. You're stuck with him. You're not going to sell him to me again, and I'm not going to try to win you away from him. If that's what you've come for—one of those two things."

"I came because I'm in town and I wanted to see you."

She embraced him while Flore watched. He felt the pressure of her breasts like the two hand-touches of an angel. Then she broke away to answer the phone.

34 ■

BACK IN Los Angeles, Nils-Frederik didn't seem surprised when Alan told him about the size of the advance. He acted as though it was about what he expected. He also gave Alan no credit for selling the book. His feeling seemed to be that the book was worth this sum of money and anybody could see it, so that what Alan had done was just to serve as a messenger to carry it to New York for him.

"What exactly is Alliance going to say about the book?"

They were in the study again. It was early evening; the sky was still light but the city below the hills was growing dark. Nils-Frederik hadn't turned on the lights in the room. Neither of them sat down. He stood across the room from Alan silhouetted against the lacework of lights from the city: a self-consciously theatrical stance.

"Your editor is Dizzy Parks. He's very enthusiastic about the book. I imagine he's going to say it's a great book. An important literary event. A sensitive commentary on the American experience in Europe. That kind of thing."

"Is he going to say it's a book by Hemingway?"

"Of course not."

"What will he say then?"

"He'll say just what we want him to say. That it's twenty stories edited by Nils-Frederik Glas. He's thought of a title for it, by the way. *Hemingway's Suitcase.*"

"I like that." He groped in his pockets and the blue flare of the butane lighter illuminated his face. He snapped the lighter off and drew at the cigarette. Slow ropes of smoke coiled around his head in the light from the window. In the middle of the shadow, at the level of his breastbone, the orange spot of the cigarette glowed dimly.

"*Hemingway's Suitcase*. Stories. Edited by Nils-Frederik Glas." This incantation seemed to soothe him, to give him pleasure. He repeated it again, with a draw on the cigarette before and after. "You say the editor thought of it?"

"That's right."

"What did you say his name was?"

"Dizzy Parks."

"He must know about the Suitcase. I mean, he must know that Hemingway's suitcase was stolen and the stories were lost."

"Of course."

"Did he say anything about that?"

"We hadn't discussed the Suitcase. Then when he suggested the title, he said, 'That's where the stories came from, didn't they?'"

Nils-Frederik smiled and was thoughtful. "You did a very nice job on this, Alan." It was the first compliment his father had paid him in years, probably the first one in his life. Alan was moved, and at the same time he felt foolish because he felt this way. He had struggled so desperately when he was a child to be accepted by him. Now he had done this thing for him, and Nils-Frederik was grateful for it. Alan basked in the warm glow of the remark.

"I am looking forward, Alan, to the publication of this book. It will be a consummation. A consummation as though I were finally going to have a woman I have desired for years. It is going to be very nice, Alan." He stood there smiling to himself, wrapped in smoke, for a while. Then he said, "Did you see Maggie while you were in New York?"

"Yes."

"What did you tell her about . . ."

"What?"

"The book."

"Nothing. She told me."

"She told you?"

Alan could tell from his voice that his surprise was feigned. It was clear that he had planted hints about what he was doing among New York writers and the literary crowd.

"She said she knew you were up to something, and it was something about publishing. I didn't tell her what it was."

"You could have. You could have told her just what you told the editor. That the book was coming out, that it wouldn't say who the author was, and that I was the editor."

"She'll find out soon enough."

"Dear old Maggie." He seemed infinitely pleased with what Alan had told him. Alan began to work out a theory that he was doing this whole thing just to impress Maggie.

35 ▪

THE PUBLICATION of the book was scheduled for the fall. This was a good deal quicker than the average publisher could move, but Dizzy was an energetic editor and good at getting things done fast. It was possible that he was afraid the Hemingway Estate or Scribners or somebody else would get wind of the thing and put a stop to it. He was always on the phone either to Alan or to Nils-Frederik, and he was full of enthusiasm about the book. He said, exactly as Alan had predicted, that it was going to be a major literary event, and that it was going to "whiz them off their perch." The question was what he would say about the authorship of the book when he published it. The key passage, when it came out on the advance jacket copy, was: "These twenty stories are unmistakably the work of a master craftsman of American fiction. There are but few hands that could have contrived them, perhaps only one." Whoever wrote the copy wrote really badly. It seemed to say that Hemingway, or Nils-Frederik, had only one hand. Still, neither Nils-Frederik nor Alan could have invented two sentences that hinted so shrewdly that Hemingway had written the stories without actually saying so and giving the Estate grounds to sue them.

"To be precise, there are only four hands that could have written the stories," said Nils-Frederik. "Two of Ernest Hemingway's, and two of mine." He put up the jacket copy on the bulletin board in his study and gazed at it with satisfaction, puffing a Sobranie Black Russian.

One evening that summer Lily and Alan went out to dinner with the Wolves. Out of an impish impulse Alan decided to take them to the Montagnola, the Italian place on North Vermont where he and Lily had gone to lunch with Nils-Frederik for his birthday. The food was not very good but the place had atmosphere. It might even be possible that they would see real Mafiosi, or at least people pretending to be Mafiosi, and that would be almost as good.

The dinner menu turned out to be better than the lunch. Everything was not smothered in red tomato sauce, and they had pasta and very decent saltimbocca and Turkey Breast Cardinal, this last a specialty of the house. The proprietor was Bolognese and it was his favorite dish, said the waiter. Alan would perhaps have to revise his opinion of Nils-Frederik's taste in restaurants. The Chianti bottles were not wrapped in straw, but otherwise everything about the meal was perfect.

They drank a great deal of Chianti, and when the bill came they piled their money with much confusion in the center of the table, disputed over who had eaten what and how much it had cost, and decided that everybody had drunk the same amount of wine. They pondered over the tip, trying to calculate fifteen percent of a complicated figure. The waiter unobtrusively set balloon glasses by their elbows and poured in each one a generous splash of Remy Martin.

"What's this?"

"Compliments of the house."

"I don't understand."

The waiter signaled the proprietor, who came over to the table. "Is everything all right?"

"Yes. Thanks for the cognac."

"It's nothing. Aren't you the son of Nils-Frederik Glas, the author?"

"How did you know that?"

"Oh, I remember when you came to lunch with him once. He comes here to dinner now and then with his wife Charmian. He often talks about you."

"He does?" Alan could hardly imagine his father talking about him, or about anything but himself. He remembered when he had pretended to cut his wrists in this very restaurant because he didn't like the birthday present Alan had given him. "Did he tell you about his book?"

"Oh yes. Everybody knows about the book Mr. Glas is writing. It's going to be a best-seller."

"Well, thank you again for the drinks."

"It's nothing. We're pleased to have Mr. Glas's son as our guest here."

When he had gone Wolf said, "Nils seems to have an excellent press agent."

"He does it himself."

"Of course. That's what I mean."

Lily said, "Alan, is Nils-Frederik's book going to be any good?"

"It's very good, Lily. The question is, is he going to get away with it."

"Get away with it? How can you get away with or not get away with a book? You just publish it and it's a success or not."

"Drink up, everybody. This is the very best stuff."

"Don't drink all that cognac, Alan," Lily told him. "You're driving. Let Wolf drink it."

• • •

When they got home, as usual Alan had to take Mrs. Quon back to her place across town. This time Kilda insisted on going along; she was still awake and hadn't yet put on her pajamas. Neither Lily nor Alan could get Kilda to go to bed at a reasonable hour. Sometimes she would go to sleep on the sofa watching TV, or on the floor in the corner of the hall, and they would pick her up and carry her off sound asleep, with one leg dangling like her dead cat, to put her away in her bed. At other times she would read books half the night in her room with the light on. She didn't seem to suffer from lack of sleep and she was always bright as a badger in the daytime, so after a while they stopped worrying about it. To-night she wanted to ride in the car to take Mrs. Quon home, in fact she sprang into the car almost before Lily and Alan had got out of it.

Mrs. Quon, adjusting to these new arrangements, got into the back with her sewing, her English book, and her police whistle, and Kilda sat perched on the edge of the front seat, looking out through the windshield with a mole-like intensity. She never had a chance to ride in the car at night, and everything looked different. She said nothing at all on the drive across town. It was Mrs. Quon who did all the talking from the back seat, in a voice so small that Alan could hardly follow it. Although her English was getting better, she still recited everything in her singsong Mandarin intonation.

She said, "Kilda show me her story. She read it to me. A story about her father. You, Mr. Glas. Not about. She say it *by* you, a story."

"What do you mean?"

"She say she read me a story you write. You not write it, but she say you write it. She write the story and say you write it."

"You mean she's writing a story and attributing it to me. She's writing it, but pretending it's written by me."

"Just pretend," agreed Mrs. Quon. "In this story, you are great hero. You tell about your heroism and all things you do. You chase criminals and make prisoner of them, and give them to police."

"It's a detective story."

"Detective, right. After giving criminals to police, you go to McConnells."

"McConnells?"

"To eat fast."

"Ah, McDonald's."

"You order hamburger with all things on it. You enjoy hamburger with money you get for making prisoners."

"The police paid me for capturing the crooks."

"Crooks." She made a mental note of this word. "And you have hero badge."

The hamburger with all things on it was a wonderful idea. It sounded like a Vietnamese myth of the origin of the world. In the beginning, God created an enormous hamburger with all things on it: cities, rivers, lands, mountain ranges, and all the beasts of the earth. The hamburger was on a plate, and the plate was resting on four saltshakers. And that is the reason why the sea is salty.

"Do you like hamburgers, Mrs. Quon?"

"I like American cooking. Also Vietnam cooking. Also China cooking. Come to dinner."

He didn't think she meant tonight. It was probably a phrase from her English book. "Not tonight, Mrs. Quon."

"Some other time," she agreed. Her English was improving for sure. As usual he gave her a larger tip than necessary when he left her off at her house, remembering her boy who died of fever, and her Sears housedress that was always the same.

As they crossed Pico and Alvarado, Kilda, still perched on the edge of the seat staring with solemn intensity through the windshield, said, "We're not far from Grandpa's house. Couldn't we go see him?"

He was amazed at how this nine-year-old infant had mastered the geography of this complicated city. Perhaps she prowled around in it more than they knew.

"Not now. It's eleven o'clock at night."

"He said I could come to see him anytime I wanted."

"He didn't mean in the middle of the night." After a thought he said, "Kilda, do you remember when you went to see Grandpa on the bus and I came and got you, and you were having lemonade and cookies in the garden?"

"Yes."

"Have you been to see him after that?"

"See who?"

"Grandpa, Honey. Pay attention. Listen to what I'm asking you."

"Have I been to see him?"

"Have you been to see him."

She seemed to be staring with great interest at a police car that was going along ahead of them in their direction a half a block ahead. The police car didn't have its emergency lights on and there was nothing at all interesting about it. After a moment she said, "How could I go to see him? You said I couldn't ride on the bus."

This was not really an answer. It was a Nils-Frederik sort of answer. Maybe she borrowed the Beast and went there late at night when he and Lily were asleep. He set his hand on her skinny leg and gave it a squeeze, while she gazed out imperturbably through the windshield. It didn't matter if she rode motorcycles, or sprouted breasts, or went out with pimply boys; he knew now that no harm could come to this charmed child in this city. She already knew every corner of it, every dangerous park, every playground the haunt of pushers, and could pass through it unscathed. He, the adult male, the pseudo-macho biker, might be in peril from the sinister phantoms and Klipspringers of the world, but she was not.

"You can't," he told her. "Not until you're older."

Later on the ride home he asked her about the story she was writing, trying to find out whether it was something she was doing in school or whether she was writing it on her own at home, but he couldn't get anything out of her on the subject.

36 ■

WOLF FOUND that he was restless and waiting for Charmian to come in with the coffee and *papillons*. It was a Sunday afternoon in the fall, about a year after Nils-Frederik had come back from Europe. In the study Nils-Frederik was standing in front of the window smoking, his face obscure and a halo of smoke coiling about his head: his most characteristic pose. Alan and Wolf were sitting in chairs at the table. It was a stuffy day in October with a band of saffron smog lying over the city.

Nils-Frederik was talking about Maggie and how she had studied art at the university, and he had always tried to get her to paint but she would never do it. "I suspect it was because she knew she had no talent."

"It was because she didn't want to compete with you. She didn't want to do anything that you could use to compare her with yourself." Alan seemed to be in a cross mood, because of the weather or because he was annoyed with Nils-Frederik about something.

"When she lived here, she kept a notebook of pencil sketches, but she would never show it to me. She kept it in her dresser drawer under her underwear and she didn't know I knew about it."

"You went through her underwear?"

He smiled. "She took no interest in my writing. She never asked to see it. Maybe she looked at it when I was gone from the house. I didn't keep it with my underwear, though."

"Why didn't she want to look at it?"

"Because it was good and she knew it. She couldn't take that. She couldn't accept the idea that I was a good writer and she was second-rate as an artist."

"You think you're a terrific writer, don't you?"

"I'm the champ." He laughed. With the cigarette in his lips, he postured like a prizefighter holding his gloves over his head. He did a little boxer's dance around the study, with surprising agility for a man of his weight. He punched Alan playfully on the shoulder and took a swipe at Wolf, who ducked. "Isn't that right? I'm the most and I'm going to whiz them off their perch. That's what Dizzy says. My editor. My big-time editor in New York."

"Sure. You wrote those terrific Hemingway stories."

He took out the cigarette and examined Alan. "If you say so."

"I didn't say so. Do you say so?"

"What are you getting at, Alan?"

"I want an answer. Did you write them or not?"

"They're what you see. They're stories. Alliance is going to publish them."

Wolf pricked up his ears; he began paying attention. He hadn't expected this conversation to take place. He didn't know why Alan was pressing the question.

"That's not enough, Father. You can tell that to Alliance, and to the readers of the book. But it's not enough for us."

Nils-Frederik's manner changed. He became wily, cautious, and thoughtful, smiling only a little now. "We've got the advance for the book. Ten percent for you and ten for Wolf-gang, as agreed. That's a hundred thousand for each of you. That must mean the stories are pretty good, doesn't it?"

"You didn't write them, Father."

"What's the matter with you, Alan? You've got some bug in your ear. Tell me what's bothering you and we'll talk about it."

"We've got to give the advance back. It's theft."

Nils-Frederik turned to Wolf and made a simulacrum of his tolerant smile. What can you do, the smile said, if you have such a crazy son? "Give back the money? What are you talking about, Alan?"

Instead of answering Alan got up and left the study. They heard his steps going down the stairs, then there was silence.

Nils-Frederik started to get another cigarette, then changed his mind. "He's upset about something. I don't know what it

is. Probably it was seeing Maggie in New York. She probably
told him all kinds of dirty stuff about me. I knew she would,
but I didn't think he would believe it."

Wolf didn't know what to say. The visit to New York had
been three months ago. Nils-Frederik seemed shaky and uncertain; his joviality had taken on an unconvincing quality.

"Maybe he really wants to know."

"What?"

"Who wrote the stories."

"You too, eh? I thought you were my friend, Wolfgang."

"I am."

"I thought you believed in me."

"You don't give us much to believe in. You want us to take
it all on faith, the way you do Alliance and the people who
are going to read the book."

"Who am I to say what the stories are?" He smiled and
spread his arms in a gesture of disavowal, of helplessness, of
innocence. "It depends on the critics. Some of them will take
them as Hemingway stories. Some of them will decide they
are fakes."

"Which is it, Nils?"

"The better critics, the ones on the literary magazines, will
decide they are fakes. But they won't be able to touch us,
because we never said they were real. In the end, everybody
will know that I wrote them."

"I knew that from the beginning."

Nils-Frederik smiled at him. He seemed to have regained
his confidence. "You *are* my friend, Wolfgang."

They heard Alan coming back upstairs, and the sound of
something bumping against the wall. Nils-Frederik stopped
smiling and seemed to become very alert. Alan entered the
room carrying a bulky object in his hand. Wolf was thunderstruck at the sight. He knew instantly what it was, even though
he had believed to this moment that it did not exist. It was a
green leather suitcase with tarnished brass reinforcements on
the corners and a green leather handle.

"Alan, you have been monkeying in my closet. I forbid that."

His anger was unconvincing. His face was milky and damp and Wolf was afraid he was going to be sick. He still wore his smile, as though he had forgotten to remove it, or as though it were pasted in place.

"This is the Suitcase. And inside are the stories that were stolen in Paris. Am I right?"

Nils-Frederik said nothing.

"You want people to believe that you wrote them, but you didn't. The original manuscripts are right here inside the Suitcase. Give me the key. I know you've got it. It's right there in your pocket along with your other keys."

"Put that away in the closet where you found it, Alan."

"Give me the key."

Nils-Frederik stared back at him. Alan was grim and angry, Nils-Frederik perspiring faintly. They confronted each other in silence, then Alan moved slowly across the room to him. Nils-Frederik was still standing against the window. Alan came up to him and stretched out a hand to his clothing. He turned away, and Alan seized him and held him. At that moment Charmian pushed through the door and came in with the coffee and pastries. When she saw what was happening she set the tray on the table and sat down, as though she were a disinterested spectator.

"The key. You've got it in your jacket pocket."

Alan, his arm around his father, gripping him in a grotesque kind of embrace, tried to reach into the pocket of the jacket with his other hand. But Nils-Frederik had two hands to oppose this single-handed assault. The two of them rotated like a strange pair of dancers, Alan's hand groping for the pocket of the jacket and Nils-Frederik pushing it away. Neither of them spoke a word. Their feet shuffled and scraped; it was the only sound in the room. Nils-Frederik lost his footing; they fell heavily to the floor and went on grappling there, slowly, painfully, tediously, with occasional sudden quick flaps of a hand or twists of a body. Nils-Frederik grunted; Alan was silent and determined. A muscle cracked and Nils-Frederik groaned. Wolf detected a musklike animal odor coming from one or the other of them, or both. The two combatants rolled on the floor; for a moment Nils-Frederik was on top, struggling to extricate himself and stand up, then Alan rolled him under again and went on straining and groping for the pocket. It seemed to Wolf that there was no hatred in the motions of the painfully struggling figures; he sensed an aura of anguished love, of destructive love, radiating from the two men and filling the room, penetrating and flooding his own emotions until his nerves stood on end. There flashed through his mind the thought of Jacob wrestling with the Angel: *I will not let thee go, except thou bless me*. At that moment he caught a glimpse of Nils-Frederik's face on the floor staring at him intensely. The face was pasty and half of it had sagged; the eye on that side was half shut. As Wolf watched, the mouth slowly opened as though moved by some inner mechanism.

"Alan!"

Alan released Nils-Frederik and got up slowly. He noticed the face for the first time.

"He's faking."

"You can't fake going green!"

Wolf went to him and looked at him. Nils-Frederik was still conscious, but he couldn't move except for small distortions of his face. Alan stood there numbly, as though bewitched.

Wolf went to the phone on the desk and dialed for the paramedics. They took the information with surprising efficiency. An unexcited voice said, "The equipment is on the way, sir."

He went back to look at Nils-Frederik. Charmian was taking care of him like an efficient nurse. She showed no signs of emotion. She took a book from the bookcase, set it on the floor, and lowered Nils-Frederik's head carefully onto it. The single open eye watched her. Taking a handkerchief from the pocket of her print dress, she wiped the foam from the corner of his mouth. Then she put the handkerchief away and sat on the floor watching him, with an expression somewhere between sympathy and curiosity.

Wolf looked around for Alan and found he had disappeared. He felt unreal and wondered if he were going to be sick himself. As in a slow-moving nightmare he saw Nana appear in the open door of the study, moving silently with her hands touching the door frame. She came to the table and sat down, as though she too, like Charmian, wanted to watch the show.

She said, "Now that you are no more I am going back to Sweden, Nils. With my money. I have a boat there and a young man to be the skipper of it."

Nils-Frederik, with his head on the book, stared at her out of his single workable eye. It had the look of an egg, a bird's egg, immovable and without life, yet perfectly aware of what it saw.

"The skipper of my boat is named Frank. I can go in the boat to the Skerries and stay there in the house of my rich friends. You don't know about them, Nils, I never told you about them. All these things here in this house will be sold. We have no need for them. All these machines, Nils, these machines for writing. If you want to write, you can use a pen and paper. My boat has an engine but it is a very simple one. Frank knows how to run it. It doesn't make very much noise, only a hum like a sewing machine. It can run all day long while we sail through the islands, black with white towns. If the weather is rough we stay snug in the cabin. We have a little stove and we can make coffee in the boat. And we will sell all these art things that you have bought too. This house is far too large, even though you have put me in a tiny room at the end of it. My friends in the Skerries have a large house overlooking the sound, Nils. It's called Sundhamn. There are many rooms, it's even larger than this house, Nils, and there are servants to take care of it. The floors are polished every day. In my room the sun comes through the window, and the servants bring me tea. I have everything I want there. They bring me my meals in my room, or I can go down to the dining room. There I eat dinner all alone, with two candles in silver candlesticks. Frank eats with the servants. Outside, if it is summer the sun can be shining through the window, or if it is winter a storm may be raging and the rain beats against the panes. It doesn't matter, because I am safe in the house, and they will take care of me there and give me everything I want. My room has a window, Nils. There is no window in this house where you have put me. And it is by the sea. By the sound. At night when I go to sleep I can hear the sea."

Charmian said, "Be quiet, Nana."

Wolf realized that he had been hearing the siren of the approaching paramedic van for some time. It ended now like a dying violin, and a pair of efficient young men in blue uniforms came into the room carrying an oxygen tank and other things.

One of them bent over to look at Nils-Frederik. The other said, "What's his name?"

Wolf just shook his head. He felt himself unable to speak. Nils-Frederik lay on the floor and the paramedics worked on him like efficient ants dealing with some larger insect. One of them held an oxygen mask over his face, and the other had opened his shirt and was massaging his chest. Nils-Frederik's face was not visible anymore under the mask but his hand was the color of milk laced with blood. He was motionless; his head moved to one side and the other as the paramedic adjusted the mask. The mask was connected to a green bottle that hissed faintly in the silence. You could not hear Nils-Frederik breathing.

Still feeling numb, Wolf went out to see where Alan had gone. He found him sitting on the stairs a few steps down from the landing, with his face cradled in his hands. Wolf made his way around him and found that his hands were wet with tears. He shook softly and silently. Wolf waited for a few moments until Alan noticed he was there. He could see him trying to control himself so he could speak. With a shaking voice he said, "I can't stay in there. I can't look at him."

"Okay, okay. You don't have to."

Alan sobbed, still holding his hands over his face as though he were trying to hold in his grief so that Wolf wouldn't notice it. Wolf tried to set a hand on his shoulder but he shook it off. Through the lattice of fingers over his face he shouted, "*Save him! God! God! God! God!*"

37 ▪

THE NEXT SUNDAY, a week after Nils-Frederik's attack, Alan went to see him at the hospital. The article by Columbine in *The New York Review of Books* was out now and he brought it along to show him. He was out of the cardiac unit and in his own room, a private room of course; nothing but the best. The room had a nice view out over the city, almost the same view as his study, although it was closer to downtown. It was full of flowers, candy, and gifts, even a gift-wrapped bottle of wine, which Alan didn't think was allowed in hospitals. He had the bed cranked up and he was lying in it watching a game show. Alan shut the television off and greeted him. It was the first time he had come to see him. There were various reasons for this: for the first few days Nils-Frederik was too sick to have visitors, then when Alan called he was told he was upstairs having tests and would be away from his room all afternoon. The truth was that Alan had put off going to see him because he didn't know how to behave to him. He was still in the state of mind he had been in on that Sunday afternoon a week ago, angry at him and at the same time terrified that he would die. Both of these emotions had grown weaker, like a storm dying down, but they were both still there.

Nils-Frederik was wearing a pair of linen designer pajamas with a monogram on the pocket. Alan couldn't remember that he had ever before seen him in pajamas. He was pale, but his complexion was always pale. At least it had lost that horrible sour-milk color that it had after his attack. The left side of his face was slack and the eyelid on that side drooped, but it opened enough so that he could see out of it. The left side of his mouth had fallen along with the rest of his face. He could only make disconnected sounds, mostly consonants, and Alan had to guess at what he was saying.

"Ot wi?"

"This? It's Columbine's article in *The New York Review of Books.*"

He showed it to him. He was standing on the left side of the bed, and Nils-Frederik didn't take it from him because he couldn't move his left arm or anything on that side of his body. The title of the article was "Wild Surmise: A New Hemingway Text." Nils-Frederik smiled at that, as well as he could with one side of his mouth. The illustration was one of those clever cartoons they used in the *NYRB* instead of photographs: caricatural figures with huge heads. In this cartoon, a bearded Hemingway was sitting at a table writing, and a crafty and shadowy Nils-Frederik, standing behind him, was copying down everything he wrote. The caricature of Nils-Frederik was done from the photo on the jacket of his novel published by Salamander Press and it showed him younger than he was now.

"I imagine you're curious to know what he said."

He read him the whole article. It took him fifteen or twenty minutes. Columbine went carefully through the stories and showed that their characteristics were typical of all Hemingway's work. He said that some of the stories were immature and not up to Hemingway's later writing, and also that there were some things that didn't appear in the later stories, for example the overt hostility to women. On the question of whether the stories were authentic he was quite precise. "The original manuscripts of these stories exist: that is known. But it is not on this documentary evidence that we can be certain that this is a new and extremely important publication by America's greatest writer. Instead it is on the quality of the writing itself: the stunning brilliance of style, the careful control, the emotion that is all the more poignant for its expression in Nick's terse and ironic language, the flashes of detail that convey an eidetic impression of the Paris of the twenties. In spite of his many imitators, the essential Hemingway is in-imitable."

Nils-Frederik looked at Alan out of his two unmatched eyes, one of them with the lid drooping. His mouth worked, he said "foo" and struggled to make some R's and W's, then he gave up and smiled lopsidedly. He seemed satisfied, but for what Alan couldn't tell: for having Hemingway's stories taken as his own, or for having his own stories taken for Hemingway's. In any case, he seemed to be saying "Fooled them."

To celebrate, Alan proposed opening the bottle of wine that somebody had given him. He rang for the nurse and asked for a corkscrew and a couple of glasses. She said that patients couldn't have wine and that wine was not permitted in the room, but he pointed out that it was already in the room. She went away and got the corkscrew and glasses. Alan filled the glasses and held one up to Nils-Frederik; he only touched it to his lips. Alan drank his and set the glass down on the bedside table.

"Ww Stcs?"

"I've got it in my apartment. I managed to open it with a nutpick and some other tools. There's nothing inside it but some old gray paper done up in bundles. No manuscripts. If there ever were manuscripts, you've done something with them. If there never were any manuscripts in it, you might have put in the blank paper to make it heavy so that people would think there was something in it. It's hard to tell some-times what you're up to."

"Mmm."

"The Suitcase itself proves nothing. It's an American suit-case and it could have been bought anywhere. It could have been bought at Bullocks in L.A. and stored for years in some-body's attic. You could have bought it at a garage sale."

"Cst stkrs."

"Yes, there are customs stickers on it, so somebody took it out of the country, but it could have been the person who bought it from Bullocks."

"Sts pt gd."

"Yes, they're not bad. But if people take them for Hemingway stories it's because you spread so many rumors about them in advance. You let Lucius Plum look at the stuff knowing that he would talk about it all over town. That hint in Dewitt Thomas's column. The rest is *nada y pues nada*. Do you know how Thomas got on to this thing in the first place? Homer Hobart, the *Times* art critic, told him, and he got it from Lucius Plum."

"Prk."

"Yes, it was just a prank. Thomas called me and wanted to know what the hell was going on. He knew I was your agent, and he thought he could get a straighter story out of me than he could from you. He said Klipspringer had been in to see him with one of the stories on some file cards. I don't understand where he got them."

"Ch."

"Charmian gave them to him? Well, it's very possible."

"Pty."

"At the party. You hired Klipspringer, didn't you? His Client and his Subject were the same person. You paid his airfare to New York, so he could tail around after me and make me nervous, and drop hints at publishing offices that what I had to show them was dangerous and valuable."

"Wrkd."

"Yes, it worked. Everyone began to get paranoid, thinking that he was a sleuth hired by the Estate. But the Alliance lawyers got into contact with the lawyers for the Estate, and they are not going to sue or bring criminal charges. They think the stories are fake. They think you wrote them."

Half of Nils-Frederik's mouth smiled.

"You planned the party, you hired Klipspringer, you told Lucius Plum about the thing. You got the Suitcase from somewhere."

"Frm Bg."

"I'll bet. A remote farmhouse in the Scheldt Valley in Belgium. You made it all happen. You control everything. You're God and we're all your people, to move around and play with as you want. There's just one thing you can't control, and that's your own mortality. It almost got you this time."

"Mm hr."

"Yes, you're still here, but not all of you. You won't be able to pull these tricks anymore. You won't be able to be so clever."

"Yr mtl tu."

"Yes, I'm mortal too; we all are. We all know that. The only one who didn't know it was you. You thought the rules weren't made for you. You thought the universe was your private possession and you could do with it what you wanted. If other people were unhappy, that was their problem. You were no more responsible than God is for an earthquake that kills people."

"Nt Gd."

"No, you're not, but you would like to be. All my life I've alternated between loving you and getting angry at you. Sometimes, I think, it's both at once. I don't know which it is now, Father. I suppose I ought to sympathize with you because you've had a stroke and are lying here helpless. But I can't help feeling that you've maneuvered me into feeling that emotion too. I know that's irrational."

Nils-Frederik muttered something with L's and T's in it.

"What did you say?"

"Lv you t."

"The hell you say. Well, it's taken you a long time to get it out. All during my childhood I waited for you to say that. Last fall, when you hugged me in the street in front of your house, it made me feel really good. But that was just because you wanted to get me to do something for you. You didn't say anything about loving me at the time."

"Ll. Kld."

"They're fine. Are you saying that you love them too? I can hardly believe that. Well, maybe you do love them in your way. It's a hell of a funny way. It's a way you've invented. Next," he said, "you're going to tell me you love Charmian."

Nils-Frederik's mouth corner went up, and he actually twinkled. He seemed to be enjoying the conversation. "Joy fkng her."

Alan smiled too. "You're incorrigible, Father. I think I'll leave you and you can go back to your TV."

"Jnk."

"Yes, it's junk. All TV is. You need something to read. In a few days you'll get a nice book in the mail. An advance copy of *Hemingway's Suitcase*, Twenty Stories, edited by Nils-Frederik Glas."

"Nc bk," he repeated.

"Goodbye, Father."

"Cm gn."

"They say you'll be out of here in another week. I'll leave the wine. You can give it to the nurse."

"Ciao."

It was the first correct word he had articulated. Alan had never been sure how much Italian he knew. Quite a bit, from all evidence.

In the corridor outside the room he met Charmian. She was coming to visit Nils-Frederik and she had brought some things for him: a cassette recorder with some books-on-tape, after-shave lotion, and a fresh pair of pajamas. They stopped in the corridor and chatted, and Alan showed her Columbine's article in the *NYRB*. She looked at it, but he wasn't sure she understood anything about Hemingway, Columbine's article, and the whole business of the book that Nils-Frederik had written or not written.

"His room is already full of things. Flowers, gifts, a bottle of wine. There's still some of the wine left. You should finish it off."

"I sent all those things to him."

"You? All of them?"

"He doesn't have any friends. You see, Nils doesn't always ask you to do the things he wants done. You have to guess what he wants and then do it without his having to ask. That's the only way to get along with him, otherwise he gets angry. I've learned to guess what he wants, and I give it to him without his asking."

"Let me get this straight. Do you mean that you have to send these flowers and other things to his room and pretend they're from friends he doesn't have? And that he knows that you're pretending, and that he doesn't have any friends?"

"God knows what he knows."

They left it at that. "How's Nana?"

"She's fine. We've moved her into a better room, one with a window. It used to be full of his books. We've put them in storage."

"Who's we?"

"Lucius Plum and I. She and Lucius are getting married, you know."

"They are?" Alan stared at her. He was dumbfounded at this.

"Yes. She's been seeing a lot of him, you know. He comes almost every day. He'll be a fine man for her, I think. He's kind and considerate. He doesn't have any money, but she has plenty of her own. She's going to have an operation for her eyes. It's just some cataracts. They can easily be taken off. It could have been done years ago."

"Why wasn't it?"

She lifted her shoulders. This question was hardly worth answering.

38 ▪

ON THE publication day of *Hemingway's Suitcase*, Alan and Lily had the Wolves over for a barbecue in their tiny patio. At the rear of the apartment building there were two small bricked squares the size of carpets, with redwood fences around them. The one on the right was their patio, and the one on the left was for the people who occupied the other ground-floor apartment. The people upstairs didn't have patios and had to make do with their rear balconies, which were festooned with ferns, vines in pots, and hanging planters. In their own patio was an oleander in a whiskey barrel, and a Biblical fig tree in a pot. Here they installed the new barbecue which they had bought at a discount store.

Nils-Frederik was at home in his wheelchair. Charmian would be fixing dinner for him, and he would eat it with her and Nana sitting at the wooden table in the kitchen. Alan and Wolf ought to have been with him on the publication day of the book, but it was a weekday and they only went there on Sundays. They would go to see him next Sunday, perhaps.

After they had finished their chicken and corn on the cob, Alan and Wolf sat looking at the reviews of the book and passing them back and forth to each other. For the most part, the critics took the stories as authentic Hemingway stories, although some of them hedged a little on this point.

"Here's a funny one. This guy in Seattle says that Hemingway couldn't have written a story called 'Down from Schruns' in 1922 because he and Hadley didn't go to Schruns until 1925."

Alan said, "Well, maybe he heard about the place and imagined going there. Here's the third or fourth one that says the stories are 'a sensitive comment on the American experience in Europe.' Lazy bastards. They got that from the Alliance promotion copy."

"If it's true, what does it matter where they got it?"

"Here's a critic in *The Washington Post* who says that 'The Trouble with People' is a little weak."

"Oh, I like it."

"He doesn't say it's not a Hemingway story. He just says it's a little weak. He compares it to some of the other weak ones in *The Complete Short Stories*. He also says that Hemingway is a woman-hater."

"He says Hemingway?"

"He says 'the writer of these stories.'"

"Then why did you say Hemingway?"

"I don't know," said Alan.

Most of the reviews were favorable, except those by critics who didn't like Hemingway and didn't see any point in publishing second-rate stuff from his early period that was better off lost. Practically all of them told the story about the suitcase full of manuscripts that had been stolen in Paris and never recovered.

The only one to make the suggestion that Nils-Frederik himself might have written the stories was the reviewer for *The New York Times*, a very astute critic named Carleton West. He came down hard on the curious circumstances of their publication, with Nils-Frederik as editor and no author indicated. If they are Hemingway stories, he argued, why not say so? Because the copyright belongs to the Hemingway Estate and they would sue? No one in his right mind would bring out a book under those circumstances. As for the rumors that the original manuscripts existed and could be produced, West said that he'd like to see them. Alan read aloud, "*Whoever wrote these stories is one hell of a writer. I don't think it was Hemingway, but that doesn't really matter. Go ahead and read them anyhow; it will be a unique literary experience. If you like, pretend that they're Hemingway's as you read them. When we finally find out who did write them—and I think I know who it was—he is going to occupy a unique place in the history of American letters.*"

"Nils will like that."

"He told me in the hospital that he'd fooled them. I don't know what he meant by that."

"There are three things that Nils really enjoys," said Wolf. "I'll put them in order of importance. The first is writing. The second is—well, it's indelicate so I won't mention it in mixed company. The third is fooling people."

Lily said, "They are all three terrible vices."

"Which is the worst?"

"I think fooling people," said Myra.

"I think writing. I'm so glad Alan doesn't do it."

"Nobody votes for fucking?"

"Alan! You pick up that sort of thing from Nils-Frederik."

Lily passed around coffee and chocolate-dipped strawberries, and they sat there eating them with the reviews piled on the table in front of them. In the middle of the dessert Kilda appeared with her boyfriend. He was a boy about her size, shy and alert, with large white eyes. His name was Garvey. Alan tried to think where he had heard this name before. Then he remembered that it was the name Kilda had given to the little Negro boy with his wheelbarrow, the antique toy that the Wolves had given her for Christmas. So Garvey had been her friend then, even though that was months ago. Garvey hardly said two words. He smiled like a timid animal when Kilda pronounced his name. Alan thought how white writers, when they want to put a sympathetic black in their stories, will always say that he's the color of café-au-lait. There was no cream in Garvey's coffee. He was black. He and Kilda filled up on the chocolate strawberries.

"Want to see my tarantula?"

"Okay."

They disappeared into the apartment, headed for her bedroom. Alan suppressed a thought that among schoolkids tarantula was perhaps a code word for genitals. It struck him that the instincts of a father with a female child are very strong, and according to those instincts a strange young male is something to be trampled on and gored.

Now that the dinner was over the two women began looking at the reviews of the book themselves. Myra said, "I don't understand. What does it all mean? The reviews are very good."

"It means that the stories probably aren't by Hemingway, but for the time no one has noticed this but Carleton West in *The New York Times,* and in the meantime the book is selling in the hundreds of thousands."

Lily said, "Alan, I told you not to get mixed up in this. No good can come of Virgos getting involved with Leos. And Wolf is a Scorpio, that's not much better. I'm not sure exactly what it is that the three of you have been up to, but I don't think I like it."

"Lily, I'm tired of your half-baked astrology. You have a pre-scientific mind. Why don't you wake up? This is the twentieth century. It's simply not the case that everyone born in a certain month is lacking in compassion, or has an aesthetic sense and is good with money. Wolf and I have helped Nils-Frederik write a book, that's all. Now it's a big success. It's what Nils-Frederik has always wanted. He's worked all his life for this. Some day I'll tell you how these stories happened to get written. Perhaps after Nils-Frederik is gone. It's a little too complicated to explain right now."

"I'm sorry I have a pre-scientific mind. I most humbly beg your pardon. Your mind is logical and scientific, is that it?"

"Well, I don't believe in astrology."

"It's a family quarrel. We'd better go, Wolf."

"Oh stay, we do this all the time. I don't imagine you want to give back the money," he told Lily.

"The money?"

"The commission on the sale of the book. Wolf got one too. Nils-Frederik agreed to pay double commissions."

"How much is it?"

"Well, quite a lot."

"Why didn't you tell me about this? Where is the money anyhow?"

"It's in the bank. You just never looked at the passbook."

"Ours is in mutual funds," said Wolf.

Myra said, "You never told me that either."

"What will Nils-Frederik do with the money?"

"He could never spend all the money he had. He didn't do it for the money. Nana will take care of it for him, as she always has."

"Nana takes care of the money?" said Myra.

"That's right. Everything he has he gives to her, and then she counts it out to him as he needs it."

"Well, I never," said Myra. "I thought she was senile."

"You mean," said Lily, "he gave her the money from the book?"

"That's right."

"How do you know?"

"Charmian told me."

"You're getting quite chummy with Charmian," said Lily.

"I like Charmian. The first time I had a really good talk with her was at the hospital when Nils-Frederik was sick."

"And you believe what she tells you?"

"She's too simple to lie. She can't make up anything. She's nothing at all like Nils-Frederik. Or Nana."

"Or like you. You're a Glas too."

"Or like me," he conceded.

Wolf said, "Nana is not as blind as she looks either."

"She can see well enough to count the money."

"She's lucky that she has Charmian to take care of her."

"She has Lucius Plum to take care of her now."

"What do you mean?"

"They're going to be married."

"Well, for heaven's sake," said Myra. "She's got one foot in the grave. How old is she anyhow? She can't last much longer."

"She's going to die at the turn of the century, just before midnight. And the same night, Kilda is going to have her first child, just after midnight, so it'll be born in the new century."

"Kilda?" repeated Myra. She had a good-natured puzzled smile, the smile of a person who isn't sure whether someone is telling her a joke.

"Kilda and Garvey."

Lily said, "Oh, Alan. Kilda and Garvey are just kids."

"So were we once."

After the embers in the barbecue died down the two women went into the house with the dishes. Kilda and Garvey were still in her bedroom and had been there for an hour. Alan knew what they were doing. She had her pants down and he was looking at her tarantula. He and Wolf sat and finished their coffee, and then Alan got up and put fresh charcoal on the barbecue. Sparks flickered around it, and occasional licks of flame, then it began to glow hotly.

Alan went into the apartment and came out with the small green piece of luggage with its battered brass corners. It was dark now and the only light came from the burning charcoal and the shaded patio lamp on the wall. He set down the Suitcase and opened it. In it were the fake original manuscripts that he and Wolf had prepared with so much work in the bookstore. Alan took out the manuscripts and set them one by one on the table by the barbecue.

Wolf fingered one of the manuscripts in its plastic cover. "Why are we doing this anyhow?"

"We were committing forgery when we made these things. I want to get rid of them. If we keep our mouths shut, no one will ever know what we did."

"Why couldn't these be the real thing?"

"You could test the paper for carbon 14 and find they were fake."

"That would prove that Nils wrote the stories. If you burn them up, then the stories might be by Hemingway."

"That's right."

"What about the Suitcase?"

"It would be hard to burn up. I think I'll just give it to the Salvation Army. It's good leather. Somebody can still get some use out of it."

There was a noise at the side of the patio and the gate of the walk to the street opened. Bumping and scraping, Nils-Frederik came through in his wheelchair. Charmian followed pushing on the back of it. She was in her usual printed housedress. Nils-Frederik was wearing his checked jacket, burgundy waistcoat, narrow flannel slacks, and Italian loafers. The wheelchair was an elaborate one, all chrome and black leather, with hydraulic controls for tilting and raising the seat. It too, like the shoes, was imported from Italy.

"Looks like you're having a party," said Nils-Frederik.

"A celebration. It's the publication day of the book."

"Why didn't you invite me? Those chocolate strawberries look good. Can I have some?"

There was only a trace of impediment in his speech now. He articulated with difficulty but correctly, as though he were a foreigner speaking the language.

Alan passed him the strawberries and he took a handful with his good right hand. "Darned good," he said, munching them.

"You have some too, Charmian."

She shook her head. She looked around the patio curiously. She had never been here before. Neither had Nils-Frederik, except once when they first moved into the apartment.

"What's that there on the table?"

"Well, there are the reviews."

"I've seen them."

"What do you think about them?"

"They're pretty good," said Nils-Frederik. "Some of them are better than the others. That guy in *The New York Times* seems to know what he's talking about."

"Yes," said Alan. "He says that Hemingway didn't write them."

Nils-Frederik could still make his jovial innocent smile, although it listed a little to one side now. "He's a pretty good critic. He reads the stories well."

"The other reviewers," said Alan, "were all taken in."

Nils-Frederik didn't respond to this. It was his chance to say he had written the stories, or he hadn't. Alan and Wolf sat looking at him through a long moment of silence.

"And what else is there on the table?" said Nils-Frederik. "I see something more."

He motioned with his head to Charmian and she wheeled him up. He shuffled through the manuscripts with his right hand and took one out of its plastic cover to examine it more carefully. Charmian got a Sobranie Black Russian out of the box in her handbag, inserted it between his lips, and lit it for him. He went on puffing it as he talked, without taking it from his mouth.

"Darn good work, you guys. They're almost as good as the originals."

"The what?"

"You could almost mistake them for the originals." He leafed through to the end of the manuscript. Scraps of brown paper fell off of it. "*I was still young and there would be other good things to do. Even when I was old I could live in my memories as they say in books. I could remember that I had talked to Madame Khlestakov in the Luxembourg, that I took her to dinner at Maxim's, and that I didn't have the money to take her to a hotel. That was the only good luck I had with women that summer.* Authentic Hemingway." He chuckled, then laughed outright.

"Sure sounds like it."

"The *Times* guy says that whoever wrote these stories is a hell of a writer."

"He is."

"Got the Nobel Prize for it," said Wolf, rather grouchily it seemed to Alan.

"For these stories? They've never been published before."

"You never are going to tell us, are you? You want it both ways. You wrote them and you didn't."

"Well, you did a good job, guys. Thanks a lot."

He gestured with his head again, and Charmian picked up the Suitcase and set it on his legs in the wheelchair. He had trouble opening it and she helped him. Then he began taking the manuscripts from the table with his one hand and putting them in the Suitcase, looking at each one briefly as he did it. "'A Friend from Detroit.' 'An Incantation Against Dying.' 'A Broken Doll.' That's a nice one. 'Snatch.' Ha!"

"That one didn't get into the book. What do you think you're doing?"

"The manuscripts are mine. I paid you for them, and quite a lot of money. The Suitcase is mine too. Did you think I was going to let you keep it?"

"It would make a nice souvenir."

"I'm the one that collects souvenirs. Every time I go to Europe I bring back something."

After Nils-Frederik and Charmian had left Alan and Wolf sat for a while in the patio, and then Alan went in and got the bottle. It was scotch, but Wolf didn't seem to mind, even though he usually drank bourbon. He put some ice in his drink and sipped it moodily.

"He beat us, Alan."

"It doesn't matter. He's got his book, the thing he's always wanted. And we've got the money."

"What are you going to do with yours, Alan? You said you might move to New York and be an agent there."

"No, I don't think I will."

"Why not?"

"Lily has her job here. And Kilda has her friends."

"Friends?"

"Like Garvey."

"Oh, that's nonsense. She's only a child. She can make other friends."

"I don't know," said Alan. "I'm a Californian, you know. I like the climate. I couldn't have the Beast in New York. I like riding it in L.A. We couldn't go out to dinner with the Wolves. Anyhow I'm a rotten agent. I'd be a rotten agent in New York too."

"All these are rationalizations. What's your real reason?"

"I don't want to leave Nils-Frederik."

"I feel the same way. I hate the son of a bitch for the way he manipulated us. He's the leader of the bad boys. He helped us rob the candy store. I wonder if he'll call again to have us come over on Sundays."

"What are you going to do with your money, Wolf?"

"Expand the store with half of it. Save the other half for our old age."

"You're a long way from that."

"Time flies," said Wolf. "I feel a little creaky now and then."

The charcoal in the barbecue was a dull red now. Alan gazed at the glowing coals, where it seemed to him that he could see fragments of old gray paper rising up in tiny sparks. Little whirling demons, the particles of his father's soul. He was a terrible sinner, a man whose own mother could look at him dying on the floor without emotion. He was the only person in the world that Alan loved enough to do something wrong for, to lie and steal and beg for, the one person whose approval he had to have if he was going to go on living. He was held in thrall by this mendacious and unfeeling egomaniac, the man he had wrestled to the edge of death and then cried for like a child.

He gave the charcoal in the barbecue a final prod. A flame guttered and crawled along the surface of the coals and then went out.

"Who do you think wrote those stories?"

"I don't know."

"I don't know either. And it doesn't really matter, Wolf. I've wrestled in my mind with this thing over and over. If somebody makes something that's so much like something else that you can't tell the difference, then there's no difference. Do you really like me? Does Lily really love me? You both behave as though you do, and that's all I can ever know. That's enough for me. I have to settle for that."

"It's extreme Kantian Idealism."

"It's what I've learned from Nils-Frederik. His world is his idea; he's created it with his thought. And my world is my idea. I've got to believe in it if I want to stay sane."

"So we'll never know who wrote the stories."

"I don't think so."

"Suppose it was Hemingway. He worked hard on those stories, the poor guy. And he thought he'd lost them forever."

"He could really write," said Alan.

39 ∎

NANA AND LUCIUS PLUM sat in two white chairs under an umbrella in the garden of the house in Los Feliz. He had a book with him and his feet were propped up on a stool. It was a bright sunny day and Nana wore a paisley dress and a sweater, with a crimson ribbon in her hair. Her hair was neatly brushed and she had new shoes.

"Which one would you like to hear now, Birgit? 'It's Marvelous, She Said'?"

"Oh, any. They're all nice."

"Maybe 'The Lady with the Dog.'"

"Did Nils write these stories?"

"No, they were written by Hemingway. A famous author."

"I'm sure Nils wrote them."

"He could have. He's a very good writer."

"You are too, Lucius."

"I've never read you anything I wrote."

"No, but your book will be coming out soon. You can read some of it to me."

"It won't be out till next year. Small presses are very slow. Still, I'm lucky to get it published at all. It wouldn't have happened if it weren't for Nils-Frederik. He recommended it to Salamander Press."

"Nils has a printer for his own book. They could have printed it."

"You see, *Strife and Charade* is not a very good book, Birgit. If it were any good, it could have been published by a real publisher. But it's not, so it's going to be published by a small press."

"You know, you're the only one in the world who has ever called me Birgit."

"You mean since you were grown up."

"No, even when I was a child they called me Nana. You're

the only one to call me Birgit. You along with Frank, the skipper of my boat."

"How about 'This Is Me, Dr. Schultz'? We haven't read that one for a while."

"I like that one."

"It's the only one that takes place in Michigan. The rest of them are all in Europe."

"It doesn't matter where a story takes place. You can see it all in your mind's eye."

"After you get your eyes fixed you can read these stories yourself. You can read my book when it comes out."

"I never learned to read, Lucius. I never saw any point to it. If there are things to be found out in books, other people can tell me about them. They always have. I have other things to do with my time. Let's hear about Dr. Schultz."

"You know, he wrote this story before all these things happened to him. It's an example of Nature copies Art."

"I don't know what that means."

"You see, in this story Dr. Schultz has a stroke. Everyone thinks it serves him right. But when he wrote this story Nils-Frederik hadn't had his own stroke. It's as though he were making a prophecy about what was going to happen to him."

"I thought you said the famous author wrote the story."

"He could have written it. Later in his life he was sick in his head. He tried to walk into an airplane propeller."

"Was he killed?"

"No, they pulled him away from it that time. Later he killed himself."

"I think Nils wrote the story. That's why it's called 'This Is Me, Dr. Schultz.'"

"What do you mean?"

"Nils was prophesying what was going to happen to him. He is Dr. Schultz himself. So the title means, 'Dr. Schultz is me.'"

"I never thought of that."

"I know everything that Nils is up to. He has no secrets from me. I'm his mother."

"To tell you the truth, I had never quite realized that either. I mean, I knew it, but it had never struck me."

"Nils is a bad boy. He always was. It was a mistake bringing him up in Los Angeles. There are too many temptations. Do you know what he does with that woman of his?"

"I don't want to know."

"Go ahead and read the story. I know how it starts." She recited in her singsong voice. *"That summer Nick lived in Petoskey in a room he rented from Dr. Schultz."*

This Is Me, Dr. Schultz

THAT SUMMER *Nick lived in Petoskey in a room he rented from Dr. Schultz. He had a girl named Trudie. She worked in the cafe that he always went to across from the Emporium. They were together a lot that summer. He was very much in love. It was the first time and it is always better then. Later he had a lot of disappointments with women, because he fell in love with them and they were not perfect. But there was nothing wrong with Trudie except the things that happened to her.*

When his father found out about it he kidded him a lot about having an Indian girl. His father and Sam were staying in the cottage in the woods, and Nick was living in town in the rented room. It was the first time he had been by himself and he enjoyed it. His father said, "Nick has a new sweetheart. Did you know about that, Sam?"

Sam knew about it too. He didn't like to discuss it because he didn't have any girl at all, even an Indian girl, although he was older.

"He got her out at the Indian camp. They sell them out there for a couple of dollars. You have to bring them back when they're worn out."

"You do not."

"I don't know how you can go with an Indian girl," said
Sam.

"I don't go with her. We go walking in the woods and along
the lake. Sometimes we fish. She's not very good at fishing.
We go hunting for black squirrels."

"They like that. That's what they eat. Black squirrels and
pemmican."

"No, they don't."

"Well, leave him alone, Sam. Get a girl of your own before
you make fun of him."

"I wasn't making fun of him. I think it's a rotten thing to
do."

"A lot of things to do with women are rotten. But everybody
does them."

It wasn't true about black squirrels. When he and Trudie
were together they didn't hunt and they didn't fish. They
walked in the woods and along the sandy road that came out
on the lake, past the cottage where the man from Boston had
killed his wife and buried her in the back lot. Nick pointed
out the place to Trudie.

"Why did he kill her?"

"Jealousy. She was going with another man."

"That's no reason to kill her."

"I don't know why he killed her. His name was Mason. It
was a long time ago. My father told me about it."

"Would you be jealous if I had another man?"

"Yes."

"What would you do?"

"I don't know. I suppose I'd cry a lot and think that I had
a broken heart. Then after a while I would find that my heart
wasn't broken after all."

"If you had another girl my heart would be broken."

"I don't have another girl."

"Where do you want to go today?"

"When we come out at the lake we'll go down the shore to
the campground."

At the campground they fooled around gathering acorns for a while, and then they sat on the sand and Trudie put her hand in his pocket, trying to steal his acorns. They had a tussle and fell over on the sand. Nick wondered where she had learned that trick of putting her hand in his pocket. It worked every time and they said it was something that the girls in the house in Petoskey did. People told stories about what happened in the house but Nick had never been there. Trudie was the first girl he had ever had, even though he had wanted to go to the house for a long time. He thought that Trudie was a lot better than going to the house.

Dr. Schultz practiced out of his house, which was out of town where the road went over the river on an iron bridge. He was overweight and had a pale face. He was a snappy dresser. He had been a surgeon in Chicago but now he had a general practice. The sign said that he did *General Practice and Diseases of Women*. Nick didn't know very much about diseases that women had that men didn't get, but probably Dr. Schultz did. He too found out that Nick had an Indian girl but he didn't think it was very funny.

"Do you know what you can get by going with Indians?"

"No." Nick had an idea.

"It's not much fun. You'd better cut it out."

"If I get something you can cure it. It would be a *Disease of Women*."

"You think it's a joke, but it's not much fun if you get it."

"I'm not going to get anything. Trudie is just a friend of mine."

"You go out in the woods with her. You'd better be careful."

Nick read books in the mornings and did a little work for the Professor from Dayton who had a big cottage on the lake. He painted the Professor's lawn furniture and fixed up the shingles on the house. Most of what the Professor paid him he spent on books. He was reading Thoreau and Emerson, and he had just found out about Leaves of Grass. The books

were all in the bookstore in Petoskey and most of them were
second hand and they didn't cost very much. Sometimes Ellen
Walsh, who ran the bookstore, let him have them free. In the
afternoon he went out in the woods with Trudie. She worked
for breakfast and lunch at the cafe and then she had to be back
for dinner. She was free in the afternoons until five.

It was a nice summer. They had just enough rain to keep
down the dust but not too much. The woods were fresh and
clean. There were not very many mosquitoes. Anyhow, his
father said that when you went with Indians you didn't have
to worry about mosquitoes because the smell kept them away.
Trudie had a smell but it didn't bother him. It was like camp-
fires and coffee and a little sweat, the kind you get from a good
game of football. Every time he smelled Trudie, it excited
him again.

They lay on the sand and she put her hand in his pocket.
Then she took her clothes off, and he did too. She lay on her
back and he explored her body, as though it was a strange land
that he had never been to before. Partly it was because he
wanted her and partly it was curiosity. He was very interested in
her body and he explored every part of it. She didn't take much
interest in his body, except to do the right thing when needed.

"Your stomach is getting bigger."

"Yes."

"When will it happen?"

"Not for a long time. Not until summer is over."

"What will you do?"

"I won't have to do anything. It will just come out."

"When did the baby start?"

"A long time ago. Before the summer. Before you came."

"You said that you didn't have another man."

"I don't. I just have you."

"Is it all right to do it when you're like that?"

"I think so. They told me it was all right."

"Who told you?"

She didn't say. "It's all right. If it doesn't make any difference
to you."

"It doesn't make any difference. I like you this way."
"You're strange. Most men don't think like that."
"You said you didn't have another man."
"I don't."

*It didn't happen the way Trudie said and it was not a good
end to the summer. Nick found out about it by accident. The
Professor had a friend staying with him, a young doctor from
Dayton, and he said that she had been brought to the hospital
and died there. It was Dr. Schultz who brought her to the
hospital. They said that Dr. Schultz was in trouble and would
be charged with something. When Nick came back to his
room, Dr. Schultz had his office closed and the door locked.
He was probably somewhere in his part of the house, but Nick
didn't care where. He lay on his bed and thought. He only
felt empty; he didn't cry a lot as he told her he would. He
wondered if it was always this way, that when you had something perfect they took it away from you. You weren't allowed
to have something perfect. The world was imperfect and there
was a rule against it. It was the first time he had really thought
about such things. It was not a good day and he didn't go out
to dinner at the cafe. Probably they would have a new girl, or
Mrs. Parton would serve the customers herself, and he didn't
want to be there. Late at night he couldn't sleep and he went
for a walk. It had rained earlier and everything was rotten with
water. His clothes were wet, and they chafed him and made
him cold and miserable. When he came back the house was
still dark except for the light in his own room. He tried the
door of the surgery but it was still locked.*

*In the morning when he woke up he could hear Dr. Schultz
in the kitchen, fooling around fixing his breakfast. He got
dressed and stole out of the house by the back door, taking his
knapsack and a sweater. At first he thought he would go for a
long walk to tire himself, but the only place to walk was down*

the sandy road to the lake and he didn't want to go there. Instead he went to the cottage in the woods to talk to his father. His father was fixing breakfast and offered him ham and eggs but he didn't want anything. Sam wasn't there and that was good. He didn't want Sam around when he was talking about it.

"Just forget it. Something hurts for a while, but the hurt goes away. By Christmas you'll be fine."

"I don't want to be fine. I want to be just the way I am. I want to hurt."

"You feel that way now. But in a couple of months you'll forget it. You won't forget it, but it won't hurt so much."

"I want to settle it with him."

"Don't be stupid. He just made a mistake. Schultz is not very good. That's why he left Chicago. He tried to do it too late. I don't know what he could have been thinking of. After they begin to swell up it's too late to do it."

"It's not because of killing her. It's something else that he did."

"What?"

Nick wouldn't say.

"Didn't you know about that?" said his father. "Everybody else in town did. He's been fooling around with her ever since she's grown up."

"Why didn't you tell me?"

"She was your sweetheart. I didn't want to make you feel bad."

"I feel swell now."

"It's not your fault. It isn't his fault either. I told you, he just made a mistake. He'll go to prison for it."

"It's not enough," said Nick.

After his father went out Nick went into his bedroom and began looking through the big old-fashioned chest of drawers they had brought up from the city. It had belonged to Nick's grandmother and it matched the bed. His father slept in the bed alone; his mother never came to the cottage in the summer. What he was looking for was not in the chest of drawers. He looked for it in his father's suitcase and finally found it in a wooden baking soda box under the bed. It was an old Colt army revolver that had belonged to his grandfather. His father shot at tin cans with it sometimes in back of the cottage. Nick put it in his knapsack and crushed his sweater down on top of it.

He walked back into town on the road, past the Emporium and the cafe where she used to work. The cafe was open but he couldn't see who was waiting on the tables. He hadn't had anything to eat since noon the day before. It was eleven o'clock in the morning. He felt floating and unreal and wondered if he was going to be sick.

When he got to the house the door of the office was open and a Ford car was standing in the road in front of it. He went up to the door and went in. Mort Closkey, the maintenance man for the town, was standing in the office looking very somber. He told Nick, "I come to have him look at my hernia and I found him. I was the first one here. A boy come by and I sent him for the doctor."

The doctor from Dayton, the one who was staying with the Professor, was there too, and some other people that Nick didn't know. They were blocking something from his view, and when he came closer he saw that Dr. Schultz had fallen off his chair at the desk and was lying on his back on the floor. Someone had put a medical book under his head. He was the color of sour milk and the left side of his face had sagged. He was still conscious; he looked at Nick out of his one good eye.

The doctor from Dayton said, "Better clear out, son. He's pretty bad. We're taking him to the hospital."

It was his Ford car. Nick wondered if they would set up Dr. Schultz in the passenger seat, staring out through the glass with his one eye. Then he remembered there was an ambulance in town. He wasn't thinking very clearly.

The doctor from Dayton said, "You're staying in his room?"

"Yes."

"Well, you'd better find another place. They'll close up the house."

"I can stay with my father."

"That would be a good idea."

Nick walked away down the road. He could feel the Colt against his back at the bottom of the knapsack. The way it had happened was a disappointment. He hated Dr. Schultz and wanted to kill him but he hadn't wanted it to turn out this way. His father was right, it was not Dr. Schultz's fault. It was that you wanted things to be perfect and they could never be perfect. He would never want that again. He was smarter now and he would be cautious and settle for things being less than perfect. If they were perfect, that would be a surprise.

"Lucius, do you think that Nils is smarter now?"

"He always was very smart. I don't know if he could get any smarter."

"Now he knows that things are less than perfect."

"What do you mean?"

"He's paralyzed now and he can't walk, like Dr. Schultz."

"He doesn't need to walk anywhere, Birgit. He can sit at his processor and write. That's all he needs. Besides he's like Nick. He knows that things are not perfect, and if they are it will be a surprise."

"I don't expect any surprises anymore."

"There are always surprises, Birgit. No matter who you are. Look at me and you. Who would have thought it?"

"Oh, I thought it from the beginning, Lucius."

40 ∎

Nils-Frederik and Charmian had gone out to the movies, a revival of a popular film of the seventies, at the Parnassus on Wilshire Boulevard. When they got back to the house it was silent and the windows were dark; Lucius Plum and Nana had gone to bed. Charmian stopped the car in the driveway and went around to help Nils-Frederik out of the car. She unfolded the Italian wheelchair and adjusted its chromium knobs and levers, and then slipped him out of the passenger seat into it. Then she wheeled him into the house, leaving the car in the drive. She could come back later and put it in the garage. Right now Nils-Frederik needed her help.

"What time is it?"

"About ten-thirty."

"My watch is on my left wrist and I can't raise it to look. I could lift it with my right hand but that's too much trouble. I'll just go on asking you what time it is for a while."

"It's about ten-thirty."

Passing through the kitchen, she trundled him on down the hall to the master bedroom. The door was half ajar and she kicked it dexterously with her foot to open it so she could get the wheelchair through it. The wheelchair was a large one and it bumped and scraped on things as it went through them. Once in the bedroom, she took him to his bathroom without speaking, set him on the toilet, pulled his pants down, and left him.

While she waited she went hurriedly into the dressing room to find her costume. She took a white linen dress with a square neck from the hanger and laid it over the chair, and got a teased blond wig from its stand. She selected the eyeshadow and liner and set them out on the counter. Then she went back to the other bathroom.

Given ten minutes, Nils-Frederik had managed to put on his linen designer pajamas with the monogram on the pocket. She eased him off the toilet and wheeled him to a position by the bed, leaving him there in the wheelchair. In the nightstand she found a Havana cigar, clipped off the end, put it in his mouth, and lit it for him. She was careful to put the ashtray by his right hand, even though she knew he wouldn't use it and would drop the ashes on the carpet.

"À *bientot.*"

"*Ma chérie.*"

They often talked French when they were alone. It was a reminder of the time when they first met, in the small town in Belgium. Charmian knew English even then but she concealed it from him. He enjoyed talking French to people who didn't know English.

Leaving him, she went back to her combined bathroom and dressing room. She took off her print dress and shoes, after some thought decided to take off her slip too, and put on sheer white stockings with white garters. Staring into the mirror at her forgettable face, the mutable face, the face without features, she smiled with the mysterious satisfaction of a sleepwalker. She began applying the makeup: a foundation to make her look pale, and the eyeshadow and liner which she applied liberally. Her eyes, as she watched them in the mirror, seemed to double in size. No lipstick; she wished to look austere. A little perfume on her collarbone, her elbows, and the back of her neck. She slipped on the simple and functional white dress with the white buttons down the front, and added white pumps with medium heels. The teased blond wig. It was hot and scratchy. As a final touch, she took a bottle of household disinfectant with a medicinal smell and dabbed it here and there on the dress.

She went out through the door and pushed the button in the dark. Here in the bedroom the odors of the perfume and the disinfectant mingled with those of the cigar. The pink lights went on overhead and the curtain opened slowly.

Nils-Frederik was sitting in the wheelchair examining the lighted end of the cigar, which he held in his right hand. His left hand rested limply on his knee. He looked at her curiously.

"Jane Fonda," he pronounced in his lightly halting way, as though he had a foreign accent. "*Coming Home.* The picture we saw tonight."

It was important for him to repeat these incantations, even though they both knew perfectly what the picture was that they'd seen. She said, "Sally Hyde. I'm just volunteering here in the hospital. You're Luke. A paralyzed Vietnam veteran. You're only an enlisted man. But my husband Bob is a stupid brute."

He smiled lopsidedly. "You're young and attractive. I'm surprised that you, an officer's wife, would work here in the hospital."

"Bob would fly off the handle if he knew I had anything to do with an enlisted man."

"What do you do in the hospital?"

"I'm supposed to do various things. Bring people magazines. Talk to them. Give them massages and take away their pajamas to be washed."

"I can't do much for myself."

"That's why I'm here."

"Okay, here we go. How do we manage it?"

She took his cigar and put it in the ashtray. "First I'll get you off the wheelchair and onto the bed. Then we'll see what comes next."

"Careful, the leg is dragging behind. Can you lift me?"

"Oh yes, I was brought up lifting heavy weights. You're lying on your arm. Here, I'll pull it out."

"You'll have to help me take my stuff off."

"I do that now anyhow."

"Yes, but this is a little different. You take your clothes off too."

"Some of them." She took off the dress, revealing herself in her underwear and the white stockings with garters. The teased wig came askew and she set it to rights. Then she lay down beside him.

"If it's a hospital bed the head is supposed to come up a little. This is awkward."

"I'll put a pillow under your head. I've been waiting and hoping for this ever since you came to the hospital."

"Me too."

"I hoped you'd understand."

"What is there to understand? Life is just the way it is."

"Was it hell over there?"

"Let's not talk about that. It's hell here."

"It's hell for me too, but not in a way you'd understand."

"It's not the same. You know, I can't even touch you. The left side doesn't work at all, and the right side doesn't work very well."

"Don't worry. I'll do everything."

"Touch me right there."

"That still works."

"Oh yes. It has its own nervous system, you know. It doesn't depend on the other nerves."

"What a contrast you are to Bob, my officer husband. You're a real man."

"Take off the rest of that junk."

She removed her underwear, leaving on the stockings and garters. This was precisely what he meant, even though he didn't say so.

"What was that smell on your dress?"

"Disinfectant. This is a hospital."

"Now, now. Hurry."

"Are you sure you're not getting too excited?"

"I'm getting as excited as I can."

"Is it good for your heart?"

"Who the hell cares? I'm a Vietnam veteran. I could have been fucking killed by the Commies. Now my life is free to throw away. Get your shit together, guys! We're going into the boonies!"

"Luke, Luke. You're flashing back."

"You said you were going to do everything. Get going."

"I love you."

"You hardly even know me."

"I don't care. I love you."

"What's your name again? Sally. I remember."

"You're an enlisted man. I'm an officer's wife."

"I'm not used to women who wear nice things. Nice underwear. Nice stockings."

She was lying on top of him. He groped with his right hand and put it on the place on her leg where the stocking ended. She took his left hand and set it on the same place on the other leg.

Charmian slipped out of bed, went to Nils-Frederik's bathroom, groped in the pocket of his jacket, and found the car keys. She opened the door of the room with infinite care not to make any sound, glancing back once at the snoring man in the bed behind her. She was naked except for the white stockings and garters which she had never taken off. Her feet glided over the expensive wool carpet; her footsteps were so silent that she could hear every sound in the house around her, the click of some insect, a faint crepitation made by the beams or the walls as they responded to minute changes in temperature. She passed the room where the old man and the old woman were locked in oblivion in each other's arms, glided like a wraith through the dining room and the kitchen, and went out the door into the garage. The garage door was open and the Peugeot was standing in the drive.

It was after eleven o'clock. In the houses across the street the porch lights were on, but there was no sign of a human presence. Quickly but cautiously she stole out to the car in the starlight, opened the door, and slipped in. When she turned the key in the lock it started with its familiar muted hum. She pulled it into the garage without turning the lights on, shut off the engine, got out, and pulled the garage door shut. In the dark, after the danger of exposing herself to the starlit night, she felt good, cozy, warm, protected. Without having to grope, knowing her way perfectly in the dark, she went around the car and back into the kitchen.

This was her domain, where the others came only on sufferance. It was the nerve center of the house. If you looked into a house with x-rays, you would see everything radiating from the kitchen: pipes, wires, conduits, drains. From the kitchen came heat and cold, sustenance, life-giving water, the smells of cooking food, permeating the rest of the house and suffusing it with life. She opened the refrigerator; from it came a Vermeer-glow of yellow light that outlined her sharply against the shadows behind her. She shut the door and turned on a gas burner. This light was dimmer, blue, trembling imperceptibly. Now she was a night priestess, a Sibyl, who rose cryptically out of the fumes of chthonic gas. She caught a glimpse of her breasts in the kitchen window; blue below, shadowy above.

The bath off the kitchen: she ran her fingers around the washbowl in the dark to verify that it was clean and free of soap scum. The wine cellar, so-called; really only a littered room behind the kitchen where a dozen or so racks held Nils-Frederik's collection of fine vintages. It smelled musty, of damp masonry, of dust and old cork, of the rotten odor of wine from a spilled bottle. It was a European smell; she took pleasure in it and stayed for some time in the dark room. It might have been five minutes; she was unable to measure time precisely and had the impression that whatever she was doing now she had always been doing and would continue to do in the future.

She left the wine cellar and made her way in her stock inged feet to the foot of the stairs. Here there was a new addition to the house: a staircase elevator with a fold-down seat. Taking the key under the blue vase in the alcove, she pulled down the seat, pushed the button, and glided smoothly upward through the darkness, with the two keys in her hand, the key to the study and the car key. At the top of the stairs she got off, careful to fold the seat up so it did not spring back and make a noise. There was another wheelchair on the landing, the one he used in the study when he was working. She opened the door to the right and entered the living room. Here there was a little more light; a faint glow from the city came through the large picture window.

She ran her hand over a bronze statuette and felt the impasto of a painting. This was the night-Charmian, a tactile creature who needed to touch things to comprehend them and assimilate them to her own; the day-Charmian lived by sights and sounds. Now, as midnight drew on, she dominated the house with her touch; it was as familiar to her as the inside of her own mind, as her own secret thoughts. Closing her eyes, she walked around the room sliding her fingers over things. In the darkness speckled with red dots behind her eyelids she recognized every object that her fingers touched. In the night the house was hers; in the prosaic daylight it belonged to Nils-Frederik. Even sound asleep in the bed beside him she knew the secure and satisfying feeling of possession. Nils-Frederik was not good in the dark; if he closed his eyes he was helpless. And he was not confident in the land of sleep. Often he turned or groaned in the night, stirring with his crippled limbs under the covers, wishing to escape from this narcoleptic prison where his possessions were invisible and slipped away from him like smoke. In sixteen hours of their life together Nils-Frederik was master; in the other eight he was enthralled, bound in cords of darkness, and her mind was free to range over their common world and possess it. The entry into this nocturnal world was the Magic Theater with its dressing room, its collection of costumes, and its curtain. He imagined that he imposed the Magic Theater on her; it was this thought that hardened his virility until it was as hot and stiff as his cigar. But in reality it was she who, detecting the secret desire in his mind, had invented it and installed it gradually in his life, as she might have carried the pieces of furniture one by one into a newly occupied house, at the same time contriving things so that he believed it was he who had imagined each detail in the rich storehouse of his lust.

And who was Charmian? How had she come to this place? In her private thoughts she often played for herself another picture, a True Movie, one that had really happened, but which became in her mind a fantasy, a fiction, an annunciation of future bliss in a far-off land. In this movie she was loitering and chatting with some other girls at the well in the marketplace of the little town of Yvellines-Vanne, near Ghent. There was a café in the marketplace, with three worn tables set out in the sunshine in front of it, and Nils-Frederik, a foreigner who was staying in a hotel in Ghent, was sitting there with a coffee and a newspaper. She and the other girls were bantering with each other about their boyfriends; the others were teasing Charmian because she didn't have one. Just at that moment an old man went by the well, a familiar town character called the Ancient Combatant, who had fought in the First World War and was now in his eighties. He wore a long military overcoat even in the summer, carried a stick like a shepherd's crook, and had a pronounced limp. He also had a terrible temper, and was a well-known woman hater. He growled and spat at the girls as he passed and waved his crooked stick at them. They responded in kind; it was an old game for them and for him. When he had disappeared down the lane Charmian began imitating him, with an uncanny skill. She lurched over the paving stones as though she were walking with a stick, she screwed up her face until she was a toothless Punch, and she cackled scratchy imprecations in two languages. In spite of her sex, her youth, and her flowery print dress, she had *become* the Ancient Combatant in every gesture and motion of her body. She had assumed the soul, the very identity, of the crabbed and crippled octogenarian, with a skill that passed beyond malice and entered the realm of pure art. The other girls laughed and couldn't stop; she went on with it for some time, limping back and forth and threatening them with her imaginary stick. Other people in the marketplace turned to look. Nils-Frederik watched her from the café.

He never touched her in the hotel in Ghent where they stayed that night, in the other hotel where they stayed in Paris

for several days, or in the house when they first got back to
Los Angeles. The first thing he did was to send her to a cooking
school, an expensive one in the French Cordon Bleu tradition.
She had learned to cook from her mother, and had been
introduced to the rudiments of continental cuisine in the restaurant in Yvellines where she worked, but now she became
an expert. She learned fast and was the best pupil in her class.
In three months she finished the beginning, intermediate, and
advanced courses and received a diploma with a blue ribbon
on it. Shortly after that, Nils-Frederik called in a contractor
and had the Magic Theater constructed.

And so it had all fallen into her hands, the chalice of her
heart's desire and her secret dreams. In this fabulous land across
the water, shiny and rich, myriad in its possibilities, its guises,
she had her house, her kitchen with its modern appliances,
her own bathroom with a Jacuzzi, and a car to drive around
on the golden streets. If anything was lacking it would be
provided; she knew how to get it. And she had become what
every girl in her town, in her country, every girl in the world,
dreamed of without daring to express it. She had become an
actress, a movie star, with her own theater and her attentive
and passionate audience, an audience she could move to any
emotion she chose. And it was she who chose her roles, in
which she became simultaneously the actress, the character
being played by the actress, and herself. She was Susan Langley, she was Myrna Loy, she was Giulietta Masina, she was
Jane Fonda. The very blood in her, the complex trickle of
emotions in her thoughts, changed as she assumed each of
these identities that he imagined he imposed on her. Somewhere along the journey of her life, somewhere on the shining
bosom of the Atlantic as she crossed it, a new spirit had declared
itself in her, a mysterious angel who commanded her, obeyed
her, and filled her with joy. In this state she knew all languages,
could unlock all doors, and knew the secrets of both sexes at
once. She could be a Negro, a bordello madam, a butterfly,
a Syrian houri, a murderer, and the executioner who executed

him. At night, running her fingers over things in the dark, she became the house. Compared to these things, the book that her crippled lover had made was a flimsy and trivial thing.

In her nakedness and sheer white stockings, she stood before the picture window looking out at the city, a polychrome diorama across which the tracks of the great boulevards, Wilshire, Western, and Vermont, stretched like illuminated jewels. From this vantage, framed in its square of glass, the city too was her possession; it was simply an extension of the darkened house, something bright to attract and entertain people in the living room, like a television screen or an aquarium of tropical fish. In the sea in the far distance was an island, blackish purple in the night, the island where Nana and Lucius Plum would go soon. So would others, but she was immortal. For immortality is simply the belief that one is immortal; mortality is only the fear of death. She herself was Princess of the Night, and she had no fear of it. It was for others to fear her. She had triumphed, she had everything her soul had sought for, while the others hungered, quarreled, and fell by the way.

She left the living room, crossed the landing, and unlocked the door of the study. Holding the keys in her teeth, she sat down at the processor. She knew how to turn it on. The green glow of the screen played dimly over her body. She pushed the space bar until the cursor was in the middle of the screen, then she tapped the letters of her name: *Charmian Berghe*. No one spoke it in the house and few knew it, perhaps only Nils-Frederik and her playful lover Klipspringer. She stared at this arcane legend for a moment. She touched the switch, the green glow faded, and the two words disappeared into the mysterious memory of the computer, in her mind to be imbedded there forever. Then she turned the machine off and stood up, stretching lazily and sensuously. She passed her hands across her breasts, her flat waist, the sculptured bones of her hips, still looking at the rounded rectangle of glass where the letters had glowed only a moment before. Then she turned and left the study, removing the key from her teeth to lock the door behind her. Feeling in the dark for the folding seat, she fitted her bifurcated flesh onto it and pushed the button. The elevator glided downward in the darkness with the sound of a contented cat, or the flight of an angel.